PRESTWI

Praise from the re

"David Hough has produced a real page turner
with this tense and suspenseful story.
A roller coaster of a ride from beginning to end."

"This would make a great disaster film."

"David Hough has conjured up an absolute cracker.
I could not put this down!"

"As the story unfolded, I found myself immersed
in both aircraft and rooting for safe outcomes.
I was flying by the seat of my pants!"

"This is a real page-turner of a novel. Reads like a 70s disaster
movie as the stakes get higher and higher,
and you wonder how it can possibly all be resolved.
But it IS resolved, with a very satisfying ending."

"I read every aviation-related book that I can get my hands on
and this one I can safely say had me totally hooked.
Excellent piece of work and the degree of technical accuracy
could come only from a professional."

"This is a thriller that gets straight down to business.
It is engaging and gives a behind the scenes insight
to air traffic and aircrews."

"Utterly riveting, sheer magnetic brilliance. Best book in ages!"

"The author really knows his subject and has used this
to maximum effect. This would make an excellent movie."

"Totally riveted by the various snapshots from various angles
as the whole plot comes together."

David Hough was born in Cornwall and grew up in the Georgian City of Bath. He spent forty years working as an air traffic controller in Northern Ireland, Scotland and England before retiring early in 2003 and becoming a writer. David has written over 30 novels and enjoys writing "a rattling good yarn with a dose of hard grit". He now lives with his wife in Dorset, on the south coast of England.

www.TheNovelsofDavidHough.com

Also by David Hough:

Danger in the Sky aviation thrillers
Prestwick
Heathrow

Secret Soldiers of World War I spy thrillers
In Foreign Fields
In Line of Fire

Historical Adventures in Cornwall series
In the Shadow of a Curse
In the Shadow of Disgrace
In the Shadow of Deception

The Family Legacy series
The Legacy of Shame
The Legacy of Secrets
The Legacy of Conflict

David Hough

PRESTWICK

Danger in the Sky (Book 1)

Cloudberry

Published by Cloudberry, an imprint of Luscious Books Ltd 2016
Morwellham, Down Park Drive, Tavistock, PL19 9AH, Great Britain

ISBN 978-1-910929-02-5

Copyright © David Hough 2013, 2016
Cover image © Moses1978 | Dreamstime.com

Prestwick was originally published in the
United Kingdom 2009 by BeWrite Books.
A revised ebook edition was published 2013 by Cloudberry.

The right of David Hough to be identified as the author of this work
has been asserted by him in accordance with the
Copyright, Designs and Patents Act 1988.

This book is a work of fiction. Any similarity between the characters
and situations within its pages and any persons, living or dead,
is unintentional and entirely coincidental.

All rights reserved.
No part of this publication may be reproduced, in any form,
without the prior permission of the publisher.

A CIP catalogue record for this book is available from the British Library.

www.cloudberrybooks.co.uk

To Henry and Oliver

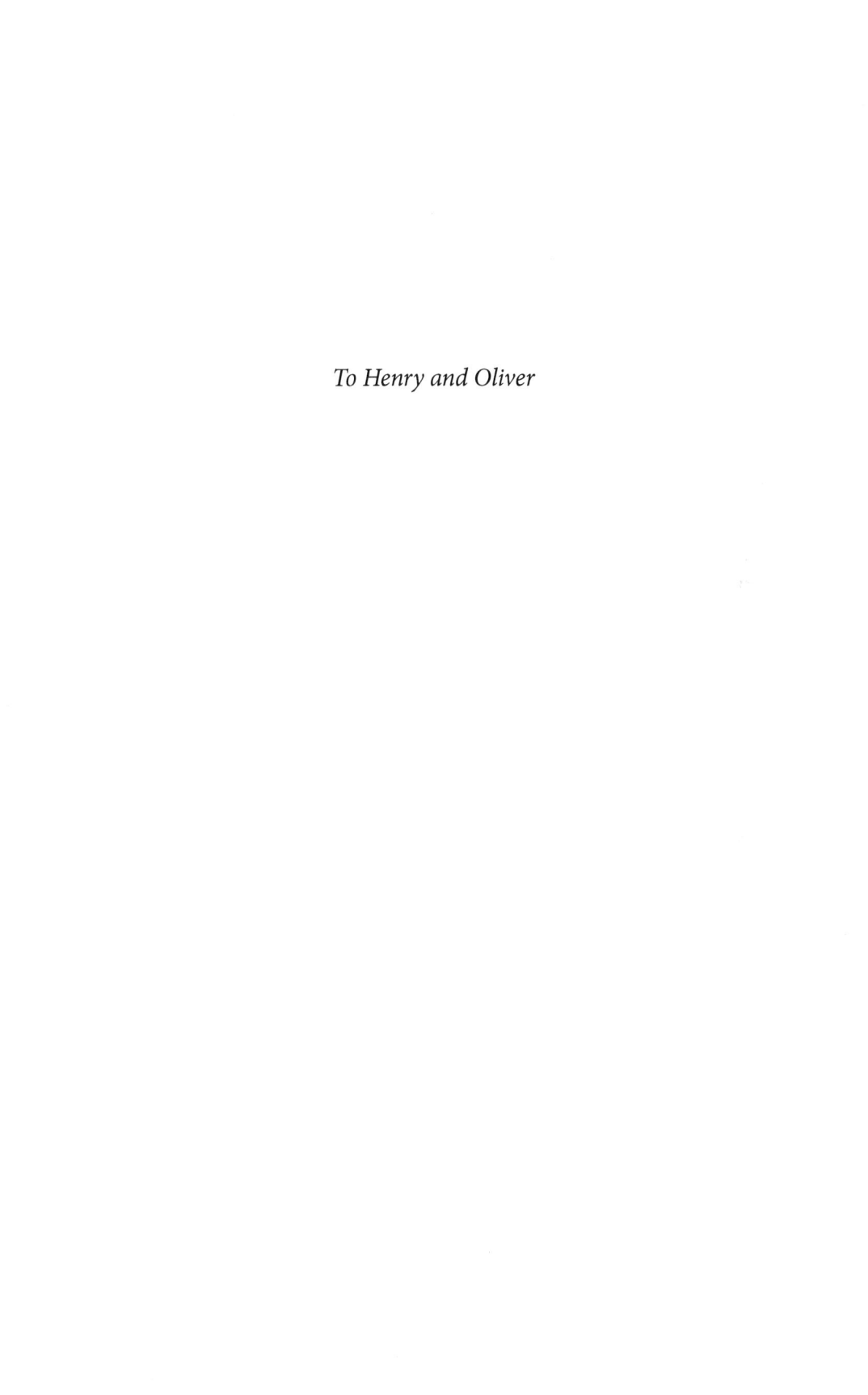

Prologue — January 1985

The mission was a failure. A gut-wrenching balls-up of a failure.

Aboard the space shuttle, the stress was evident in George Sharpe's voice. "Houston, this is *Washington*. Guess this is your last chance to come up with another option. What can you offer us now?"

He knew as well as the Mission Commander that there was *no* other option, but he had to make the point anyway.

"*Washington*, this is Houston. Sorry guys, this is the only way down. Start your manoeuvre to burn attitude." The voice was firm, the instruction predictable, inevitable.

Sharpe nodded to Peter Guthrie, the shuttle pilot in the right-hand seat. "Okay, Pete. You heard what the man said. Let's get this ship turned round. Like it or not, we're going down with the bomb."

The shuttle pilot's face was tense as he initiated the manoeuvre to turn the shuttle for the engine burn that would slow it down for re-entry.

He turned his attention to the instruments and ran his mind over the problem once again, hoping against hope for some vital clue that would help them avoid the granddaddy of all explosions.

"*Washington*, your burn attitude looks good. You are go for de-orbit burn."

"Roger, Houston."

This was it. No turning back now. Ronald Reagan would be starting the first month of his second year in office worrying over a dramatic fault in his Strategic Defence Initiative.

Star Wars was backfiring. Badly.

Either the shuttle would land safely, or a lot of people were going to die in a nuclear holocaust that would make Hiroshima look like a Fourth of July firecracker.

Chapter 1

Dougie Nyle peered through the heavy rain pebbling against the 747's front screen and wondered again what it was about flying that made him come back for more.

He tried to reassure himself that the delayed take-off to Sinclair International flight 984 was not a portent of something worse. They were already three hours late starting engines at Kennedy. The cabin crew had distributed free drinks and forced smiles, but the passengers were restless and growing more so by the minute.

Dougie had thought the police might insist on a complete crew change. Detectives from the New York Police Department questioned everyone, compared notes and then questioned many of them again. The second time round, a fat lieutenant confronted Dougie in a grimy office at the heart of the terminal building.

"Did you ever fly with this girl?" As he spoke, he shifted a wad of gum from one side of his mouth to the other and then back again. His gaze never wavered from Dougie's face.

Dougie drew back his shoulders and held himself upright in the hard wooden chair. He tried to present an air of calm maturity. He was the first officer, but he was only twenty-nine years old. "I really don't know. I don't remember her."

"Did you ever meet her outside of work?"

"I don't make a point of meeting stewardesses in my own time. I'm a happily married man." He immediately regretted the word 'happily'. He conjured an image of Jenny back home in Ayrshire, sobbing over her knitting.

The lieutenant paused, mouth half-open, revealing the pink gum. "Do you know anything about the girl's background?"

"I told you, I don't remember her." He flexed his fingers, unsure which was more annoying, the questioning or the gum-chewing.

The policeman poked a finger at a head-and-shoulders photograph of the dead girl, the stewardess found stabbed in a New York subway. "You sure?"

"We must have come here on different flights."

"But you've flown with her at some time?"

"Maybe I did, maybe I didn't. How many times must I tell you? I don't remember her. Do you know how many cabin crew the company employs, Lieutenant?"

The policeman's voice turned acid. "This girl had been in deep trouble before she died. Her body was covered with bruises."

"I don't beat up women. Do you want a signed statement from my wife?"

"Don't get smart with me, buddy. We've got a dead Brit on our patch and we could make things awkward for you if you don't cooperate." He swallowed his gum and rubbed a chubby wrist across his lips.

*

Fergus MacNabb was interviewed for much longer than the others. Maybe because he was the captain and the dead girl was one of his crew. Dougie felt uneasy about every long minute the older pilot spent in the interview room. MacNabb had a quick Celtic temper.

But the interview ended abruptly and a senior officer gave permission for the crew to board the aircraft. Whoever killed stewardess Sally Scrimgeour didn't appear to be on flight 984 bound for Scotland. Now Dougie could go home to Jenny and get down to the talk they should have had weeks ago.

"Bloody cops!" MacNabb wriggled into his seat at the left-hand side of the flight deck. He was a giant of a man with a broad Glaswegian accent, a wide craggy face and a shock of grey hair that refused to lie flat. He set his huge hands on the yoke at the top of the control column and stared ahead, his teeth gritted together.

Dougie held back from replying. The captain was a good flier but a poor communicator.

MacNabb swung his gaze round. "This place stinks. Be glad to get home again."

"We could be in for a rough ride, Captain. More turbulence reports are coming in."

"I've flown in worse. You'd better get us our start-up clearance."

Dougie contacted the control tower while the captain switched on the inertial navigation system. Once it was running, laser gyros and accelerometers would detect every movement of the aircraft in flight and give a constant read-out of their location.

"Damn!" MacNabb swore loudly.

"Problems, Captain?"

"Finger trouble."

MacNabb cleared down the panel and started again, inputting the vital coordinates. When he was done, he grabbed his flight bag, pulled out a wad of documents and thrust a copy of the flight log across the console. Dougie took it as he acknowledged a call from the tower.

He removed his headphones and hung them about his neck. "We're cleared to start engines."

"About time. The police give you a grilling, did they?" MacNabb kept his eyes focussed on the instruments.

"They were very thorough."

"No clues as to what they thought?"

"No, Captain. None at all." As he spoke, Dougie ran his gaze over the technical log sheets. "There's a problem with the drinking water supply in one of the economy cabin galleys. It should have been fixed."

MacNabb shook his head fiercely. "It's not important. Ignore it."

"But the company rules—"

"Stuff the company rules. We're not going to get tied up in paperwork because of the bloody drinking water in cattle class. Let them drink beer."

*

That Friday evening, they should have started engines at six o'clock Eastern Standard Time. The seven hours' flight across the Atlantic, together with the five hours' difference between New York and Europe, meant they were scheduled to land at around six o'clock Greenwich Mean Time: Saturday morning breakfast time in Scotland. A fresh crew would be waiting to take the 747 on to London, but that crew would likely have a long wait after the delays at New York.

Dougie pulled his flight bag onto his lap and flicked through the documentation. The weather reports made grim reading. Anticyclones over Greenland and Scandinavia had caused a cold front to move south. In Scotland the temperature had dropped to minus twenty-seven degrees Fahrenheit at Braemar. Even in England the blizzards were the most severe of the century. Prestwick airport was still open, but the weather was deteriorating. Conditions at Glasgow and Edinburgh airports were already below limits for landing, with no improvement expected.

Dougie read the reports again. His father's love of aviation had rubbed off on both his sons, but Dougie had a healthy respect for the inherent dangers. Bad weather had contributed to the mid-air collision that killed his brother in a military accident.

With the pre-flight checks complete, he eased himself into a more comfortable position while waiting for clearance for the aircraft to push back from the stand.

Sinclair International Airways had bought the Boeing 747, *Tartan Arrow*, second-hand from another European airline. The airframe was fitted with RB211 engines, the engine whose birth had bankrupted Rolls Royce. They were a fine combination, Dougie thought, the 747 and the RB211.

"Got your fuel flight plan completed, Sammy?" He turned to the flight engineer seated at right angles behind the two pilots.

"Aye." Kovak's father had escaped wartime Poland to fly with the RAF, but Sammy's accent carried no trace of Eastern Europe. It was pure fishing coast Fife.

"Things could get a bit awkward if we run into headwinds."

The flight engineer shrugged. "We're late anyway, Dougie. And I had a lunch date tomorrow."

"She'll just have to wait." Dougie turned his attention back to the captain who sat, ramrod straight, staring at the rain-splattered screen.

There was something puzzling about Fergus MacNabb this evening, puzzling and disturbing. It wasn't just the delay caused by the police questioning, although that had undoubtedly not helped, it was something deeper. It had bugged Dougie earlier in the evening while the crew packed away their documents in the flight briefing office.

Before they boarded the aircraft, he had quietly asked the flight engineer, "D'you think the captain looks troubled, Sammy?"

Kovak had whispered back, "Sure. It's this business with the stewardess. There's rumours about him screwing her."

Dougie shook his head. MacNabb had a reputation for playing the field, but it was none of his business.

"Sinclair 984, this is Sinclair Operations." Dougie pulled his headphones over his ears and adjusted his microphone boom.

"Go ahead, ops."

"Sinclair 984, we've got a message here from the police. They want to talk to Captain MacNabb. You're to shut down engines and ask him to return to the ops office."

Dougie looked across the flight deck at the senior pilot who was staring ahead into the cold night, his face set hard. "I think you're mistaken. The captain has already been interviewed by the police."

MacNabb looked up suddenly. "What's that? What's going on?"

"They say they want you to go back to the operations office, Captain. The police want to speak to you again."

The radio buzzed once more in Dougie's headset. "No mistake, guys. Tell Captain MacNabb to get his ass over here as quick as he can."

MacNabb's eyebrows rose as he picked up his headphones and caught the tail end of the message. Dougie waited for the famous temper to flare. It didn't.

"You have control, Mr Nyle. Shut down the engines." MacNabb looked pale as he climbed out of his seat and vacated the flight deck.

"Maybe they know all about him and Sally Scrimgeour." Sammy Kovak raised his voice once MacNabb was out of earshot.

"That's none of our business."

"Sally's husband's an air traffic controller at Prestwick Centre," Kovak said. "They say MacNabb wanted her to get a divorce and marry him, but she was stalling."

"Who told you that?"

"One of the stews. The brunette, Trudy Bodenstadt. The German girl. Boy, I could do things with her!"

"How does she know about it?"

"The usual rumour machine." With the engines winding down, Kovak leaned back and put his hands behind his head. "It's the same in every airline. The stews know everything there is to know about everyone. The company grapevine wouldn't work without them. I tell you, if the chairman picks up a woman tonight, it'll be common knowledge by breakfast. Especially if the woman works for Sinclair International."

"You don't seem to have a very high opinion of the company's female staff."

"High opinion?" Kovak laughed. "I've had a high opinion of every stew I've ever slept with."

"Including Trudy Bodenstadt?"

The flight engineer grinned. "I'm working on it."

Dougie didn't reply.

To pass the time at his flight engineer station, Kovak pulled out a copy of *Playboy*. He whistled loudly. "Jeez, Dougie, would you get a load of these!"

*

Half an hour later, MacNabb barged onto the flight deck, roughly elbowing his way past the flight engineer.

"Everything all right, Captain?" Dougie asked.

"Let's get this ship airborne."

"We're cleared to depart?"

"That's what I said, dammit!"

*

The climb out from Kennedy Airport was rough. Heavy clouds and gusting winds buffeted the aircraft as it clawed its way into the marginally calmer upper airspace.

Most other eastbound transatlantic flights had departed their Stateside airports on time and an armada of long-range jets was already winging its way across the ocean, well ahead of Sinclair flight 984.

"Would you like me to get the oceanic clearance, Captain?" Dougie gently reminded MacNabb that they had yet to be cleared into the vast spread of airspace beyond the North American coast. It was normal to ask for the oceanic clearance after take-off, but not to leave it too late.

"Ask for a clearance on track Victor at flight level three three zero." MacNabb's curtness was not lost on Dougie.

Victor was one of the six parallel flight tracks for aircraft crossing the North Atlantic that night. Dougie selected the clearance delivery frequency and transmitted the request.

When the reply came, he noted it on his log. "We're cleared on track Victor, Captain. Flight level three three zero." The Canadian oceanic control centre at Gander had allocated the exact flight profile they requested, a northerly route at thirty-three thousand feet.

MacNabb's affirmative was a grunt.

Dougie waited a few seconds before asking, "Shall I update the navigation?"

"I'll do it."

"Very well, Captain."

Passing twenty-two thousand feet, the Boeing climbed out of the tops of the thick, turbulent clouds into clearer air. Then the crew saw the lights of another aircraft five or six miles ahead and about two thousand feet below.

"A KC135 tanker, heading into Gander, according to his ATC reports," Dougie said.

MacNabb shrugged.

The flight engineer took up the comment. "Ever been into Gander, Dougie? It's a hole, like the back of beyond. And as for the women—"

The young pilot turned in his seat. "Concentrate on your instruments, Sammy."

Kovak sat back, melting into the dimness behind the two pilots. "I prefer to spend my time with women in warmer places. They wear less."

Across the flight deck, MacNabb moved uncomfortably in his seat.

Dougie glanced out at the lights of the other aircraft. It was going to be a long night.

*

The passenger in the front business-class section sank another large, neat whisky in one. It burned his throat, but it made him feel better.

Too many meetings had lasted into the early hours. Perspiration glistened on his bald, clammy scalp. His light grey suit was crumpled as if he had been wearing it day and night. A black leather briefcase was spread open on his lap and he fiddled with bundles of papers: reading, checking and comparing information, occasionally adding small pencil marks in a rough, hurried hand.

One of the cabin crew had made a public address warning about turbulence during the flight, but he ignored it and left his seatbelt loose, one half spread out on the empty seat beside him. He had too many air miles under his belt to worry about rough weather. When one of the smiling stewardesses leaned over and politely asked him to fasten up, he snapped an order for another Scotch and waited for her smile to fade and the girl to leave before he complied.

He stared down at the documents on his lap. Within an hour of landing he would have to brief the board on the possibility of an American offer for a major interest in his company. It irked him that some of the board members were in favour of their main British rivals taking a stake in the company. That would almost certainly mean the bidders taking a controlling interest, undermining his position. The Americans wanted him to remain at the helm.

"Miss! Where's that Scotch?"

The girl frowned at him as she placed the glass on his tray. He grabbed at his new drink and quickly downed it. The tightness in his chest started to loosen, though the perspiration was heavier now and he unknotted his tie. The stewardess paused, as if she was taking in something about his appearance.

"Bring me another," he told her.

"Sir, are you—?"

"Another one, lassie. Now!"

That damned tightness in his chest gripped him again. He fumbled among the papers inside the briefcase where his wife said she had packed his pills. He couldn't immediately find them. Where the hell were they? He cursed. He'd just have to cope without them.

*

Maggie Loughlin also needed a drink. Her father had taught her to drink heavily whenever trouble loomed — may he rest in hell.

She glanced down the length of the economy-class cabin before she slipped into the forward galley and poured herself a stiff whisky. Then she poured another. Finally she slipped a peppermint sweet into her mouth.

Maggie had felt nervous when MacNabb was called back for a second police interrogation. He wouldn't talk, she told herself. He was too clever to give anything away. He had too much to lose.

The mint cracked between her teeth. She put the heel of her hand to her chin and breathed into her palm. The whisky smell was masked. As senior stewardess on this flight, she had to set an example.

"Maggie?"

She jumped as one of the other girls came up suddenly behind her. "Oh God, Trudy, you gave me a shock."

The girl spoke softly, with just the hint of German accent. "What's the matter with you, Maggie? You look like a ghost."

"Just a bit under the weather. It's coming up to that time of the month, I guess." She turned towards the galley trays.

The younger stewardess took a step closer, too close for comfort. "We've got a problem in business class. There's a funny-looking old guy. He's had a number of stiff drinks and he wants more. I think he's had enough, but he's turning nasty."

Maggie wiped a hand across her damp brow before turning to face the other girl. "All right, Trudy. I'll handle it."

At thirty-five, she was one of the most experienced stewardesses aboard the aircraft and she had seen them all at one time or another: the drunk, the frightened, the downright rude. She had a formula for dealing with each. She strode into the business-class section and approached the passenger from behind. His head was slumped sideways across his seat, his arms were spread wide, one into the aisle and the other into empty seat beside him.

Coming alongside him, she looked into his staring eyes. His mouth was gaping open.

Chapter 2

"The winds are stronger than forecast." MacNabb glanced back at the flight engineer. Was it his imagination or had Kovak just thrust a magazine out of sight? "Check our fuel burn, would you. Work on the basis of a ten knot average increase in tail wind."

"That should help us make up a bit of time," the engineer said.

MacNabb turned back to the blackness in front of the aircraft and kept his thoughts to himself.

He knew better than any of the New York cops that he ought not to have taken this flight. It was too soon after Sally's death and he was too full of remorse for allowing things to get so far out of control. The depth of detail in those police interrogations unnerved him. That last time — when he had been called back from the flight deck — he thought they were ready to pin something on him. It had shaken his confidence in his own ability to stay calm under pressure. Even when they released him again he had been trembling inside.

He tried to relax as the 747 droned steadily through the night skies on full autopilot at flight level three three zero. They were now flying above the worst of the weather, but the aircraft hit an occasional rough patch. It was enough to upset one or two passengers, but MacNabb ignored it.

He glanced around at the other two crew members and reassured himself that they were settled into the routine of the flight.

First officer Nyle was finishing his meal, his face inscrutably unruffled. MacNabb always felt uneasy when flying with him. The younger man gave the impression of being too calm by half and his manner was always so courteous and formal, as if he was looking down his nose. MacNabb preferred the easy-going guys who called him Fergus on the flight deck.

Kovak was reclining in his seat at the flight engineer station, checking through the fuel flight plan. The edge of his cheesecake magazine was just visible beneath his desk. Was there no one here he could actually talk to?

MacNabb jerked himself upright in his seat at the sound of a call from the galley. He grabbed the handphone.

It was Maggie Loughlin. "We have an emergency, Captain. A sick passenger in business class. I think he's had a heart attack."

MacNabb forced his thoughts into sharper focus. "Have you checked whether there's a doctor on board?"

"No joy, I'm afraid. This is a serious one, Captain. He's just about conscious, but his breathing is erratic and his pulse is weak."

"All right. Keep me informed. I'll come back to you as soon as I can." He slammed the handphone back into its cradle.

Nyle pushed his meal tray to one side. "Trouble, Captain?"

"Passenger with a heart attack, and there's no doctor on board." MacNabb reached for his route charts and thrust them across the console to the first officer. "You have control, Mr Nyle. I'm going downstairs to check on the sick passenger. In the meantime get us a clearance for an emergency diversion to Gander. Make sure they have an ambulance ready for us when we land."

"Right away, Captain."

*

"Shit! What I wouldn't give for a bath right now." Major Paul S Judson scratched his ear and rubbed the back of his sweaty hand across his forehead. He was pooped. More than that, the entire crew of the United States Air Force KC135 Stratotanker was pooped. Dog tired. The order to divert to Gander for refuelling had come at the end of a long, gruelling exercise which had taxed them to the limit. Now the strain was telling.

Judson threw the dregs of his coffee down his throat. He waited for the tepid liquid to settle in his stomach, belched loudly and then eased himself out of his seat.

"You've got her," he announced to Lieutenant Lou Youngman, the second pilot. "I'm going to the john."

Youngman raised a thumb and looked pissed off. He was a junior pilot, but he looked older than his mid-twenties. His face had hardened with the job, grown dark and grim.

Behind the two pilots, at his navigator station, Lieutenant Brian Hewson had his head down low. Judson wondered whether he was asleep or just studying the small print on his charts. He didn't give a hoot as long as the course changes came on cue.

Judson shook his head clear. Flying was fun when it came in reasonable doses, but not when it was rammed down your throat by the jugful. And what in hell was it all about anyway? An emergency, they had been told. What emergency? You'll be briefed when you refuel at Gander was all they were told. It had better be one goddamn humdinger of an emergency or he was sure going to kick ass. All the way to Missouri, he was going to kick ass.

Shit! Pull yourself together, Judson. Majors didn't kick ass. They do as they're told and they fly their airplanes until they fall down dead with exhaustion. That was what being in the Air Force was all about.

Or was it?

Deep down, he knew that doing what he was told was his problem. Always had been. He'd just slipped into the way of it.

"You'll give up your vacation and fly this route exercise, Judson."

"Yes, sir."

"You'll take the longest route through the worst of the weather, Judson."

"Yes, sir."

"You'll lick my ass, Judson."

"Yes, sir!"

Doing what he was told had taken him to the rank of major, but it was also why he would never rise beyond that. He didn't have the guts to turn the tables and do what his brain told him was right. The generals in Washington promoted men with vision, but that was not the style of Major Paul S Judson.

As he left the flight deck, he ran his hand back through his short-cropped hair and reached into his pocket for gum. He would have preferred a reefer, but that was out of the question while he was flying this goddamn heap of aluminum. Even he could see the sense in that. He pulled out the sticky gum wrapping and swore softly. It was empty.

"Hey, Bryzjinsky!"

The burly sergeant was curled up at his rest station. Like the rest of them, his face was grey with fatigue. He glanced up from a well-thumbed magazine he had picked up back at base.

"Major?"

"Gimme a stick o' gum, willya?"

"Not again. Fer Chrissake, you bin cadging gum off o' me fer weeks now."

"Quit the cackle, Bryzjinsky. Gimme the gum."

"Okay Major. But this gotta be the last time."

"I know, I know."

Judson snatched the gum from the burly sergeant's fist and stomped on back towards the john. Goddammit. He was reduced to cadging from a lousy sergeant. How low can a guy get in this man's Air Force? He put a hand to his head again and felt the stress of so many hours' flying wash over him. The stress of flying and the stress of his wife walking out on him.

He wasn't too sure which pissed him off more.

*

"Why don't you call him 'sir'?" Brian Hewson leaned back in his navigator seat, rubbed his eyes and stretched his arms. "You know, Lou, I never once heard you call the major 'sir'."

Lou Youngman half-turned towards him. "Nope. Reckon I never did call him 'sir'. Not ever. But then, me and Paul, we're buddies."

"You go back a long way, huh?"

"Not so long." Youngman focussed his eyes on the flight-deck instruments. "But we're still buddies. I was there when Paul and Ruby were married."

"She weren't none too easy with him, from what I heard," Hewson said.

"Reckon she left him 'cos she was like that. Never one to settle down. But don't you say nothin' about it to Paul. You hear me?"

"Touchy subject, huh?"

"What do you think?"

*

Gander was not Fergus MacNabb's favourite place. But for the booze they called Newfoundland Screech, he would have classed it as a first-class dump. There was nothing else to interest a man. Once a week they had a stripper at one of the drinking clubs, but she had to be imported from St John's or even flown in from the mainland. On both the occasions when MacNabb had been forced to divert into Gander and make a night stop, he had been bored out of his mind. This time he hoped the delay would be minimal.

He made his way down to the business-class cabin and confirmed Maggie Loughlin's assessment of the passenger. Damn bad luck there was no doctor on board this time; there usually was. He stood up suddenly and felt tension pounding in his temple.

The tension got worse as he returned to the flight deck.

"They've given us a priority straight-in approach to Gander," Nyle announced. "But there are a lot of other aircraft on the approach control frequency. Mostly United States Air Force transport flights. It's as if there's some sort of military exercise going on round here."

"Nothing about that in flight briefing at Kennedy." MacNabb promptly put the matter out of his mind. After a cursory glance around the flight deck, he went back down to the business-class cabin and sought out Maggie Loughlin.

"We'll be landing at Gander soon," he said with forced calmness. "They'll have an ambulance meet the aircraft."

The stewardess bent over the sick passenger and wiped the sweat from his face. "His pulse is getting weaker. I've given him the medicine I found in his briefcase. There's nothing much more

I can do."

MacNabb patted her arm. "Shite! Why did this have to happen now of all times?"

The stewardess looked up at him. "S'pose we're just unlucky this trip."

MacNabb shook his head and turned away. He went back to the flight deck and took his seat. It was turning into one pig of a night.

"You have the landing," he told Nyle, more because he felt unsure of himself than as a favour to the first officer. His mind was crowded with thoughts of Sally Scrimgeour, no matter how much he tried to blank them out. Was it only four days ago they had had that big bust-up? The evening before he took the New York flight from Prestwick? She came over on the next flight, still angry when they met in the Big Apple.

She could have been more cooperative, much more cooperative that evening before he left Scotland. The more he thought about it, the more convinced he became: everything that happened was *her* fault.

*

Marriage. That was what he offered her. Okay, so he didn't offer it, he thrust it upon her without warning. It was what he thought she wanted, so he made a big thing of it. So big that he wanted to announce a planned engagement at a lavish dinner party in his parents' Ayrshire coast mansion.

What was so wrong about that?

All the right people were there: the board of Sinclair International Airways and one or two Scottish politicians, men of influence. Sally was happy to go to the party while her husband was conveniently away from home on an air traffic control training course in Bournemouth. Fergus thought she would be delighted.

She wasn't.

"For Christ's sake, Fergus, I'm a married woman. You can't announce my engagement to you!"

"But I want to marry you, Sally. I love you, you know that."

"No you don't, Fergus. You love flying, and you need some stupid woman to stick around and make things easy for you. You're not in love with me at all. And I'm still married to Jock. Remember?"

He flinched and turned away. "It's time we sorted out Jock, one way or another."

"What do you mean?"

He stared at the floor. "We're going to see him when he gets back from Bournemouth. You and me together. I've arranged a roster change so we can be on the same flight back from New York next Friday night. Jock will be home by then and we can tackle him together. You and me."

"You've done what?" She stood rigid at the door. Her voice rose to a scream. "How dare you! How bloody dare you!"

"Calm down, Sally. You'll bust a gut if you're not careful. If we face up to Jock together, we can persuade him to give you a divorce. Once we've sorted everything out—"

"Sorted things out? Fergus, it's *my* job to speak to Jock. Not yours."

"You're no good at that kind of thing, Sally. A little help won't go amiss."

"I've had enough of this. I want you to take me home."

"But Sally—"

"Now!"

The angry look in her face reminded him of Lindy. The way his first wife had looked just before he had beaten her to the ground. The desire to strike a fist at Sally was overwhelming. He had to turn away before he lashed out.

"Later. I'll take you back later," he said.

"Now!"

"All right, damn you!"

They drove away in silence. He felt uncomfortable because the excuse for leaving — a forgotten appointment with friends — was so obviously lame. As his powerful BMW headed back up the coast towards Ayr, he remained grimly silent. She didn't have the right to humiliate him. Even if she did think she was a princess and not a mere stewardess.

He slammed his foot down on the accelerator pedal.

"Slow down, Fergus!"

"Slow down? Shite! You want to drive the car for me, too?"

"You're going too fast."

He braked hard. "Okay, damn you. I'll slow down." He pulled off the road at a wild spot overlooking the sea, switched off the engine and sank back into his seat.

"Why have you stopped here?"

"Because you're a bitch, Sally. A right bitch. You know that?"

She refused to be drawn and sat staring out into nothingness.

He grasped the wheel tightly. "Get out of the car."

"What?"

"Just do as I say. Get out."

Her voice wavered. "Please, Fergus. Take me back to my flat."

He shook his head. "Not yet."

And his hand trembled as it curled into a fist.

Damn the woman! She deserved what she was about to get.

*

"This place stinks."

Major Paul Judson's words were carried away on a biting wind as he strode across the apron towards the Gander control tower. The whole goddamn business was getting up his nose and he was ready again to start kicking ass.

It wasn't ever as cold as this back home, not ever. The thought of a hot bath came back into sharp focus. That was followed by thoughts of Ruby. Flame-haired Ruby had the body of a goddess, the face of an angel and the temper of the devil himself. He wondered whether he would ever see her again.

An airman stood at a half-open door at the base of the control tower, his parka drawn forward over his head.

"Can I have your name please, sir?" The bored airman held a clipboard in front of him, his hand raised ready to check off each new arrival.

"Judson. Major Paul S Judson. KC135 number—"

"Okay, Major, I got all your details here. You just go in there. They're expecting you. First room on your left." His breath condensed in the freezing Canadian air like puffs of steam.

"What's this all about, airman?"

"You'll get a full briefing inside, sir. They'll tell you what to do next."

"Sure they will." They'll tell him what to do and he'll go out there and do it. He'll do it because he always did, even though he and his crew were tired beyond reason and common sense told him to say no.

He kicked the door as he entered.

Twenty minutes later, he emerged from the building holding a large portfolio in one hand and a heavily sealed envelope in the other. He paused at the door, gasped as the cold air sawed down into his lungs, and gave the airman a grim look.

"You okay, Major?" The airman's face was pinched and drawn beneath the parka hood.

"Sure, sure. I just finished a goddamn pig of a route exercise, my whole goddamn crew is whacked out. And now this."

"We all got our problems, sir."

"You bet your goddamn boots we have. And this one sure takes the biscuit."

"That's the way the cookie crumbles, sir. It ain't gonna be no picnic up there for the *Washington* guys." He raised his eyes heavenward.

Judson stared out into the icy, damp night air, blinked and then returned his mind to reality.

"That's right. It ain't gonna be no picnic. And this time the goddamn cookie is likely to crumble with one helluva mighty bang."

*

The 747 broke through the cloud base at fifteen hundred feet.

"Lights in sight," MacNabb said.

Dougie looked up and caught the converging lines of runway lights, piercing the darkness. After landing, he taxied the aircraft to the terminal and closed down the engines.

"Wow, take a look at that," Kovak chirped. A wide spread of American military aircraft, mostly transports, was arrayed across the apron. Dozens of well-wrapped figures darted about among the armada.

"I've never known Gander so busy," Dougie said. He peered through the front screen.

"What d'you think's going on here?" Kovak stretched forward from his flight engineer station.

MacNabb shot him a grim look as he climbed out from his seat. At the flight-deck door, he paused and looked thoughtfully towards the first officer. "We'll need to refuel. See to it, will you?"

When he was gone, Kovak whistled through his teeth. "Wow. There goes one helluva disturbed pilot."

*

Maggie Loughlin shivered. The senior stewardess had to accompany the ambulance crew when they stretchered the sick man from the aircraft.

Down on the apron, the chill wind hit her like a solid block of ice and she wrapped her coat tighter about herself. When the passenger was safely aboard the waiting ambulance, she stood back and watched it drive away across the frozen tarmac. The sound of the vehicle's engine was whipped aside by the biting wind. She was barely aware of MacNabb standing beside her until he touched her arm.

"I'm going over to flight briefing," he said. "Come with me." It was more of a command than a request, and Maggie knew better than to argue. No one argued with Fergus MacNabb, just as no one dared suggest that he had been promoted because his father sat on the company's board of directors. Nevertheless, it was common knowledge that he had been ten years in the promotion queue with British Airways before starting his swift rise to a senior post with Sinclair International.

They bent their heads into the freezing wind and said nothing more until they were in the warmth of the terminal.

"What did you tell the police at Kennedy, Fergus?"

"Nothing. At least, nothing to link either of us with Sally's death."

"You're sure?"

"Of course I'm sure. For chrissake, do you think I don't know how to handle a few damned cops? Just keep your cool and the whole business will blow over."

"I'm afraid."

"You can't afford to be afraid. Especially you, and especially not now. Just pull yourself together." Something behind his steady, glaring eyes frightened her.

"I hope you're right."

"Of course I am. The whole thing will disappear into the unsolved crime files. Dammit, there's a murder or a bloody mugging every day down on the New York subway, this one will soon be forgotten."

"What about—?"

"Look!" He grabbed her arm and pulled her closer. "Just get a grip on yourself. If you don't pull yourself together, you'll let something slip." He glanced around and saw people looking in their direction. Then he released the woman and hissed, "Go and buy me a bottle of Screech from duty-free and meet me in the briefing office."

She backed off slowly. She was in this business up to her ears and she had to be strong enough to see it through. If she didn't, she could expect no mercy from MacNabb.

*

The 747 sat quietly on the apron, a single civil airliner surrounded by an army of military aircraft.

MacNabb remained in the terminal for half an hour, leaving Dougie fretting at the further delay. When the captain returned to the flight deck, he looked angry and worn. A silence settled over the crew, broken only by the communication needed to prepare the aircraft for its continued flight.

Dougie's discomfort grew with each passing minute. MacNabb's impatience was becoming more and more like the behaviour he had learned to accept as normal from his father.

Eric Nyle had been a legend in the RAF. He was a man born to be a fighter pilot: hard, daring, forthright and unforgiving. When others hesitated, Eric Nyle always stepped forward. His elder son, Ian, was from the same mould.

When Dougie began his RAF pilot training, he was immediately compared with his father and brother, and found wanting.

"So, you're Eric's son, are you?" the flying instructors would say. "You're not like him, are you? Not like your brother, either. Reckon you don't have the right stuff to be a fighter pilot. Stick to flying transports."

Dougie took the advice to heart. He left the RAF and worked hard for his commercial pilot's licence. But he never forgot that his father and Ian were made of the right stuff. When he encountered a difficult situation, it came naturally to him to wonder how his father would have coped. If there was a good way, a right way of handling a problem, his father would know it.

An hour after they landed at Gander, *Tartan Arrow* was refuelled and ready for take-off. It taxied towards the runway, carefully inching along behind a Lockheed P-3B Orion maritime reconnaissance aircraft. An old KC135 was at the head of the queue.

MacNabb was at the controls while Dougie ran through the pre-flight check. He glanced at his watch: approaching 0600 Greenwich Mean Time, five hours ahead of Eastern Standard Time. Whatever steps they took to make up some of the loss, they could not now expect to arrive at Prestwick until after midday, well behind the breakfast time arrival the company had promised.

After take-off, the aircraft was gobbled up into the thick, bumpy cloud. It bucked and strained as it clawed its way towards the upper airspace. A continual stream of air traffic control directions bubbled in the flight crew's headsets, directions designed to separate the 747 from the large number of military aircraft mysteriously crowding the Canadian skies.

"I've been thinking, Captain," Dougie commented, "about the USAF activity: there must be a major exercise going on. Did they say anything about it in the briefing office?"

"Didn't ask. It doesn't concern us. You'd better contact Gander Oceanic again and get us a new ocean clearance. Ask for track Victor, same as before."

Dougie leaned across the centre console to change his radio frequency. He tuned into the Gander clearance delivery channel and requested a new clearance for an oceanic track. MacNabb took no notice of him until he announced, "We can't get a clearance on track Victor, Captain."

"Why not?"

"The track is no longer available for military reasons. We're cleared on track Whiskey at flight level three three zero."

"Military reasons! What the—?"

"That's what they say, Captain."

"Shite! Alright, you stick with the radio and I'll sort out the paperwork and the waypoints." MacNabb breathed out loudly as he reached for the navigation charts. The aircraft's navigation computer was set up for track Victor and would need to be re-programmed for track Whiskey.

Dougie glanced at him as the captain began to operate the navigation computer keyboard, feeding in the waypoints for the oceanic flight. He was stabbing at the buttons with undisguised annoyance.

When the 747 levelled out at thirty-three thousand feet, it was clear of the worst of the turbulence, but Dougie left the 'Fasten Seatbelts' sign switched on as a precaution. Then he settled down for a routine end to an otherwise eventful flight.

"I hope it's quieter than this out over the ocean," he said as another gaggle of military aircraft checked in on the radio frequency. "The Americans seem to be putting everything they've got in the sky tonight."

*

"Bryzjinsky!" Major Paul Judson howled into the intercom.

"Waddyawant?" the sergeant's voice snapped back.

Judson grimaced. The bastard could be court-martialled for that sort of insubordination. "Get your ass up here with some fresh coffee."

"Okay."

Judson felt his mind spinning, like a fly buzzing inside an empty bottle. Tiredness seeped through his every bone and joint.

He glanced across the flight deck. Youngman had his eyes closed, his head angled forward onto his chest. The whole darned crew was in no condition to be flying. Even the airplane wasn't equipped to be out here. It was an early model KC135 with old, smoky engines that would be banned from any civil airport in normal circumstance. He could imagine the base commander saying, "Give Judson the oldest shit we've got and he'll fly the damned thing. Judson never complains. Judson is an *ass-licker*. Judson does what he's told."

It wasn't just the engines that were clapped out. The navigation equipment wasn't up to it and the high-frequency radio equipment was minimal.

But this was an emergency.

It was an emergency? So what? They should not be doing this. But they would do it anyway because Paul S Judson always followed orders.

He looked at his watch. Another forty-five minutes and they should be on station to begin refuelling the other aircraft engaged in the emergency. He would give Youngman half an hour before waking him. Hewson also. Then what? Then they would try to make the best of whatever mess they found out there. What a screw-up the government had made. There was no way the president was going to ride out this one. Not if the press got hold of it.

"You wanted some coffee?" The burly sergeant appeared between the two pilots. He had moderated his tone and he looked as bad as the rest of them.

"You had some shut-eye, Bryzjinsky?"

"No, sir. Never could sleep on these old ships."

"Nor me. Guess we'll have to slug it out till we drop."

"Guess so, sir."

Bryzjinsky shuffled away and Judson took a sip of the coffee. It tasted dreadful. He leaned his head back and half-closed his eyes. What he wouldn't give for a long, hot bath.

*

For Fergus MacNabb, the night was longer than usual, drawn out by a dark foreboding that pressed constantly on his thoughts. He checked their position over the oceanic waypoints like an automaton, his real thoughts elsewhere, and he left the high-frequency radio calls to Nyle. The rest of the time he sat back, staring out into the night sky.

They passed out of the jurisdiction of Gander Oceanic air traffic control at a position on the thirty degrees west line of longitude, halfway across the North Atlantic Ocean. The aircraft then entered the Shanwick Oceanic Control Area under the joint jurisdiction of radio communicators at Ballygireen radio station near Shannon and controllers at the Scottish Air Traffic Control Centre in Prestwick town.

Nyle passed a routine message to Ballygireen at the midway point, using the outmoded system of high-frequency radio. The Irish communicators relayed the aircraft's message to controllers at Prestwick along a teleprinter link. One day the system would be brought up to date, but it was a long time coming.

At 0930 GMT they were flying in full daylight. Instead of an ocean below, the captain stared down at a carpet of cloud with occasional towers of cumulonimbus clouds rising majestically like giant mushrooms.

As the flight droned onwards, MacNabb bemoaned the cabin crew's lack of diligence in keeping his cup topped up with black coffee. As if in response, Nyle left the flight deck to visit the latrines.

Sod him, MacNabb thought.

*

In the cramped toilet, Dougie splashed cold water over his face and allowed it to dribble down his cheeks and neck. He stood, half-bent over the wash basin, staring into the stainless steel bowl. As the water drained away, he felt the tension begin to ease.

He was glad of a few minutes' respite from the pressure of the flight deck. He had come up against MacNabb's crass behaviour on previous flights, but this time it was different. Much worse. He looked upwards and his reflection came into view in a small mirror mounted above the basin. Is that really me? How tired I look.

Still gazing into the mirror, he allowed his thoughts to drift away from Fergus MacNabb and settled upon Jenny's behaviour just hours before he left home.

*

He'd picked up his black leather flight bag, hoping Jenny would curtail her tears for the next few minutes. At least until he left the house. With his free hand, he buttoned his uniform jacket.

He looked away from her, overcome with guilt.

The early morning television news chattered in the background and he glanced at the screen as a way of avoiding Jenny.

"At a news conference, NASA spokesman, George Henry, denied rumours of a secret space shuttle mission involving President Reagan's Star Wars Strategic Defence Initiative. When questioned, he said—"

"I wish you didn't have to go." Jenny sat hunched forward in her armchair, her head bowed, eyes focussed on her knitting.

Dougie turned away from the television set as the newscaster introduced the next story: the disappearance of British Prime Minister Margaret Thatcher's son, Mark, on the Paris-Dakar car race across the Sahara.

Dougie sighed. When did Jenny change from the fun-loving outdoor girl of just a few months ago?

"I really need to be off now. It's going to be a difficult drive in this weather." He straightened his jacket and forced himself to take a step closer. "It's my job, love. It pays the mortgage."

"If only we could…" Her words tailed off and the needles moved furiously, as if her heart and soul were being incorporated into a pale pink sweater that she didn't need. Her black hair looked dull and matted, as if she had not washed it in a week or more.

Could he put a protective arm about her without provoking a squeal of protest? Probably not. "I understand," he said.

Day after day, she said she wanted another baby, a child to heal the wound of their loss. They needed time to adjust, he told her. Time to get over the period of grieving. But the problem went deeper than that. Much deeper. Sometimes, not often, he was able to admit to himself that he was afraid of risking further hurt.

The clock chimed on the mantelpiece, a tinny sound that was out of place in the big lounge. Beyond the picture window, the cloud had dropped lower in the past hour, obscuring the view of Ailsa Craig.

Dougie leaned forward and hesitantly pecked at Jenny's cheek, still soft and pliant but pale even in the flickering glow of firelight. She flinched, something she had never done until after the funeral. How could he deal with his guilt when she refused to offer him comfort? Tears welled in her eyes but she hastily brushed them aside with the back of one hand.

"I'll call you as soon as we arrive in New York."

"Might not be here. Might go up to Alloway to see Mum." She sniffed and wiped again at her eyes. "The weather's getting worse so I might stay a while."

"That's fine. You need to be with family while I'm away." He straightened and his glance swept past her to a photograph beside the clock. Jenny and him, with two-year-old Edward.

It was a summer holiday picture of a happy young family on a sunny beach in Tenerife. Just six months ago. Jenny looked happy and so beautiful in her skimpy white bikini, her hair shimmering in the sunlight. Dougie, tall and broad-shouldered beside his petite wife, held his son in his arms. Edward and he had the same straw-coloured hair and the same square jaw that was a trademark of the Nyle family line.

It had been Jenny's twenty-eighth birthday and they had spent a week in an expensive hotel to celebrate. They had never been happier.

It was the last picture taken before Edward died of meningitis barely a month later. He went to bed one night a happy and contented little boy, by midnight they had rushed him to the children's hospital in Ayr. By morning it was all over.

Dougie wished Jenny would let him put the picture in an album, somewhere out of sight.

"You take care," she said hoarsely, eyes still focused on the unnecessary pink sweater. The needles flashed even faster.

"I always do." He bit at his lip and glanced back at the television. The news broadcast was coming to an end. The weather forecaster was predicting heavy storms coming in from the north.

He walked away with a muttered goodbye.

A light flurry of snow played about his face as he strode to his car. He opened the door, shivered and then stared up at black rolling clouds. Could he bear the agony if they went through another loss?

*

The 747 bucked in turbulence.

Dougie looked again into the mirror and saw that his face was grey and pinched.

He splashed more water across his forehead.

*

On the flight deck, Fergus MacNabb sat quietly in the left-hand seat. He squinted out through the front windscreen, but tiredness was getting the better of him. All he could see was the distant horizon and the blurred images of endless clouds.

The high-frequency radio telephone was switched off. The

oceanic communicators would use the SELCAL system to alert him for routine radio reports. One VHF radio was tuned to the emergency frequency, 121.5 megahertz, but no sound came from it to disturb his thoughts.

His attention was drawn back into the flight deck by the appearance of the stewardess called Trudy Bodenstadt. He had once asked Maggie Loughlin to arrange a casual meeting between Trudy and himself at a party. It hadn't worked out as he had planned because she claimed to have a boyfriend flying for British Airways. Lying bitch. Truth was she had no time for older pilots like Fergus MacNabb. Tonight the girl looked red-eyed and uneasy. Probably the reaction to Sally's death. They had been roommates.

"Would you like some more coffee, Captain?"

He turned in his seat to better study the girl's figure, wincing when she avoided his face, as if she was ill at ease in his presence.

"No thank you. Not just now." It annoyed him to be so polite.

"Put me down for a cup, sweetheart," Kovak said from his flight engineer position. "I like it black and sweet, like my women."

The stewardess tried to raise a smile, but failed. Her face was pale in the subdued light of the flight deck.

"What about Mister Ny—" The stewardess's voice tailed off as she stared, suddenly wide-eyed, out of the front windscreen. "Oh, no! Look! Look!" She dropped the tray and brought her left hand up suddenly to her face. "Look!" She thrust out her right arm, pointing towards a flashing wingtip light framed in the screen beside the captain's seat.

MacNabb swung round. "What the hell!"

A large aircraft was flying close alongside them. Far too close. The fuselage markings — *US Air Force* — were briefly seen and then lost to sight. He grabbed instinctively at the control column yoke with one hand and deselected the autopilot with the other. He swung the big Boeing over into a steep turn to take it away from the other aircraft, but he knew that it was too late.

The fuselage of the Sinclair aircraft shuddered as the other aircraft's wingtip sliced into its nose just ahead of the captain's seat. MacNabb screamed as the wingtip carved a devastating path across the metal fuselage skin. Before he could fling up his hands to protect himself, it ripped through the front screen, smashing the glazing into a million parts.

He screamed again as the sharp splinters of glass lanced into his face. Any rational thoughts were dragged out of his mind by a wall of cold air blasting through the broken screen.

Seconds passed. He wasn't sure how many. Then a loud explosion followed. A flash of flame, a thundering noise, a violent reverberation.

MacNabb tried to think.

His head was filled with noise, loud burning noise. What had happened? He turned his barely-seeing eyes to the left and watched, incredulous, as the other aircraft swung away.

The explosion! He knew now what the noise was. That damned wing had torn through one of the 747's port engines. He swung his damaged gaze to the right, across the flight deck towards the stewardess. She seemed to have her arms tight about the first officer's seat to stop herself being sucked out of the aircraft. Oh, God! What have we done?

Chapter 3

A burst of anger rippled through Maggie Loughlin, an uncontrollable dragon she shared with Fergus MacNabb. It was also anger born out of the stupidity of Sally Scrimgeour, the girl who died because she knew too much. She gritted her teeth and clenched her fists. She had to keep herself under control.

"Miss! Come here. Quickly!"

What the hell was the matter now? She swung round as an irate passenger raced up to her, shouting incoherently. Damn! She'd had enough of passenger problems.

She had been sorting empty meal trays in the rear galley, taking her time as an excuse to keep away from the passengers. She could have asked one of the other girls to do the job, but she wanted to be out of sight when she took a few much-needed shots of vodka.

Then the alarmed passenger came rushing into the galley.

A smartly dressed young man with wild eyes, he used his high-pitched voice at blast level. At first she thought he had been drinking heavily. She cursed aloud and then thrust out a hand towards him. But he sidestepped it like a dancing boxer.

He waved his arms wildly before grabbing the front of her uniform jacket. "There's another aircraft alongside us!"

"There's what?"

"Come and see!" Keeping his grip tight on her jacket, he hauled her into the economy-class cabin.

She needed a moment to adjust her thoughts. The vodka had numbed her brain to the point of lethargy. And yet something was obviously wrong. Passengers were gathered excitedly at the port-side windows. A burst of anxious voices rose to greet her and the young man thrust his fist towards the view outside the aircraft.

Maggie gasped.

She knew enough about aircraft to recognise it. The tail end of a United States Air Force KC135 Stratotanker. The image filled the window. Her heart thumped as she pushed herself into an empty seat space and peered out. It was flying on a parallel heading, just yards away from the 747.

Seconds passed as she stared out at the Stratotanker, seconds spent in numbed shock. Then her mind cleared suddenly. In the same instant, a cold sweat broke out over her body. The other aircraft was moving at about the same speed as the 747 and edging slowly nearer.

"You must tell the pilot!" The passenger's eyes bulged from his head.

"Yes, tell the pilot!" Another passenger grabbed her arm.

Maggie tried to edge away, but her coat was trapped in the young man's tight grip. His mouth opened to shout, but he got no further. Before the words formed in his throat, the fuselage bucked like a frenzied horse. Metal impacted fiercely upon metal.

Thrown aside by the collision, he and Maggie Loughlin fell into each other's arms.

*

Major Paul S Judson had been dreaming about home. Not as it was now, an empty apartment strewn with dirty clothes and the re-mains of half-eaten meals. He dreamt about it as it had been before Ruby left, when their lives had been one long round of parties. Days spent flying and nights spent in Ruby's arms. He should have realised it would never last.

He had met Ruby at a mess party. She arrived with another officer and left with Paul Judson, both of them headed straight for her bed. Ruby was dynamite. She always took the lead and she rode him until he was drained. Sometimes she demanded more than he was able to give in one session and lovemaking became an episodic serial throughout the day. They married one weekend on a high of booze and sex.

What hit him most was the way Ruby left. Not quietly, but with one helluva bang, just like everything else Ruby did in life. On a whim, she phoned all her friends on the base camp and told them what she thought of him. She told them she couldn't live with a man who was always doing what he was told, like some goddamn prep school kid out to please his teachers. And then she took off with his car and his credit cards. The news was all round the base before Judson got back to the apartment and found she had left him without a dollar to his name. A week later she wrote to say she was shacked up with a film director on a ranch in California. But she never did send back the credit cards.

The dream ignored those days of pain. It stuck to the time they had been happy together, that short period when Judson's life was good.

Then it happened.

He woke suddenly, punched forward in his seat.

The blast echoed back through the fuselage. The KC135 kicked savagely and Judson grabbed at the jerking control column in a vain effort to steady himself.

His mind went into a spin.

"Jeez! We gone and done it this time!" Youngman shouted across the flight deck. He was struggling violently with the column. Beyond him, framed in the starboard window, was the unmistakable outline of a 747's nose.

"What the—?" Hewson, pale-faced and frightened, swung round in his seat. Had he been asleep, too?

Judson tightened his grip on the juddering column and followed through on Youngman's control movements. They were going into a left turn, away from the other aircraft.

"We hit them!" Youngman shouted between clenched teeth. "We goddamn hit the bastards!"

Judson felt his blood curdle.

*

MacNabb's mind ran haywire, powering into uncoordinated overdrive. The 747 was diving. The gushing airflow inside the flight deck was misting up.

He tried to work out what had happened in between loud panic-stricken screams for help. His own screams. His brain was running between blind terror and reason. He couldn't make out the readings on the instrument panel. Why? The mist was getting worse. And something sticky was lathering his eyes.

Blood.

And pain. Pain was everywhere.

Never mind. Forget the physical hurt. What went wrong with the aircraft?

Think. What happened in the moment of collision?

Cushioned. Yes, the impact between the two aircraft had been cushioned. Why? Think. Because the two aircraft were flying on parallel headings at similar speeds. But they were badly wounded. How? Think again! The sharp tip of the military aircraft's wing had torn through the upper skin along the nose of the Sinclair 747's fuselage like a surgeon's knife slicing open a body on an operating table.

More pain. What was wrong with him?

Never mind. What happened to the aircraft?

He imagined the scene as if it were a re-run: the 747's metal skin peeling back, the skeleton of the aircraft beneath suddenly revealed, cruelly exposed like twisted and broken bones. The image grew more vivid: the rear edge of the tanker's wingtip grating back along the nose and catching the 747's front windscreen a sliding blow. Only a glancing blow, but plenty powerful enough to shatter the glass in front of the captain's seat.

The four RB211 engines were running at high speed. What had he done wrong? He had handled the whole damned thing badly, that's what. He had turned the 747 to starboard so that the port wing rose and the port engines came up level with the military aircraft's wing. Having scythed through the 747's nose section, the rear of that wing had cut backwards into the port inner engine cowling, smashing into the big fan blades inside.

That was the explosion he heard: the noise of the engines disintegrating.

The fan assembly had shattered with the force of a small bomb and pieces of hot, jagged metal had flown off in all directions.

Some would have fallen through the clouds into the cold ocean below, lost forever.

And the rest?

Once again his imagination took over: debris from the shattered engine ripping through the 747's fuselage. He visualised large holes stabbed through the 747's skin causing explosive decompression. Air rapidly sucked out of the cabin. The fine mist forming inside the aircraft as moisture in the air condensed.

The picture grew in his imagination. Overhead lockers bursting open. Cabin luggage bouncing off panels and passengers alike. Oxygen masks hanging and swinging wildly. Passengers crying out, tumbling into the aisle. Bodies banging against bodies. Passengers riveted to their seats, unable to move. Piercing screams echoing down the fuselage.

Hysteria.

What should he do now?

Think, brain, think!

But his thoughts turned cloudy, his vision tunnelled away from him. Where was his own oxygen supply?

*

Dougie was leaving the toilet on the upper deck when the first collision occurred.

He had just pushed the door shut when the fuselage shuddered violently. Caught off balance, he fell to one side and grabbed out for support. The heavy crash didn't sound like the effect of turbulence, and it certainly didn't feel like turbulence. He tried to regain his feet.

Staggering upright, he registered a brief shocked silence. It was quickly followed by the sound of alarmed voices.

He grabbed at the toilet door handle with one hand, wobbled on his feet and took a giant step across the aisle. And then! Another aircraft was silhouetted in the port-side windows. A long silver tubular shape. A brief glimpse of lettering on the side: *US Air Force*.

His thoughts suddenly stopped, blanked out by a thundering

explosion. His ordered mind was overbalanced by confusion. And noise. Impossibly loud noise.

Then logic returned and his innate sense of discipline brought him back to reality. But what was happening now? A violent rush of air burst through the cabin, the sound of a subway train coming out fast from a tunnel into an underground station.

The fuselage had been ruptured. He turned to the rear of the cabin where a gaping hole had opened up on the port side. What had MacNabb done?

He had to get back to the flight deck.

Gritting his teeth, he pulled himself along the aisle towards the front of the aircraft. It was imperative that he be back in his seat.

He had taken only two steps before the floor moved again as the aircraft went into a steep turn to starboard. He flung out his arms to protect his face and bounced against the cabin partition. Then he was thrown backwards into the lap of a large woman in one of the aisle seats.

The emergency oxygen masks had dropped from the ceiling, but panic was now rife among the passengers. A sports bag fell from a nearby locker and scattered clothes and toiletries. A packet of tampons bounced across the cabin floor.

Dougie paused momentarily, struggling to formulate his next move. He swung his gaze up and down the cabin. Where were the crew? Further down the aisle, a stewardess lay on the floor, her back towards him. Her face was hidden from his view. She half-struggled to her knees and then twisted and fell, face down with her head jammed against an aisle seat.

Someone ought to help her get to her feet. Maybe he ought to go to her? No. It was more important that he should get back to the flight deck.

He forced himself out of the maternal woman's lap.

"What's happening?" The woman snatched at his sleeve. Her face was white with fear. Dougie patted her hand and reached for her dangling oxygen equipment. He took several deep breaths from the face mask and then pushed it over the woman's mouth.

At first she struggled, but she relaxed a little when she saw what he was trying to do. With a quick check that her seatbelt was secured, he levered himself upright and continued on down the angled aisle, stumbling towards the front of the aeroplane.

*

Just moments before the collision, Simon Devereaux had been studying the previous day's *New York Times* and sipping at his coffee. Soberly dressed in grey turtleneck sweater, dark grey jacket and light-coloured slacks, he sat on the starboard side of the upper-deck first-class cabin.

Then the world went mad.

Earlier in the flight, Maggie Loughlin had appeared in the cabin in the course of her duties. Not bad for a Brit, he decided. He allowed his attention to envelop the senior stewardess, mentally stripping away layers of clothing from the tall, well-endowed young blonde. Enjoyable, but that was not his purpose in being here. With an effort, he focussed his attention on her behaviour, especially her contacts with the other crew members. When she left the cabin, he felt a tinge of disappointment.

He jumped at the sound of a loud explosion, behind him and to his left. As he spun round in his seat, a flash of flame shot through one of the windows. An engine exploded, sending shattered remnants through the fuselage skin. A passenger, who had been sitting in the rear window seat on the port side, was suddenly reduced to a bloody pulp as shards of hot, jagged metal speared through his body.

He tried to think, to concentrate on what was happening. His head whirled but he forced himself to scan up and down the cabin. That guy — the aircraft's first officer — what was his name? He was at the front of the cabin, using a passenger's oxygen mask, cupping it over his mouth.

Devereaux clasped at his head. He must do the same. Must get some oxygen. He reached up for his own dangling mask and took a long breath.

What now? The first officer had staggered on towards the flight deck. Who was left in charge here? Anyone?

Still sucking in the oxygen, Devereaux turned his attention to the other passengers and the single stewardess who had been on the upper deck. The poor girl was near the rear of the cabin, lying face down and motionless on the floor.

He turned his attention back to the gaping hole in the side of the aircraft. The nearest row of seats still held the gory mess of the dead man in the window seat and the two other passengers, both screaming.

The whole thing was moving! Torn from its mounting, and tugged by the force of the cabin decompression, the seat row began to scrape across the floor until it slid into the hole. The passenger in the centre seat had his hands across his face as the violent draught sucked him and the assembly farther into the void. A small, grey-haired woman, writhing in the seat beside him, screamed soundlessly against the roaring chaos.

Devereaux clutched at his arm rests. Directly opposite him, a dark-haired young woman stumbled to her feet and struggled back down the aisle towards the three doomed people. She grabbed the end of the assembly and pulled. Devereaux strained to see back down the cabin, the detail imprinting itself on his mind like a frozen moment in history: the young woman's worn jeans and white T-shirt, the legend *Jesus is Love* emblazoned across her chest, her look of intense concentration as she pulled at the seat assembly.

Devereaux instinctively removed his oxygen mask and shouted at her to get back. There was nothing she or anyone could do to help those passengers. But his words were drowned by the cacophony.

The fuselage shook violently and the woman fell to her knees, still grasping the seats. He gaped at her, helpless, as the row of seats, the passengers and the young woman were tugged farther out through the hole.

Slowly, painfully, the whole assembly slid out into the cold, empty sky. At the last moment the young woman appeared to understand the folly of what she was doing. She opened her mouth to scream and then shut it again. No one moved to help her. No one *could* help her now. As a jagged edge of the fuselage tore into her body, a spurt of blood leapt across her T-shirt, obliterating the message of heavenly hope. The last thing Devereaux saw of her was the surprised look on her face.

*

Dougie fought his way down the steeply sloping aisle towards the flight deck, his hands tightly grasping each seat row as he passed by.

The 747 was still in a steep dive, but that was fortunate. With the loss of pressurisation, it was vital to get the aircraft down below ten thousand feet before the passengers and crew alike collapsed from hypoxia. He had about one and a half minutes of consciousness left before he would collapse through starvation of oxygen to his brain.

The emergency masks had automatically deployed from the ceiling, but many of the passengers were too confused, too shocked or too frightened to use them.

He stopped and grabbed at a mask dangling above a thin, middle-aged woman who was silently weeping into her hands. He clamped it over his mouth and gulped down the oxygen. When he felt able to move on, he placed the mask over the woman's face and pulled her hands upwards to hold it in place. For a moment, he thought she was going to push the mask away, but when he removed his own hands, she kept it in place and stared at him, red-eyed and frightened.

Oxygen was now the uppermost thought in Dougie's mind. Would he be able to get to a portable breathing set in order to fight the rest of the way to the flight deck? He had no idea how far the aircraft had already descended, but his brief intake of oxygen would only keep him conscious for a short time.

A stewardess was struggling towards him.

*

Trudy Bodenstadt felt as if her brain was slipping in and out of gear. She vaguely noticed the first officer as she climbed up the steeply sloping aisle away from the flight deck, but he meant little to her just then. He was coming towards her out of the hazy mist that filled the cabin, approaching her like a ghost from a graveyard.

She had to get away from the front of the aircraft. Had to. Her place was back here in the passenger cabin. But the truth went deeper than that. She was too frightened to stay on the flight deck where all hell had broken loose.

The first officer came closer. He was using a passenger oxygen mask. Of course! That was why she was feeling so woozy. She had to get to a mask, had to get oxygen. Steadying herself against the seats, she grabbed at the nearest unused mask and inhaled.

After a few deep breaths, her thoughts swam into sharper focus. What now? She cast her gaze about the cabin. Chaos, nothing but chaos. And appalling noise. As bad as the noise on the flight deck.

If only she could strap herself into the nearest seat and wait until this whole nightmare went away. If only she could just close her eyes and wipe out the horrors about her. But she couldn't. She had to do something to help the passengers.

She dropped the mask and struggled on up the aisle. As she came closer to the first officer, he shouted at her. His voice barely registered.

"There are serious injuries at the back of the cabin." He tried to point with one hand while holding onto a passenger seat with the other, but he had difficulty keeping his balance. All about them, the swirling mist gave the cabin an eerie atmosphere.

"I'll see to them," Trudy mouthed and struggled on past. Her eyes stung as her gaze darted about the cabin, taking in the confusion in the faces of some passengers and the terror in the eyes of others.

She stopped suddenly. What had happened back here?

She stared at the gaping hole in the fuselage and felt the roar of wind as it howled through the opening. In the adjacent passenger seats, people were moving, shouting, screaming or lying dead in

47

their seats. Several long swathes of blood were painted about the inside fuselage walls. Large ugly red pools swilled about on the floor.

Trudy gulped. She put a hand to her mouth. Dear God, what should she do? Then she saw the prostrate body of another stewardess on the floor.

Anxiously, she struggled on up the aisle to where the girl lay. She stopped, horrified. A jagged piece of metal protruded from the stewardess's forehead. Her face was a sticky red mass where blood had poured from the ugly wound. Beneath the flow, brain tissue oozed down her face. Trudy turned away, retching.

She shivered violently as she pulled herself upright. Her long, brown hair whipped wildly in the bitter rush of air through the cabin.

*

MacNabb swallowed hard, drawing oxygen into his lungs. A wall of air pounded in through the shattered screen, threatening to rip away his face mask.

The autopilot was disconnected and the flying controls were responding to his violent inputs. His own spilled blood fogged his vision and more blood was splattered down his left arm. He had no idea where it had come from.

The aircraft was in a steep dive with thrust levers closed, speed brakes selected and gear down. He had got that bit right. It was the standard procedure for this sort of emergency, the procedure he had practised many times in simulators.

His pulse raced as he squeezed the juddering control yoke and eased it gently backwards to reduce the rate of descent. They had been going down fast, too fast. Maybe ten thousand feet per minute. He wiped the blood from his eyes and peered at the climb and descent indicator. When he eased back again on the column, the instrument's arrow moved in response.

Another quick swipe across his eyes, then another scan across the instrument panel. Most of the instruments on his side of the flight deck were no longer working.

His vision clouded once more.

The roaring air continued to beat into his face. He brought his right hand back to tighten the strap of his oxygen mask. Again, he seized the column with both hands and pain shot through his left arm. He glanced at his jacket sleeve. Blood seeped through the black material and dripped to the floor.

If only Nyle were there to take the pressure from the column. But the first officer's seat was empty.

MacNabb shook his head to clear his thoughts, fighting against the greyness creeping over him. Numbness was masking the reality of the catastrophe. He was drifting away.

"I can't see the altimeter!" He wasn't sure to whom he was crying out. Wasn't even sure who was on the flight deck with him. Wasn't sure if the greyness engulfing him was caused by the mist that filled the aircraft or by loss of blood. Whatever it was, he couldn't stop his slow descent into unconsciousness.

*

Sammy Kovak had been daydreaming before the stewardess appeared on the flight deck, conjuring up fanciful images of young, attractive women. Thoughts of Maggie Loughlin and Trudy Bodenstadt were interspersed with memories of other, more amenable stewardesses who had caught his imagination. Trudy's appearance — especially her shapely young figure — had added yet another source of inspiration.

Then his world fell apart.

"What the hell's happening?"

He gripped his seat with one hand and used the other to hold his oxygen mask tightly to his face. The strap was broken.

The 747 was diving towards the ocean. He heard and felt the shudder of a badly wounded aeroplane, creaking, shouting, complaining. Metal ravaged against metal and broken fittings banged loosely but heavily against the fuselage. Air roared through the jagged hole in the front screen.

His view of the engineering instrument panel was blurred. The dials shook violently, the air was turned opaque by the mist. But he didn't need a sharp focus on the instruments to see that they were running wild. The aircraft was losing fuel, probably through lines ruptured in the collision. But which lines were ruptured? And which valves should he try to shut off?

A warning bell rang and an indicator light on the right side of the panel showed an engine fire. Was that the port inner engine? He peered closer. Probably the port inner. Instinctively, he reached towards the fire protection switches. At the same time his oxygen mask fell away, blown aside by the rush of air.

"Captain!" he screamed against the roar of cold air. "Captain, we have a fire!" But his words were dragged off into the maelstrom.

Kovak stared at MacNabb, willing him to do something. Anything. Slowly, as if he was unsure of what was going on, the pilot reached for the port inner thrust lever. It was already closed. Kovak watched the captain's laboured movements and wondered if he was fully conscious. At least he had shown some reaction to the warning bell.

Breathing heavily, Kovak jabbed at one of the fire switches and reached for his mask.

The warning bell stopped. One less thing for him to think about. He wasn't sure why the alarm had stopped. Maybe the fast descent had blown out the fire. Should he continue with the full emergency drill? The fuel flow to that engine was still switched on. Should he shut off the fuel to the port inner? Or not? Logical thought came only in short snatches.

He breathed in the oxygen and tried to concentrate before it was too late. Too late? It was already too late for all of them. Too late to stop *Tartan Arrow* plunging into the cold waters of the North Atlantic.

He directed his vision back towards the vibrating panel in front of him and forced himself to concentrate on the fuel flow valves and gauges. Hesitantly, he reached out a hand towards a fuel switch and hoped he was about to shut off the supply to the damaged engine.

*

Dougie half-staggered and half-fell onto the flight deck. He had been unable to get to a portable oxygen set and his lungs were heaving, his vision clouding. He had to get to his emergency supply as quickly as possible. He struggled back into his seat, clamped his face mask in place and breathed deeply.

As the oxygen worked its way down into his lungs, his brain slowly cleared. He turned his attention to the rest of the flight-deck crew.

"Are you all right, Captain?" The intercom was dead, so he pulled aside his mask and shouted. But his voice was only a murmur against the loud roar that filled the air. "Captain! Are you hurt?" Again, the rush of air carried his words away like petals in a gale.

MacNabb was slumped in his seat, his head lolling forward. Dougie gritted his teeth and grasped the convulsing control column. The autopilot was disconnected and the aircraft was diving under manual control.

No. This could not be called control.

Gritting his teeth, he eased back on the column. Were the long lengths of hydraulic piping still sufficiently intact to bring about a response? For certain, much of it would be ripped open and leaking fluid into the air.

Slowly, painfully slowly, the aircraft began to respond. The dive became shallower.

He swept his gaze across his own instrument panel. What a mess. Major damage to most of the primary instruments. He averted his gaze to the captain's panel. Some of the instruments registered wildly improbable readings, others registered nothing at all. The centre console? Most of those instruments were running haywire.

For a moment he felt an inclination to panic. No, he mustn't allow that! What would his father have done? In a similar situation, he would have acted courageously and done all the right things. If his father could ride out such an emergency, so could he. He had to, if only because he owed it to the name of Nyle.

Subdued in the knowledge that he was in virgin territory, Dougie paused for just a second to allow his rising blood pressure to stabilise and then he began to study the panel — instrument by instrument — working out what was intact and what was destroyed.

*

Maggie Loughlin stopped dead in her tracks, horrified. Just ahead of her the cabin floor had opened up.

Wearing a portable oxygen mask, she had been making her way along the main deck, the economy-class area. The worst damage was in the centre section around the leading edge of the wings. A gaping hole had been torn through the fuselage from floor to ceiling on the port side, the result of flying debris from the engine ripping into the 747's thin metal skin. Some passengers who had been seated near the hole were dead. Their bodies were mangled by pieces of hot, jagged metal. Blood and grisly human remains were splattered across the cabin ceiling and walls.

Maggie put a hand to her mouth as her stomach lurched.

She closed her eyes until the nausea began to subside. She eased her eyes open again and looked about the cabin. Slowly, painfully, she took in the extent of the damage. It would be important to make an accurate report to the crew up on the flight deck. Assuming she lived long enough to make such a report.

While she stood staring at the gaping fuselage hole, the floor heaved beneath her feet. She looked down to see a split open up in line with the hole in the fuselage side. Dust and smoke began to billow through the gap. Then, incongruously, items of passengers' clothing erupted into the cabin: a pair of trousers, a flowery dress, a white shirt. They billowed about the ghostly spirits of the dead passengers come back to haunt them all. The forward baggage hold was beneath her feet, directly below the ruptured floor. The gap in the floor must go right through to the hold.

*

Upstairs in the first-class cabin, Trudy Bodenstadt felt her senses reeling as she reached out for a face mask. Too long had elapsed since her last gasp of oxygen.

At first, the image of the dead stewardess's face stood out clearly and everything else was a fuzzy grey. Then the greyness swirled about until even the face was an indistinct mess of dark, ugly colours. She was barely conscious as she fell into an empty seat and struggled to find the dangling lifeline above her.

Was this how life ended? Fading away into a loud noise?

She blinked as someone pulled her upright in the seat. Who? Who was manhandling her? She couldn't tell. She blinked again but was unable to focus on the person holding her. Was it a man? Whoever he was, he held a mask over her face.

She breathed deeply.

"Can you hear me?" a voice shouted at her above the confusion, an American voice.

She blinked and tried again to focus on the figure beside her. It was no good. She needed a few more moments to recover. She closed her eyes once more, relaxed for a few seconds and then took another look.

A shudder went through her body as she realised she was in the arms of a stranger.

"Are you feeling all right now?" he asked. His head was bent to her ear, trying to make himself heard above the noise.

She nodded and attempted to sit upright. What on earth was she doing in the arms of a strange man while the aircraft was falling apart about them?

"I'm all right," she tried to say beneath the mask, but the words came out blurred and muted.

She breathed in deeply once more and felt her senses swimming back to normality. Normality? Back to the reality of a crippled aircraft diving towards the North Atlantic Ocean. Back to the blood and gore splattered about the cabin.

Suddenly her ears popped and the noise intensified.

*

Dougie had no idea of the aircraft's altitude. Both altimeters were dead.

On his own side of the flight deck he had, by some small miracle, a working artificial horizon which enabled him to keep the wings level. That, he reflected, could be a lifesaver. If he remained calm and kept the wings on an even keel, they just might have a chance of survival.

He checked the airspeed indicator. It showed 250 knots. Another useful instrument still working. Another gift from whichever god was watching over them. It was a reassurance that MacNabb had pulled the speed back below 270 knots, the upper limit for extending the landing gear. A quick flick of his eyes and Dougie registered the green lights that confirmed the undercarriage was down.

They were still descending, still in cloud with no means of determining what the cloud base might be. If the swirling grey mass went right down to sea level, they would probably continue the descent straight into the ocean. The thought gave him a momentary sense of concern. Not for himself or the remaining passengers in the damaged airframe, but for his wife. How would Jenny react to the news? How would she cope with being left alone, deprived of both her son and her husband? Was that why she wanted another baby? Did she need a child in the house to guard against dark thoughts of being left alone in the world?

No time to think about that right now. Keep calm and work out a plan of action to save the aircraft and the passengers who had trusted their lives to Sinclair International.

MacNabb was unconscious in his seat, his head angled sideways towards the centre of the flight deck, his hands clear of his control column.

Dougie tightened his grip on the column at his side of the flight deck. It shuddered in his grasp, as if it were about to shake itself free. How much farther should he allow the aircraft to descend? As long as he had no visual horizon and no altimeter, it could only be a guess. He could try to level out and hope that they were below ten thousand feet, the altitude at which they could all breath safely without oxygen. As soon as the thought entered his head, he prepared to level off in the cloud. Then another, more reasoned thought followed on: If he levelled off now, they would be flying blind without adequate instruments. On reflection, he had to let the 747 go on down. With luck, they would break out of the cloud before they hit the water. Luck? It was all he had to go on. Below cloud, he would be able to see sufficiently to navigate the *Tartan Arrow*. If they were lucky.

Still the cloud bubbled and streamed past the side panels like an evil potion churning out of a witch's cauldron. The torrent of air still blew straight in through the broken front screen and blasted into the unconscious pilot in his left-hand seat. In front of Dougie, the screen was cracked but still intact. Pray god it stayed like that.

And then... what was that? Yes. He caught a sudden brief view of the sea below. Just the merest glimpse, but enough to tell him that they were in steeper dive than he had imagined and also a slight port turn. He straightened up on the turn and eased back on the descent. Then he waited for the sea to appear once more.

With little warning, the 747 burst out through the cloud base with the sea close enough for him to make out individual waves. They were well below ten thousand feet.

He pulled back on the column, eased forward three of the thrust levers and felt the crippled giant level off. It was a fair guess that the port inner engine was the one that had exploded, so he kept that thrust lever shut. His breathing became easier as the aircraft shuddered into a reasonable approximation of normal flight.

He sighed softly, cleaned up the airframe by deselecting the speedbrakes and selecting the undercarriage up, and then he pulled off his mask. The noise was lessened now the aircraft was in level flight.

"What's our fuel state?" he swung his head around and called back towards the flight engineer.

Kovak shook his head, his face pale. "We've lost one whole damned lot. I'm still trying to find out which engines are running normally."

Dougie focussed again on his instrument panel and grimaced. A green warning light! The port main undercarriage was still indicating down. He reselected the landing gear sequence, knowing that most of such indications were false alarms. But the green light remained on. With the speed down to 250 knots he could afford to let the problem ride for the moment. He scanned the other instruments, slowly piecing together the fragmented picture they showed him.

Tartan Arrow was a 747-200 series. In front of him, there should have been a total of 971 working instruments, lights, gauges and switches. Each would have to be checked. Two of them were working, might even continue to work, but as for the rest... he would check them out one at a time.

"What's happened to the captain?" he shouted.

With no response from Kovak, Dougie continued to check his instruments. Whatever had happened to MacNabb, it was less important than what had happened to the aircraft.

He scanned across the engine instruments on the centre panel between the two pilot seats. Something was now working there. If the dials could be believed, they told him that the port inner engine was quite dead but the other three were still delivering enough thrust to keep them airborne. At that moment he had no option but to believe what he saw. He remembered what he had seen in the passenger cabin and decided that the port inner engine was probably now a wreck. Certainly, there was no point in trying to restart it.

He shouted, "Shut off all fuel to the port inner."

"I have." Kovak's voice was high-pitched, strained with panic. "We had a fire in that engine, but somehow we've managed to douse it."

"God help us all."

"He'd better. We're still losing fuel somewhere out there in the wing."

"Try to stop it."

"I *am* trying!"

Dougie glanced once more at the captain. MacNabb was still slumped in his seat. It was one hell of a time to lose the senior man on the flight deck. He needed help up here. A quick glance across the flight deck showed him the smashed remains of the cabin handphone. He tried the cabin public address. It was dead.

He half-turned to the flight engineer and shouted, "Go and get someone up here to see to the captain, will you?"

He vaguely noticed Kovak leave the flight deck. His gaze was once again scanning across the rest of the instrument panel, trying to make some sense of it. At least, he consoled himself, they were still airborne. But how bad was the damage? How much longer would they continue to fly? And what of the other aircraft, the one they had hit? His mind flashed back to the big silver shape that had appeared alongside them. American military. Probably a tanker.

For the present, the 747 was holding steady in level flight. Would he be able to engage the autopilot? If that worked, it would allow him to concentrate on the airframe and the extent of its damage. Autopilot switching was a complicated procedure, far removed from the simple 'push button' operation depicted in Hollywood movies. A check about the centre console told him that the inertial navigation platform was inoperative and that put paid to any hopes of directional control through the autopilot. A further check confirmed his suspicion that the autopilot was also devoid of altitude hold.

Like it or not, he would have to fly the huge 747 manually, by the seat of his pants, until they reached land.

If they reached land.

He selected his high-frequency radio on the overhead panel. It was also dead. There was no way he could communicate with Shanwick Oceanic Control, either to inform them of what had happened or to ask for help.

He looked again at the console between the two pilots' seats. The VHF radio receivers located alongside him might be operating.

He would not be able to contact Shanwick because they were beyond the range of VHF radio, but he might be able to call another aircraft. It was worth a try. The emergency radio frequency, 121.5 megahertz, was already dialled up on one of the VHF frequency selectors. Standard company practice.

Dougie donned his headset, took a deep breath and pressed the transmit switch. "Mayday! Mayday! Mayday! This is Sinclair 984. Does anyone read me?"

No reply. A bleak emptiness filled the airwaves about him. He tried again, and again received no reply.

What now? It would be nigh on impossible to get such a badly damaged aircraft back to dry land without some form of help. He had to get two-way communication with someone. Even then their chances were small. He flinched as a muffled voice cut through his thoughts. "Sinclair 984, this is Gasser 29. I read you strength three. How do you read me? Over."

A rush of blood filled Dougie's head as the voice crackled inside his headset. Any response would have been a welcome sound. This voice came across with a deep, Southern drawl.

"Gasser 29, I read you strength three also. My aircraft has been damaged in a mid-air collision. I am at low level and my position is uncertain. Please relay an emergency message to Shanwick. Over."

The following pause lasted no more than a couple of seconds. To Dougie it seemed like minutes.

"Roger, Sinclair 984. I guess we're the guys you hit. How bad is the damage to your own airplane?" The voice sounded despondent rather than angry.

Dougie's hopes plummeted. If there was one aircraft that was least likely to be able to help them, it was the one with which they had collided. He breathed deeply and searched his thoughts before replying. It was an inopportune moment to ask who had been responsible for the collision.

"I'm not sure, Gasser 29. We've lost one engine and a lot of fuel but we're still flying at the moment. I believe we've had a number of injuries back in the passenger cabins."

"Roger... uh, are you able to hold on down there?"

What a dumb question. "I guess we have to, Gasser 29."

"Sure... uh... okay, Sinclair 984." The other voice sounded indecisive. "Look, we'll... uh... we'll call Croughton Airways and get back to you in a moment. You just listen out on this frequency, okay?"

"Roger. We'll do that."

That was one little bit of help, Dougie reflected, and every little bit was going to be important from now on. American military aircraft relayed all their North Atlantic position reports through Croughton Airways, the USAF radio communications base in the heart of England. The Croughton people would tell the Shanwick controllers about the collision. It was a longwinded process, but the message would get through.

Dougie turned his attention back to the flight-deck instruments and shook his head. The standby compass located at the top of the central windscreen post showed him that he was heading roughly east. At least they were aiming in the general direction of Europe and the UK. But he had no accurate means of telling exactly where they would make their landfall. Assuming, of course, there was enough fuel left to make a landfall.

The VOR and DME radio navigation instruments, which worked on land-based transmitters, showed nothing. That was understandable. They were beyond the range of the nearest radio beacons sited on the Scottish Western Islands.

Dougie looked down at the inertial navigation equipment on the central console. It was dead. That left him with only the standby compass to navigate the aircraft towards a landfall. It wasn't much. He reminded himself that Alcock and Brown had flown the Atlantic with even more primitive instruments. But they hadn't collided with another aircraft.

Kovak returned to the flight deck alone. He pushed his way between the pilots' seats and bent over MacNabb's inert body. "It looks as if he's badly injured. I'll use a tourniquet on that arm, but I think he's already lost a lot of blood."

"He'll have to be moved into the passenger cabin," Dougie shouted back. "Get a couple of the stewardesses to move him. Where are they anyway? I thought you went for help."

"A couple of them are supposed to be coming up here shortly."

"Tell them to remove the tourniquet after a few minutes or he'll lose his arm. In the meantime, you concentrate your mind on the fuel problem."

"Yeah, sure. Look, first I'll go back and kick those stewardesses' asses. Where the hell are they?"

Kovak disappeared again from the flight deck and Dougie suddenly felt alone and helpless. He was in charge of a badly damaged aircraft and the safety of all on board depended upon him. What would his father have done in a situation like this? He wouldn't panic, of that Dougie was certain. Eric Nyle never panicked because he never had the capacity to panic. It was, at times, as though his mind was devoid of all human feeling and he became a part of the flying machine he was strapped into. He was there to do whatever was necessary to achieve his fighting mission and he acted as though his own life never came into the equation. But just *how* would his father tackle an emergency like this? It suddenly struck him that it was a problem his father had never had to face. Eric Nyle flew only single seat fighters and thought only of his own life. He had never been saddled with responsibility for the lives of hundreds of others.

Dougie drew a deep breath. He had to keep cool and think carefully before doing anything, and then reason through a sensible course of action. The trouble was, he had never before experienced anything like this. Flying only transport aircraft, he had never been shot at. He had never even lost an engine.

"Sinclair 984, this is Gasser 29, do you read me?" The deep Southern voice on the VHF receiver sounded even weaker than before.

"Go ahead, Gasser 29. I read you."

"Roger, Sinclair 984. We've contacted Croughton Airways. They're asking for your present position. Over."

"Our position is uncertain." Dougie thought quickly and then added, "Based on our last position report to Shanwick, I think we're probably around fifteen degrees west and fifty-five degrees north. I think we must be down below five thousand feet. That's as much information as I can give you at the moment."

There was a short pause.

"Roger. That position sounds, uh... it sounds a bit unlikely. We reckon we were at fifty-*eight* degrees north at the time of collision. You wanna check that again?"

Dougie felt a quick spasm of annoyance. Keep calm. This was a time for rational behaviour. "Gasser 29, I confirm we were at fifty-*five* north at the time of the collision."

"Uh... okay, buddy." Standard radio-telephone phraseology was rapidly disappearing from the American's repertoire. "Have you anything more on the damage to the aircraft?"

"Standby, Gasser 29."

"And just check that position again, will ya? There's no way you can be where you say you are."

Dougie shuddered. Fifty-eight degrees north, the man had said. They had no business being at fifty-eight degrees north. They were cleared on a more southerly route because of that supposed military exercise. A sudden thought struck him. Had they been off course? But how could they have been? MacNabb should have fed in the new coordinates when they were re-cleared on track Whiskey.

Then the obvious truth dawned.

MacNabb had made a mistake when keying in the new oceanic waypoints. His mind had not been on the figures and he had goofed. He had fed in the *old* coordinates, not the *new* ones.

Dougie clenched his teeth as realisation set in. The captain had clearly been in a troubled frame of mind, just the sort of mental state in which mistakes are made.

Summoning up a degree of calmness he did not feel, Dougie pressed his transmit switch. "Gasser 29, I think your wing tip took away our port inner engine. The fuselage damage seems to be quite extensive and we have a number of casualties, including the captain. But we are still flying." As an afterthought, he added, "What is your own condition?"

"Uh, okay, Sinclair 984. We... we've lost a section out of one wing. But no one on board is hurt. I reckon we can survive until we get to landfall."

"Roger, Gasser 29. I'll keep listening out for you on this frequency. But we have only three working engines and I will probably lose you as you pull ahead of us."

"Good luck down there, buddy. There's an E3A airborne command post in the area. We've reported the collision to them and they're heading this way. I guess they'll be calling you when they're in VHF range."

"Roger and thanks." Dougie frowned. An airborne command post out here over the Atlantic? What was an American military command aircraft doing out here? Obviously it was connected with the intense military activity in the area, but what was behind it all?

He pushed back into his seat and stared ahead. The howling wind pulled at his hair and his clothes. A few snatches of driven rain slammed like arrows through the smashed screen. Three engines, a VHF radio, an airspeed indicator, a standby compass, a badly damaged aircraft. And luck. Would it be enough?

In the distance, the cloud base was getting lower, as if they were running towards a bank of the stuff. It was difficult to tell what lay ahead, but the forecasts for the UK were bad. Either they would be able to stay below cloud and maybe land at Prestwick. Or they would run into low cloud and that would be the end of flight 984. On balance, he didn't give much for their chances.

*

Judson felt an unreasonable sense of relief. Dammit! He had a damaged airplane and he felt relieved?

It wasn't his fault.

The other guys were off course, the other guys were responsible, not Major Paul S Judson. Not the guy who always did as he was told and kept his ass clean with the senior base commanders.

They wouldn't like this back in the States. In fact, the generals would go ape over the damage to a US airplane. There would sure be one huge investigation over who was going to carry the can. But Paul S Judson was fireproof. The other guys had goofed.

He shook his head savagely. The KC135 was back on an even course and all four engines were running. At the very least they would all survive this goddamn collision.

"You sure that position is correct?" he called back to Hewson.

"Would I lie to you, Major?" Hewson's voice held a hint of scorn. "It weren't us that was off course."

Judson ignored the insinuation. He jabbed the intercom switch. "Bryzjinsky?"

"Yes, sir?" The insolent attitude had gone. Probably wiped away by fear.

"You okay back there?"

"Sure thing, sir. The main tanks are secure and there don't seem to be any fuselage damage. Just the wingtip as near as we can judge. We got the fuel lines shut off just in case, but I reckon we caught lucky with that one."

Thank God for that. Judson's sense of relief increased. If the damage was kept to a reasonable level, maybe the generals wouldn't create too much fuss after all.

"No one hurt?"

"No, sir."

"Good. One more thing, Bryzjinsky..."

"Sir?"

"You just get your ass up here with some hot coffee."

"Yes, sir!"

Judson rubbed the back of his hand across his forehead and felt the sweat drip away from his skin. Goddammit, he was tired and he needed hot black coffee to revive his brain. His thoughts had been too woolly and that was why he had fallen asleep. That was why he hadn't seen the other airplane until too late.

His heart suddenly stopped.

He hadn't seen the other airplane! No one on board Gasser 29 had seen the giant hulk of a Boeing 747 as it closed in on them? They had all been too whacked to be looking. Maybe they had all been asleep.

Trouble was, they should have been looking. They should have seen the 747 before it hit them. Tired or not, they should have had their eyes open. The generals would sure have a field day with them on that score.

Chapter 4

Early morning half-light hung over the white Ayrshire countryside. Already, the hilly road outside Jock Scrimgeour's flat was impassable. A carpet of ice lay hidden beneath a thick mantle of snow, turning the steeply inclined road into an urban ski slope.

A police car slowed at the bottom of the hill and then pulled up alongside a slushy pavement. Detective Inspector McKee and Detective Sergeant Hastie eased themselves out of their car, their breath condensing into white clouds. They stopped for a moment while the senior man studied his notebook, then they trudged through the snow towards the block of flats. The sergeant, a sad-looking man with a thin, pinched face, rang Jock Scrimgeour's doorbell several times with no response. He drew his lips together while McKee breathed into his hands. Eventually the two men tramped back to the patrol car where they discussed their next move.

Their mission was not the sort of thing that should be left to a telephone call. Much too personal, too painful. Judging from the detail supplied by the New York police, it was the sort of tragic happening that had to be revealed with care.

*

Snow was falling heavily four miles along the coast in Prestwick. Jock Scrimgeour paused to watch as a trail of military vehicles crawled along the town's main street, each throwing up a sheet of slush from its wheels. Most were painted uniform RAF grey, but two camouflaged troop transport trucks were slotted into the middle of the convoy. An RAF Land Rover took up the rear, the driver wiping at his misted windscreen. The uniformed airman alongside him was armed.

The convoy turned into a side street leading inland, away from the town centre and towards Atlantic House, the Scottish Air Traffic Control Centre. What were they doing? Jock had no idea, and after a few minutes he ceased to care. A cold mist formed on his breath as he bent his head into the snow, pulled up the collar of his fleecy lined coat and walked on towards Pamela MacReady's flat.

Saturday morning, the morning after returning from a course at the College of ATC in Bournemouth, and already he had been partying as only a Scotsman knew how. Yesterday evening, he had arrived home tired and miserable, dumped his luggage at the flat and phoned his wife in New York. She was out according to her roommate, who went on to divulge things that had unnerved him. Still feeling angry, he went straight to a friend's house where an all-night humdinger of a party was planned.

The revelries were still going strong over a fried breakfast, but Jock had other plans for this morning. His intention had been to take a bus home and freshen up before Sally got back from New York. He should have known better. The weather had turned so ugly the local buses were no longer running, and his car was garaged for much-needed repairs.

The snow settled on Jock's mop of untidy red hair. Rob Roy in miniature, they had called him in his youth, on account of his short stocky build. Often he wished for a return to those long-gone days when life had been a casual adventure which took him from bed to bed with no long-term commitments.

Sally told him he looked younger than his thirty-five years, but he rarely felt it.

"You still look like a twenty-year-old, Jock. A pity you act like a stupid old git." She had uttered the words with a heavy dose of acid in her voice. He wondered if that was her reason for hinting at a divorce. Or was it all brought about by her infatuation with one of the Sinclair International pilots?

They had an odd sort of marriage, with Sally often away in New York on stopovers between flights. He had no positive proof that she had been playing around with one of the pilots, nothing he could conclusively put his finger on. Just a strong suspicion. And a name.

Fergus MacNabb.

Well, he too could play that game. Pamela MacReady was the comforter in his life, his reassurance that he was not entirely unattractive to women. She was always there for him when he needed female company in Sally's absence. Someone to take away the coldness of the long winter nights.

He looked up and wiped the back of one hand across his eyes. The military convoy had disappeared from sight. A trail of deep wheel ruts was left in its wake, pointing directly towards Atlantic House. Jock had worked there since it opened in 1978. So had Pamela. He was an area sector controller and she was an assistant on the same team. Was it surprising that they had become good friends? Was it wrong that they had become close enough to confide in each other's ideas and opinions? Close enough for Jock to talk openly about his marital difficulties. Close enough for her to fill in the gaps in his life when Sally was away.

His teeth chattered as he approached her ground floor flat in an elderly tenement block. He chapped the door with some trepidation, blew into his hands and waited. Pamela took a couple of minutes to answer, minutes in which Jock stood shivering and stamping his feet on the cold concrete doorstep.

"Oh. It's you." She looked past him to the heavy snow and added, "You've been out in that?"

"It's bloody freezing."

She was strikingly proportioned. Short even by Jock's standards, she was perfectly formed like a Greek Goddess reduced to eighty per cent full size. She gave him a warm, self-conscious smile. "You'd better come inside."

She wore a short nylon dressing gown and thick carpet slippers. Her hair — damp, as if she had recently taken a bath — hung loosely round her shoulders and her face bore no trace of makeup.

"I know it's very early." The words tumbled out as if he was no longer able to contain them. "I was at the party last night and now

I can't get home because of the weather. The buses aren't running."

"Ah, yes. The party." She compressed her lips. "A night of boozing and honking."

"More or less. Anyhow I thought you wouldn't mind if I called on you."

"Because you couldn't get home?"

"I thought you might let me hang around here until Sally's flight gets in. Then I could meet her at the airport and maybe find a taxi willing to risk the roads."

Pamela shut the door firmly behind him. The cold air was suddenly banished, replaced by a warm glow. "When's the flight due?"

"It's running late. Very late. I called by at the airport on my way here, but they're not allowing anyone into the terminal. Something about the building being unsafe. So I phoned the Sinclair head office and they said to check with them again in an hour or so."

She raised an eyebrow quizzically. "The terminal building is unsafe?"

"Don't ask me. That's what they said. Sounds suspicious to me."

Pamela sniffed pointedly. "What about you? Are things any better between you and Sally?"

"Not really."

"There's something else, isn't there?"

"Why do you say that?"

"I know you well enough, Jock. You didn't come here just for a casual chat. What's it all about? Did something happen while you were away in Bournemouth?"

He shrugged his shoulders. "Not really. It's just that—"

She eyed him sternly. "Yes?"

"I've decided to resign from the job."

"Resign?"

"Yes."

"And you came here because you thought I'd talk you out of it? Or perhaps you thought I'd offer you a shoulder to cry on."

"Is that what you think?" He looked away, trying to hide his embarrassment. Why did she always have to be right?

She inclined her head, gesturing him into the small sitting room. "Have you had any breakfast?"

"Not really. I was at the party and—" He shrugged.

"And I'm on duty soon. I've swapped onto a day shift to do someone a favour. How would bacon and eggs suit you?"

"Heavenly."

"Good. Sit over there by the gas fire. You can talk while I'm cooking."

The room was small but cosy with a pervading air of femininity in its simple decorations.

Jock hunched over the fire and instantly felt better. "You weren't at the party," he said.

"Not my scene, Jock. Heavy boozing and honking on the floor isn't my idea of fun. You know that. What's all this about you resigning?" She ambled into the kitchen.

He sensed straightaway that she was giving him the chance to get the whole thing off his chest without having to face her directly.

"I've been thinking about it a lot while I was away." He rubbed his hands in front of the fire. "I suppose I'll have a problem getting another job. But I have to make a stand."

"Why?"

"It's a matter of principle." He thought for a moment before adding, "People are walking all over me. I can't let them get away with it. It's breaking up my marriage."

"Who, Jock? Who's walking all over you? Who's breaking up your marriage?" The voice from the kitchen sounded unconvinced.

"People. Everyone."

"That's a matter of debate. I suppose you think resigning will make the whole thing right? Is that what you're saying?"

"I'm not sure I like your line of attack," he said firmly.

"What will Sally think about you resigning?"

"This is my decision, not hers."

"Have you told her yet?"

"No. Last time she called me from New York she seemed to be in a bit of a funny state of mind. She gets like that. I tried to call her yesterday evening, lunchtime over there, but her roommate said she was out. She couldn't... *wouldn't* say where."

Pamela walked into the sitting room carrying a breakfast tray which she set down on a glass-topped coffee table, handing him a plate and cutlery without meeting his gaze. "I think you're wrong to resign, Jock. Why on earth give up a good career?"

"I told you. A matter of principle."

She sat directly opposite and faced him squarely. "That's a load of balls, Jock. And you know it."

He looked up suddenly, holding a fork halfway to his mouth. "What do you mean?"

"I mean that you're thinking of getting out because you can't stand the pace. Traffic levels are up and it's all a bit of a bugger over at the centre. You've lost your nerve, haven't you?"

"You think so?" His voice was slow, laboured. The controllers at Atlantic House had been feeling the strain for some time, but they never admitted it in public.

"Have you lost your nerve, Jock?"

He set his knife and fork back on the plate. This was not the way he had expected the discussion to develop. "Maybe I should go."

"Why? Are you afraid of the truth? Eat up before it gets cold."

He began to eat again. Leaving so soon wasn't really such a good idea. "I've been thinking about it for some time. It's not just a casual idea."

"I don't suppose it is. But that doesn't make it right. Think about it a bit longer." She rose suddenly and slipped away to the kitchen. Moments later, she called back to him, "At least put off your decision until you see how things pan out between you and Sally."

"I've already decided," he mumbled at his plate. Then he lifted his head and said clearly, "I've already made my decision."

"That's a very great pity. Excuse me while I get dressed."

The sound of her bare feet padded through the sitting room behind him, followed by the slam of the bedroom door. This was not how he had intended the discussion to go. Feeling angry and frustrated, he sat forward in his seat, about to get to his feet. Then his gaze caught the television.

The set was tuned to a morning news programme, the sound turned down. The presenter's lips moved noiselessly alongside a library shot of a space shuttle blasting off from Kennedy Space Centre.

His attention caught, Jock stretched out a hand to turn up the volume and the presenter's voice burst into the small room. "The US Defence Department has so far refused to comment on the purpose of current United States Air Force manoeuvres over the North Atlantic. And NASA denies rumours of a link with any secret space shuttle mission. However, informed sources claim the operation is a joint effort codenamed Project Washington."

Jock swung his head round suddenly at the sound of a wardrobe door banging in the bedroom. Was it meant as an indication of Pamela's thoughts and feelings? He stood up and switched off the television with a quick, decisive movement. What was the point in staying longer at the flat? It would be just as warm over in Atlantic House, and less confrontational. He grabbed his coat and was striding towards the front door when Pamela emerged from the bedroom.

"Going already, Jock?" she said. Her mouth was beginning to curve down, as if she was deeply concerned.

"I think it would be best."

"I wish you wouldn't go while you're in that frame of mind. Let's start again." She put a hand to his arm, touching him lightly. "Why don't you get your head down here for an hour? Have a rest before you ring to find out what time Sally's flight is due. You can use the bed until I get back."

He grinned wryly. "Thanks. You're an angel."

"I'm not. I'm a fool, just as I'm always a fool when you're around. But we'll let it pass this time."

He felt a sense of relief begin to take control of his thoughts. "When you get into Atlantic House, perhaps you could find out when Sally's flight's coming in."

"Which one is she on?"

"Sinclair 984. New York to Prestwick."

"I'll watch out for it."

"Thanks."

Pamela took a warm coat from the hall cupboard. "I hope you get it all sorted out between you. For her sake as well as your own."

"I'll let you know how it goes." A sudden thought caught him. "Watch out for the military. I saw a convoy of trucks heading towards Atlantic House."

"Trucks? What for?"

"Haven't a clue."

"That, Jock, seems to be the story of your life."

Chapter 5

Sammy Kovak's hands shook uncontrollably as he helped two worried-looking stewardesses manhandle MacNabb's unconscious body out of the captain's seat. Blood from the captain's uniform jacket rubbed off on the flight engineer's white shirt.

He stood back while the two young women eased the body through the flight-deck door. A cold expression, now set hard in the pilot's pale face, seemed to mock Kovak, as if the devil had taken up residence behind the closed eyelids.

"What are things like back there?" he asked the stewardess nearest to him.

"As bad as it can get. A lot of people got hurt when the engine exploded. Some are dead. The fuselage is ripped wide open."

"Yeah." He imagined the scene. "Explosive decompression. Was there much panic?"

"What do you think? We couldn't warn anyone. It wasn't our fault. The PA system isn't working. We couldn't tell them what to do."

"Aw, shite! Look, get us a detailed report on the damage, will you. How many people killed? How many holes in the fuselage? That sort of thing."

The stewardess nodded.

Kovak waited impatiently for them to clear the door, and then he slammed it shut. Cold air still filled the flight deck and the captain's smashed screen dominated the forward view, but the closed door kept MacNabb out of sight. Kovak went forward to the left-hand seat and leaned across to peer out of the port-side windscreen panel.

Somewhere in the fuselage behind him a spar broke apart. A sudden loud crack, like a firecracker at a bonfire party. The airframe juddered and Kovak grabbed hold of the captain's seat back.

"Can you see a sick engine out there?" Nyle shouted across the flight deck.

"I can see a sick-looking space where the port inner used to be," Kovak called back. "This whole damned plane is sick!"

Nyle kept his eyes focussed ahead and his hands rock steady on the control column yoke. "You'd better go back to the passenger cabin and inspect the damage." He paused. "No. Not now. Do it later. Right now I need another check on the fuel loss. How does it look?"

"Not good." Kovak staggered across to the flight engineer's panel and strapped himself into his seat, determined to be secure if the aircraft made any further violent manoeuvres. "We're still losing fuel from somewhere in the port wing. The trouble is, I'm having to cross feed from the starboard wing tanks to keep the port outer alive. The more we feed to the port side, the more fuel we lose."

"You think I should stopcock the port outer?"

"You're in charge."

It was a huge dilemma. Lose too much fuel or lose the power of the remaining engine on the port side. Not the sort of decision for a mere flight engineer to make. Kovak ground his teeth. Thank God he didn't have to make the choice.

He felt a brief — very brief — moment of relief as he reflected that Nyle was an experienced pilot, despite his age. He was turning out to be one cool customer when the chips were down. Yes, Nyle could handle this one. Kovak breathed deeply and then shivered in the knowledge he was kidding himself. No one could handle anything this bad. No one.

"Sammy, can you monitor the amount of fuel we're losing?" Dougie's voice strained to rise above the cockpit noise. "I need to know how much we're throwing away on the port side."

The flight engineer considered for a second and then shook his head. "Only very roughly. The gauges are going mad."

"Well then, give me a rough idea. How much longer can we

continue losing fuel and still stay in the air?"

"I'll try." Kovak's brain snapped into a sudden violent mood change. He knew it had happened, but he did not know why, nor could he help himself. He felt angry, unreasonably angry Why was the first officer putting pressure on him? He hadn't been responsible for the collision, he hadn't been in charge of the aeroplane. For all that he was older than Nyle, he was still technically the junior man on the flight deck. Dammit, what the hell could he do about it all? His sense of confidence in Nyle vanished as quickly as it had appeared, replaced by fear. Outright fear.

"Don't just try, Sammy, *do it!*" Nyle's voice was even more insistent. Almost as if he too was beginning to lose his nerve. Don't do that, Dougie. For chrissake, don't you crack up on us. Not now.

"Alright! I'll do it." Kovak forced himself to calm down. "I'll do it," he repeated as he leaned towards the instrument panel.

Was this what flying was all about? Was this why the captain was paid so much more than anyone else? Was this, he wondered, the sort of responsibility he would have to shoulder when he made it to the captain's seat? *If* he ever made it to the captain's seat.

*

Trudy stood up slowly, checking her limbs for signs of damage. She moved awkwardly, her eyes still refusing to come into sharp focus. She blinked and tried to gather her wits.

Her vision slowly sharpened. The man who had been sitting beside her helped her into a standing position. His hands supported her powerfully, but he had a strange look, as if he too was only just coming to terms with the enormity of what had happened.

"Thank you," she said formally, drawing away from him. "I think I can manage now."

"Are you sure?" He continued to hold her arm, keeping her in range. "You passed out for a few minutes, you know."

"I did?" Trudy put a hand to her head. She had not been aware of passing out, nor of coming to again. How could that be? Surely she would have felt something?

"Why don't you sit down again, for just a little longer?" The man's voice was insistent now, as if he knew what he was talking about.

Trudy looked about her, staring blankly at the wild devastation of the cabin. Suddenly, it all came back to her. The collision, the dramatic dive, the struggle to breathe. Her temple throbbed and, at the same time, her eyes grew hazy once more. She stared up at the passenger as he eased her into the seat.

"Give it a minute or two," he said calmly. "You sit here while I scout around. I'll come back again when I find you something to drink."

Trudy closed her eyes, not because she wanted to sleep again, but because she was too frightened to look at the horror about her. She sensed that the man was moving away from her, faintly heard the rustle of his clothes for just a second before he was quickly swallowed up by the noise and activity inside the cabin. Who was he? Why did he appear to know what to do?

She kept her eyes tightly shut and decided that someone must have made an enormous mistake for the two aircraft to collide. Was that the fault of Fergus MacNabb?

Forget about MacNabb. This was no time to be thinking of him. But ugly memories invaded her mind anyway. Unwanted, unhelpful, but persistent. She hated MacNabb, but she hated the senior stewardess even more. It was Loughlin who had made the threat against her after Sally died. The woman was mixed up in that terrible business, right up to her eyeballs.

Forget about Maggie Loughlin. Concentrate on the horror here in the aircraft. No, she couldn't fix her mind on the horrors around her. Just couldn't. Her thoughts drifted, spiralling away from the present reality. Anywhere. Back to New York. What went wrong there? When the police interviewed her, she held her tongue because it was more than her life was worth to speak out. She told the police that she and Sally shared a hotel room. She told them about her own dull routine when stopping over in New York. But she said nothing about Sally's affair with Fergus MacNabb.

Then her thoughts drifted irrevocably back to the present. This terrible collision. She felt alone. And very afraid.

"I told you I would be back."

She snapped her eyelids open to reveal the passenger leaning across the seat, reaching for her hand.

"Here. Grab hold of this." He pressed a miniature brandy into her hand. "Go ahead. No one's going to complain about you drinking on duty."

She lifted the open bottle to her lips and sipped, slowly at first and then hungrily. Seconds later she coughed as the alcohol bit into her throat.

"Good girl. How do you feel now?"

"I think I'm going to die," she moaned weakly.

"No you're not. I need your help. There isn't another stewardess alive on this deck."

"No one alive?"

"There was another stewardess at the rear of the cabin, but she's dead. A couple of others came up from the main deck but they've gone back downstairs. Now there's just you in charge up here."

"Me? Oh, no!"

"Look, miss—" His voice became firm. "There are a lot of people needing help around here. Even the captain is hurt and they've stretched him out on the seats at the front of the cabin."

"Captain MacNabb?"

"A couple of stewardesses carried him out of the cockpit. Before someone called them back downstairs. I guess things are even worse down there. More passengers than up here. They've left the captain in our care."

"But things are bad up here," Trudy protested.

"Yes. But it's only a small cabin. We can cope. There's a woman — one of the passengers — looking after the captain. I reckon the rest is up to you and me until the cavalry arrives. Think you can stand up now?"

"I don't know."

He grabbed her arm and gently eased her out of the seat. "Come on. I have this feeling you ought to take charge around here. There doesn't seem to be anyone else qualified."

"Oh, no. Please, no."

Trudy felt her legs crumble as she put her weight onto them. She should have got out of flying while the going was good. There was no way she could take charge in an emergency like this. No way.

"Don't worry, I'll stay with you."

Why was he able to keep calm when she felt so lost? She reached out to grasp his outstretched hand, trying to get a firm reading on her wildly buzzing thoughts. All the while, her pulse raced and her heart thumped.

She gazed around. Confusion was rife. Some passengers were strapped in their seats, some wandered about in the aisle looking for help, others lay trapped beneath the wreckage on the port side. And a loud rush of cold air penetrated Trudy's brain, no matter how hard she tried to blot out the noise.

"We'll start by getting the survivors to help the injured." The man squeezed her hand. "It's best you and I deal with the dead."

Dead?

Trudy stared at the blood-soaked area around the hole in the fuselage, at the mangled remains of metal, plastic and human flesh.

"What must we do?" Her voice came out hoarse and choked.

"Leadership. The first thing we must do is to show a sense of leadership. Make them think we know what we are doing. Even if we don't. Let's get them organised, shall we?"

"Organised? Doing what?"

He pulled her round so that he could look her straight in the eye. "There are people hurt... trapped... injured... they need help. You and I can't do everything that needs to be done, but if we can get the survivors organised into some sort of rescue party, they can help."

"I suppose so. What should I do?" She rubbed her hands round her cheeks, extending the fingers so that they ran up over her eyes.

"Get all the able-bodied men together. Send them back there to deal with the worst damage." He pointed to where wrecked seats had fallen towards the hole in the fuselage. "I'll organise them."

"You said we would have to deal with..."

"Bodies? Yes, it's best we get them moved out of sight. There's enough horror in this airplane without them."

*

"I reckon it's a fair bet the rate of fuel loss will give us something around ninety minutes flying time." Kovak shouted the words with less than certainty. "We sure as hell won't stay in the air for more than one hour forty-five minutes. After that it's in the lap of the gods."

Dougie kept his eyes focussed on his remaining instruments. "What do you mean by a fair bet?"

"I mean, dammit, that I can only guess. You think you can do better, you come and read these damned gauges."

Dougie glanced across the back of his seat long enough to shoot the flight engineer a sharp, angry look. He didn't need a bout of temper from Kovak, just information. Accurate information.

"Aw shite!" Kovak banged his hand against the panel in front of him. "You think I'm enjoying this? Dammit, I'm doing my best!"

Dougie concentrated his attention again on manually flying the 747.

Behind him, Kovak took a more calculated attitude. "If we continue to lose fuel as we are, we should be able to stay in the air for about an hour and a half. Even at this speed, that means we may be able to reach the Scottish coast. That's if we're lucky. So how about we get some met reports for the Scottish airports. How about Glasgow and Edinburgh, as well as Prestwick?"

Dougie cast his gaze across the instrument panel. Could he keep the aircraft flying for another hour and a half? He didn't give much for his chances, but he would keep that opinion to himself. "I can't take my hands off the column," he shouted back. "If you look in my flight bag, you'll find some area forecasts and some reports for UK airports."

Kovak left his seat and stretched down to where the flight bag lay beside Dougie's seat. "You'll need something more up to date. Those blizzards reported over the UK were looking pretty nasty and forecast to get worse."

"I know, I know. I'll see what sort of information our military friends can come up with." Dougie kept his gaze focussed on the flight instruments while Kovak went through the flight bag and withdrew the met charts.

The flight engineer slumped himself down in the captain's seat and spread the charts across his lap. "According to this, the blizzards are widespread throughout Scotland. There's a marginally better cloud base at Prestwick, but it always did have a better weather record. That's why they built the airport there. Knowing our luck, it's probably got worse by now."

Dougie nodded. "I'll get it checked."

Kovak put most of the papers back in the case, but he kept the main area chart for Scotland. His voice turned sour. "All of this supposes that we can make it to the mainland."

Dougie angled his head towards the flight engineer. "Stop moaning, Sammy. Someone should have come up here by now to report on how things are in the cabins. Maybe you ought to get back and check on the damage. I think I can handle things up here for a short while, but don't be too long."

"Okay. What's the score with those Americans? Are they going to help us?"

"Dunno, Sammy. They're taking their time."

"Maybe they've got something else on their minds right now."

*

Kovak readily agreed to the first officer's request. Anything to get off the flight deck for a short while. He pulled the door tightly shut behind him and made his way back to the upper-deck cabin.

MacNabb was stretched across the front row of seats, a large woman in a fur coat kneeling beside him.

"How's he doing?" Kovak crouched down beside the woman. It was in his mind to say that they might need the bastard alive if they were ever to get the damaged aircraft down in one piece. But the passengers didn't need to know that.

"He's unconscious," she replied. "But he keeps mumbling to himself. I've got a tourniquet on his arm to stop the bleeding."

Kovak patted her arm as he stood up. "You're doing a good job. I think you're supposed to loosen the tourniquet every few minutes."

"But he's bleeding badly."

"I guess he is. Don't want to let gangrene set in, though, do we?"

"The stewardess said she would hurry back," the woman replied. "But she didn't come. I'm just a passenger, you know."

Kovak frowned. "Just do what you can, love. Someone will come and help you when they're able. We've a lot of problems at the moment."

Towards the rear, the cabin was a scene of confusion. Several dead and injured passengers lay near the long, jagged hole in the fuselage. Kovak looked away. The sight appalled him.

Where were the cabin crew? They should be helping to clear up this mess. Kovak gritted his teeth, scanned again over the area of worst confusion and recognised a pretty young stewardess. She was shifting a body with the aid of one of the passengers. Trudy Bodenstadt, the girl who told him about MacNabb and Sally Scrimgeour. She was a good kid, he could go for her in a big way. A bit more introvert than he would prefer, but she had one peach of a good body.

His gaze swung back to the fuselage hole. He took half a step towards it and his foot stumbled against a body. He peered down at the remains of a young woman passenger and a prickly shiver ran through him. Her clothes were ripped apart, one arm was almost severed from the shoulder and her face was contorted in the pain of death. Blood was spread everywhere. He felt a sudden urge to vomit.

He hurried down the stairway to the main deck. Nyle would want him to assess the extent of the fuselage damage down there. He must concentrate on the damage to the aircraft and ignore the dead and dying people. Ignore the screams and sobbing of those still alive.

He raced down the main cabin to the economy-class section where a powerful draft of cold air rushed in through another gaping hole in the fuselage. A symphony of clattering aluminium rattled through the cabin. For some moments he stood looking aghast at the wreckage. How could an aircraft this badly damaged still keep flying? Nearby, the cabin crew attempted to shift the dead passengers, but Kovak ignored them. He stared at the twisted and ripped metalwork and saw the inevitability of his own end. Within the open wound, the stark fuselage skeleton was outlined by rushing grey clouds.

Was there any chance he could survive this? The 747 was one of the strongest airframes built, a legend in aviation manufacturing. He had heard stories of failures in quality control, especially in systems wiring, but the huge beasts still kept on flying safely. Was it possible they might get this one back on the ground before it fell apart? In aviation, most things were possible. But there was a limit to structural damage beyond which no aircraft could survive.

He shook his head to clear his thoughts, studied the extent of the damage again and turned to race back up the stairs.

"It's bad!" he shouted as he came back into the rush of cold air that filled the flight deck. He slammed the door shut behind him.

"Tell me about it."

Kovak leaned against Nyle's seat. "There's a large tear in the fuselage on the port side where the engine exploded. It extends through the upper and the main deck cabins."

"Could you see the damage to the wing?"

"Not really. But it's a fair bet that the underside will be shot to hell."

"What about the injuries?"

"Lots of dead and injured down on the main deck. And a few more on the upper deck. The cabin crew are dealing with it."

"How many dead?"

"I don't know. I went to look at the aircraft, not the passengers."

Nyle made no immediate reply, his face hard-set in concentration.

Kovak made a quick calculation. They had left Gander with 405 passengers, sixteen cabin crew and three flight-deck crew. A total of 424 human beings. How many were still alive? He had no idea and, on balance, he thought it best not to consider the matter further.

"All right." Nyle sounded unbelievably calm. "How bad is the structural damage? What are our chances of nursing the aircraft to a landfall?"

Kovak shrugged his shoulders. "How should I know?"

"Because you're supposed to know all about this aircraft."

"Only when it's in one piece. The main damage to the fuselage is in that area on the port side a little way in front of the inner engine. Just ahead of the wing. It's extensive and probably goes right down into the holds."

"Has it damaged any of the main fuselage frames?"

"I didn't see any sign of that. The fan must have spewed its guts slightly forward when the other aircraft's wing hit it. The fan blades have cut into the fuselage at the port wing leading edge, just behind the number two passenger door."

"It doesn't sound good."

"Too bloody right it doesn't."

"You think it's bad enough to warrant me taking a look?"

"And who's going to fly the aircraft while you're gone?"

Nyle grunted. "I get the idea you want me to stay where I am."

"Yep. You get the right idea."

*

Simon Devereaux swallowed hard. He took the shoulders of a severely mangled passenger and pulled, dragging the heavy body out from where it lay wedged between two seats. Parts of the body were no longer recognisable as human.

As the corpse tumbled free, the seats collapsed. The watery-eyed stewardess grabbed the legs and heaved the body along the aisle. Devereaux gave her a hand. Three other corpses were already stowed in the upper-deck galley at the rear of the cabin: the dead stewardess and two passengers.

Blood spilled over them as they pushed and dragged the body down the aisle. On either side, white-faced passengers watched in silent horror or shielded their eyes from the gory scene. Most of them looked numb and the few who watched were staring stupidly with little real comprehension of what was happening.

Devereaux risked a lengthy gaze at the stewardess. How much longer could she cope with this? He would have preferred the help of a hard-nosed steward, but as long as the girl was alive and on her feet he had to make use of her. They had a job to do and she was the only crew member on hand.

They stowed the body on top of the others. It was no occasion for formality.

"Take a moment to catch your breath," he told the girl and put a comforting hand to her shoulder. It wasn't just the girl who needed a break. He needed it, too.

She shivered and wrapped her arms about her chest. How very different she was to Diane Redmond. They both had positions of responsibility, but one was confident while the other was emotionally fragile. And the wrong one was here.

Twelve hours ago he had been lying in bed beside Diane, a dark, Spanish-eyed beauty. She was new to the Drug Enforcement Agency, but Devereaux was quick off the mark and she had responded to his overtures with equal conviction. They both knew that they were taking a chance. The DEA did not like staff to form personal relationships, especially not when they were working together on operations of national importance. It was risky. But Devereaux was too intoxicated with Diane to be constrained by the Administration's preferences. He wanted her and she wanted him. They were both free of complicated relationships and they were going to enjoy one another.

It was Diane who had made the first breakthrough on Fergus MacNabb, upstaging Devereaux in a big way. He didn't resent that, he was too much in love with the girl, but he was eager to get himself one jump ahead, if only to impress her. She had made the first break but he was determined that he was going to make the arrest.

"Reckon you'll get lucky on this trip?" she had asked as they lay side by side in her bed, feeling the warmth of each other.

"Reckon so," he told her.

"Wanna lay a bet on it?"

"What's the odds?"

"You nail MacNabb and Loughlin, especially MacNabb, and I'll move into your apartment. You goof up and you move into my apartment."

"Sounds like I can't lose."

"You think so? In my apartment you obey *my* house rules."

"Oh." He had turned towards her and drawn a line down her arm with his finger. "In that case I'd better nail the bastards."

He scanned around the cabin. Not much chance of that now.

He brought his thoughts quickly back to the task in hand. "I think that's all the dead from this section."

"I don't want to see any more!" The girl ran a hand across her forehead, leaving a smudged red trail in its wake.

Devereaux stared at the blood. Some dead person's blood. The life fluid of someone who had been, not so many minutes ago, a living being with thoughts and plans, loves and hates, friends and enemies. Someone like himself.

He nodded to the stewardess. She was near the limit of her endurance, on the verge of cracking up. He was surprised that she had coped so well this far.

The giant rip in the side of the aircraft was outlined behind her. Sharp edges of torn metal flapped and clattered in the force of the gale that blew through the opening. Inside the cabin, loose fittings were beating in time to the macabre music of death.

"Let's take a look at the injured now," he said, tightening the comforting arm he still held around her shoulder. "What's your name?" He knew the answer because the DEA had already linked her to Sally Scrimgeour, but it was a good move to ask anyway.

"Trudy. Trudy Bodenstadt."

"Okay, Trudy, my name's Simon Devereaux. Simon. Now, let's go and do what we gotta do." He held her for a few more seconds and thought he detected a soft glow in her eye, but the moment passed so quickly he decided he must have been mistaken.

They concentrated first on the passengers on the port side, those nearest the fuselage damage. Devereaux led the girl to where a group of relatively uninjured men were attempting to lift a fallen baggage locker from the wrecked seats immediately behind the hole. He had set the uninjured passengers to the task some minutes earlier, but they had no coordination in the way they worked. Some had dropped out from sheer horror.

The seat rows in the vicinity of the hole were twisted and buckled, but most remained roughly intact. Just behind the hole, three sets of seats were toppled forward with the force of the decompression. Devereaux felt a sudden gripping fear that the seats and anyone standing nearby might, even yet, be pulled out of the aircraft through the hole. He fought down a retching feeling in his gut. Keep calm. The danger of being sucked out must now be past. They were flying low enough for the pressures inside and outside the aircraft to be balanced.

He cast around the scene, impatient with his own frailties. Injured limbs littered the wreckage, trapped and jutting out like surrealist art forms. Bodies lay crumpled below fallen lockers and plastic mouldings that had come away from the interior of the fuselage.

"Let's give a hand here." Devereaux gritted his teeth. He was taking charge again in a situation where he had no right to be in charge.

He pointed towards a small trapped figure, the deathly white face of a young child staring out from beneath the wreckage of the seats. Her face was pathetic, almost rigid with shock. A straggle of fair hair played about her bloodied forehead in the icy slipstream, but her deep blue eyes continued to stare straight ahead.

"Let's get this little girl free." The words choked in his throat. Why hadn't someone seen to the poor mite before now? Why had they left her trapped for so long?

The child made no attempt to cry out. Her chubby hand was stretched out from under a heavy metal support, the tiny fingers splayed like twigs on the branch of a tree.

"One of you grab that length of metal and pull." Devereaux tried to sound decisive as he addressed the uncoordinated group. He looked askance at the stewardess, hiding the fact that his mind was wracked with pain for the suffering of the injured passengers, especially the child. They all needed far more help than he could supply.

"Hold it there!" Trudy held up a free hand as the wreckage moved. "I think I can reach her now."

While Devereaux and the other passengers held the metal support clear of the seat, the stewardess knelt down to grab the child's outstretched arm and pulled.

"Soon have you out of there, honey. Just you take it easy."

The arm came away suddenly, jerking free from the wreckage like a piece of rag. Trudy held it out in front of her, her whole body rigid with shock. For a second or so she stared silently at the severed limb which ended in a jagged mess of flesh, bone and bloody gore.

Devereaux felt his flesh creep as he looked down at the child's wide, staring and lifeless eyes. Then he heard the stewardess scream.

*

Dougie took a deep breath as he studied the instrument panel in front of him and shook his head in silent despair. His eyes blinked against the blast of cold Atlantic air. Despite his determination to keep a grip on himself, his mind began to wander.

Would Jenny be still asleep? Would she be blissfully unaware that her husband was fighting for his survival aboard the stricken aircraft? Would she be alone in the house they had planned and built for three: himself, Jenny and Edward? Had someone from Sinclair International already called and told her the news that flight 984 was in trouble? How would she react when she found herself facing the prospect of life alone, a childless widow?

In the house they had built for three.

"Sinclair 984, this is Gasser 29. Do you read me, buddy?" The VHF radio crackled.

Dougie's headphones had been dangling about his neck. He dragged them back over his head to better hear the radio above the noise of the rushing air. "Gasser 29, I read you strength three. Go ahead."

"Okay, Sinclair 984. We, uh... we ain't forgotten you down there, buddy. Airborne command have taken control of the situation and they, uh... they're directing a British Nimrod towards you."

"Roger, Gasser 29. The command aircraft hasn't called me yet."

"Roger, uh... not to worry, buddy. They got an even bigger problem on their hands. Reckon they'll call you shortly. We, uh... we just heard they've picked up a radar contact they think is you. Once they've confirmed that, they'll bring in the Nimrod to get an eyeball on you and shepherd you to a landfall."

Radar! Dougie felt a surge of hope. Radar could only mean that the command ship was an E3A AWACS aircraft. The E3A, with its huge rotating radar on top of the fuselage, was just the sort of help they needed.

"Roger, Gasser 29. We'll keep a look out for airborne command and the Nimrod. It'll be nice to have some company down here."

"Sure thing. You just hang together, y'hear?"

"I hear you, Gasser 29. And thanks for the thought. There's one more thing you could do for us, if you would."

"Sure we will. What is it?"

"We'll need some up-to-date met reports for the mainland Scottish airports. Can you get them for me?"

"I reckon that sort of information is going to be uppermost on a lot of people's minds right now. Leave it with me, buddy, and I'll come back to you in a couple of minutes."

"Roger. And thanks."

Dougie clamped his teeth firmly together and looked out towards the lowering cloud base in front of the aircraft. If they were to find a way to navigate *Tartan Arrow* through that cloud, they would need very precise assistance, the sort of assistance a Nimrod was well equipped to provide.

But, what were all those other aircraft doing out here?

It was not unusual to find a British maritime reconnaissance aircraft out on the western approaches to the UK. What was unusual was to find a USAF E3A AWACS aircraft out here, along with all those other American aircraft. It didn't make sense.

"Sinclair 984, this is Gasser 29. Over."

Dougie was surprised at the speed of the KC135 pilot's response. "Go ahead, Gasser 29."

"Roger. The latest met reports show that Glasgow and Edinburgh airports are both closed. At Glasgow they have eight eighths cloud right down on the deck and the visibility is nil. At Edinburgh they have eight eighths cloud at one hundred feet and a visibility of fifty metres, and it's deteriorating fast. Aberdeen and all the other northern airports are out as well. Your only hope is Prestwick. They have snow conditions, but the cloud base is five hundred feet and the visibility two kilometres."

"Roger, Gasser 29. Thanks for your help. That was quick."

"Like I said, a lot of people are studying the weather right now. Especially at Prestwick."

"Roger, Gasser 29. Say, just what is going on out there?"

"Standby." The pilot's voice came back as a sharp snap.

Dougie wriggled in his seat. He was getting uncomfortable under the strain of flying the 747 manually. He stared ahead through his cracked screen. What were their chances of making a landfall? Not great. And even if they did reach the Scottish coast, what were the odds that they could make a safe landing? Pretty slim. He glanced back at Kovak. Best keep that opinion to himself.

"Uh... Sinclair 984... you copy me, buddy?"

Dougie thumbed the transmit switch. "I read you strength three, Gasser 29. Go ahead."

"Say, uh... we got a bit of a problem up here. We're, uh... we're gonna close down on this frequency for the time being. The command ship will call you shortly. Okay?"

"Roger, Gasser 29. Good luck to you."

"And you, buddy. And you."

Amen to that, Dougie thought.

*

Maggie Loughlin clasped a hand to her forehead. The blood pounded in her ears as she scanned the scene of chaos about her. She took a deep breath before striding purposefully towards the front of the main deck centre cabin. Shock was rife in among the passengers, but most of the cabin crew were now going about their emergency duties. White faced and trembling, but at least they were doing their jobs.

Two stewardesses and one steward had been injured on the main deck. Maggie had heard that one of her girls had been killed on the upper deck, but she had not yet found time to get up there. Too many dead and injured passengers down here demanded her attention. The dead upstairs could wait.

"Please, someone, help me!" A pitiful cry breached the all-enveloping noise about her. It came from the front of the economy-class section where the worst damage had occurred. The cabin crew were busy freeing injured passengers from the wreckage; no one had responded to the cry.

Maggie hurried forward and scanned around the devastated cabin. An old man was trapped in his seat beneath a fallen baggage locker, almost opposite the gaping hole in the fuselage. He looked frail, white-haired and pasty-faced, with thin, straggly arms that reached out from beneath the fibreglass moulding.

"All right, I'm coming." She breathed deeply and reached out to grab at the fallen wreckage. The broken edge of the locker cut into her palm and she winced with pain. With the weight lifted from his chest, the old man struggled to help himself out. The effort was too much and he fell back under the ruins. Maggie tried to pull him with one hand while holding the moulding clear with the other.

"Can you push yourself clear? Push a bit harder..." Her words were cut short by a violent thump beneath her feet and the impact of a hammer blow throughout the cabin.

She stumbled as the floor trembled beneath her, reached out a hand to grasp a seat back and then fell across the debris pinning down the old man. He yelled in pain as the extra weight landed on him.

Maggie threw herself sideways, rolling awkwardly onto the floor. With her arms flailing wildly, she came down heavily on her face and immediately felt a cold damp liquid splash onto her neck and chest.

"Oh, my God!" The floor beneath her was wet. Liquid was bubbling up from the baggage hold beneath the floor, spurting into the cabin in short, erratic splashes.

"What is it? What's happening?" The old man's voice called to her weakly, as if from a distance.

"I don't know. God help us, I don't know!"

She struggled up onto hands and knees and crawled closer to the gap in the floor. Suddenly the whole cabin shook again with a juddering, hammer blow. The senior stewardess fell back against the seat beside her. She snatched at it and held tight. The floor shifted beneath her, shifted again and then vibrated. The tear that had ripped open across the width of the cabin floor was getting wider. More jets of liquid spurted into the cabin from the hold below.

*

"Sinclair 984, this is Highball. Do you read me?"

Dougie pushed his skewed headset back over his ears and adjusted the boom microphone. This was the call he had been waiting for, the confirmation that the airborne command aircraft had positively located them.

"Highball, this is Sinclair 984. I read you strength five."

"Roger, Sinclair 984. This is an airborne command post. We have all your details and we've been asked to look for you. We think we have you on radar, but we're getting no squawk code.

Would you please check your transponder."

Dougie felt his mouth twitch involuntarily. He was lucky to have three engines still working, let alone something as minor as a transponder. He wiped the thought from his mind with a query. Why had the Highball pilot not announced his reason for being out here off the Scottish coast? Perhaps it would be best not to ask. For the moment he was glad enough to have the assistance of the American radar aircraft.

"Highball, my transponder does not appear to be working. Most of my flight instruments are damaged."

"We copy that, Sinclair 984. What is your heading?"

"We're heading due east on the standby compass."

"Roger, turn right thirty degrees onto heading one two zero."

"Wilco. Turning now." Dougie eased the giant airliner round, a gentle turn in case the fuselage or wing structures were severely weakened. The thirty degree turn was a standard technique for identifying aircraft where a radar transponder was not available. It would also take them onto a better track for Prestwick.

Had they been on their correct course, down at fifty-five degrees north, then the easterly heading would have been more appropriate. But there was a distinct chance the 747 was far to the north of that position.

"Sinclair 984, this is Highball. We have you identified at position fifty-eight degrees north, eleven degrees west. Over."

"Roger, Highball." Fifty-eight degrees north! The pilot of the KC135 had been right; they were well off track. It would be of little comfort to the tanker pilot that he was not at fault. The error lay with the 747 crew and they had seemingly come off worst. He pressed the transmit switch again. "Can you give us radar vectors for Prestwick?"

"Affirmative, Sinclair 984. Continue on your present heading. We'll start you off with a heading towards Prestwick, but the airport may not be available to you. We'll talk to command operations and keep you advised. In the meantime a Nimrod is being diverted towards you. He will call you shortly."

Dougie's cheek twitched. A new sense of alarm crept into his thoughts. "Highball, this is Sinclair 984. Why can't we use Prestwick? And what exactly are you guys doing out here anyway?"

"Sorry, Sinclair 984. I can't tell you more at the moment. We've got another emergency on another frequency. We'll keep you advised."

Keep you advised? Like hell they would. It was the same old story where military matters were concerned. Tell nothing now and promise more later. He slammed a fist against his control column.

*

Maggie Loughlin rushed headlong up the stairs to the upper deck. She stopped dead when she caught sight of Fergus MacNabb lying across the front row of seats on the upper deck. He looked badly injured.

She scanned the cabin. Who was in charge here? At least one stewardess should have been on hand, calming the passengers, dealing with the dead and injured. And looking after the captain. Instead, MacNabb was being tended by a female passenger in a fur coat.

She clenched her fists. No time to worry about that now. She rushed on towards the front of the plane, burst open the door and stumbled, wide-eyed onto the flight deck. Nyle and the flight engineer turned to face her from the two pilot seats.

Maggie's hair whipped across her eyes as the chill air rushed past her.

Kovak half-rose from his seat and bellowed, "Shut the door!"

Maggie slammed it shut and turned back to the first officer. "We're falling apart back there." She gestured to the rear. "And something is splashing into the centre cabin."

"What do you mean, splashing?" Nyle looked back over his seat, frowned and used his head to beckon her closer.

"Liquid. It's spurting into the cabin. But that's not all. We're falling apart." She waved back towards the rear of the aircraft. "I was down by the hole on the main deck, where the engine blew up. There was a thump and a bang, and now the gap has opened up farther in the main cabin floor. I tell you there's something very wrong back there."

*

"Highball, this is Gasser 29. We, uh... we're in real trouble now. We've got a fire."

Judson leaned forward and selected the emergency code on his radar transponder. It was an automatic reaction.

"Roger, Gasser 29. Can you contain it?"

"That's one big negative, Highball." We've got one mighty huge fire out there in the starboard wing. We can't get it under control."

Judson's hands had turned cold and clammy. Outside, the grey sky looked even more ominous. Off to the right, a red glow in the cloud reflected the fire that was burning away his starboard wing.

"You sure you tried everything, Gasser 29?" The voice had a tinge of accusation, as if the KC135 pilot was to blame.

Judson felt his dander rising. What a damn fool question. "Look, buddy, I... uh... I tried everything except standing on the wing and pissing on it. You hear me?"

A short pause followed, and then, "Sure, we hear you, Gasser 29. Standby."

"Standby, nothing, Highball. I need to get this ship down on the ground fast, and I mean fast! You give me a steer for Prestwick."

A cackle of static spluttered in his ears and Judson's hands grasped the control column like it was about to be taken from him.

Come on, Highball, get your finger out!

"Gasser 29, sorry but we can't give you a diversion to Prestwick. They can't take an emergency diversion in there right now. Their card is marked by the guys in the *Washington*. We can give you a steer for a ditching in the sea near Benbecula."

Shit! They wanted him to ditch. A trickle of cold sweat dribbled down his cheek and he brushed at it angrily. But they were right. Judson knew that if he were the Highball commander he would have to say the same thing. Prestwick was one big no-no for the

KC135. They couldn't risk blocking the runway with a burning tanker.

Not now.

"Where's that place, Highball? What did you call it?"

"Benbecula. It's one of the Scottish islands. They used to have a British military base there. We reckon you could ditch in the sea, in sight of the airfield. They've got a zodiac rescue launch to pick you up."

"Jeez. You guys don't figure on making things easy for us. Unless we can dump all our fuel in time, this ship could go up like a bomb when it hits. You know that?"

Highball's voice came back cold and sober. "Affirmative. We know that, Gasser 29. But the other guys have got a bigger bomb than that."

That was true. Judson felt a throbbing pain begin to creep across his forehead. He wiped the back of his hand across his brow and noticed with some surprise that it came away dripping with sweat. He sensed rather than heard Bryzjinsky shuffle onto the flight deck and tuck in between himself and Youngman.

"Well?" he snapped.

Bryzjinsky came straight to the point. "You wanna know the bad news, Major, or the real bad news?"

"Gimme the real bad news first."

"We can't dump the gas from the main tanks. The vents won't open and the emergency cocks ain't playin' ball."

The pain across Judson's forehead turned suddenly into a stabbing above his eyes. Sparks of white light flew across his vision. "What's gone wrong?" he bellowed. "Why the hell can't you fix it, Bryzjinsky?"

"Christ, Major!" Bryzjinsky took a step backwards from the central console. "I'm only the goddamn messenger. You wanna see the headache they got back there, you go back and see for yourself."

"I thought the main tank system was still intact."

"Yeah. You thought it. Them guys working back there thought

it. But we was all wrong, Major. The system just ain't playin' ball."

"Shit! Tell me why, damn you."

"I don't know why." Bryzjinsky took a deep breath. "Look, maybe we got more damage than we thought when we hit that 747. Maybe, when that other ship's engine blew up, some o' the debris hit us in the fuselage. Maybe there's damage to the fuel lines inside the hull. Dammit, Major, I'm only guessin'. Ain't that enough?"

"Okay, okay. So we can't dump the gas in the main tanks. Now, what's the bad news?"

Bryzjinsky sighed loudly. "The bad news, Major, is that we got one helluva lot of fuel still in them tanks."

*

Dougie frowned as he pressed his radio-telephone transmit switch. "Highball, this is Sinclair 984. Over."

The response came back almost immediately. "Go ahead, Sinclair 984. We're still here and listening out."

"Roger, Highball. We were wondering… why are there so many military aircraft out here over the Atlantic? What's going on? Over."

The response was guarded. "There's an emergency situation, 984. We're preparing for an emergency landing."

"Roger Highball. I take it all this is not for us?"

"Negative, Sinclair 984. It's not for you."

"Roger." Dougie thought for a moment. "Who's in trouble, Highball?"

"Sorry, Sinclair 984. That's restricted information."

"Understood, Highball. But I'm not likely to call the press just now."

"I guess not." The voice paused, followed by a click on the frequency. Another click followed before it went on. "All I can tell you is this: If the other ship goes down, there's a real risk we can all kiss our asses goodbye."

Chapter 6

The flat felt strangely empty after Pamela left. Jock lay awake in the bed, staring at the ceiling and turning over in his mind disturbing thoughts and memories. At first he tried to ignore them, but the more he concentrated on dislodging those thoughts, the more they demanded his attention.

The blizzard outside robbed the room of daylight. With his hands clasped behind his head, Jock lay on his back, wrapped in the spread of a gentle glow from a bedside lamp. It cast soft, warm shadows around the delicately decorated room, illuminating the flower-print furnishings with a soft tint and emphasising the femininity of the owner's taste.

A tangent thought about Pamela MacReady made him smile to himself, a smile that spread as he shifted slightly in the bed. It rapidly faded when his mind returned to the subject of his uncertain future. Recent events began to crowd his mind, and the most demanding event was Sally's last telephone call from the States.

Ultimately, there was a pretty good chance that he and Sally would end up getting divorced. They had never discussed it in depth, never talked the matter through to its logical conclusion. They left it to hints and the odd one-liner to describe their thoughts to one another. He avoided the subject as much as possible because he didn't want things to go the way of the divorce court, but that was the very way they appeared to be heading. He felt his body tense as he considered the implications.

Sally's last phone call had come at a difficult time. It had been a tiring week and he was ready to go home.

*

He had set his portable alarm clock for six o'clock Friday morning and booked an early breakfast. A taxi would collect him from his hotel at seven. The course at the College of ATC was finished and he planned to catch an early train up to London. He'd spend an hour or two shopping and then catch a Glasgow train. A local train down to Ayr should see him home by early evening. Just in time to head out again and enjoy a party.

He was woken just a few minutes before six by the sound of his bedside telephone dragging him from a deep sleep. His eyes were still half-closed as he grabbed at the receiver. "Yes?"

"Jock? Is that you?" Sally sounded disturbed. Frightened. As if she was the victim of something terrible.

He screwed up his face. What was the matter with her?

"Jock? Are you there?" Her voice swam into sharper focus and she sounded suddenly close, as if she was calling from another room.

He sat up and pulled the telephone onto the bed. "Sally? What are you doing calling at this time of the morning?"

"I just wanted to talk to you."

"Oh. Right. How are you?"

"I'm fine." She was lying. Of course she was, even though the fear had almost vanished from her voice. Now it had a detached air, as if she were thinking other, deeply troubled thoughts. "I just thought I'd give you a call."

Sally rarely, if ever, phoned just to pass the time of day, or night.

"When will you be back?" he asked.

"At the weekend." She was hiding something. He was sufficiently awake to detect the obvious signs, the wary tones.

"How are things over there?"

"So-so. I've been out and about quite a bit."

"Anything interesting?"

"Not really. Fergus took me to a club. A place called Labelle..." Her voice checked suddenly. "We were with a group of others, of course."

"Of course." What else could he say? She was obviously lying again. She and MacNabb had been alone together, but this wasn't the time to make an issue of it.

"What are you planning on doing today?"

"Today, Jock?" Sally's voice came back dull and uninspired. "It's the middle of the night here." She paused. "Just coming up to one o'clock Friday morning."

Middle of the night? What was she doing ringing him in the middle of the night? He kept the questions bottled up. "I see. And did you have a good time?"

"Good time?"

"At the place MacNabb took you."

"Oh." A deep, hollow breath echoed down the line. "I miss you, Jock."

His lip trembled. "You seem to be spending quite a bit of time with this guy, MacNabb."

"Not really," she replied guardedly. "He likes to keep an eye on me."

Keep an eye on another man's wife? The bastard. Jock forced himself to speak evenly. "I figure we have to talk, Sally. Really talk. What time do you get back?"

"I'll be home Saturday morning. Around breakfast time."

"Okay, I'll see you then."

"Sure."

"Sally... just why did you call me?"

Again, the pause. Uncomfortable and embarrassing. "I told you. I just wanted to speak to you. I wanted to be sure you're all right. Look, I'll see you at the weekend, Jock. We can talk then."

"We need to."

"You're right. We have to sort out our future, Jock."

"Do we really have any future?" It surprised him that the thought uppermost in his mind had finally been spoken. "We're virtually living apart as things are. We might as well be strangers for all the time we spend together."

"Is that what you want?" she asked. "To be strangers?"

"You know damned well it isn't!"

"It might be the answer."

"No. It's not the answer. Look, we really do have to sort this thing out once and for all, Sally."

"Yes. You're right."

"I'll see you at the weekend."

The call didn't end there, but he chose not to dwell on that.

*

Pamela MacReady trudged angrily through the snow towards Atlantic House. She liked Jock Scrimgeour. She admired his skill as a controller and she felt an odd flutter of her heart when she met him socially. It would have been foolish to imagine there could ever be anything serious between them, but the thought was there. It came as a blow to learn that he was prepared to throw his career to the wind. Jock, of all people.

She was only yards from the main gate of the Air Traffic Control Centre compound before she detected something was wrong. The site was owned by a civil organisation, National Air Traffic Services, and was normally guarded by civilian personnel. But two armed RAF Regiment policemen now stood guard at the gate, stamping their feet to keep warm.

Pamela swept her gaze through the gates to where more military personnel hurried to and fro, as if the site had suddenly become a military base. Outside the main building, a line of grey drab vehicles was drawn up neatly, an attendant group of airmen pacing up and down in the snow beside them.

Pamela stopped beside a small security cabin and offered a puzzled expression to a uniformed guard seated behind an open window. The two military policemen standing nearby watched her warily.

"Your pass, please," the seated man snapped.

Pamela pushed her plastic ID card towards him. "What's going on?"

"Wait here a moment." He picked up a telephone and spoke quietly. After a short pause for a reply, he turned back towards her.

"You're not a controller?"

"No. An assistant."

"All right, love. You won't be required for duty today. It's controllers they need upstairs. You can go home."

"But, why?"

The man shook his head. "Just go home. If you cause any trouble, we'll have to keep you here."

"Keep me here? I don't understand."

"Don't argue with me, love. Just go home."

*

Jock jumped when he heard Pamela let herself into the flat. Even with an 'early go' — that illegal perk so widely prevalent in ATC — she should not have come back so soon.

He lay in the quiet solitude of the bedroom and tried to concentrate his wavering thoughts. Maybe she had forgotten something. She would leave again shortly, he was sure of it. He relaxed and waited for the slam of the front door.

But she didn't leave. Minutes later, she brought him a cup of coffee and switched on the room light. "Come on, you. That's my bed and I'm home again."

He sat up and glanced at the bedside alarm. It was only ten fifteen.

He stifled a yawn. "You're home early. I thought you were on a day shift."

"I was. But there's something odd going on at Atlantic House. The RAF have taken over and posted armed guards all over the shop. I didn't get past the main entrance before they sent me straight home again."

"Who sent you home?"

"An armed guard. Looked like a rock ape. You know, the RAF regiment type."

"What's it all about?" Jock rubbed his hand across his stubbly chin and realised he had no shaving kit with him.

"God knows. I didn't wait to find out. But it's odd, very odd.

Whatever it is."

Jock leaned back against the bedhead and kneaded his bleary eyes. Whatever was going on at Atlantic House, it was not his problem. But something had to be very wrong if the RAF had taken over a civil establishment. A sudden thought hit him. Was this in any way connected with that fishy story about the airport terminal?

"It's one shitty morning out there," the girl continued as she backed away out of the room and out of sight. "The snow's as deep as I've ever seen it, and it's still falling heavily."

"Were the rest of the staff allowed on duty?"

"I don't know. I suppose so, but I didn't see anyone else before I left." Pamela's voice echoed from the sitting room. "They said something about needing controllers. They didn't want me to stay because I'm only an assistant." She was moving around, but her voice came back evenly through the open doorway.

Jock rotated his shoulders to bring the muscles back into use. "Thanks for the use of the bed anyway."

"You're expected to pay for it."

"Yes?"

"I figured you could cook the lunch. I did some shopping on the way home so there's no excuse for you not to do your share."

He grinned and pushed aside the cosy duvet. "I suppose it's the least I can do for you. Porridge or black pudding?"

"I don't have either in the larder. Make it bacon, egg and chips."

"As you please. Give me a moment to get dressed."

"Not just yet."

She appeared in the doorway in what Jock later remembered as a hazy dream sequence. She must have been undressing in the sitting room while she was chatting to him. It never occurred to him to ask himself why she was about to climb into bed with him. His thoughts were orientated more towards the actuality of the situation than the reason behind it. Naked, she was beautiful, and that was enough for him to think about right then. He sat, stunned, on the edge of the bed, his toes playing a disbelieving tune on the warm carpet. As she walked towards him, he knew that his eyes were transfixed, but there was nothing he could do about it. He didn't even trust himself to speak.

Then another sudden memory fell into place.

Sally's phone call.

"Just one thing before you hang up, Jock." Sally's voice sounded eerie, almost as if she were haunting him.

"Yes." His hand gripped the telephone more tightly.

"I never meant to hurt you."

"What do you mean?"

"I never meant any of it. Oh, dammit! Let's talk about it when we meet."

"It's MacNabb, isn't it," he snapped accusingly.

"I'll try to explain when we meet. Honestly."

"It's bloody MacNabb. You bitch!"

The next sound he heard was the hum as the phone line went dead. He shivered. It was not a memory he wanted to think about.

"Jock, you look so angry." Pamela sat on the bed beside him and stretched an arm about his shoulders. "Is it because of me?"

"No, it's not you. Something I have to sort out at the weekend."

"Something important?"

He nodded savagely. "I reckon so."

Chapter 7

"For God's sake!" Kovak glowered at Maggie Loughlin, not too sure whether he was annoyed with her or with the urgent information she had brought onto the flight deck.

"You must come," she insisted, her arms waving wildly. "Please come and look."

"You go and check it out, Sammy," Nyle snapped. His gaze never wavered from the instruments in front of him.

Kovak wanted to protest. Hadn't he enough to cope with at his flight engineer station? Dammit! But what was the point of arguing? With no working autopilot, the first officer had to remain in his seat until the aircraft was on the ground and the emergency was resolved. One way or another. That left only the flight engineer to deal with complications in the passenger cabin.

Kovak groaned and rose from his seat. "Come on, then. Show me what's worrying you."

The stewardess grabbed him firmly by the arm, half-leading, half-dragging him down the stairs to the 747's main deck, and on through the devastated cabin area.

"That's where it starts." She pointed to the hole in the fuselage side where jagged metal framed the view of the dark clouds outside. Then she moved her finger down to the floor, in line with the hole. "Now look down there."

Kovak knelt down. Maggie stood back as he studied the tear in both the carpet and the pressure-bearing cabin floor beneath. Something damp discoloured the carpet.

"See? The liquid. It's all across the floor. What is it?"

Kovak bent closer to inspect the dark stains spreading out across the carpet either side of the giant tear in the aluminium floor. He ran his hand gingerly across the wetness, put one finger to his nose and sniffed. No obvious smell, or was his nose fooled by the other strong odours lingering about the wrecked cabin? Whatever the liquid was, it was no longer seeping into the cabin.

"There's not too much of it," he said.

"But it came up from below the floor. It shouldn't do that!" Maggie's lack of cool was out of character for a senior stewardess. He glanced round at her. Had she been drinking again? He had heard enough rumours about her boozing habits. Or was her behaviour simple panic?

What the hell. He had more important things to think about than a stewardess's drink problem. He turned his concentration back to the liquid on the floor.

"If we're lucky, it's water from the fresh water tanks. They're just below here."

"And if we're unlucky?" Maggie countered.

"If we're unlucky, it's fuel from the centre section fuel tanks. They're also under the floor near here."

*

The clogging mass of cloud enveloping the KC135 made the front screen look like a bubbling grey caldron. A view into hell and beyond. Major Paul S Judson kept his eyes focussed ahead, looking for a break, while Youngman called out the altitudes.

"Two thousand feet." The altimeter was winding down fast and Youngman's voice was growing ever more taut.

To the right-hand side of the airplane, on the periphery of his vision, Judson could still make out the red glow of the burning wing. How much longer would it burn before the fuel tanks exploded? He gripped the control column even tighter.

If they had been given permission to make an approach to Prestwick, they would be landing soon. Just a little longer, not too long, and Judson would be following the needles of the ILS — the Instrument Landing System — for a safe touchdown on a firm runway. But Prestwick was out of the question. It was just bad luck.

"One thousand feet."

Judson began to ease back on the column. "There's the cloudbreak," he shouted.

One moment they were descending through the thick, grey gloom and then the KC135 broke through the cloud base still in a dive. With the angry sea below and the bubbling cloud above, they had descended into a dangerously slim layer of indecision, halfway between certain death and probable death.

Judson pulled farther back on the column and brought the jet into level flight just a few hundred feet above the sea. Ahead of them was the stark outline of a group of islands, slate grey against the heavy cloud formation. It didn't look too enticing.

"All crew to ditching positions." Judson tightened his seat harness and offered a short, poignant prayer. "And cancel that darned noise!"

Youngman obliged by silencing the undercarriage alarm, a warning that they were flying close to the surface with the wheels up. As he leaned back in his seat, the second pilot scanned across the instruments. "Shit. We're losing oil pressure in number two."

Judson ignored him. Within a few minutes they would have no oil pressure in any engine, no goddamn life in any system on board the flying gas tank. *Burning* gas tank.

He pressed his intercom switch. "How does the fire look from back there, Bryzjinsky?"

The sergeant's voice came back slow and dour. "It's sure spreadin' fast, Major. You gonna get us down soon?"

Spreading fast? He gasped. The sooner he got the ship down in the water, the better.

"Okay, Bryzjinsky. All crew stand by for ditching."

He eased the nose down towards the heaving waves. "Highball, this is Gasser 29. We're going down now."

"Roger, Gasser 29." The voice came back calm, too calm by half. "Rescue boats are being launched from Benbecula."

"Roger, Highball. We're gonna need 'em. We're..." His voice choked in mid-sentence. "Aw, shit, Highball, we... we got another problem... uh, I don't think we're gonna make it."

*

MacNabb forced his eyes open. Someone was leading a uniformed figure hurriedly out through the flight-deck door. Who was it? His mind was too confused by far. Perhaps it was one of the stewardesses grasping the man's uniform sleeve, or perhaps it was someone else. He wasn't sure of anything.

His head was spinning, almost as if he had been on the granddaddy of all benders, but far more painful. It had taken a while before he was able to fully appreciate the magnitude of the shambles inside the aircraft. There was so much noise. So much activity that appeared quite out of place on board a Sinclair International flight. And why was he not up on the flight deck anyway? Why was he not in control of the 747?

Fergus MacNabb had grown used to being in control. It was his natural place in life. His father had instilled in him at an early age that control was everything. "The guy who's in charge is the winner. Always grab the winning hand, laddie. Whatever it takes. Whoever you have to step on. Always be the one with the finger on the button. The one who makes the decisions."

MacNabb always lived up to his father's expectations. Until now.

Now he was no longer in control. He was stretched out on a row of seats at the front of the upper-deck cabin and someone was sitting beside him, gently mopping his forehead. His whole body ached, especially his left arm. He tried to raise himself to get a better idea of what was happening, but a hand was immediately put out to restrain him. Who was holding him back?

He turned his head to one side and focussed on the strange face staring back at him. Maggie Loughlin? No, it was some woman he had never seen before, a woman wearing a fur coat. A passenger?

A sudden thought. Perhaps it was Maggie Loughlin but, in his confused state of mind, he was unable to recognise her. Yes, that had to be it. In his swirling thoughts, the fur-coated figure was indeed the senior stewardess. The more he tried to concentrate, the more convinced he became that he was being tended by Maggie Loughlin and his mind frantically searched for recent memories of her.

A hand went to his brow, calming him, helping to bring back the recollections he sought. Recollections of the senior stewardess.

The last time he had seen her from this angle, leaning over his prostrate body, he had been in his own bed. The sudden memory of the occasion attacked his brain with a sharp snap. Memories poured back.

*

He woke up slowly that Thursday morning. Was it only two days ago?

In the first few moments of consciousness he thought he could feel Sally's soft, warm body lying beside him. He reached out his arm to wrap it around her naked breasts and he held her tightly, wondering why he felt so protective towards her.

Then full awareness crept over him and he realised with surprise that it wasn't Sally who shared his bed. It didn't even smell like Sally. But the breasts felt warm and comforting and he squeezed the soft tissue anyway. Why did he automatically imagine it was Sally who lay beside him and not his erstwhile wife? Could it have been a sense of guilt?

Then the warm feminine body stirred in the bed.

"Goddammit, Fergus. Do you have to squeeze so tight?" The girl spoke with a pronounced Glaswegian accent. It took him only a second to register that it was Maggie Loughlin. He had arranged to meet her at a bar in Manhattan.

It wasn't exactly a casual pick up. He slept with Maggie frequently. Their relationship had begun when they both worked for British Airways. She had been an attractive and innocent young stewardess then, but she had soon changed under his influence. She had also learned enough about pulling strings to get herself a senior job with Sinclair International. She had to make the move because MacNabb had also moved to Sinclair and he had such a heady hold over Maggie, a hold which bound her to his will and command. All it took for her to get the job was a couple of nights of persuasive lovemaking in the bed of a senior manager, and MacNabb had engineered that also.

He closed his eyes while Maggie stirred and reached her arms across him. She traced her finger across the tattoo that was emblazoned on his chest. She was fascinated by the tattoo which depicted two aircraft in a dogfight.

She yawned. "It's time we were out of bed, Fergus."

"Piss off," he replied. At the same time he grabbed her and swung her further across his own body. "But not before you've done your bit."

She had a warm smell about her, which he liked, and it made him feel horny. When she rose up and straddled him, he grinned to himself, opened his eyes and reached out to capture her breasts. Maggie wasn't the world's best sex, but she was free and she belonged to him whenever he chose to say so.

Having done her bit, she slipped out of the bed. He heard her move about the hotel room as she dressed, but she said nothing more for the moment. He pulled the bedclothes tighter about him as he heard the sound of the bedroom kettle coming to the boil and he smelled coffee.

"Bring me the first cup!" he bellowed.

A few moments later, she slapped a mug down on the cabinet beside the bed.

She pouted her lips as she spoke. "I'm going now."

"Good. Make sure you shut the door on the way out."

"Why did you bring me here, Fergus?"

"I needed a screw and you were available."

Anger took hold of her voice. "You know, you really are the bastard they say you are. You won't be sleeping with me again."

He leaned up on one elbow and stretched out a hand for the coffee. "I'll sleep with you whenever I choose. And don't you forget it."

"I'll see you in hell first."

"Will you? I'll make you suffer before we get anywhere near hell."

"Like you made Sally suffer? Beat me up like you beat her, will you? Don't even think about it."

He frowned. "Beat her up? I did not!"

"You bloody well did. She told me. Told me how you made sure all the bruising was hidden beneath her clothes. Showed me some of the marks. You must have known what you were doing. It wasn't just blind anger, was it? You're a bastard, Fergus."

He snorted. She would change her tune pretty damn quick if he turned the screws, which he had the means to do. Her job, even her freedom might depend on him one day. She couldn't afford to rub him up the wrong way and expect to get away with it. Anyhow, she would be on the flight back to Prestwick Friday night so she had better be nice to him. It would be one pig of a flight if he had to cope with two bad-tempered females — Maggie and Sally — on the same trip.

He sat up when he heard the bedroom door slam behind the stewardess and he took a long pull at the hot coffee. She was a cow and he never could work up much enthusiasm for manners. Certainly not for a casual plaything. What he wanted right then was to make someone pay for the feeling of bitterness that was tearing him apart.

It had been all Sally's fault, of course. She had refused his offer of marriage. She had let him down in front of his parents. The humiliation had stung him to the core. MacNabb didn't take kindly to the experience of humiliation. That was why he had been forced to beat her.

*

He turned his head at the sound of a loud crash nearby. One of the stewardesses was helping a man to pull a dangling section of an overhead locker. It was the young woman, what was her name? The one he had tried to date through Maggie Loughlin. Hell's teeth, what was her name? He couldn't remember. Other passengers were now coming forward and helping her rip the broken locker from its remaining mountings. Helping the stewardess to pull apart his aircraft.

*

A dull orange glow appeared some distance ahead of the 747, right down on the waterline. For just a second, Dougie thought he saw flames, but he couldn't be sure. He leaned forward to get a better view through the cracked screen. While it lasted, it was too bright to be a flare, but already it had faded to just an afterglow. Then a lingering remnant.

It was often the most painful things that lasted. Like memories of Edward. The child's behaviour had been almost a carbon copy of Jenny's. When he did wrong, as any child will, he had that same way of holding his head, looking over his shoulder, smiling and yet not smiling. Melting any risk of chastisement stone dead. Dougie had cherished him when he was alive, but that was what being a father was all about. Wasn't it? After Edward's death he had ached so much for what was lost that he began to wonder if any tender memory could ever again bring peace.

It had been the same for Jenny. He knew that well enough. She had grieved for her son with equal intensity. Maybe, when her husband was dead, along with everyone else on flight 984, she would grieve again.

He felt suddenly alone on the flight deck and wished Kovak would hurry back.

He jerked back into his seat as a new voice came across the airwaves. "Sinclair 984, this is Watchdog on 121.5. Do you read me? Over." The voice came across with a straight, unflappable English accent. Like a pukka gentleman reading the BBC evening news. At other times, it amused Dougie that the English could still put up their 'piece of cake' image when the war was so long ended. Right now he needed some decisive help, not a Bertie Wooster act.

He responded with equal calm, wondering if his light Scottish accent would be picked up by the other pilot. "Watchdog, this is Sinclair 984. I read you strength four. Over."

"Good morning, sir." The English voice suddenly developed a spurt of enthusiasm. "I believe you've had a spot of bother."

"You could say that. Are you the Nimrod come to shepherd us?"

"Affirmative. We have visual contact with you, and we're approaching from your port side, presently about two miles behind you at the same altitude."

Despite the seriousness of the situation, despite the cut-glass accent on the radio-telephone frequency, Dougie sensed an immediate wave of comfort. Someone was there to help. He was surprised that Bertie Wooster could have that effect on him.

"What's your plan, Watchdog?"

"First thing, old chap, is to give you a once-over and try to assess the damage. I'll tuck in just below you on the port side to start with and then work my way around the rest of your fuselage."

"That'll help, Watchdog. I think most of the damage is on the port side. The port inner engine is a write-off."

"Roger. I can see that already. Someone gave you a black eye, did they?"

"Caught us off guard."

"Most unsporting. How many casualties do you have?" No allegation of blame, just a bland, off-hand comment and a pertinent question.

"I don't know exactly," he responded, "The captain is injured and is no longer on the flight deck. A number of passengers are dead. Not sure how many."

This time the voice was more restrained, almost apologetic. "I'm sorry, old chap. It sounds pretty bad in there. We'll do what we can to help you. I'm just coming up under your port side now."

Dougie held the aircraft level and waited for the Nimrod pilot to call again. When the message came, it was deliberate and calm.

"Sinclair 984, this is Watchdog. We've made a close inspection of your port side. It doesn't look good."

"Roger, Watchdog," Dougie replied calmly. "Give me the worst."

"There's a whole line of damage to your fuselage starting with a nasty hole just in front of the wing and extending back to a point behind the undercarriage bay doors. There is some structural damage to the port wing in front of the inner engine. Farther back it seems to be mainly dents and scratches, but you do have the odd puncture hole through into your cargo bays. There is also one nasty bit of damage to the lower fuselage just above your main body undercarriage bay doors. Have you tried lowering your undercarriage?"

"The wheels were lowered when we made our emergency descent, but they should be up again now."

"I think you should try lowering and raising them again. Try it after we've inspected the rest of your fuselage. Your port undercarriage bay doors are slightly open."

Dougie looked at the telltale green light on the panel in front of him and felt his blood run chill. If there were problems with the undercarriage, they would have difficulty getting down on the ground safely.

"Watchdog, how far open are the doors?"

"Enough to show, but not enough for us to be able to see the undercarriage itself."

"Thanks, Watchdog. That's just what I don't need."

He stared ahead, thinking frantically, until his eyes focussed again on the bank of cloud directly in the path of the aircraft. With the weather radar inoperative, it was almost impossible to guess how far ahead the bank lay, or how extensive it was. He had already lost two or three thousand feet in height since breaking through the cloud base, and the 747 was now flying at what he guessed to be about two thousand feet above sea level.

He thought for a moment longer and then he asked, "Watchdog, can you guide us around that cloud ahead."

"Affirmative. Around it, over it or beneath it. But first I'll just pop round to your starboard side to see if there's any damage over there."

"Roger. But the cloud is getting closer."

"We see it, old chap. Stick close beside us and we'll take you home to Scotland."

Dougie shook his head and wondered what the Englishman was like, sitting inside his shiny big Nimrod. The disembodied voice gave no indication whether the owner was young or old, tall or short. The only clues to the pilot's character lay in the apparent stiff upper lip. And that was probably just an act.

He said, "I guess I'm not doing anything else at the moment, Watchdog."

"Jolly good. I'll call you again when I get in position along your starboard side."

"One more thing, Watchdog." This one was bugging him, he had to ask. "What was that flare I spotted earlier? It was some way ahead of us and very low down."

After a short interval the Nimrod pilot replied, "I don't think that was a flare, sir. I think that was an aircraft on fire."

"Roger." He had suspected it. "Who was it?"

"An American tanker aircraft. He had a fire in his wing."

Dougie cleared his throat. "Was it the one we hit?"

"Affirmative."

"What happened to the crew?"

"We don't know. The aircraft was in real trouble, but someone else is dealing with it. The USAF people are looking after their own."

"Keep us informed, will you."

"Affirmative. We'll do that."

*

"Well? What do you think it is?" Maggie Loughlin's voice was shrewish in its cutting edge, as if all her past experience as a stewardess was beginning to wear thin. She was, after all, just as human as the rest of them. Just as frightened as everyone else. Just as likely to resort to the bottle in an emergency. Kovak was convinced now that she had tackled her fear with alcohol, probably from the duty-free supply.

He looked up at her and breathed a long sigh of relief. "Water." He placed another drop on the end of his tongue and nodded, satisfied with his judgement. "It's all right, it's only water from the fresh water tanks."

"That's bad enough, isn't it?"

"Maggie, at this moment everything on board this darned aircraft is bad." He stood up slowly and deliberately. "A spot of water in the bilges is likely to be the least of our worries."

She clamped her hands around an adjacent seat back. "I heard some loud noises as well. Loud bangs beneath the floor. I thought we were falling apart."

"Where did the noises come from?"

"I'm not sure." She released one hand to spread it round the scene. "Somewhere underneath the floor."

"All right. If it happens again—"

He froze as a shuddering boom reverberated through the cabin floor beneath him. He put out a hand to steady himself and watched, silent but fascinated, as the torn edge of the wet carpet flapped in reaction to another deep thump.

Maggie took a step backwards and grabbed at another seat to retain her balance. Nearby, the passengers sat rigid with fear, holding onto one another and to the seat rests. One cried out in alarm. A young child threw itself into its mother's arms, weeping while the mother looked to the crew for reassurance.

Kovak waited until the noise had subsided and then announced, "It's not coming from directly below this area. It's coming from farther back."

He felt angry with Maggie because she was openly exhibiting her fears while he was doing his best to hide his own. Was that another price to be paid for his career ambitions? He pushed past the senior stewardess and made his way back down the cabin, past the galley units, and stopped at the front of the next section. He had hardly come to a halt before another noise echoed through the cabin floor.

"It's coming from below here."

Maggie raced after him, pulling herself along from seat to seat. She came to a halt alongside where he stood and followed his eyes to the floor at a point directly beneath them. While they stood, watching and waiting, another concussion reverberated beneath their feet.

"What's under here?" she asked.

Kovak's voice was edged with shock. "Something far more important than a couple of water tanks. Under here are the main body undercarriage bays."

*

MacNabb's thoughts drifted in and out of reality so that he had no clear idea of what was now and what was past. He felt the 747 buck and heave at each angry encounter with air turbulence, but the motion was unreal, as if it was part of his more transient dreams and recollections. As if the aircraft was the mattress of his bed, and the turbulence was Maggie Loughlin's violent sexual manoeuvres. But it couldn't be, because he had ordered her out of his hotel room. He remembered doing that. Remembered lying in bed afterwards as his thoughts swung between Maggie and Sally.

The image suddenly snapped into sharp focus.

*

He pulled himself out of bed lethargically. His clothes were scattered about the floor where the stewardess had left them after disrobing him. She was pretty good in the act of seduction, he told himself, not as perfect as some of the whores he had bedded, but good. He felt a minor spasm of regret at his brusque manner towards her. Then he remembered again his more violent behaviour towards Sally and his hand instinctively tightened into a balled fist. He'd really gone too far that time.

He didn't want her forgiveness because she deserved everything he gave her, but he did want to see her again. And she was here in New York. She'd come in on a different flight but he knew where to find her.

He grabbed the telephone and dialled her downtown hotel. The company always put the cabin crew in cheaper hotels. He had once offered to get Sally something better, but she had refused with the excuse that her husband would get to hear about it. Stupid bitch.

He tapped impatiently on the wall while he waited. When the

hotel switchboard put him through to her, she sounded cautious, frightened.

"Who is it?"

"It's me. Fergus."

For a second he thought she might disconnect, but instead she answered slowly, "What do you want?"

"I wondered how you are."

"You've got a nerve phoning me, Fergus."

"Oh, come off it, Sally. How are you feeling?"

"I suppose I'll be alright again in a few days."

"Yeah. Sure you will. Say, can we meet? I have to talk to you."

"No, Fergus. We mustn't meet again. Ever."

That was stupid, he thought. They were bound to meet again in the course of their jobs. They would meet again Friday evening. He went on, "Please, Sally. Let's be reasonable about this."

"Reasonable! You beat me up and then you ask me to be reasonable?"

He felt his anger swelling again. Why wouldn't she see it from his point of view? "You provoked me, Sally. You humiliated me in front of my folks."

"You're wrong, Fergus, I didn't provoke you. And I don't want to talk to you or see you again. You really are a bastard of the first order."

"Come off it, Sally. How can you say that when I wanted to marry you?"

"I'm sorry, Fergus. That sort of self-pity cuts no ice with me now. In some ways, I feel sorry for you. I really do."

He heard the click as she disconnected. Without any rational thought, he slammed down his own receiver and stood rigid with fury.

He needed a drink and this was one occasion demanding something with guts and determination. He ferreted into the base unit of his drink cabinet and pulled out a bottle of single malt. Then he poured himself a generous measure and drank it neat, gasping as he felt it tear at his throat like no other drink he knew.

The second pull felt even better.

The bitch would have to pay for what she was doing to him, on that point he was certain. He took another large measure of whisky and poured it down his throat so fast he choked as the bite of the liquor ripped into him. The bitch would pay.

Around midday he decided to contact 'the big man', the one who arranged the New York end of their drugs shifting business. He needed to collect enough coke for his own personal use. He always moved his personal supply as a separate package. Safer that way.

He dialled another New York number. A gruff voice answered.

MacNabb kept his reply short. "I'm visiting mother Friday night. I think I should take her a present."

"Better see me soon. Be here in thirty minutes."

MacNabb grunted a quick acknowledgement and rang off. Half an hour later he left the hotel by a rear exit and took a taxi to an address in the Bronx.

The big man was looking grim, even more grim than usual. Something was wrong and MacNabb wasn't surprised when he began pouring out his problem.

"We gotta be more careful," he said ponderously. "The Feds are getting too close."

"They watching you?" MacNabb asked.

"Not a chance. I got more sense than that. But they've been watching my mules. Some o' them're no longer any use to me. You'll need to fix your own mule for this small package."

MacNabb grimaced. Then he grinned. Of course! He knew just the right person to be duped into carrying his personal coke. The beating-up wasn't enough; there had to be some more satisfying form of revenge.

Sally could carry his supply on this trip, only a small quantity, easily hidden, and she could do it without being aware. Perfect. And if it worked, he would confront her with her crime and warn her of what would happen if she ever breathed a word of it to anyone. She would keep her mouth shut; that was for sure. Then she would be under pressure to carry the load again and again.

He pictured her face when he confronted her at the other end. It made him feel better. After that she would be bound to him for life. His slave. The more he thought about it, the more appealing the idea became.

An hour later he was back in his hotel room, his brain slowly moving back up into automatic. He slipped a polythene-wrapped package into his desk, then carefully and deliberately locked the drawer. When he left the hotel the second time, he took a taxi across the Brooklyn Bridge to Midtown Manhattan, the shopping area between Third Avenue and Seventh. He knew exactly what he was looking for and he found it at the third place he tried. With a sense of cautious triumph further lifting his spirits, he returned again to the hotel.

It was almost six o'clock that Thursday evening when he telephoned Sally's hotel a second time. He got through to her straightaway.

"Sally, it's me. Fergus."

She sounded weary. "Not again, Fergus. I told you—"

"I know. I know. Look, I want to say I'm sorry, that's all. Just an apology and nothing else."

"Okay, Fergus. You've apologised."

"Not like this. Will you let me buy you dinner? We could meet at Labelles. It's a public place and you won't come to any harm there."

"I already told you, Fergus. I don't want to see you."

"Please, Sally. Just this once. Just let me say sorry before we part for good."

"Oh, I don't know, Fergus."

"Honestly, Sally, I only want to see you to apologise. That's all."

"Didn't you hear what I said? I don't want to see you again." But her voice was less insistent this time and he knew he had won.

"Just this once and then it's all over. I want us to part on good terms."

An audible sigh was followed by a telling pause. Then, "Alright.

But it's going to be the last time."

"Make it seven o'clock. I'll be waiting."

He rang off in triumph.

It occurred to him to wait until the following day before giving her the present. But, on reflection, he thought that might be too dangerous. Better to let her get used to having it before she boarded the aircraft. Just in case anyone noticed. He went to his desk and took out the package.

*

MacNabb's senses reeled.

Somewhere nearby, the young stewardess yelled, "Hold onto that broken end!" Then he felt the crump of yet another damaged locker falling across a section of seats.

A man shouted, "Grab hold of it, someone!"

People were milling about nearby.

As he turned to see what was happening, a sharp spasm of pain shot through MacNabb's arm and he cried out suddenly.

*

Devereaux pushed the broken locker aside and helped a young woman climb out from beneath the wreckage.

"You hurt?" he asked, dragging her into the aisle space.

"Hurt?" The woman swept her hair from her smudged face. Her eyes blazed fiercely. "Am I hurt? What the hell do you think?"

"Take it easy, lady," he said.

"Take it easy? Shit! What kinda flight is this?" Her hands shook as she tried to stand upright.

Devereaux looked behind him to where Trudy Bodenstadt was trying to calm a hysterical elderly woman near the back of the cabin. What kind of flight indeed?

He almost laughed to himself as he recalled Diane Redmond's parting words. "Goddammit, Simon, do you always get the cushy numbers?"

"Luck of the draw, I guess," he had replied. "I'll bring you a bottle of duty-free Scotch from Prestwick."

"Sure. You get the free trip to Scotland, and I get a lousy bottle of Scotch."

"And the chance to move in with me when I get back."

"You ain't arrested the guy yet."

"Trust me."

His only qualm about the assignment was that he would be making it without his partner — the police .38 Special he always carried in a shoulder holster under his jacket. The boss had made a semi-formal deal for cooperation with the British cops, but they had drawn the line at Devereaux carrying a firearm on a British flight into Scotland.

*

Kovak burst onto the flight deck with Maggie Loughlin close behind. He waited for the first officer to acknowledge him with a short nod before he continued. "There are loud noises coming from the port main undercarriage bay."

Nyle shook his head. "What sort of noises?"

"Banging noises. Loud banging noises!"

The first officer replied dully. "There's a British Nimrod flying alongside us. The pilot says our lower fuselage is damaged around the port undercarriage bay doors, and the doors are not fully closed."

Kovak lurched forward to the windscreen and scanned the view outside for sight of the Nimrod. He saw nothing and flopped down into his flight engineer seat.

"What do we do now?" he asked.

"I think you'd better take a look down inside the undercarriage bay."

"Me!" Kovak's brows rocketed. "Can't you do it?"

"No, I can't. You should be able to see that. I have to stay here to fly the aircraft. You must go back and take up the inspection panel. Then find out what's happened down in the undercarriage bay."

"I could take the column while you go back there."

"Sammy!" Nyle was getting ruffled. "Go and take a look. That's an order."

"Okay. I'll go." He swung round to Maggie. "You'd better come with me. It was your bloody discovery."

*

MacNabb felt the fur-coated woman's warm hand grasp his own and he heard her voice saying, "Gee, honey, I'm glad to see you're awake. You sure gave us a bit of a shock, you know. What with you being the captain, and all."

Stupid cow. He'd not been responsible for the shock. It was the other guy, the one who flew his aircraft into them. He stared into the woman's face and found himself looking at Sally Scrimgeour, although he knew it wasn't her voice. Poor Sally. The girl had died because she got herself into something she hadn't understood. If only she hadn't caused such a fuss at his parents' home. If only she had behaved more reasonably towards him. Then he wouldn't have felt obliged to get his revenge by using her as a drugs mule. There was no ignoring the fact that she had died as a direct result of that bag. And its contents.

*

"I brought you a present," he told her in the restaurant.

She threw him a sudden suspicious look. "A present?" Her face was pale, her mouth turned down grimly at the ends. The restaurant was dimly lit but not enough to hide the sadness in her eyes.

"Are you okay?" he asked. Of course she wasn't okay, how could she be?

"Yeah. I'm okay."

"Well, anyway. I bought the present to say that I'm sorry for what happened."

"You didn't have to do that." She leaned back in her seat, as if she were about to play one of her futile feminine games with him.

"I wanted to buy it. I want you to have it." He brought the parcel up onto the table and pushed it towards her.

She stared at it for some seconds, apparently unwilling or unable to reach out and accept his offering. "I wish you hadn't," she said.

He caught her eye. "Open it, will you."

Hesitantly, she took it in her hands and slowly peeled away the fancy wrapping paper. Inside was a white, soft leather handbag. She held it up and studied it carefully.

"It's very nice, Fergus."

"Very nice? Look at the label, Sally. That thing cost me a bomb."

"But I'm sure you can afford it."

He had a vague suspicion this might turn into a re-run of their last date. But at least the important task of the evening was accomplished. Maybe he could drag out the rest of the meal without any recourse to acrimony.

They left the restaurant shortly after nine, Sally easing ahead of him to avoid any physical contact. He tried to offer her a lift back to her hotel, but she refused.

"No thank you. I want to be alone now." She looked determined.

"Thanks for coming, anyway," he said.

Her response was strained. "Thank you for the meal. And the present." Her fingers held the bag lightly as if she felt unconvinced about accepting it.

"Be careful how you go. I'll call you a cab."

But already she was striding away from him. "I can do that myself."

MacNabb shrugged his shoulders. Damn the stupid woman.

*

He looked up again but this time he was staring into the eyes of the matronly passenger in the fur coat. Big, worried and frightened eyes looked down at him from a puffy, round face. All about them, the row continued unabated.

*

Maggie Loughlin bent down to lend a hand while the flight engineer pulled up the carpet, exposing the aluminium inspection panel. Her heartbeat increased as Kovak unscrewed the pressure caps. He gasped as each one came loose. Then he lifted the panel. Straightaway a jet of bitingly cold air rushed up from below, a sure indication that the bay doors were not fully closed. The stewardess shrieked as the wind swirled about her legs and blew her skirt high around her thighs.

"I'll have to take a closer look into the wheel bay to see what the hell's wrong. Hold onto me in case I fall." Kovak reached out his hand and Maggie grasped it tightly as he leaned forward into the opening. He flinched as he aimed a torch down into the semi-darkness. She pulled tighter still on his hand and gritted her teeth.

"Shite! There's some real bad damage down here."

"What sort of damage?"

"One of the tyres is ripped. And I can see hydraulic fluid leaking down the oleo. Looks as if some bits of wreckage from the engine have flown back into the bay doors. One or two bits have gone right through into the undercarriage itself."

"That's bad?"

"It is if we aim to land this crate." He straightened up, leant back on his haunches and turned towards her. "One ripped tyre we can cope with, but I don't like the look of that hydraulic leak. The oleo's our shock absorber. If we don't have hydraulic pressure, we may not be able to get this set of wheels down."

"What about the other wheels?"

"God knows. If they don't come down, or if they collapse on landing, there's going to be a lot more dead bodies inside this aircraft."

Chapter 8

Daylight rolled slowly over the horizon and, with apparent reluctance, it spread its wintery illumination across the eerie landscape of Prestwick airfield.

From the visual control room on the top floor of the control tower, the aerodrome controller studied the scene in amazement. As the crawling edge of daylight advanced across the airport, it revealed the once familiar pattern of taxiways and runways now littered with a strange clutter of unreality.

Trisha Ruskin sat left of centre at the wide aerodrome control desk in the visual control room. It had been dark when she came on duty that morning and the mysterious transformation of the airport had been hidden from view. Now she swept her gaze in a wide arc, taking in the broad vista. As the aerodrome controller, she was responsible for arriving and departing aircraft as well as the safety of vehicles moving around the runways and taxiways. Despite twenty years of experience, what she now saw alarmed her. It smacked of something far more dangerous than she had been led to expect.

Away to her left, the apron was empty, lifeless except for a continual fall of snow. Not even a vehicle trail marked the virgin mantle. On the opposite side of the main runway, the aircraft factory and the flying school were equally lifeless, both closed down for the duration of the emergency.

Directly in front of the tower and stretching from one endpoint, slightly to her right, to another endpoint more than two miles away to her left, the main runway stuck out like an ugly grey scar against its pristine surroundings. Snow blowers pounded up and down the strip, endlessly spewing out white streams. Vehicles scurried about on the cleared area like uncoordinated beetles. Fire appliances stood alert at strategic points just off the runway.

Trisha turned to her right and stared out through the tower window. The short subsidiary runway ran almost at right angles to the main in a line parallel with the right-hand wall of the control tower building. It had not been cleared of snow and its outline was only discernible by low, white banks at its edges. But it was host to a whole army of people, vehicles and parked aircraft.

Three RAF Hercules transports, incongruous in desert camouflage, were parked side by side just below the visual control room, their noses pointed in towards the control tower building. A little farther down the runway, two large C141 jet transports of the United States Air Force sat in the same sea of snow, each disgorging vehicles and equipment through their tail loading platforms. Beyond them sat a pair of F15 Eagles, intended for use as chase planes when the need arose. Other aircraft were involved in the emergency, but they were now airborne over the North Atlantic.

Despite the appearance of activity, no aircraft moved upon the airport. Inside the control tower, figures hurried about the building with a purposeful gait, but the control staff sat at their desks.

Waiting.

Trisha sat hunched forward in her swivel seat, leaning on the aerodrome control desk, casually twisting her pen between her fingers. An unfinished newspaper crossword lay on the desk while she watched, fascinated. The army of military vehicles and personnel moved about in the snow below, drawing long snaking lines in the white mantle. After some time, the area around the parked aircraft became just grey pools of slush.

The atmosphere inside the visual control room was unusually tense. A background of shadowy figures came and went, busily setting up unusual equipment. Cameras, tripod mounted binoculars and a host of measuring instruments appeared around the room. At first the invasion of foreign personnel had disturbed Trisha's concentration, taking her thoughts away from her job. As the shift progressed, she put the disturbance to the back of her mind.

It took her some seconds to react when a deep, commanding voice addressed her. "I guess you ain't never seen a space shuttle before." A big American, looking immaculate in United States Air Force uniform, stood near the centre of the long control desk and stared at the scene outside. Trisha deduced that the words were meant for her.

"No," she said in her husky voice. "I've never been to the States."

"Never?"

"Not adventurous enough, I suppose."

He turned and gave her a wry grin. He was tall, broad-shouldered and towered over her like a gentle giant. She guessed he was about forty, possibly a year or so younger. Just about her own age, she reasoned, and instinctively looked towards his hands. Not a sign he had ever worn a marital ring, but that was no guarantee that he was available. She pushed her spectacles back up her nose and flicked a curl of dark hair from her eyes.

Trisha had once been married, very briefly, to Tim Ruskin, a young Englishman brought up in a wealthy area of the Home Counties. The marriage lasted just over twelve months and would have collapsed long before that if they had not had such a good sex life together. They quarrelled constantly.

One day Tim drifted into the arms and the bed of a girl from London and that was the end of the marriage. The other girl was calm and undemonstrative, understood Tim intimately and was submissive in any debate. Against that, Trisha hadn't a hope in hell.

She accepted the divorce with some measure of stoicism but she never again came near to any potentially lasting relationship. In time she began to wonder if she ever would.

"It ain't goin' to be no picnic here. I guess you know that." The American was talking directly to her now. "This runway ain't rightly suitable for *Washington* to put down on. We'd go someplace else if we could."

"There are longer runways down south," she pointed out. "Longer and wider."

"Yeah, we know that, but we can't use them. Not this time. Closed in by weather, every one of them."

"You get an emergency like this and the only place it can land your top secret space shuttle is here in Scotland?"

"Yeah. There just ain't no other option. Once it enters the atmosphere, *Washington* is just one big glider and it has to come down somewhere. Either it comes down here or it comes down in the sea off the coast hereabouts. Either way we've got real problems."

"It just can't go elsewhere?"

"It's gonna re-enter the atmosphere in the wrong place and it ain't gonna land where we really want it to. Whatever them guys try to do up there, the ship just don't seem to want to cooperate."

Trisha grimaced. "Was it computer trouble or engine trouble?"

"I don't rightly know." He turned away to stare out of the window, as if the scene outside would give him comfort. "We think it was the damned computer system, but until we get some guy with a screwdriver to poke his nose inside... well... you'd think by this time we'd have got the thing sorted out. When I was a kid, we never had computers and guys managed to fly without them. My pappy used to fly Mustangs and they didn't know what computers was in them days."

"Times change," she said. "Nowadays, school kids know more about computers than I do."

"Yeah. Same with me." He gave her a mischievous grin. "Guess I'm showing my age." Then he added, "You're Mrs Ruskin. Right?"

She shrugged. "Mrs isn't really an appropriate title since my divorce, but I haven't got round to changing it."

"What's your first name?"

"Trisha. That's if you're allowed to get on first name terms with us natives."

"Sure, we're allowed." His grin widened, showing an expanse of white teeth. "And if we ain't, I just changed the rules. I'm Colonel Lawrence, but you can call me Dan. Unless the General happens to be listening to us."

She smiled self-consciously. Was that his opening shot? "I

suppose if this hadn't happened, you'd be watching the landing out in the sunshine at Edwards Air Force Base."

"Nope." He shook his head. "If this hadn't happened, I'd be sitting in an office in our London embassy, waiting for some other emergency. That's my job. The US air force always has some sort of emergency on its hands. Whatever it is, I guess I'm the one who gets lumbered."

"This one seems like a big operation," she commented.

"You bet your sweet life it is. We got a whole load of aircraft out there over the Atlantic, just waiting for that goddamn shuttle to come down. We got radar aircraft and we got tankers to refuel the radar aircraft. We got rescue control aircraft and we got tankers to refuel the rescue control aircraft. And we got tankers to refuel the tankers. It's the biggest operation I've seen since... well, since I don't know when."

Their conversation stopped at the sudden sound of a group of people entering the visual control room. They came in via a short flight of steps behind and to Trisha's left. Leading the group was the ATC Business Manager, a short grey-haired man called Keating. A senior RAF officer followed him, then came two more Americans in USAF uniform and a smartly dressed civil servant from the Ministry of Defence. All five ignored Trisha but the military officers saluted in formal recognition of the big colonel beside her. Wearing severe expressions, they went directly to the supervisor's desk at the rear of the room.

Trisha sneaked another quick glance at the American colonel and was surprised to see him remain standing at the control desk, grinning at her, almost as if he was enjoying himself.

He nodded in the direction of the official group behind them and leaned towards her to whisper, "Don't be surprised if they call you over to the desk. They'll want you to stay on duty when the time comes. But they'll have to ask you nicely."

"Why should they need to ask me? Like you said about yourself, it's my job."

He glanced about before answering softly, "Not exactly, Trisha.

It's not part of your job to get involved in something as dangerous as this."

"Dangerous?" Her voice rose an octave.

"Yeah, dangerous. Things could get a mite hot around here and it ain't your job to put your neck on the line. We thought of most things that could go wrong with that darned space shuttle, but we never imagined this." Lawrence stared out of the control room window with his hands thrust firmly into his uniform jacket pockets.

"They didn't tell me it was going to be dangerous," Trisha said.

Outside the snow continued to fall, steadily and obliquely, blowing back against the tower window. Lawrence studied it. "We planned for the possibility of an early abort back to the launch site. We planned for an Atlantic abort farther south with a landing in North Africa or Spain. But we didn't expect this. Not on this particular mission."

"You must have known its orbit would take it this far north," Trisha adjusted her spectacles as her interest intensified.

Lawrence shook his head. "It shouldn't have been this far north. That's probably because of some damned fault in the computers. Like I said before..."

"These things didn't happen when you were a kid?" Trisha smiled broadly.

"Okay, so I tend to labour the point. But at least in those days we didn't make such monumental cock-ups as this."

"Didn't you?" Trisha leaned back in her seat. "I seem to recall an American pilot called Douglas Corrigan who set out from New York to Los Angeles and ended up in Ireland."

"He was a civilian."

"That makes a difference?"

"Sure. When you've dedicated your life to the United States Air Force, you kinda get convinced no one else does it better."

Trisha angled her head sideways and tapped the end of her pen against her lips. "That accolade was accorded to James Bond. Not John Wayne."

"That's as maybe. The fact is we had important reasons for wanting this mission to go without a hitch. You know, this is about the worst thing that could have happened."

Behind her, someone called, "Trisha, would you come over here please?"

She turned quickly and noted Keating, the ATC Business Manager, beckoning to her. Just as the big American colonel had warned her, she was being summoned across to join the group at the ATC supervisor's desk. She nodded silently, left the radio selector switched to a desk loudspeaker and quietly joined the anxious group of visitors.

"This is Mrs Ruskin, the aerodrome controller." Keating made only a brief attempt to introduce her to the assembled group before he went on, "Trisha, you know the rudiments of what's going on here?"

She nodded.

"The thing is, we would like you to stay on duty until the shuttle lands. You don't have to, I must tell you that. We could try to get someone else to do the job."

"But there isn't anyone else qualified to do it that you could immediately get hold of? So you want me to take the risk."

"You know about the risk?"

"No, but I have the impression you're about to enlighten me."

"We have an obligation to tell you." He hurried on, "Obviously, there's some degree of national security involved in this. In fact, we're going to have to keep you out of public reach even if you choose not to stay in the tower. The thing is…" He looked around at the group for some support, as if he were unsure of his facts and needed someone else to take over.

"Perhaps you'd better let me explain." One of the Americans stepped forward to interrupt. He was dressed in a smart uniform and Trisha noted two stars on his lapel. "You are security cleared, Mrs Ruskin?"

"You must know that I am."

The American nodded. "The *Washington* flight was vital to our national defence programme."

"Your *American* defence programme," Trisha interrupted.

"You sound critical."

"No. Just making a point."

The American studied her with a firm-set mouth and piercing eyes. "This mission was supposed to launch a laser experiment. It's a scheme to use X-ray lasers to bring down enemy missiles before they re-enter the atmosphere. The *Washington* was due to place a device into orbit but the mission had to be aborted before the device could be released. It's still on board."

"Are you telling me that having the laser on board is the dangerous bit?"

"In a sense." The General shook his head as if he was growing tired of the conversation. "I can't tell you anymore. It's enough that you're aware how vitally important this mission is to our defence system."

"You're telling me that this laser is vital to the United States and that's why you want *me* to stay on duty?"

"You've a very caustic manner, Mrs Ruskin."

"Maybe. What exactly do you want me to do when it lands?"

"Just your job. You're an experienced controller."

"But this isn't going to be like controlling a civil aircraft."

"No. We could bring in military controllers but they don't know Prestwick airport like you do. Will you help us?"

Trisha set her face in a look of resignation. "At this sort of notice, there isn't really anyone else. Now come clean and tell me about the danger involved."

"You'll be fully briefed when the time comes."

"When it's too late for me to back out?"

A look of annoyance creasing his face, the general took a step back into the protection of his peer group. "That's all I can tell you now, Mrs Ruskin."

*

The mission was finished. A failure. A gut-wrenching balls-up of a failure. But the worst of it was yet to come.

"Houston, this is *Washington*. Guess this is your last chance to come up with another option. What can you offer us now?" Aboard the space shuttle, Mission Commander George Sharpe held his breath. He knew there was no other option but he had to make the point anyway. He figured that, down on the ground, they would expect nothing less of him.

The response was terse and predictable. "*Washington*, this is Houston. Sorry guys, this is the only way down. Start your manoeuvre to burn attitude." That was it, predictable and inevitable. And delivered in a no-nonsense, no-argument style. Sharpe had been expecting it.

He nodded to Peter Guthrie, the shuttle pilot in the right-hand seat. "Okay, Pete. You heard what the man said. Let's get the ship turned round. Like it or not, we're going down with the bomb."

Guthrie replied pensively. "I had me a date for tomorrow night. Reckon she'll have to wait."

"You'll make it."

"Hope to God, George."

"Amen to that."

"Here we go." The shuttle pilot's face was tense as he initiated the manoeuvre to turn the shuttle around for the engine burn that would slow it down for re-entry.

Sharpe turned his attention to the instruments and ran his mind over the problem once again, hoping against hope for some vital clue that would help them avoid the granddaddy of all explosions.

There was nothing new about flying a broken ship with a nuke on board. It was simply a matter of degrees. He'd been a schoolkid back in February 1957 when a B47 bomber was damaged after colliding with an F86 fighter. The crew had been lucky on that occasion: they'd managed to jettison their Mark 15 hydrogen bomb into the Atlantic Ocean off Tybee Island. If Sharpe and his crew had been able to jettison the experiment on board the

Washington, they would have done it. And they'd have cheered when the device drifted away harmlessly into space. But they couldn't do it. The payload bay doors were jammed shut.

Houston interrupted his thoughts. "*Washington*, your burn attitude looks good. You are go for de-orbit burn."

"Roger, Houston." Sharpe looked down at his hands, steady as a rock despite the terrible fear running through him.

This was it. No turning back now. Ronald Reagan would be starting the first month of his second year in office shitting bricks in a White House toilet over his crazy Strategic Defence Initiative. Star Wars was backfiring.

Either the shuttle would land safely, or a lot of people were going to die in a nuclear holocaust that would make Hiroshima look like a Fourth of July firecracker.

Chapter 9

Fatigue was beginning to show on the young stewardess's face as Devereaux helped her carry yet another body to the rear of the cabin.

Devereaux stood back and stared at the blood-stained corpses, the mangled limbs and the white faces permanently twisted into excruciating expressions of pain. Friends and relatives would be waiting for them to arrive at Prestwick.

The last body had come to light only when they cleared away some of the wreckage near the hole in the fuselage. Now, five of them lay in a tangled heap in the galley at the back of the cabin.

On his way back up the aisle, Devereaux stopped beside each of the injured passengers and offered words of comfort. He felt inhumanly tired, but he had to play the part of knowing what he was doing. There was no logical reason for his tiredness; he was a fit man who exercised every day. With a small, concentrated sigh, he sprawled back in the seat and pulled thoughtfully at his chin. He tried to keep his vision sharp, on guard despite the chaos that surrounded him, but further waves of weariness swept over him. Closing his eyes, he leaned back into the hard cushion, temporarily relinquishing his unauthorised role.

While he and Trudy Bodenstadt had been disposing of the last of the bodies, another stewardess had come up from the main deck. Trudy had cried out, "Thank heavens you're here, Wendy."

The new girl had a commanding manner that overshadowed Trudy Bodenstadt's indecisiveness and she quickly took control of the passengers on the upper deck. For a few minutes, Devereaux could relax. But his mind remained active.

Trudy puzzled him. He had studied some of her personal background from the Drug Enforcement Administration files. They had very little detail on her, certainly nothing incriminating, and in most respects she was just another airline stewardess. She should have been the one to take charge when the emergency happened, but the task was beyond her. Poor kid.

He would need to talk to her in depth if they survived the accident, ask her a few pertinent questions about her relationship with Sally Scrimgeour. But they would have to survive first, and that was nowhere near a foregone conclusion.

The DEA could have stopped MacNabb at Kennedy Airport and pinned a good deal on him. The NYPD was in favour of doing just that. But that plan left too many unanswered questions. Who was supplying the coke? What was Sally Scrimgeour's role in the main setup? Who were the contacts in London? Who was the real mastermind behind the ring?

They would only find the answer to those questions by launching a joint operation with the police in the UK and keeping an eye on MacNabb during the flight.

He had a sudden ironic thought that the captain of the aircraft was now only two seat rows in front of him, still being tended by the woman passenger in the fur coat. He opened his eyes and studied MacNabb, wondering whether to get closer.

It had not been easy getting this far. He and Diane Redmond had spent hours examining the financial dealings of a number of suspect New York companies, looking for the cover operation that hid this particular intercontinental cocaine racket. Night after night, they drank gallons of coffee, smoked endless cigarettes and pored over thousands of detailed documents. He joked to Diane that they had probably used more legal drugs — caffeine and nicotine — in the course of their investigation than the hard stuff the gang were smuggling across the Atlantic.

They cottoned onto Maggie Loughlin and Fergus MacNabb early in the investigation. The surprise was Sally Scrimgeour. Devereaux was convinced she was no more than a foolish young woman who had got mixed up with the wrong people. He had virtually written her out of his investigation until her body was found on a subway platform with a deep knife wound in her back and a package of coke lying nearby. Then they had to think the whole thing through again.

That was when he was assigned to this flight at the last minute. A couple of uniforms had let themselves into his tiny East Side apartment to pack for him (thanks for the Hawaiian shirt and shorts, you joking bastards) and rush the overnight bag and passport to the squad house.

He shivered at the cold wind rushing through the cabin. He had not recovered his jacket after the collision. He glanced around and found it lying on the floor beneath the adjacent seat, a grey soft leather coat with worn elbows and one torn pocket. Diane had remonstrated that it was not really the right sort of dress for flying the Atlantic, but Devereaux wore it anyway. As he pulled it from the floor, he noticed that his ID, with the badge and the photograph, had fallen from his inside pocket and was spread open under the seat in front of him.

"Ah, there you are. I wondered where you had gone." Trudy Bodenstadt stood over him; he hadn't heard her approach. She sounded more self-assured now, as if she was winning the fight to recover an outward display of confidence. "I thought I ought to come and thank you for your help."

"My pleasure." He was leaning forward, his hand outstretched beneath the front seat when he realised what a stupid reply that was.

Trudy bent down to help him. "What have you lost? Oh!"

Devereaux sat back in his seat with the ID clearly visible in his hand. He smiled self-consciously. "Nothing important."

"But that's a police badge, isn't it?" Her eyes were wide open, her jaw sagging.

"Sort of." He hastily returned it to his jacket pocket.

"You're a New York cop?"

"No. Nothing like that." He shook his head. "Look, it's not important, so I wouldn't worry yourself about it."

"But it is important. If you're a cop—" She spoke loudly. With other passengers nearby, he didn't want that. He thought frantically and made a very quick decision.

He gestured to the adjacent seat. "Sit down for a moment, and don't say anything." He pulled out the ID again, glanced up and down the cabin, and then showed it to her. He waited until she had read the detail and studied the photograph before he continued. "You must keep this to yourself. I can't explain why, but it is very important that no one else knows about this. I don't want you to tell anyone else on board who I am. No one. Do you understand?"

She nodded violently, but her face was even whiter than before.

*

Paul Judson looked over his shoulder. Brian Hewson's blank expression stared back at him. The navigator was scared out of his wits, just like the rest of them.

Judson turned to the front again and jabbed his transmit switch. "Highball, this is Gasser 29." Even to himself, his voice sounded faint and distant.

"Go ahead, Gasser 29."

"Jeez! We thought we'd lost it, Highball. There was an explosion in the starboard outer engine. The fuel line must've gone up."

"You still hanging in there, 29?"

"Guess so. The fire seems to be burning itself out. We shut off all systems on that side and it's now starved of fuel."

"Okay, 29. You ready to ditch now?"

Judson gritted his teeth. No, he was not ready to ditch. Somehow, that explosion had jerked him into a clearer awareness of what was happening out here. The fire was burning out fast, so why the hurry to ditch? The longer he could keep the KC135 in the air, the better were the chances of survival. Maybe that sudden jolt of adrenaline, the shock of the engine exploding, had made survival seem more important.

"Negative, Highball. I don't figure on ditching just yet."

"What's the problem, Gasser 29? You gotta get it down soon."

Judson tightened his fists on the control column. He was beyond tired now, beyond accepting every instruction at face value, beyond doing whatever he was told without question.

He punched the transmit button. "Look, buddy. There's no way we can put this ship down safely in that sort of sea. It would be plumb crazy and we'd all end up fish food. I figure it would be a better bet if we head on towards the coast and try to make a landfall."

"Standby, Gasser 29."

Through the following two minutes, the radio frequency was silent. Youngman looked across at Judson with an expression of surprise, but nothing was said.

Then the voice of Highball returned. "Gasser 29, we got a message for you from Ocean Command. They say you are ordered to ditch off the coast of Benbecula. Over."

Ordered to ditch? They were *ordering* him to ditch in the sea! Who the hell was in charge of this airplane? They must know that the crew's chances of survival down there would be pretty small. So there was an emergency at Prestwick? So what? That didn't give them to right to order him to kill everyone on board.

Major Paul S Judson, the guy who always did as he was told, ground his teeth. He darned well wouldn't do it. So he was being rebellious? So what? Maybe if he had been a bit more rebellious before now, he wouldn't have lost Ruby. Well, he wasn't going to obey any more stupid orders.

Angry and tired beyond reason, he jabbed again at his transmit switch. "No joy, Highball. We're not gonna kill ourselves just yet. You tell Ocean Command that Major Paul S Judson is not ready to commit suicide. You hear me?"

"I hear you, Gasser 29."

From across the flight deck, Youngman looked at him, open-mouthed, as if unable to believe his ears. "Paul, are you sure?"

"Shut up!"

The airwaves went silent again. That little outburst was giving them something to concentrate their minds. That should ruffle the shirtsleeves of a general or two. If only Ruby could see him now.

He had the KC135 flying straight and level. He didn't know what was keeping the old lady in the air, but he thanked God for whatever it was. By rights, the goddamn airplane should be down at the bottom of the North Atlantic, split into a million small pieces. Thank God they were still alive and kicking. And thank the guys at Boeing who built the old cow.

He inched the thrust levers slightly forward to increase power on the remaining engines. The airspeed was just nudging two hundred knots and he wondered whether he could notch up to a higher speed. The problem was the damaged starboard wing. The fire had subsided, but the destruction it must have caused had to be extensive. You don't get explosions like that without substantial structural failure. And structural failure meant the wing was now no longer capable of taking the strain it was designed for. It could fold away from the fuselage at any time.

Hold it at two hundred knots, he decided.

"What's your plan, Paul?" Youngman's face looked ghostly white as he spoke. He'd never had to take executive command of an airplane, not even in normal circumstances. Probably never would if things went on like this. And he had never before seen Paul Judson take such a commanding attitude.

Judson grimaced. "I sure don't fancy ditching. Not in *that* sea. Jeez. Look at them waves!"

"We sure wouldn't have much of a chance," Youngman agreed.

"Nope. We sure as hell wouldn't." Judson had made up his mind, but it helped to have Youngman's cooperation. "I guess we head south-east and hope to make a landfall before we fall out of the sky." He glanced around the flight deck, looking for any disapproving signs. There were none. Hewson nodded. It was done with apparent reluctance, but he didn't disagree.

Youngman asked, "What about that sonofabitch Ocean Command, Paul?

"Ocean Command can go take a running jump. They ain't up here with us and I ain't gonna put this ship down in the sea unless we got no other choice."

The altimeter was stuck solid on three hundred feet and the grey cloud base raced by above them. Too close above them for comfort; just as the sea was too close for comfort below. The Outer Hebrides island chain was very close to them now and the cloud over the land dropped to the ground. This was where Ocean Command wanted them to ditch, wanted them to sacrifice their lives for the good of the United States Air Force. Like hell they would. They would fly on past the island chain and hope to reach the mainland. He stared at the dark mass in front.

His mind worked in overtime. Shit, it's only a chain of islands. We could climb a little way into the cloud, just enough to clear the land mass, and then there's most likely just water on the other side. Once we descend again on the other side of the islands, we'll just have to hope there's a higher cloud base.

It was a real risk, of course. Only two of the Pratt and Whitney engines were now running, and they had more than ten thousand gallons of fuel back there in the fuselage tanks. If anything went wrong now, they could all kiss their asses goodbye.

He continued to study the forward view for some minutes before he stretched out a hand to the VHF receiver. With a deft flick, he clicked the selector channels to a random frequency. Then he turned the volume control down to minimum.

"Reckon there's somethin' wrong with the radio," he said flatly. "We can't hear Highball no more." He glared at Youngman, daring him to disagree. "Can you hear 'em?"

"Nope. Must be a malfunction caused by the fire." Youngman gave him a knowing look.

"Yep. Reckon it is."

Both men leaned back in their seats and Judson sniffed expressively. The decision was not only made, they were now acting on it.

Youngman puffed out his cheeks. "Just one thing, Paul. Who's going to help us? We're sure gonna have a problem when we hit that cloud."

"We'll think about that later." Judson chewed at his lower lip. It was something he hadn't yet figured out. "Where are the European information documents?"

141

"Dunno," Youngman replied.

"Well, see if you can dig them out. Then start lookin' for the frequencies of any airfield on the Scottish coast with a big runway. The bigger the better."

"Sure thing."

"After that I reckon we better figure out what we can do about that fuel load. We sure don't want to end up as Kentucky Fried."

*

Dougie groaned. His arms were aching and his eyes were streaming in the cold blast of air coming in through the captain's shattered screen. The physical and mental pressure of being in sole command of a crippled aircraft was wearing him down.

Like so many other pilots, he had eased through from being a seat-of-the-pants flier to being an aeroplane systems manager, a human monitor of the on-board computer. In time he had grown used to the principle of allowing the aeroplane to fly itself while he kept a watchful eye on what was happening. He had practised many times handling emergencies on flight simulators, but this was for real in the worst of all circumstances.

His hands were growing numb with the strain of keeping the aircraft straight and level. He tried to concentrate his thoughts on the aircraft systems and how they might be reacting to the emergency. Now and then he found his mind distracted by the thought of his own death.

And how Jenny would cope without him.

He had no fear of being killed when the 747 finally gave up the ghost and plunged into the cold ocean. His worry was solely for Jenny's future. He could picture her sitting at home knitting, just as she had been when he left the house. Or slumped over the kitchen table, sipping a coffee without even being aware that she had the cup in her hand.

Grieving.

He remembered how they had stowed away Edward's toys. Neither of them could bear to have them in sight, so they sealed them in boxes and stacked them in the attic. Then they packed all photographs of Edward, except that one on the mantelpiece. To a stranger in the house, it was almost as if Edward had never existed. But he never ceased to exist in their minds, never would cease to be there in their thoughts night and day. The toys were still there, locked away in the attic, but they never went near them, never referred to them.

Neither could they bring themselves to dispose of them.

With a sudden loud crack, another section of front windscreen broke away. The glass blew back into the vacant captain's seat and Dougie's thoughts were cruelly rammed back into the present.

The Nimrod pilot's voice cut into his headphones. "Sinclair 984, this is Watchdog. Sorry to trouble you, old chap, but the cloud base is getting lower. We'll have to drop down to a lower altitude. I think we should go down to five hundred feet and see if we can creep underneath."

Dougie stared ahead. The angry ragged bottom of the thick nimbus cloud was only a few feet above them at times.

"Roger, Watchdog. I have you in sight. I'll follow you down."

The grey porpoise shape of the Nimrod was ahead and to the left of the 747. If they did have to ditch in the sea, the presence of the RAF jet aircraft with its on-board supply of rescue equipment would be crucial in saving lives. It sank slowly away below the 747 screen hood, coming into sight again as Dougie eased down the *Tartan Arrow*'s nose.

They were getting very low now, low enough to see the white-topped waves in detail. He would have preferred to keep some height in hand as a measure of safety, but he could not risk taking the 747 into cloud unless he had no choice. In cloud, he would have no visual means of navigation. He couldn't do that without fully functioning equipment.

He noticed with some satisfaction that the VOR radio navigation receiver seemed to be back on line. If it functioned correctly, it would receive signals from the VOR beacons located along the west coast of Scotland. He tuned in to the Stornoway beacon with no clear confidence that it would work, but there was nothing lost by trying.

"Work, damn you," he hissed.

The needle flickered and then came on line. The beam bar slid into place indicating the Stornoway beacon off to their left.

Dougie let out a long sigh of relief. The associated Distance Measuring Equipment remained obstinately dead for the time being, but maybe it would come on line later. Or maybe not.

"That's it, Sinclair 984. Five hundred feet." The calm English voice almost crooned in Dougie's headset. The Nimrod had levelled off, but the cloud base ahead of them was still lowering.

He stared at a darker patch, straight ahead and right down on the horizon. "Watchdog from Sinclair 984, I see some sign of land ahead of us. Is it one of the islands? Over."

"Affirmative, Sinclair 984. You're looking at the shoreline of Benbecula. There's higher ground on the islands to left and right of us, but I reckon we can cross the island chain safely at Benbecula."

Dougie pictured the line of Outer Hebridean islands as he had seen it on so many maps and charts, the hills of North Uist and South Uist to left and right, and the smaller island of Benbecula lying smack in between.

"Roger, Watchdog. I'm in your hands. I'll follow you through."

"Stick with me, Sinclair 984. There is a small aerodrome on the island and I'm in contact with ATC. They tell me that the cloud base over the island is less than one hundred feet and there's a four-hundred-foot-high hill sticking up into the cloud two and a half miles beyond the aerodrome. The cloud base is too low for us to go under it, so we'll have to stay at five hundred feet and fly straight through the cloud."

"That sounds dodgy, Watchdog. Only a hundred foot clearance with the hill, if we're lucky. How far does the cloud bank stretch?"

"At that low level, it's only in the vicinity of the island. The cloud base goes up to about six hundred feet beyond the island. If we stay level at five hundred feet and charge through the cloud, it'll only take a few minutes."

"If you say so, Watchdog." He paused and then jabbed the

transmit switch again. "Watchdog, couldn't we land at Benbecula airfield?" It was probably a stupid idea, but he had to give voice to it, in case he had missed something important.

The response was immediate. "Negative, Sinclair 984. Not a chance. Unless you have no option, of course. It's just a small island aerodrome. The runway isn't nearly long enough and they've only a minimal emergency service. And besides, the cloud is much too low for you to even attempt a landing."

Dougie grunted to himself. He didn't need an Englishman telling him about the Scottish islands. "That's understood, Watchdog. I know it's very small, but it is an airfield."

"Affirmative. And at the moment you are an aeroplane. Try to put down there and you'll be a pile of broken aluminium. If we had no choice, I'd say have a go. But your best bet is to continue towards Prestwick in the hope you'll be able to land there."

"Is there any improvement at Glasgow?"

"Negative. Nor at Edinburgh. If anything, the visibility is still dropping there."

"In that case I guess we press on for Prestwick."

"Roger. Good show."

"Let's go for it, Watchdog." He understood now how the Englishman was able to keep up his calm manner. His image was as much play-acting as his own measured responses. Behind the facades, both pilots were equally appalled by the implications of the game they were playing.

"Sinclair 984, this is Watchdog. I have just received a message from Scottish Control." This time the Nimrod pilot's voice carried a sharp edge of uncertainty.

"Go ahead, Watchdog."

"It's not very helpful. They say Prestwick will not be available to you for a landing. I'm trying to sort out where they want you to land and I'll give you another call in a moment."

"What's it all about Watchdog? Why isn't Prestwick available?"

After a short pause, the Englishman's voice came back with much less restraint. "It's a bit of a bastard, old chap. They have another emergency on their hands at the present. Stand by while I try to sort this out."

"Roger." Dougie thought quickly. "In that case maybe we should consider an emergency landing at Benbecula?"

"For the present I think we should continue towards the mainland. Landing on a dangerously short runway in bad weather is no fun at the best of times. Far too risky."

"Roger. But we'll have to keep it in mind."

"Perhaps. Can you keep steady on your present heading for a couple of minutes while we dive through the cloud?"

"We'll give it a go, Watchdog."

The 747 followed the Nimrod into the cloud bank; two express trains disappearing into the same dark tunnel. Dougie held the aircraft as straight and as level as he was able with his limited instruments. He kept his gaze firmly fixed on the panel. Outside, the cloud enveloped them like a giant gloved hand. The roar of wind through the cracked screen became a blast of thick mist. Dougie blinked as it spewed out across the flight deck and hit him. He screwed up his eyes and tried to focus on the instrument panel. Keep the wings level, watch the altimeter and the airspeed indicator. And pray that they have a little bit more luck in their account. Just a little more luck.

Barely two minutes passed and then they burst out into the same dull and dismal scene they had been watching before, heaving waves and ragged cloud base.

With the island chain behind, the Nimrod regained its position just ahead and off the 747's port side. Dougie eased the plane into close formation, jiggling with his three serviceable engines.

The Nimrod pilot's voice interrupted his thoughts. "Well done, Sinclair 984. I'm turning slightly south now to avoid the island of Mull. There's some very high ground in the middle of the island and it's hidden in low cloud. We'll pass between two more small islands shortly."

"I'm still in your hands, Watchdog. But what will we do when the cloud meets the sea."

Ten seconds passed before the Nimrod pilot replied. "We'll have to solve that problem when we meet it. I'm rather hoping we'll be able to creep down through the gap along the line of the Crinan canal."

The Crinan canal? This was going to be more of an aerial stunt than commercial flying. If he lost contact with the Nimrod at low altitude along the canal, he would be unable to navigate safely towards Prestwick.

He tried to cover his fears. "You sound optimistic, Watchdog."

"Optimism is the only thing going for us. You worry about your aeroplane, old chap. Leave the navigation to me."

*

Trudy's hands shook as she grasped a shattered seat back and pulled it clear of the aisle. How had she got herself into such a mess? Within the past forty-eight hours she had become mixed up in Sally Scrimgeour's problems, felt the unspeakable shock of Sally's death, lied to the police at Kennedy Airport — albeit under threat from Maggie Loughlin — and now she was likely to die any minute.

She had never harboured any long-term intent to stick with this job. She had simply drifted into it as a temporary measure after graduating from university and coming up against a brick wall with other job applications. She had joined the company with a vague notion that she would drift onto some other employment before long. But, as one comfortable flight followed another, she began to forget her career plan.

A tear ran down her cheek and she brushed it away angrily. Was the DEA agent here because of the trouble Sally had got herself tied up in? There couldn't be any other explanation. If only she had got out of the aviation business earlier. It was too late now.

She had liked Sally, even if the other girl was a naive fool in her association with MacNabb. The pilot was not the right man for her to be sleeping with, and Trudy had felt inclined to tell her so. The two stewardesses usually shared a hotel room on the New York stopovers and Sally was sensible enough not to bring MacNabb into it. Trudy was thankful for that.

But that didn't prevent her from getting caught up in MacNabb's insidious game.

*

She had been out shopping early that Friday morning, picking up a birthday present to take back to her mother. She paused in the corridor outside the hotel bedroom, discovered she had forgotten her key and knocked loudly.

Sally opened the door fractionally. "Who is it?"

"Only me." Trudy pushed into the room and slammed the door. Sally had been taking an afternoon nap and she habitually slept naked.

"Dear God! What happened to you?" Trudy stared. She knew well enough what had happened. Sally's torso was a mass of ugly bruises and it had to be the work of that bastard, MacNabb! It just had to be him. And he must have known what he was doing because Sally's face, arms and lower legs were unmarked.

"It's nothing." Sally turned away hurriedly.

"Don't be stupid, Sally. Get dressed before one of the other girls sees those bruises. Bloody MacNabb! I've told you often enough, he's no good."

"I suppose I've learned that now, so let's not talk about it anymore." She looked too contrite not to be believed.

"Okay. I suppose it does no good to say I told you so."

"None at all." She opened the wardrobe and pulled out a dress.

"In that case let's get out of here and find somewhere to have a drink, even if it is early in the day."

"How could I have been so stupid?" Sally threw the dress onto her bed, slapped her forehead with an exaggerated blow and turned away towards a big wall mirror. "Oh shit!" she groaned, "I look such a mess."

"What will Jock say when you get back?" Trudy asked.

"I don't know." Sally slumped down onto her bed. "Fergus was sorry after he did it." She picked up a soft leather bag. Her eyes took on a wistful expression as she turned it over in her hands before throwing it across to Trudy. "Last night, he gave me this. His way of saying sorry."

"Looks expensive," Trudy observed.

"Very expensive. I'd been admiring one like it and he must have remembered."

"Bought with conscience money." Trudy admired the touch of the soft leather while, at the same time, hating it because it had come from MacNabb. It felt heavy, even for a leather bag, but she knew that someone like MacNabb would not settle for anything cheap and lightweight.

Who the hell did that man, MacNabb, think he was that he should try to buy Sally's forgiveness with a present like this? Trudy threw it to the floor. "You mustn't see him again, Sally."

"I don't intend to." Sally sank her head into her hands and was silent for a minute. Then she stalked away into the bathroom.

The telephone rang while Sally was under the shower but Trudy felt inclined to ignore it, afraid that it might be MacNabb. She felt too angry to even risk talking to him. But the jangling sound of the bell continued until Sally called out, "Take that call, will you, Trudy."

Trudy grabbed the receiver and that act of giving in to the noisy intrusion made her even angrier. She had barely put the thing to her ear before Sally threw open the bathroom door and stormed naked into the room leaving a trail of wet footprints on the carpet.

"On second thoughts, I'll take it. It might be Jock." One wet foot kicked the handbag lying on the floor, knocking it against one of the beds. As she took the telephone from Trudy's outstretched hand, Sally kicked the bag again, this time in deliberate anger. Not satisfied with that display of temper, she slammed one foot down on top of it.

"Yes!" she snapped into the telephone.

A rather abrupt way to address the caller, Trudy thought, but said nothing. Worried about intruding on a private conversation, she turned away from Sally and her attention was drawn towards the handbag. It had burst open and something had spilled out. She stared.

It was a white powder.

"Oh, it's you, Maggie." Sally's voice lowered as she too spotted the mess spilling out onto the floor. "What do you want?"

Trudy bent down to pick up the handbag. The bottom interior lining was burst and the end of a polythene package poked out from behind the torn material. More of the white powder spilled out onto her skirt.

"Christ!" Realisation suddenly burst into her head and she stared up at Sally, her words halting and hoarse. "You know what this is? It's— it's a packet of drugs!" She fought for some rational thought, something logical she ought to do in a situation like this.

Sally's mouth hung open. She was only half-listening to Maggie Loughlin on the telephone. Her voice returned in tiny, horrified snatches, little more than a whisper. "We've got... got a problem here, Maggie. Can... can you come over..."

Trudy put out a hand to stop her saying more, but Sally ignored her. "It's something serious. Please come over to our room. Quickly, Maggie."

Trudy held the bag gingerly with one hand. She had a feeling that this was something best kept quiet until they had talked it over between the two of them.

But it was too late now.

*

A passenger cried out in pain, a sharp screeching sound.

Trudy stared at a short, middle-aged woman whose arm was wrapped in a bloody bandage. Wendy Yuell, the other stewardess, was doing her best to comfort the woman, but with little success. Even Wendy was not infallible.

Trudy stared down the length of the shattered cabin. Broken fittings creaked and swayed in the breeze as the aircraft shuddered with the thump of turbulence. She allowed bitter tears to flow.

Chapter 10

It was impossible to make out where the pavement ended and the road began beneath the thick, white blanket. With each step Jock studied the ground before him, placed his foot carefully into the snow and felt his shoe sink below the surface. At the same time he bent his head down into the wind to stop the icy snowflakes biting into his numbed face.

In an odd sort of way he was glad of the mortifying effect of the weather. It was a punishment, meted out by a god-like hand in response to his misdemeanour. And that made him feel just a little less guilty. There was no doubt in his mind that Sally had been farther — much farther — down the road of deceit. But that wasn't the point. The degree of unfaithfulness was irrelevant. He had done wrong and he had to be punished.

Yet, despite the guilty feelings, he retained a warm feeling towards Pamela, picturing her naked elfin figure kneeling over him on the duvet. Eight tenths of a full-size lover. Beautiful legs, beautiful breasts, beautiful face. Beautiful love.

If only Sally had called him again, as he had hoped she would. Perhaps, after talking things over, he would have been able to generate enough mental reserve to resist the temptation of sleeping with another woman. Or perhaps not. The trouble was, he told himself, things had probably gone too far off course on too many occasions before now. After that disturbing phone call from Sally, he had brooded for a while, wondering what she was hiding from him. He had tried to speak to her when he arrived home Friday evening, midday over there. The call was answered by Trudy Bodenstadt. He remembered the strange conversation clearly.

*

"Hello, Trudy. It's Jock Scrimgeour here. Is Sally in?"

"Jock? No, I'm sorry. She's out at the moment." The voice was hesitant, worried, a clue to things unsaid. And immediately he began to tense up for unwelcome news.

"Has something important cropped up?" he asked.

"Well, actually she's gone to meet someone. But I'm not sure who."

This time he definitely detected an air of alarm in the girl's voice. Something was seriously wrong.

"Is Sally alright?"

"She's just gone out to meet someone. Maybe she could phone you when she gets in."

"Yes. Ask her to do that, will you, Trudy. Look, you must tell me, is something wrong?"

"It's best you talk to her yourself, Jock."

"Why? What's happened?"

"Oh dear. I don't know what to say."

"Something has happened, hasn't it?"

"It's nothing important, Jock. It's just that... well, it's just that she had a present from Fergus MacNabb and—"

"A present? Why?"

"Oh no. I shouldn't have said that. Look, you must ask her yourself, Jock. It's none of my business."

"What did he give her?"

"It was a handbag, Jock. And there was... oh, dear."

"A handbag! What was he doing buying my wife a handbag?"

"I'm sorry, Jock. I shouldn't have told you that. I'm making a mess of this. Perhaps it would be best if you talk to her when she gets back. I'll tell her to call as soon as she gets in."

"It sounds like you should."

But she never did phone back.

*

Fergus MacNabb again! The bastard was giving presents to his wife. No wonder Sally hadn't phoned back. Maybe she had repaid the present by spending the night in MacNabb's hotel room.

A tight knot formed in Jock's stomach as the memory replayed. He could not explain to Pamela his feelings of anger because they were based upon a deep-seated sense of shame. He had been upstaged by a pilot. When Sally failed to phone him, he wanted to call her once more, but his sense of shame held him in check.

"Bloody weather!" He blew into his hands and wished he was somewhere warmer. It could be damnably cold in his native land, and that added to his conviction that he had to get away from Prestwick. Somehow or other.

The Atlantic House car park was filled with a mixture of civil and military vehicles. The military transport looked forlorn under a blanket of snow, static at the end of parallel tyre tracks. The civilian cars had been there longer, devoid of telltale fresh tyre marks in the snow, waiting for the next shift change.

He stepped up to the security post at the main gate and withdrew his plastic ID card. Instead of the civil security guards who normally manned the gate, an RAF military policeman leaned through the gatehouse window and peered at his outstretched pass.

"You're a controller?"

"Yes."

"In that case, report to the guard inside the building." The policeman waved him on.

Guard? What guard? Behind the misted-up gatehouse windows, Jock noticed a second uniformed MP. Both were armed.

He stuffed his pass back into his pocket and shuffled on through the snow. It seeped into his shoes, making his feet as numb and as wet as his face. He kicked the shoes against the entrance steps to dislodge some of the clogging grey clumps before he stamped his way into the foyer.

A big, sombre-looking military policeman stopped him, directing him towards a much smaller man who sat at a desk furnished only with a telephone and an open log book. This man wore a sergeant's stripes and an anxious look.

"Your pass please, sir." He spoke with a Home Counties accent.

Jock frowned. "I showed it outside." He felt into his pocket once again and withdrew the plastic ID card. "What the hell is going on here?"

The sergeant ignored the question and studied the card. "Are you going on duty Mr... is that pronounced Scrim-ger?"

"Maybe I'm going on duty, maybe not. First, I want to go up to the oceanic operations room to check on a flight."

"I'm sorry, sir. Only oceanic controllers are permitted into the oceanic operations rooms."

"Hang on a minute, sunshine—" Jock's hackles rose suddenly. "This is a civil establishment and I work here. I'm a civil air traffic controller."

"But you're not an oceanic controller, not according to your pass."

"So what?" Jock fought to suppress his irritation while he quickly thought up a different approach. "Look, why don't you call the watch manager in the domestic operations room and tell him I'm here. Tell him—" He searched his brain for an excuse. "Tell him I'm offering to help out if he needs me."

The sergeant studied the rising anger in Jock's face before he lifted the telephone and tapped out a number. "I have a Mr Scrimger here, sir. He says he's offering to help in the ops room."

A bubble of sound echoed from the instrument.

"Very well, sir." The sergeant replaced the instrument and turned back to Jock. "The watch manager will be down in a moment."

"I know the way up to the ops room."

"Please wait here for a moment." The voice was firm, insistent.

Jock grunted and stomped away towards the glass entrance doors. Outside the snow still fell relentlessly. Despite his sense of annoyance, the warmth of the building had rarely felt more inviting. He stamped his feet to knock more slush from his shoes and rubbed his hands together.

He swung round at the sound of a voice behind him. "What are you doing here, Jock?" The watch manager, Angus Cameron, was a tall, intelligent-looking man.

Jock grinned at him. "I heard there was something afoot and I was in the area so I thought I might be able to help you out."

"Help us out? Man, you're a welcome sight. You know what's going on here?"

"It looks as though you're having a bit of bother."

"Too bloody right, Jock. Four controllers sick, another three stuck at home by the weather, and now this! Come on upstairs. If you really want to help out, you can take a sector for a while."

"Sure. But what the hell is going on, Angus?"

"Bad things, Jock. Bad things." The watch manager led the way up the stairs. Behind him the RAF sergeant half-rose to speak, and then thought better of it.

"It's a real humdinger, Jock. An American space shuttle. This is highly hush-hush, but you'll have to know about it. The *Washington—*"

"The what?"

"Military space shuttle. You've never heard of it? Neither had any of us until this morning. And now it's making an emergency return to earth. Coming down out of orbit in the wrong place." Angus Cameron spoke quickly but easily. "From what we can deduce, they've got engine trouble, computer trouble and who knows what else. Anyhow, it's headed for a re-entry position somewhere off the west coast of Scotland. The military are going ape."

"I had noticed."

"There's more to it than they're telling us, but we're supposed to help them without asking questions. You'll see some USAF people in the ops room. Part of their emergency operation to try to get the shuttle down at Prestwick."

Jock stopped in his tracks. "Prestwick? You're joking!"

"I wish I was, Jock."

"Shit!" Jock shook his head. Of all his guesses on the likely reason for the military presence at Atlantic House, this was not on the list. He slid his tongue along his upper lip and then remembered one of his own reasons for coming to the centre: Sally's flight.

"I'll help you out, Angus, but my wife is flying back from the States. Do you mind if I just pop into the geriatric ward and check on the flight time. Then I'll come and join you."

"Go ahead, Jock. But don't be surprised if they're busy in there, too."

The oceanic room had been known as the geriatric ward long before Jock was posted to the Scottish Air Traffic Control Centre. This was where older controllers worked at a slower pace than their counterparts in the domestic operations room next door. It was less like an air traffic control operations room, and more akin to a large open-plan office in a city finance house.

Damned if I want to end my career in that place, he had once told Sally.

He poked his head through the operations room door and immediately sensed an unusual air of tension. A small group was gathered round the watch manager's desk: an RAF officer and two men in USAF uniform. Another uniformed American sat alongside one of the oceanic controllers. This was not the geriatric ward he was used to seeing.

Standing out among the tense atmosphere in the room, one controller lounged in his seat. Jock strode towards him.

Chas Campbell lay back with his hands clasped behind his bald head. His spectacles reflected the glare of the fluorescent lights in the ceiling, but Jock was pretty sure there would be a pair of closed eyelids behind the glasses.

"Hi, Chas. Sorry to wake you."

The old man awoke slowly and unwound himself like a serpent creeping out of its nest. As the oceanic planner, his job was almost finished for the next few hours. He stretched his arms. "What are you doing here, Jock? You work next door."

"Lost my way."

"You radar boys couldn't navigate your way from a brothel to a whore shop. What can we do for you?"

Jock pulled up a seat. "What's happening here, Chas? I heard you've turned this place into a mission control centre for NASA."

"If some silly bugger in his space ship thinks he can land at Prestwick Airport, why should I care? Personally, I think they ought to splash down in the sea. It's a bit softer than Prestwick's main drag. But my opinion doesn't count."

"Maybe they don't want their toy to get wet. They must have paid a lot of money for it."

"Maybe. Whatever it is, they won't tell us. Anyhow, you didn't come here to talk about bloody space ships, did you?"

"Not really. It's Sally—"

"Time you got your woman sorted out, Jock. How are things between you at the moment?"

Jock measured his words carefully. "Not too good. I got a phone call from her while she was in New York and she sounded pretty fraught. Then I heard some bloody pilot has been buying her presents. The bastard bought her a handbag, would you believe?"

"A handbag? Most female airline staff carry French letters in their handbags. Did you know that? So they can screw their way round the world. Sounds like a case of more money than sense, Jock, my boy. Anyway, why should you worry if a pilot buys her presents? Wish some bugger would buy my missus a present. Like a one-way ticket to the States."

"You don't mean that, Chas."

"P'raps not. Anything I can do?"

"I wanted to check on Sally's flight. It's coming back from New York and it should have been here by now."

"Jock Scrimgeour!" A rough hand came down on his shoulder and a thin voice interrupted the conversation. "What are you doing here?"

Jock turned towards a grey-haired figure. The oceanic watch manager's face was tired and worn with responsibility.

"I just came in to speak to Chas."

"Did you, now?" The heavily creased, sagging face returned a look of annoyance. "We've got an emergency on our hands. I can't allow visitors in here at a time like this."

"Visitor? Oh, come off it — I work here."

"You work in the domestic ops room, not in here. You can see we've got an emergency to cope with, so be on your way, will you."

"Okay, okay. If you say so." Jock retreated. "You're the boss." He gave Chas Campbell a noncommittal wave and headed for the door.

He still had no idea when Sally's flight was due.

In the domestic operations room, the heady atmosphere of tension was even more prominent. Jock paused at the first control position inside the door. The label on a green canopy above the controller's radar displays read: HEBRIDES SECTOR. The controller looked tired and drawn. He was hunched over a circular radar screen that displayed an electronic outline of the west coast of Scotland.

Jock looked around the room. At the outer edges — down the two outer walls — controllers sat facing their displays in two long ranks with their backs towards the centre of the room. Some stared at pairs of side-by-side radar screens mounted into the consoles in front of them. Others concentrated on complex traffic information written on paper strips and mounted in plastic holders. Military personnel stood behind them. United States Air Force uniforms were mixed in with RAF grey. Voices were hushed, as if they were attending a funeral.

Air traffic assistants sat in the centre of the room, passing information to the controllers and waiting for them to act upon it. Pamela MacReady usually worked here.

Jock turned back to the Hebrides Sector, a huge chunk of airspace covering the west coast of Scotland and a portion of the North Atlantic out as far as the ten-degree west line of longitude. Beyond that line, aircraft were controlled from the oceanic control room.

"You busy here?" He leaned over the sector controller's shoulder.

"Too bloody right, mate. The sector planner's gone sick and my relief's stuck in the snow."

"Give you a break in a jiffy."

Jock hurried on to the watch manager's desk at the top end of the room. "All right, Angus. I'm here now. Shall I give the guy on Hebrides a break?"

Cameron looked around the room. "I was just thinking of putting an extra man on that sector to handle the emergency when it arrives. Would you mind taking the radar until I can find a planner to help out?"

"Sure. What about the emergency?"

"Which one?"

Jock frowned. "You mean there's more than one emergency?"

The manager nodded sadly. "You heard about the collision on the ocean, didn't you?"

Jock felt a shiver run up his spine. "No. What happened?"

"A 747 collided with a KC135. From what we can make out, the 747 was well off course and entered the military restricted area they've set up for the shuttle's descent."

"Are they both down in the ocean?"

"No. Miraculously, they're both still flying as far as we know. The last we heard, the KC135 came off relatively lightly. But the 747 is badly damaged and it's flying at a low level."

"Whose aircraft was it?"

The watch manager glanced down at the scrap of paper in front of him. "The callsign is Sinclair 984—"

The blood froze in Jock's veins. "Oh no! My wife is on that flight!"

*

A buzz of anxious voices bubbled up from the Prestwick approach control radar room, disembodied sounds wafting into the visual control room on notes of wavering tension.

Trisha Ruskin glanced over her right shoulder to the short flight of steps leading down to the darkness of the radar room. Near the top of the steps, Colonel Lawrence stood facing the subsidiary runway, as if he was studying the activity outside the tower and, at the same time, listening to the voices from below. Trisha noted the stiff, vertical angle of his back, typically military. His part in the emergency seemed to be mostly inactive supervision, as if the man from the American embassy was a lone agent among the organised chaos that had taken over Prestwick Airport.

It crossed her mind that she had never really known a man like Lawrence, never known someone who embodied the American ideal, a real live image of John Wayne. After Tim, there had been one or two boyfriends in her life who gave an initial impression that they might measure up. But it never worked out. Those who did meet her expectations soon lost interest in her, and those who hung around turned out to be less appealing than she'd anticipated. In consequence, her planned moments of intimacy rarely had been truly intimate. Sex became a way of saying 'thanks for the meal' just a little too often. Sometimes she wondered if, at her age, anything more was too much to expect.

"The thing you must bear in mind..." Lawrence's voice broke the atmosphere so suddenly that she started and dropped her pen. He was turned towards her now, speaking thoughtfully and precisely. "This will not be like any other landing you've seen before. *Washington* will land at a speed of 224 miles per hour."

"That's fast."

"The final approach angle will be twenty degrees. Much steeper than the three degree glide slope of your average civil airliner. That means some very precise flying on the part of the pilot. Normally it would all be done automatically, but this time he'll have to play it the old-fashioned way."

Trisha sniffed and retrieved her pen. "That's all very interesting, but what's the real problem? The one you're not telling us about?"

"Real problem?" He gave a short laugh. "You think we should tell you all our national secrets?"

"No, not all. Just a bit more about this shuttle mission. And why the whole business is causing so much bother. It's not just because the *Washington* is coming down in the wrong place, is it?"

"If you need to be told more, I'll tell you."

"Don't leave it until too late. You know I can never tell a soul that the *Washington* exists, let alone what it's doing here. So you might as well confide in me." She twisted her head suddenly as a movement in the radar room doorway caught her eye.

Keating, the ATC Business Manager, hurried up the steps into the visual control room. He looked at his watch as he paused alongside Trisha's console. "We reckon it will touch down fifty-six minutes from now."

"The main runway should be clear of snow by then." Trisha re-directed her gaze to the long grey strip. It was still snowing steadily, but the mechanical blowers had more than kept pace with the weather.

"Yes." Keating's jaw hung open as if he was unsure how to continue. "We're not too sure how much runway length they need, what with the payload still being on board and the runway being wet. And the crosswind from the north."

"Not like the open space they're used to at Edwards, is it?"

"No. There is another problem." Keating stepped to the next console and sat down gingerly on the wide desk section. "There's another emergency out over the ocean."

Trisha raised her eyebrows.

"A mid-air collision," Keating continued awkwardly, as if he felt responsible for the all troubles that had beset them. Behind him, Lawrence moved in closer, his hands jutted firmly into the pockets of his uniform jacket.

"The Sinclair 747 that was delayed out of Kennedy has collided with a KC135. It looks like the 747 was way off course and it's badly damaged. They're trying to divert into here."

"Into here?" The big American colonel came up behind Keating, dwarfing the ATC Business Manager with his broad, bulky frame, catching both the British controllers off guard. "When? When is it going to arrive here?"

"That's the problem. As near as we can judge — which isn't easy because the aircraft is flying low on three engines — it'll be here in about fifty minutes or so. About the same time as the shuttle."

"The hell it will!" Lawrence suddenly became insistent. "You can't allow that."

"It's an emergency, Colonel. Your senior commanders are looking at the problem, but really we don't have much choice. There are more than four hundred people on that plane."

Lawrence pointed a finger at Keating, as if he was about to argue the point, paused, and then turned away to hurry down the steps into the radar room. Keating watched him go and then his voice went suddenly hushed. "I don't know what we're going to do, Trisha. Every other airport within range is closed by the weather. If we refuse them landing clearance, we're as good as signing their death warrants."

"We couldn't do that, surely? Why shouldn't they land here?"

"The aircraft is badly damaged. It's also losing fuel and it won't be able to hold off when it gets here, so the pilot will want to make a straight in approach and landing. But when it lands, there's every chance that it will either break up and block the runway with debris or that it will have to stop on the runway to evacuate the passengers. That will stop us getting the *Washington* down on the ground."

"Suppose we allow the space shuttle to land first?"

"We've thought of that. The problem is that it can't taxi clear of the runway under its own power, so it'll block the runway as soon as it lands. Added to which, it's heavily loaded. And with this bad weather there's a possibility that the shuttle might make almost as much of a mess on the runway as the 747. So if we let the *Washington* land first, we'll probably prevent the 747 from landing."

"So, whichever one lands first, the other probably won't get down safely."

"Most likely. Yes, that's about the size of it. There's every sign it's going to be a straight choice between trying to save the lives of the four hundred or so people on board the 747 or trying to save the space shuttle."

Trisha breathed in deeply. "That's not an easy choice, I know. But surely the four hundred people on the 747—"

"No." Lawrence came running back up the stairs, closely followed by the General. "At all costs, the shuttle must take priority. At all costs!"

*

Jock's heart thumped as he ran down the length of the operations room and came to an abrupt halt alongside the Hebrides Sector controller.

Breathlessly, he asked, "Can you see the Sinclair aircraft? The emergency flight."

The sector controller, a bearded man named Price, pointed towards the left-hand screen. "Not yet. It's below radar cover. This tube is set up with the Tiree radar." His finger jabbed at Tiree, an Inner Hebridean island, on his radar map. "We should get a primary blip from the Sinclair aircraft on here. When it gets in range. But Sinclair's transponder isn't working so we won't see it on the Stornoway secondary radar."

Price jabbed a finger at an aircraft on the right-hand display. "That's an E3A, the airborne command post for the space shuttle recovery. Their on-board radar has picked up the 747 and they've directed a Nimrod onto it. I did have the Nimrod on the display earlier, but now it's descended below radar cover."

Jock pulled forward a swivel seat and eased himself in alongside the other controller.

"My wife should be on the damaged plane," he whispered. "Do you mind if I watch what's happening?"

"Your wife? I'm sorry. You'd better grab a headset and listen in."

"I was going to give you a break."

"Not if your wife's on board that aircraft."

Jock stared at the radar screens, helpless and sick. Suddenly, the fact that Sally had been unfaithful to him was unimportant. His hands shook.

"Do you know if anyone was hurt or... or if anyone... anyone was hurt aboard the 747?"

"No idea, Jock. The aircraft is pretty badly damaged from what we hear. One engine ripped off."

Jock's lip trembled and he put a hand to his face. He forced himself to study the two radar displays. With the Sinclair flight not visible, he diverted his attention to the mainland area. The screen showed a single aircraft heading, somewhat hopefully, towards Glasgow from the south.

"He's wasting his time," the Hebrides controller observed calmly. "There's no way he'll be able to land at Glasgow in this weather. He'll have to divert somewhere else. Heaven knows where at the moment."

"Prestwick?" Jock suggested.

"No. Nothing's being allowed to land there except flights involved in the shuttle emergency."

"What are the chances of an improvement in the weather?"

"Not much."

"Wouldn't like to be in that pilot's shoes."

"Hello. Looks like Angus is in a hurry." The Hebrides controller glanced over Jock's shoulder and directed a finger at the watch manager as he strode towards them with a black expression creasing his face.

Jock swivelled round in his seat. Cameron's face was filled with anxiety. He came to a halt at the Hebrides Sector suite and spoke haltingly. "Will you go down to the General Manager's office as quick as you can, Jock. They want to see you straightaway."

"Me?"

"There are a couple of policemen waiting to talk to you. It's about your wife. I think you ought to get along there as quickly as possible."

Chapter 11

Not for the first time, Kovak wished he were back at home in his own apartment, curled up with a warm, responsive girlfriend and watching a premier division football match on the television. He swore out loud as the airframe shuddered and groaned.

The air outside was getting rougher by the minute. A ragged cloud base, invisible air pockets and a blustery wind shook the aircraft like a mouse clamped between the jaws of a vicious cat. Kovak looked around at the passengers. The survivors were now strapped into their seats and tightly grasping the arm rests. Only the cabin crew were on their feet.

A wailing wind blasted through the cabin. Beside the open undercarriage bay hatch, the sound was frightening, like the cry of a Celtic banshee.

Kovak peered down into the bay, trying to clear his mind of the noise around him. He was unable to block out the sound of a teenage girl seated nearby, vomiting into a sick bag. A large woman in a thick, blue coat was doing her best to comfort the girl, but not succeeding. The stench of the vomit whipped past the flight engineer before it was lost in the blizzard of cold air.

Kovak concentrated his attention on the port main undercarriage. The entire wheel assembly sat at an angle some way between the raised and the lowered position. The bay doors were clearly open, a glimpse of the wild, grey sea visible between them. As he studied the angle of the leg, Kovak suspected that the wheels had fallen further since the Nimrod pilot had inspected the airframe. It was going to be a major problem when... *if*... they reached land. The undercarriage was not raised sufficiently for them to attempt a belly landing. Neither was it lowered enough for Nyle to attempt a wheels-down landing.

He drew back and stared at Maggie Loughlin. She knelt at the

165

opposite side of the opening, her face a mask of horror. Was this the first time she had been forced to confront a situation over which she had no control? The first time an aircraft had fallen apart beneath her? Of course it was. Kovak had no sympathy. It was a first time for everyone aboard.

If rumour was to be believed, the senior stewardess had a drink problem — and other problems on top of that — but she was supposed to be able to cope with any situation. Maybe she was not the right sort of young woman for his bed.

"If you look down there—" He leaned forward again into the open well, pointed a shaking finger and raised his voice to counter the howling wind. "That's the main load-bearing part. It's called the oleo and the wheels are mounted on the bottom of it. This part — up here in front of the oleo — this is called the breaker strut."

"It looks frightening from here." Maggie put a hand to her billowing hair and averted her eyes.

"If you can't stand heights, you shouldn't fly."

"Pig!"

Kovak ignored her and pointed again, this time to a small component mounted just beside a cross-member between the oleo and the breaker strut. "That's the actuator. It's one of the parts I want to get a good look at. The trouble is I can't reach it."

"Why not?"

"Because I would have to put my own weight on the oleo or the breaker strut to reach down there. There's a risk that the whole thing would open up underneath me."

"And drop you out like a bomb."

Kovak looked up suddenly to check whether the stewardess was mocking him. Her face remained cold, white and shocked. It had been no joke.

"Yes. Like a bomb," he muttered. He leaned forward again into the well.

Maggie eased herself onto her haunches beside him and wrapped her billowing hair back into place. "What else do you need to see down there?"

"The hydraulic lines. Look, you see those pipes down there, the ones that run down the oleo leg? I want to see if any are leaking."

Maggie looked once more, leaned back and shook her head. "You really have to get to that actuator and the hydraulic lines one way or another?"

"That's Dougie Nyle's orders. He wants me to get a good look at them to see whether they're damaged. If they are, we'll have to rethink how we're going to get the wheel assembly lowered before we land the aircraft."

"But you can't get down there to look at those things. You said so."

"That's right."

"So what do we do now?"

"Let me go and talk to Dougie again." Kovak jerked back into a kneeling position and cocked a thumb over his shoulder. "Maybe he can suggest a way."

"Do you have to bother him? He's got his work cut out just flying this damned thing. Can't you decide what to do?"

"Why should I? He's in charge. It's his problem. He has to take the decisions. I'll be back"

*

Left beside the open hatch, Maggie Loughlin felt deflated and helpless. Her hands shook in the cold wind that whistled up from below. She leaned farther back on her haunches, drawing away from the opening, and peered at the passengers' faces. She was surrounded by frightened people who depended upon the crew for their survival.

If only she could get away to a quiet place and take something to calm her nerves. She had a small packet of white powder secreted in the lining of her uniform jacket. On second thoughts, perhaps alcohol would be a better answer. She wrapped her arms around herself and hardly noticed Trudy Bodenstadt until the younger woman was almost touching her.

"Maggie. I must talk to you." The voice was uneven, but she had grown to expect that from Trudy.

"Is it important?" Maggie stood up slowly.

"It's terrible. There's an American drug enforcement agent up on the top deck." The younger woman's already dull eyes suddenly glazed over.

Maggie froze. Something she had long dreaded was suddenly about to attack her. She spoke quietly and shakily. "How do you know what he is?"

"I saw his identification. It fell out of his coat. There's a DEA badge and a photograph of him."

"What's he doing on board?"

"I don't know. He told me not to tell anyone about him. He made me promise. But I had to tell *you*. I'm so scared, Maggie, honest I am. So scared."

Maggie clenched her fists. Her mind was working again in overtime.

You're scared, Trudy? How do you think I feel?

She forced a deep breath and then spoke slowly, feeling the heaviness of the tone in her own voice. "We're all scared, Trudy. Why should you be any different?"

"Let me stay down here on the main deck." Trudy grabbed her by the arm, her fingers twisting into Maggie's coat. "I'm frightened the man up there might start questioning me. I know too much, Maggie. I might say something I shouldn't."

Maggie put a hand to the girl's shoulder and nodded. In that state of mind, it would be too dangerous to risk her going back upstairs. "All right, Trudy. You stay down here and Wendy can cope with things up top. I told some of the girls to sort out hot drinks for the passengers. You go and give a hand. Find out who's bringing the drinks up from the galley and say I sent you to help."

"Thanks, Maggie. I haven't let anything slip, honest. Not to anyone else. Only you."

"I hope not, Trudy. For all our sakes, I hope not." Maggie shook her arm loose from Trudy's grasp. "Where exactly is this man sitting?"

"Right-hand side, three rows back, aisle seat. Leather jacket."

"All right, leave it to me. But remember what I told you before we left New York. If you squeal to anyone, you're as dead as Sally Scrimgeour. There's nothing I can do to help you if you talk."

Trudy blinked and backed away. Maggie watched her thoughtfully as she edged back down the aisle towards the main-deck service centre. Could she trust Trudy under pressure? Maybe it would have been better if the girl had died along with Sally Scrimgeour in that New York subway. Maybe it would have been better if they all had.

As the thoughts whistled through her mind, she reminded herself that Fergus MacNabb would never have sanctioned the killing of both girls. It had been difficult enough convincing him that Sally had to be eliminated. He had too much residual affection for Sally, a dangerous trait for a man in his position. But there had been no choice.

*

The phone call from Sally rattled her. Maggie clenched and unclenched her hands as she made her way to the girl's hotel room.

She found Sally in a state of shock and Trudy little better.

"Why did he do it? Why did he do it to me?" Sally sat on the bed with tears streaming down her face.

"For chrissake, calm yourself!" Maggie told her angrily.

Sally's eyes were red. "He did it! It was Fergus, wasn't it? He planted that stuff in my new bag."

"What if he did?" Maggie snapped unsympathetically. "There's more going on in this world than you're aware of, you poor little innocent. Now, pull yourself together and we'll work out what to do."

"I want to speak to Jock." Sally reached towards the telephone. "I want to speak to my husband. He'll know what to do."

"You mustn't do that." Maggie grasped her arm and dragged her back to the middle of the bed. "Whatever you do, you mustn't tell anyone about this."

"I want to talk to Jock!" Sally shook herself free, a wild look in her eyes.

"Sally, if you talk to anyone, they'll kill you."

"Kill me—?" Her voice faded away to nothing. Her mouth hung open.

Maggie patted her arms. "Do nothing. Let me sort this out. I will, I promise you."

"But—"

"No buts, Sally. Just let me see what I can do." She wanted to hit the girl, make her suffer, but what was the point in that? Nevertheless, something would have to be done to silence her. And quickly.

Having extracted a promise from both girls that they would do nothing straightaway, she took a taxi to Fergus's hotel. In her rush, she forgot the handbag.

She barged into his room, her head already working on half-formed plans. "Your little bed mate has found the coke. She knows what it is." She slammed the door behind her.

MacNabb's face fell. "What about the other girl?"

"Both girls have seen it, but it's Sally who's the biggest threat. She's a liability, Fergus. She could see us both behind bars."

MacNabb hesitated, just as she had expected. "She'll be all right," he said half-heartedly.

"She won't, Fergus. Call the man and ask him. He'll tell you the same. You've got to do something. Fast."

In the end the cocaine supplier tipped the balance, levered enough pressure to convince MacNabb that Sally Scrimgeour had to be eliminated. She was too great a threat to the whole operation. Even then, his courage wavered until the last moment.

Maggie kept up the argument. "She not only knows about the cocaine, she also knows important names. Worst of all, she hates your guts enough to go to the cops."

"You don't know that," he roared back, his eyes blazing.

"Everyone knows it! There's too much of a risk that she'll blow the whistle on all of us."

The argument was too conclusive and the risk too heavy. Sally had to go.

"You know what we have to do, Fergus."

"Shite! I can't do it."

"Fergus, she's your responsibility."

"I can't do it. You know I can't."

"You creep. All right, I'll do your dirty work for you this time. But you're in this as deep as anyone."

She picked up Fergus's phone and called Sally's hotel room. "Sally, this is Maggie. Listen, we've found a way of dealing with this. We've got to be careful. If the cops find the stuff on you, you're in real trouble. You understand? They'll think it was you who was dealing in the stuff."

She understood.

"Good. Now, listen carefully. I want you to wrap up that bag and everything inside it. Then, this is what I want you to do. Go to the nearest subway—"

"This is a terrible business," MacNabb wailed when she put down the phone.

"Sure it is. But it has to be done. And one of us has to do it, Fergus. One of us has to silence her. You or me."

The question of how to deal with Trudy Bodenstadt had been a different matter.

"Okay, so one stewardess dies and it looks like a simple mugging gone wrong," Fergus argued. "It isn't even news because it happens every day. But if two stews from the same airline die at the same time, the police will get suspicious and we can't afford to have them sniffing round."

"I know how to handle the other girl."

Maggie left MacNabb's hotel with the determination of a lioness defending her patch. An hour later, it was over. Driving a knife into Sally's back on the crowded subway platform was easier than she had expected. She escaped from the subway station without being seen and hurried back to the stewardesses' hotel.

There, she cornered Trudy.

"If the police should ever find drugs in your luggage—"

"In my luggage! I've never had anything to do with drugs."

"That won't stop cocaine being found in your bags. It can be put there just like it was put into Sally Scrimgeour's bag. You think you could talk your way out of it?"

"No one would do that to me."

"Don't you believe it. Certain people would do exactly that. Set you up with incriminating evidence stacked against you. That's exactly what they would do. Just like they did to Sally. If you value your life, you'll keep your mouth shut."

The threat had appeared to work, although Maggie still held a nagging suspicion that, sooner or later, Trudy would have to be got rid of.

*

She shivered in the cold air wafting up through the open hatch and wished she had a stiff drink in her hand. Another stiff drink, dammit! Anything to calm her shattered nerves.

Trudy was coming back towards her, carrying a tray of soft drinks for the passengers. Soft drinks? What the hell was the point in soft drinks?

"Maggie, you look dreadful. Are you all right?" Trudy stopped beside her, balanced the tray on one hand and put the other to Maggie's arm.

A comforting gesture? Stupid girl, with her innocent expression. Just listen to her! "You look like you've seen a ghost, Maggie."

Ghost? No, not a ghost. Maggie flinched. She was staring at a weak girl who could put them all behind bars.

"There's something wrong down in the wheel bay," she muttered and pointed towards the open hole.

Trudy leaned forward and stared down into the void. "What is it? What's wrong?"

Oh, but it was so easy, easier than she had expected. Even with passengers all around them. One foot in front of Trudy and then just a small push. A nudge, and over she went. The younger girl didn't scream until she was falling through the hole and the tray of soft drinks was tumbling across the cabin floor. The high-pitched scream quickly faded.

The nearest passengers jumped to their feet, but Maggie soon calmed them. "She tripped. I couldn't stop her. You saw how I tried to save her. There's nothing you can do now. Please sit down again." Yes, it was so easy. Easy to do, easy to forget about. After all, what was one more victim when they were surrounded by so much death? Maggie drew back her shoulders and turned her attention to the other passengers seated nearby. They would soon forget about this little incident. And so would she.

*

Judson felt alone. Even with Youngman sitting only a few feet away across the flight deck and Hewson sitting behind them, he felt alone. Maybe it was because he was saddled with all the command decisions, including disobeying Ocean Command's instructions. Or maybe it was because he was so damned tired. One way or another, he felt like he needed someone to be there with him to take away the responsibility. To tell him how he could land his burning airplane on a nice clean, long runway with fire crews ready to spray the wing with foam. But there was no one to help him. No one at all.

Why had he disobeyed orders? Why had he not just ditched the aircraft in the sea? Maybe he should get back to Highball and do as he had been told. Like hell he would! He had lost his wife, his car and his money. After this fiasco he would probably lose his commission. So why worry about what anyone else told him to do?

They were going on.

He had grown used to silence from the radio and the sudden burst of intercom beat on his eardrums. "Major. This is Bryzjinsky."

I'd never have guessed, he thought. "What you want, Bryzjinsky?"

"Sir, there's an island down there on the starboard side."

He sighed. So, you've got your eyes open now, have you, Bryzjinsky? He pressed the intercom switch. "Sure, I see it."

"Well, sir. I thought maybe it would have an airfield. Looked like there was a glimpse of a runway, but I couldn't be sure."

"It sure does have an airfield, Bryzjinsky. We looked it up and we know all about it. It's called Tiree and it's too darned small for us. The runways are much too short. We're headed on south towards a bigger airfield called Machrihanish."

"Mac— what, sir?"

"Machrihanish."

"Jeez, sir. You still got your teeth glued in?"

Judson silently mouthed: Very funny, Bryzjinsky. Get lost, will you! Aloud, he said, "Thanks for the information, Bryzjinsky." Then he turned towards Hewson. "How're you doin' with the course?"

"We should get to Machrihanish on this track, sir. Just you keep flying that same heading."

"For how long?"

"I'll have an ETA for you in a minute."

"You mean you don't know."

"Just gimme a minute, sir!"

Judson put a hand to his aching brow. Couldn't he trust anyone on this damned ship?

*

A numbing ache crept down Dougie's arms. His concentration began to wane and his thoughts flashed back to more comforting images of Jenny. The news media must have latched onto the story by now and it would be on every television channel. She could not fail to have learned that Sinclair flight 984 was engaged in a life or death battle. How would she react? With a measure of calm and thoughtful appraisal? Probably. There would be no emotional outburst as long as she was uncertain whether her husband had survived the collision, no tears until she was certain she was a widow.

And that possibility was a strong one.

The rush of air through the flight deck increased to a gale as Kovak threw open the cabin door and bounded in. It subsided again when he slammed the door behind him. Dougie gave him only the briefest of glances. He had more important matters on his mind. He brought his concentration back to the instrument panel.

Kovak came up alongside him. "It's the port main body undercart all right. It's not fully retracted."

That was no surprise. "What do you suggest?" Dougie kept his response calm and to the point.

"Me? I came back to ask *you* what we should do? Can you knock it down with a bit of G?"

Dougie shrugged. The undercarriage might be forced down by violent aircraft manoeuvres, increasing the gravity pull. But moves like that would put additional stress on the weakened fuselage and wings. Could the aircraft stand up to it?

He considered the proposal for a second. "I can try it if I have to. But the airframe might not take the strain."

Kovak gestured despondently and turned back to his flight engineer seat. "It's a straight choice, Dougie. Either we try to force the gear down or we try to land with that leg halfway extended."

"That's no real choice, is it?" Dougie stared ahead and juggled with the multitude of conflicting demands being made on his brain. He had to keep calm and sort out each difficulty as it became critical. Prioritise every problem and deal with each of them in sequence. That was the way to cope with a situation like this. The undercarriage could wait for a little longer while he thought about it. "Let it ride for the moment," he said. "You just concentrate on your job up here, Sammy."

Ahead of the aircraft the cloud base was sinking lower — much too low. In places it was almost touching the heaving waves. He noticed that the Nimrod had led them down lower in the past few minutes.

A voice suddenly cut into his headphones. "Sinclair 984, this is Watchdog."

"Go ahead, Watchdog."

The English pilot sounded concerned now. "We've got serious problems, I'm afraid. The cloud base is much lower here than I was led to expect. I thought we'd be able to creep in to Prestwick underneath the cloud, but it looks now as if that's a no-go."

"Roger, Watchdog. What do you suggest?"

"We've no alternative but to climb up into the cloud. Can you maintain IMC?"

Dougie closed his eyes for a second and cursed. IMC — Instrument Meteorological Conditions — meant flying blind on instruments. The aircraft had few enough instruments still working. He had an artificial horizon which would enable him to keep the wings level and he had an airspeed indicator. But he had no altimeter.

"Only with difficulty, Watchdog. I told you I have no altimeter, and I won't be able to see you in the cloud."

"I understand that, Sinclair 984. But there is no other way."

"Roger. I'll need some assistance in maintaining a steady safe altitude."

"Understood. We'll monitor you with our on-board radar and tell you when to level off. I'm afraid I have nothing better to offer you."

"Roger, Watchdog. When do I start the climb?"

"Please begin your climb now. Are you picking up the Turnberry VOR?"

Dougie checked his VOR receiver. "Affirmative."

"Jolly good. Continue climbing straight ahead and homing towards that. I will tell you when to stop the climb."

"Roger. What's the situation at Prestwick now? Can we land there?"

The reply was not immediate. Neither was it said with any confidence. "They still refuse landing permission, but there's really nowhere else for us to go. I'm arguing the point with them quite forcibly."

Dougie kept his voice calm, but determined. "You'd better try being even more forceful, Watchdog. If there's nowhere else for me to land, I aim to put this aircraft down at Prestwick. One way or another."

"Roger. I'm doing my best. Just stick with it for the moment."

"Affirmative, Watchdog. I'll do that anyway. In the meantime, have you any other suggestions?"

"Negative. To be honest, I think the air traffic people anticipate that you will ditch in the sea off the coast."

"I'd rather not do that." As Dougie spoke, his mind went back to the small island airfield they had passed earlier. "If we had to, could we turn back to Benbecula?"

"It's your choice, old chap, but I wouldn't recommend it because of the weather conditions over the island. It's getting even worse by the minute. In any case, Tiree aerodrome is nearer to Prestwick. If you have to put down on a small island, you'd be better advised to land there."

Dougie flinched. Another small island airfield. He recalled all he knew about Tiree from his school geography lessons — small, flat and windy — and didn't like the idea one little bit. "What are conditions like there?"

"Just marginally better than the weather at Benbecula. The runways are much too short for a 747 and the bearing strength is not nearly high enough. And you would have to make as near a crash landing as makes no difference. Quite honestly, old chap, it would be much better if I can persuade our friends at Prestwick to allow you to land there."

"Roger, Watchdog. I'll continue towards Prestwick for the present. Keep me informed, will you."

"Affirmative, Sinclair 984. I'll do my best for you."

As the aircraft began its climb up into the clinging cloud masses, Dougie peered at his shattered gauges and called to the flight engineer, "Check the fuel, Sammy. How much more time do we have?"

Three minutes passed before Kovak replied. "It looks like the fuel loss is getting worse. We have about forty-five minutes of fuel left. Maybe less."

"That's not much, is it?"

"It's enough to get us to Prestwick."

"They may not allow us to land at Prestwick."

"Shite!"

"Go back into the cabin and take another look at the under—" Dougie got no further.

The aircraft went into a sudden sharp yaw. Instinctively, he tried to counter with the rudder. He scanned across the few remaining instruments on his panel and cursed as his eyes caught the reason for the jolt. Behind him, he heard Kovak's voice erupt into an alarmed cry that echoed across the flight deck.

"The port outer engine has shut down! We're dead!"

Chapter 12

Colonel Lawrence had no misconceptions about himself. He had a love of flying which had never progressed much beyond the piston engine, making him an anachronism in the high-tech modern world of military aviation. But he understood politics. He had been flown up here to Prestwick because he understood the implications of what was happening. He knew what the political fallout would be. And he had no doubt that the politicians in the White House would be chewing at their fingernails over this one.

According to the progress documents he had read, the plan to put X-ray lasers in space as part of Reagan's SDI policy posed one major problem: how to build a large enough power source. Reason said that if you can't get a huge power source up there, you might as well not bother to develop the weapon in the first place. But there was always a way around reason.

In one report he read, "Multi Mega Watt (MMW) power systems will be needed in Burst Mode for laser weaponry. These power requirements can be serviced only by a nuclear detonation."

When he first read the report, it frightened him.

A movement nearby dragged his attention back to the Prestwick aerodrome controller. She was leaning across her console, seemingly allowing her mind to drift at random. The clue to those wandering thoughts was the pen that she held lightly between her fingers, allowing it to tap rhythmically on the control console desk top.

Lawrence wasn't sure whether he approved of women air traffic controllers. It was not the sort of job he would trust to a woman's flighty mind. Women were for minding homes, having children, making love. Not for controlling aeroplanes. The trouble with women nowadays was that they thought they could do a man's job, and employers too often tended to go along with them. The US Air

Force even allowed them to fly planes. Okay, so they mostly flew transport aircraft, but that was still flying. A man's job. Someone once told him that he would have to change his ideas if he hoped to ever find a woman willing to live with him, but he doubted that. There had to be women in this world who knew their place. He just hadn't met one yet.

Forcing aside his reservations, he pulled up a swivel chair and sat down alongside the aerodrome controller. Perhaps she might be available for other, more female tasks, more socially orientated tasks. Bedroom tasks.

If they got through this day.

"Have you been working here long?" he asked.

"Fifteen years. Most of my career, in fact." She sat back in her seat and grasped her pen with both hands, as if it needed that much effort to stop herself tapping the desk top.

"And you're not married?"

"No." She looked up sharply, as if he had hit a raw nerve. "I was, but it didn't work out. Besides, it's not a qualification of the job."

"Sorry. Didn't mean to be offensive," he said gently. "I thought we might have a drink together when this is all over. Couldn't really make the offer if you were married."

This time she looked surprised. "Oh. No offence taken. I'd love to. Have a drink, that is."

"Good. I wouldn't want you to think we're not grateful for what you British are doing."

"Is it that important?"

"You'll never know, Trisha," he drawled. "There are some things I can't tell you, but it must be pretty damned obvious that this is a major operation by any standards."

She blinked and adjusted her spectacles. "Do you think the shuttle will get down all right?"

Lawrence looked away for a moment before he answered, not too sure how much he ought to divulge. "I sure hope it does. And there are one whole lot of people praying it does. We've never had to consider putting a shuttle craft down at an airfield covered in snow. So far, we've never had to put down outside the States."

"How much runway length will you need?" She was probing now, looking for answers.

"For this particular landing, we're not too sure," he said huskily. "At Edwards we have four and a half kilometres. All being well, we can put a normal shuttle mission down in about two and a half. Here at Prestwick you've got—"

"Nearly three thousand metres. Two thousand, nine hundred and eighty-seven, to be exact."

"Quite." he said, redirecting his gaze towards the scene outside, "That should, in theory, be enough — in normal circumstances. But, like I said, this isn't a normal mission." He hoped his answer would be enough and that he could change the subject.

But she immediately went on, "I read somewhere that you can manoeuvre the shuttle over a two thousand mile area once it re-enters the atmosphere."

"Yes. Its lateral manoeuvring capability is about two thousand miles. But that still puts us well off course for a recovery to base."

"Okay, but why do you have to use Prestwick?" She was getting insistent now and the pen was tapping once again, louder and faster. "Surely there are other landing grounds you could use? Surely you could find some other place for the shuttle so that we can save the lives of the people on the 747. Why can't you use your reserve landing field at Saragossa in Spain?"

He realised then what was bugging her, why she was beginning to get a little rattled. She didn't understand why the shuttle had to take priority over those four hundred people on board the 747. Why they were condemning those four hundred people to save the *Washington*. Of course, there was no way she could understand.

"Yes, I see your concern. But there are reasons—" He began firmly enough, but his words petered out into an ominous silence.

"Come on, Dan. There's more to it, isn't there. Tell me what it's all about. I am security cleared, you know."

He hesitated. How much could he reveal? Officially he was

allowed to divulge very little. But if the press got hold of the story, they would probably ferret out the truth. So why shouldn't he tell the woman now? Let her see what she was letting herself in for. It was, after all, part of his job to make sensitive decisions on who should be told what.

"The truth is, the Spanish and all the other European governments have refused us landing permission. The British government was the only one willing to put its head on the line. The others were afraid."

"Afraid of what?"

He looked her in the eye and allowed a long, deep breath to escape his lips. "All right, Trisha, I'll tell you what it's all about. But this is top security information. You know that the payload is still on board?"

She nodded.

"That payload is an X-ray laser experiment. You've heard of the X-ray laser?"

She shook her head and frowned. It meant nothing to her.

"Well, it's a pretty hot piece of hardware. The big thing about it is the power source. Most laser weapons need huge power sources, and the X-ray laser needs even greater reserves of power to drive it. In fact, the only viable power source for an X-ray laser is a thermo-nuclear detonation." He paused for effect. "In other words, Trisha, if you want to power up such a device in space you have to detonate a thermo-nuclear device."

"You mean—"

"I mean that our scientists had to build a nuclear bomb into the structural fabric of the experiment."

Trisha's head jerked upwards. "A nuclear bomb? But surely, when the bomb explodes it will blow up the laser weapon."

"That's right. It disintegrates the weapon a split second after the laser has fired. By then, we hope, the enemy missile is already destroyed."

He watched her face for some sign of reaction, but after that initial reflex action she kept her expression composed, as if waiting for him to go on.

He drew breath and continued. "The crew was able to arm the bomb before things started to go wrong. Then the shuttle went off course and the experiment computers went haywire. The scientists are saying that maybe the experimental equipment had some effect on the ship's computers. I don't know. Anyhow, one of the consequences was that the crew was unable to disarm the bomb."

"It's still armed?"

"It's still armed. There's a primed nuclear device on board the shuttle, and if the craft were to crash-land, there is a very real risk of the thing detonating. I don't need to spell out what that means."

Once again he focussed his eyes on her face, and this time Trisha stared back at him with a wide-eyed sense of horror. Clearly this was not the stuff of British civil air traffic control, not the sort of emergency she was trained to handle. Neither was it the sort of thing the British College of Air Traffic Control had ever thought fit to simulate on their training computers.

Lawrence said softly, "You can see now why we have to get the *Washington* safely down, Trisha? If that ship crashes into the sea, or tries to put down on rough land away from an airport, there could be one hell of an explosion. The sort of thing you've never ever known in this country. Hiroshima magnified many times over."

"And the four hundred people on the 747?"

"I'm as sorry about them as you are."

Trisha screwed up her face and her spectacles tilted on her nose. "Surely you could have put the shuttle down at one of the USAF bases in England."

"The weather is below limits at all our bases. You know that."

"It's also pretty well marginal here." She began to stand up as realisation seeped into her mind. "It's a *political* decision isn't it? They don't want the risk of a nuclear explosion in highly populated England so they've offloaded your bomb onto poor old half-empty Scotland. That's it, isn't it, Dan?"

"It's a matter of the weather," he said firmly.

183

"But not entirely. Is it?"

He turned away, unable to deny the accusation. Political, she had said. Well, politics was his game, his reason for being here. He hoped he'd got it right.

*

Jock swept his gaze between the two police detectives. They looked uncomfortable in the semi-formal environment of the General Manager's officer. In all probability, neither had previously been inside the Scottish Air Traffic Control Centre. It was as if they were working in an alien environment.

The older of the two, Detective Inspector McKee, nervously twisted the end of his bristled moustache. He leaned forward to speak with an air of fatherly concern. "Perhaps you would like us to drive you home, Mister Scrimgeour. We have a car just outside."

Jock shook his head. He looked straight through the policeman, fighting to keep his quivering lower lip from betraying his horror.

Sally was not on board the 747 over the Atlantic, she never had been. Sally was dead. A cold corpse in a New York mortuary.

"No. Not yet." he whispered. "I don't want to go home just yet."

McKee addressed him with an air of compassion. "I understand how you must be feeling. I'm sorry to have to bring such terrible news."

"I'll be all right." But his voice shook as he spoke.

"Yes, of course. Do you feel up to answering a few more questions? You don't have to, of course, not in the circumstances."

"What questions?" Jock was surprised at how hollow his own voice sounded.

"About your wife, sir. I wondered if there was anything you could tell us which might help to solve the question of her—"

"Her murder?" Jock bit his lower lip and turned to face the policeman.

Out of the corner of his eye he saw the younger cop, Detective Sergeant Hastie, open his notebook and lick the end of a short stub of pencil. He watched fascinated as the man struggled to avert his gaze while writing. Embarrassment was spread across his face.

"We have to ask," the older man said, screwing up his mouth while his face turned red with discomfort.

"What exactly do you want to know?" Jock asked, turning his attention back to McKee.

"Well, sir. Who did she know in New York? Who did she associate with when she was off duty over there?"

"Associate with?"

"Who did she see or go out with? Perhaps there was another stewardess she was friendly with?"

"She shared a hotel room with another stewardess. Apart from that, I don't know." Jock lowered his eyes. Of course he knew who she associated with. And he knew where Sally had been the night before she died. Or, if he didn't actually know, he strongly suspected. But he wasn't yet prepared to reveal to the police that he was being two-timed by an unfaithful wife and a bastard of a pilot. Later he would tell them, when he was better able to compose his emotions. But not yet.

"I'm sure the New York police know about the woman your wife shared with. What we really need to know is, did she often go out with other members of the crew while she was abroad?"

Jock's head snapped up suddenly. "Why? What are you suggesting?"

Detective Inspector McKee looked taken aback by the severity of Jock's reply, momentarily lost for words.

"Are you suggesting, officer, that my wife had some sort of affair going on with another member of the crew?"

"No, sir. Not at all. I merely wondered..." McKee looked down at his own notebook, scanning the open page for help. "Did she ever speak of someone called Fergus MacNabb?"

"MacNabb? Yes, he's one of the senior pilots. Why? What's he got to do with this?"

"We're trying to follow up every lead, sir. The New York police have asked us to find out who your wife knew over there. They want to know if there was someone she might have known sufficiently well to have arranged a meeting with the night she died."

Jock choked back a cry of anger. "They think she might have arranged to see MacNabb that night? Is that it?"

"We really don't know, sir." The detective chose his words with care. "Look, I really do think we ought to give you a lift home, Mister Scrimgeour. We can ask you more questions later."

"More questions? What other questions do you want to ask?" There was something they weren't telling him, he was certain of it. Something to do with that man, MacNabb. Whatever it was, he wanted to know. Now. Almost growling, he said, "If you have questions to ask, fire away. Let's get it all over with."

"This is going to be a little difficult, sir. A white leather handbag was found alongside your wife's body. It contained a package of cocaine."

Jock's mind reeled as if he had received a blow to the head. The present from MacNabb! Trudy Bodenstadt had said that MacNabb gave her a handbag. The bastard had given her a present of cocaine.

"No, not drugs. My wife had nothing to do with drugs."

"I'm sorry this had to come out now, Mister Scrimgeour. The information has come to us from the New York police and they have asked us to investigate it. I realise it must be very painful for you."

"She's never had anything to do with drugs. Never."

"Have you any idea where the cocaine might have come from? Any idea at all?"

"No," he lied, emphasising the word. Whatever inclination he had felt to reveal Sally's liaison with MacNabb, it was now firmly held in check. For Sally's sake. If she was mixed up in the drugs scene, he had to protect her. Or her memory. And his lies, even now, had gone beyond the point of no return. He'd stick to his story. If he could.

"It seems quite possible that these drugs were connected with her death."

"You mean she was killed because she was carrying cocaine?"

"Maybe. But whoever killed her didn't then take the package from her, even though it was a valuable haul. It's possible it was just a random killing. We need more information about your wife and her associates."

Jock forced his reeling mind to settle, to concentrate on what the policemen had told him. Something didn't add up. "But you have some other information, don't you? Why did you ask me about Captain MacNabb?"

"I can't tell you any more yet, Mister Scrimgeour. All we can do is pass on to the American authorities any information you can give us."

The two detectives looked at one another, silently indicating that there was nothing more to be gained and the interview was best ended now. The sergeant folded his notebook shut.

As the two men made to stand, Jock looked up suddenly. "Do you know who is piloting that flight? The one my wife should have been on?"

"I don't see where this is getting us, sir. I really do think we should continue the discussion some other time."

Jock stood up slowly while the policemen watched him hawkishly. He found himself wondering what was in their minds. What else did they know about this business? What were they not telling him?

McKee addressed him hesistantly. "Let's call a halt to this matter for the time being. We can talk about it again later when you've had time to come to terms with what has happened. Are you sure we can't take you home, sir? The snow's rather bad."

"No." Jock brushed a hasty hand across his eyes. "Thank you, but I don't want to go back there just now. It's only an empty flat. I'm better off here among friends."

"I quite understand. Perhaps we could get your manager to help in some way?"

"I'll talk to him when I've sorted things out in my own mind. Are you sure you don't know who's flying that aircraft?" Was it

MacNabb? If it was, he would see the bastard dead.

Neither detective answered, but the older one shook his head unconvincingly.

*

Jock shuffled into the staff canteen with his head bent low. The General Manager had begged him to go home, but he couldn't face the idea of being cooped up in the flat on his own. He needed people about him, people who would avoid discussion about Sally's death, people who would comfort him by their presence, not their words.

The atmosphere in the canteen was frantic. The stress in the domestic operations room was too great and a half-hour break came nowhere near lowering adrenaline levels. Animated arguments were going on in the coffee lounge area. Arms were being waved, hands were levelled to represent conflicting aircraft. Another airmiss? Probably. Nearby, smokers were puffing their way through a ritual fag-and-coffee session. In the dining area, food was being consumed fast. Not because it was necessary, but because knotted nerves demanded it.

Jock carried a coffee to an empty table in a quiet corner. He cast about the room. People were watching him out of the corners of their eyes, speaking carefully out of his earshot. He had no doubts about the subject of their conversations; they would have heard the story about Sally's death now. Something like that wouldn't remain a secret in a place like this. He wanted to shout at them, tell them to mind their own business, but he ignored them, hoping they would have the courtesy to leave him alone.

His sipped absently while his mind struggled to recall all that the policemen had said. What was the significance of their words? What had Fergus MacNabb got to do with Sally's death? Why did they ask about MacNabb in the context of the drugs? They knew something they were not telling. Was it because MacNabb was implicated in Sally's murder?

Someone nearby raised his voice. Jock flipped his eyes open and looked up. Another controller was standing up and nodding in his direction, an older man given to long pointless conversations. He didn't need that right now. He drained the last of his coffee and left the canteen before the man came any nearer.

Back in the operations room, he sensed rather than saw that other people were watching him. Maybe they pitied him, or perhaps they were simply morbidly curious at how he would react to the news of his wife's death.

At the watch manager's desk, Angus Cameron stood up. His face was a picture of genuine sorrow. "I really am sorry about the bad news."

So it was true enough, they all knew about it. Jock waved a hand to stop the statement before it became too emotional. All he wanted now was practical help, not expressions of sympathy.

"Wouldn't it be best if you went home?" It was said almost as an order.

"No. I want to see what happens to the 747. It's about the only tangible link left with Sally. I won't get in the way."

Cameron nodded reluctantly. "If you say so. Can I do anything to help?"

"Just one thing. Have you got the flight plan details for Sinclair 984?"

"Yes." The watch manager put his hand straight to an A4 sheet on his desk.

"What's the pilot's name?"

Cameron held the paper up to his face and peered down the rows of information. "Ah, here it is. Captain Fergus MacNabb."

MacNabb. So, it was him! Just as he expected. A sudden twinge of pain ran through his muscles. Fergus MacNabb: the man that Sally had been unfaithful with. He was sure of it now. But in what way was he linked to her death? MacNabb had given her the handbag, that much was clear. The handbag contained cocaine — assuming, of course, that it was the same handbag. Assuming it was given to Sally complete with drugs. Yes, it had to be the same bag. It had to be MacNabb who had given her the drugs. Far too

189

much coincidence otherwise.

The policemen had wanted to know about Sally's relationship with him. Why? They obviously thought there was some link. The more he thought about it, the more the idea took hold inside his troubled mind. Someone had killed Sally because of those drugs. MacNabb had been responsible for the drugs, therefore MacNabb was responsible for the killing. It was only a short hop to that inevitable conclusion. It didn't really matter whether MacNabb had actually killed her, he was *responsible*. Jock suddenly realised he didn't know the details of how Sally died. He didn't want to know. He simply needed a focus for his anguish. And he hated MacNabb.

He walked away down the room, clutching his hands together to stop them from shaking. He had never before realised just how powerful hatred could be. It consumed him, hiding all his rational thoughts behind a curtain of intense emotional pain. He pictured the pilot in front of him, pictured himself choking the life out of him. He would do it, if MacNabb were here now, he would kill him without a moment's regret.

He stumbled against a desk, then staggered on. Someone spoke to him; he vaguely noticed a controller's lips moving. He ignored the man. To hell with all of you. You don't know what it's like any more than those cops know what it's like.

The control room doors opened, allowing someone to enter. He blinked. Without warning, something inside finally snapped, taking away the last of his sense of reason.

"Let me out!" He hurried towards the opening... had to get out... had to get away. Most of all, he had to find some way of avenging what had happened to Sally.

MacNabb was to blame for Sally's death, and MacNabb would have to pay. Some way, any way, MacNabb would pay for what he had done.

Chapter 13

Dougie pressed down hard with his right foot, using full rudder to counter the effect of two inoperative engines on the aircraft's port side. At the same time, his right hand on the column held the aircraft in a steady attitude and his left pulled back on the port outer thrust lever.

"Straighten up, damn you!" Dougie growled between clenched teeth, searching his mind for a reason behind the power loss. But his brain was finding it increasingly difficult to cope with so many problems at once. He was fighting a losing battle.

"Sammy!" he shouted, keeping his eyes focussed on the instrument panel. "Get into the captain's seat. Quickly. I need your help."

"What about the engines?"

"Never mind them just now. Get into the left-hand seat and help me hold this beast straight."

"But I think I may be able to get more fuel to the port outer."

"Do as I say! I need your help up front."

The scene outside the aircraft looked lethal. Thick, turbulent cloud flushed past the aircraft, cutting off all sight of sea and sky. Some of the cloud misted into the flight deck through the smashed screen.

In the back of Dougie's mind was the nagging thought that he had been wrong to follow the Nimrod pilot into cloud. While he was flying at low level there had been some small chance to navigate the aircraft visually. Inside the cloud, he had little chance of navigating anywhere and the sooner he got back out of it the better. It was one thing for the Nimrod pilot in his fully serviceable aircraft to climb into the thick, buffeting cloud, but for the occupants of the damaged 747, it was a different story. With two engines, he could maintain level flight, but if he lost any more power, they would likely never see their families again.

The sooner he descended again, the better.

To hell with this, he would take the 747 back down before the situation got any worse, even if it meant abandoning the route towards Prestwick.

He pressed the transmit button and called, "Watchdog, this is Sinclair 984. Do you read me?"

"Affirmative, Sinclair 984."

"Watchdog, I've lost my port outer engine. I want to descend below the cloud. I'll turn back towards the ocean if I have to."

"Roger, Sinclair 984. Can you maintain height on your two remaining engines?" There was no sense of surprise in the reply. It was almost as if the English pilot expected problems. Or had he even more nerve that Dougie imagined?

"I could maintain height if there's no other choice, but I don't want to. Is it safe to descend here or shall I turn back?"

"Standby."

Dougie waited, holding the aircraft steady while Kovak slid himself into the left-hand seat and put his hands onto the captain's control column. Straightaway the pressure was eased on Dougie's arms. Moments later, he felt the pressure on the rudder pedal ease off as Kovak took his share of the strain.

The educated English voice cut through the confusion inside the noise-filled flight deck. "Sinclair 984, this is Watchdog. You will be clear of high ground in two minutes. If you turn right now onto heading 170 degrees, you will be heading almost directly down Loch Fyne. Once you're clear of the high ground, you can descend."

"Roger, Watchdog. I'm turning onto heading 170 degrees now." He conjured up an image of Loch Fyne. A long stretch of relatively sheltered water. A good place to ditch? Yes, if he really had to, but ditching in water was a last resort. Hitting the water at 130 knots was like hitting concrete, with the added risk that the big engines mounted below the wings would scoop up tons of water. There was a real chance that would rip the wings off. Right now he had no intention of ditching just as long as there was a chance of putting down on dry land. Dry land meant a better chance of people walking away from the aircraft.

"Good show. We'll continue to monitor you on our radar and I'll tell you when you're over Loch Fyne. Then you can start your descent. But I should warn you the cloud base is very low."

"How low, Watchdog?"

"It's down at ground level over the land. Over the water it's a bit more difficult to judge, but it seems to be about two hundred feet."

"Is that information based on reliable reports?"

"As reliable as we can get. We're in contact with a US navy warship heading down the loch. They have a two hundred feet cloud base above them."

Dougie screwed up his face. An American warship in a Scottish sea loch? What was going on here? "I guess that means I ought to believe it."

"Your choice, old chap. But it's a very low base, even if it is accurate. You're not exactly built for sea skimming, you know."

Dougie's thoughts raced through a series of unpalatable options. Should he continue in cloud, should he descend over Loch Fyne, or should he turn back towards the ocean? He didn't really want to do any of those things.

He glanced at Sammy Kovak but the flight engineer was not listening to the radio conversation. He pressed the switch again. "Watchdog, I don't want to continue flying IMC in case I lose another engine. What do you suggest?"

"Quite honestly, old chap, I think you should stay up at altitude. Apart from the weather problem, I still can't get Prestwick to agree to your landing there."

"Why not, Watchdog?" Dougie was rapidly losing his remaining composure. He could feel the anger rippling through him. "Don't they know how badly damaged we are?"

"I've spelled it out in detail. But they have another emergency on their hands. Look, old chap, I'm doing my best to get you landing permission, but there seems to be some reluctance down there to see our point of view."

A stab of anger pierced Dougie's brain. He responded sharply. "Okay, I've made up my mind, Watchdog. I want to descend again. As quick as we can."

"Fair enough, old chap. I understand your problem." The Nimrod pilot's voice was calm. "Can I suggest it might be best if we go down first to check out the conditions down there?"

"Thanks, Watchdog. I'd appreciate that."

"Don't mention it, old chap. You maintain your present altitude until I call you."

The same old stiff upper lip, Dougie noted, but he made no comment. He was dependent on the Nimrod pilot's help. After a moment's thought, he flipped the transmit switch again and asked, "Watchdog, what exactly is going on at Prestwick? What's the other emergency there? What can be more important than the lives of four hundred people?"

"Something rather big, old chap. I've suggested to them that they allow you to land after they've dealt with the other problem. Do you think you could hold off for a while once you get to Prestwick?"

Another sharp stab of annoyance hit him. "You expect us to hold off? Look, we're badly damaged, we're losing fuel and we've some seriously injured people on board. Haven't you told them that?"

"Affirmative, I've told them." The voice sounded apologetic. "I'm sorry, Sinclair 984, old boy, I really am. But if it comes to the worst, I think you may have to ditch in the sea."

*

Maggie Loughlin tried to put all thoughts of Trudy's death from her mind. Killing her had been a necessity and there was no point in brooding over it. She had, after all, killed before.

After the first time she had been forced to quickly abandon Sally Scrimgeour's body, merging herself into the milling crowd on the subway platform. She hadn't been so clever that time. In the New York subway, she should have recovered the handbag, but she had failed miserably. When Sally's body slipped to the ground, the crowd closed in, ghoulishly eager to see what had happened. Two men bent down to help the girl and one of them grabbed the handbag. Maggie hesitated and then melted away into the background. Fergus MacNabb had been furious. So had the big man.

This time she hoped she had handled things better. She turned away from the opening in the floor, brushed down her uniform skirt, straightened her jacket, and ran her fingers through her hair. Her hands felt sweaty and she rubbed them again down her clothes, took a quick deep breath and stepped away down the aisle. Almost immediately one of the other stewardesses, Ros Dyson, approached her with an empty tray.

"Did you see Trudy?" Ros's voice sounded tired and harassed. "She was supposed to help me make the hot drinks."

"You'll have to cope by yourself." Maggie forced herself to remain cool as she hurried on past the stewardess. A growing tightness across her chest warned her that her nerves were getting too taut. If she stayed longer, she might say or do something suspicious, something out of character that would draw attention to herself. She couldn't afford that. She had to appear in control, whatever happened.

Meanwhile, had she covered all the possibilities?

Maybe First Officer Nyle would land the aircraft safely in which case Trudy would be listed as an innocent victim of the collision. Maggie would be in the clear. The alternative was, of course, that they would all die. But she preferred not to dwell on that.

She walked through the shattered cabin, slowly at first, but within seconds her feet were taking her at a faster pace towards the upper deck. Uncontrollable panic was setting in. There was nothing she could do to prevent the haste, it was a subconscious reaction. As she paused at the top of the stairs her gaze fell first on Fergus MacNabb, still sprawled across the row of seats. Then she took in the DEA agent who was striding purposefully towards the captain. She clasped a hand to her chest as she felt another tight spasm of alarm.

*

It was, Devereaux decided, time to take some decisive action. The situation aboard the aircraft was clearly getting more critical by the minute and the chances of their survival did not appear to be improving. If MacNabb died, a great deal of crucial information would go with him, information that might take the DEA years to discover from other sources.

There was no denying the obvious possibility that MacNabb's death could easily also be accompanied by the demise of the rest of the aircraft's occupants, including himself, but Devereaux chose to put that thought aside for the moment. He preferred to consider the more palatable outcome: that he would survive even if MacNabb did not. If that happened, he wanted to be armed with all the relevant data he could glean from MacNabb, vital evidence concerning the death of Sally Scrimgeour and the cocaine. With those thoughts clearly to the forefront of his mind, he acted.

The woman who had been tending the captain had walked away after a short conversation with one of the stewardesses. That alone told him that the captain was not in imminent danger of death from his injuries.

Devereaux cast about the cabin, saw no obvious attention being directed towards MacNabb, and slid out of his seat. He had no exact idea of what he would say to the pilot, just a general impression of the tactics he might employ. Much would depend upon MacNabb's reaction to him.

Calmly, he made his way forward.

*

MacNabb's moments of lucid thought came interspersed with random and disjointed periods of confusion. Sometimes he thought he was up on the flight deck, flying his aircraft across the North Atlantic. Other times he thought he was back at home making love to the soft and inscrutable Sally Scrimgeour. Or that bitchy whore, Maggie Loughlin. And sometimes he just knew that he was lying uncomfortably across a row of passenger seats on the upper deck of a 747, and that was when his thoughts came clearest. In those brief periods he saw Sally and Maggie as real people, and he remembered the last few days as real times crowded with real events, including the most vivid and frightening happenings he could ever recall.

Maybe, if he'd had more sense, he would never have got caught up in the drugs business. But it was in his nature to go beyond the legal boundaries. He first became aware of that at boarding school. Other boys were content to use that period of their lives as an academic learning experience, but not Fergus MacNabb. He used it as an opportunity to learn how to become top dog in a small enclosed beehive of society. With various devious devices, he manipulated the other boys to ensure his work was done for him at minimal cost to himself. By the time he left school, he was a master of using others to his own ends.

Sally had become a liability. Whatever his own thoughts and feelings about her, he had been left with just one simple choice: her life or his freedom. Maggie Loughlin also had seen the logic of it. She had had the wit to warn him before that stupid girl could talk. Despite her bitchy nature, he could rely on Maggie. When it came to putting pressure on the other stewardess, Trudy Bodenstadt, it was Maggie who took the initiative and tightened the screws to prevent her talking. Yes, he could rely on Maggie, bitch that she was.

He was cold and his thoughts went dull for a few seconds. Then the pain receded and some degree of clarity returned. He had no real idea what exactly was happening, but it frightened him.

He looked around for the passenger who had been tending him since the collision. She was nowhere in sight. Did anyone here care about him any longer?

He started as a shadow fell suddenly across his face.

"How are you feeling now, Captain?"

MacNabb looked up to see another passenger, a tall man. In

a brief moment of lucidity, he recalled seeing him help the stewardess calm the other passengers. At least someone was able to keep his wits about him in an emergency.

"Reckon I'll live."

"Reckon we all will if your crew keep their heads. They're doing a damned good job, you know."

"Yeah. Guess they are." MacNabb felt a sudden spasm of suspicion, nothing he could put his finger on.

"Your senior stewardess certainly seems to know what she's about." As he spoke, the man sat down on the armrest of the aisle seat, as if he was practised in talking to people in a seemingly casual manner. For some imponderable reason, another burst of alarm rose in MacNabb's mind and grew rapidly to fever pitch.

"You're not doing so bad yourself," he said. "I saw you helping the cabin crew. You know something about aircraft?"

"A bit." The man grinned, keeping his gaze tightly pinned on the pilot. "I guess I've spent more than a few sleepless nights working at Kennedy Airport. All in the line of business, you know. You get to pick up bits and pieces about aviation just by working near airplanes."

"Oh yeah?" MacNabb shifted his body to better study the man's face. "What sort of business are you in?"

"Investigation work."

"Yeah?" MacNabb choked heavily as he replied.

"That's right, Captain MacNabb. I'm what the DEA like to call a special agent. Dunno why they stuck the 'special' tag on me, but there you have it."

"What the blazes—?" MacNabb's voice tailed off. He understood now why his instincts had been so strongly reactive.

"What the blazes am I doing on your airplane?" A sharp, acid grin twisted the edges of the man's mouth. "Investigating narcotics. Chasing the bad guys who deal in drugs."

MacNabb's vision suddenly collapsed into a narrow tunnel. At the end of it, he saw only the man's staring eyes. Those eyes told him everything. Somewhere inside he felt his body begin to tremble as the past caught up with the present and the truth began to spill into the future.

"Reckon you've struck unlucky this time, Mr... whatever your name is"

"Devereaux. Special agent, Simon Devereaux."

"You should have stayed on the ground at Kennedy." MacNabb forced the words out so that they emerged thickly. "You might have lived."

"That's the way it crumbles, I guess. We all have to pay the price sooner or later. It's been a bit of a bastard for *you* one way or another. Hasn't it?"

"What do you mean?"

"First one of your stews was murdered on the New York subway, now this bloody calamity. It's not exactly your birthday treat, is it? In fact, I'd say things are pretty bad for you at this moment."

"It wasn't my fault."

"What wasn't? The collision or the murder?"

"The collision."

"What about the murder?" The man's eyes pierced into MacNabb's head like two boring drills. "Rumour has it you had something going with the girl who was killed. What was her name? Sally Scrimgeour."

"I had nothing—"

"Bullshit. You were screwing the ass off her."

"That's none of your business." MacNabb turned his head away from the agent and tried to concentrate.

"Maybe you're right. Or maybe not. When did you last see her?"

"I already told the New York cops all I know. I don't have to take any crap from you. 'Specially not now. Shite, you're not even within your jurisdiction."

The DEA agent stood up slowly and half-turned away. "Yeah. If you say so. But the law has a long arm, as you Brits say. I can't exactly force you to talk to me, Captain MacNabb. But I suggest you think it over for a while."

As MacNabb's head lolled to one side, he saw, in the background, Maggie Loughlin standing rooted to the floor near the stairway. Devereaux gave her a quick glance and then leaned over the pilot. "Maybe I should come and see you again after I've talked with Miss Loughlin. Or do you want her to take you down with her?"

*

The Nimrod pilot's voice sounded confident, the sort of confidence that Dougie found reassuring despite the danger into which he was being led.

"Sinclair 984, this is Watchdog. We're now down at two hundred feet. Over."

Dougie flipped the radio-telephone switch. "Roger, Watchdog. Is it safe enough for us to descend now?"

"It's a bit turbulent down here, old chap. I hope your wings are glued on tightly. We're flying in and out of the cloud base at this altitude, but we have the sea reasonably clearly in sight. If you must come down and join me, make a slow descent on your present heading and be prepared to level off as soon as you break through the cloud."

"Roger, Watchdog. It's turbulent up here, too. I'm starting my descent now." He pulled back gently on the two starboard thrust levers and gave Kovak a quick nod. He received a worried look in return.

"Keep your eyes fixed straight ahead, Sammy. Shout out as soon as you catch sight of the sea."

The nose dipped and then they were descending. Dougie kept his eyes firmly on the instrument panel, cursing his bad luck in not having an altimeter. He would have no clear idea of his altitude until they broke through the cloud base and gained visual contact with the ocean waves. To prevent him diving on into the sea, he was dependent upon Kovak's vigilance and eyesight.

He aimed to take the aeroplane down into VMC — visual meteorological conditions — but, in doing so, he would be breaking the basic low-lying rule that limited him to five hundred feet above person vessel, vehicle or structure. In the circumstances, he decided, the rules were meaningless.

The misty cloud still billowed in through the cracked front screen, blowing back directly into the crew's faces. Dougie squinted as he stared ahead, concentrating hard on the few instruments still available to him. He was now picking up a strong signal from the Turnberry VOR.

Suddenly Kovak's voice rose into a high-pitched scream. "Shite! Level out, for God's sake! Level out!"

"What the—!" Dougie looked up and felt the heavy tug on the column as Kovak grabbed his control yoke and hauled sharply back.

"Level out, Dougie! Level out!" Kovak heaved again on the column, this time throwing the aircraft into steep port turn.

Dougie followed through with the turn, allowing the flight engineer to take control of the move.

"Jeez!" Again, the shattering cry shrieked across the flight deck.

Dougie stared out of the front screen. Directly ahead of them the dark grey sea was flecked with white spume. A huge, dark shape sat upon it, dominating the view. It was a warship, bristling with tall radio masts and radar antennae. Despite the steep turn, the 747 was flying directly into the masts.

A second later, the stall warning indicator started blaring above the noise in the flight deck.

*

MacNabb turned awkwardly in his row of seats and watched the narcotics investigator walk away. Maggie Loughlin was still at the head of the stairway and the man homed directly onto her. For a few moments they talked, and then they both went down the stairs to the main deck. MacNabb gritted his teeth and swore silently.

After a while he heaved himself up, grasping his wounded arm. A stabbing pain shot up through his shoulder and added to the fuzzy grey sensation inside his head. He would much rather remain where he was, but that option was no longer open to him. In fact, there was now nothing left for any of them. The sequence of events had run their full course and had to be ended once and for all. If the DEA knew about the cocaine run and the truth behind Sally's murder, his life was not worth living. In his woolly thoughts, one idea stood out above the rest: it would be best if the aircraft never reached safety. Best if the truth about himself and his illegal activities went to the grave with him, along with all the others who had chosen to fly on Sinclair International flight 984.

He curled his lip. For all his failings, he was no coward. If he had to die, he would go down with some degree of honour remaining, something his parents could hang their hats on when they carved his memorial stone. Better that than a prison cell.

He'd take control. Then make sure they all died.

He staggered forward towards the flight deck, grasping the passenger seats on each side to steady himself. Then his feet suddenly fell away from beneath him. The cabin floor swung over and the aircraft went into a steep turn.

Before he could stop himself, he crumpled to the floor, crying out in pain. From farther down the cabin came the startled cries of passengers who were caught equally unawares by the sudden manoeuvre. A sharp jolt of pain shoot up through his injured arm. He cried out loudly again.

*

Kovak screamed. "Bloody hell, Dougie! We're going to hit!"

Dougie kept his lips firmly compressed and forced his mind to ignore the sound of the stall warning alarm. The 747 was turning steeply at an altitude of no more than two hundred feet above the waves. At any moment it might stall down into the grey, cold sea below. A dead aircraft filled with dead bodies. The high masts atop the warship filled the cracked windscreen.

There were seamen on the deck of the warship, he could see then, running, waving, terrified at the prospect of their ship being rammed by an out-of-control Boeing. If they hit, those men's chances of survival would be as marginal as the occupants of the aircraft. Minimal. Zero.

The ship grew rapidly bigger and then, slowly at first but building in speed as they came closer, the dangerous array of masts moved away to the side of the screen and the 747 raced past the ship with only feet to spare. Trickles of sweat rolled down Dougie's face. He felt the moisture drip from his lips.

*

As the floor swung back onto an even keel, MacNabb forced himself up into a seated position. Whatever was happening up on the flight deck, this was not the way to fly a 747. Angrily he staggered to his feet and started to totter again towards the flight-deck door. He had to get up front if he was to stop this aircraft reaching dry land.

He had taken only a few steps before another stabbing pain shot through his body. He fell once again to the floor, grasping his left arm.

"What are you doing, Fergus?" Out of nowhere, Maggie Loughlin raced up to him. "You shouldn't be on your feet. Christ! Look at that blood." She put her arms about him and tried to drag him into a semi-seated position. "You'll bleed to death if we don't do something."

The shadow of another figure fell over them both. MacNabb wasn't sure who it was until he heard the voice. "Let's get him back to the seats."

Devereaux, the damned DEA man, had raced up directly behind the stewardess. MacNabb glowered at him and then closed his eyes as a wave of nausea swept over him.

*

"For chrissake, Watchdog!" Dougie's reserves were wearing thin. This was not the reaction they would have had from his father. Eric Nyle was above panic.

"Sorry about that, Sinclair 984."

"Why the hell didn't you tell us there was a warship in our way?"

"We weren't too sure exactly where you would break cloud."

"You were watching us on radar, weren't you?"

"Affirmative. We were watching you, old chap, until we lost you in radar clutter. Like I said, we're sorry about the gaffe. I'll make sure someone gets a bollocking for it."

"That won't be necessary."

"At least let me buy you a beer when we land."

Dougie forced his blood pressure to stabilise. He breathed out long and deep. "That is something I'll accept. Just don't put us in a position like that again."

"We'll do our utmost, Sinclair 984. For what it's worth, that particular vessel happens to be a US destroyer, the same one that gave us the cloud base information."

"Another mistake like that and they'll give you the conditions on the sea bed."

"The destroyer commander has just made a similar comment. He put it quite strongly, actually. Not the sort of language one likes to hear on the radio."

"I know how he feels." Dougie stared out of the cracked windscreen and felt a sudden raw hope. In the distance he could just make out a line of darkness down at the interface between sea and cloud. It had to be land. "Watchdog, are we safe to continue flying this low from here on?"

"Affirmative. As safe as you can be at such a low level. I'm about a mile behind you coming up on your starboard side. If I tuck in just ahead of you, you can follow me visually towards Prestwick."

"Roger, I'll do that, Watchdog. And get those people to understand that I want to put this thing down on a runway."

"I'm still trying. Much more of this intransigence and I'll be tempted to use the sort of language I got from the American warship. The trouble is the guys on the ground have another emergency to worry about and they seem to think you rank second in the order of priorities."

"Don't they know how badly we're damaged?"

"Affirmative. But it doesn't seem to be top of their priority list right now."

Dougie sighed. His cool was rapidly disappearing behind another growing storm of anger. "Tell them, if they don't get their priorities right soon, I'll put this thing down on their airport without their help. Tell them I'll land with or without their permission. Tell them that, Watchdog."

"Wilco, old chap."

*

Maggie Loughlin shook her head as she watched the captain.

MacNabb had lapsed into a semi-conscious state, probably a reaction to his exertion, she decided. She called Ros Dyson to the upper deck and made sure the stewardess understood the importance of staying with the pilot, whatever happened. They couldn't afford the risk of him blundering onto the flight deck in his present state.

More important than Fergus MacNabb, right now, was the DEA agent. He wanted to talk to her and that could only mean one thing. He knew the truth.

When she was sure that there would be no further trouble with MacNabb, she led the narcotics investigator down to the main deck and forward to a row of empty seats in the front section.

"Okay," she began, "what exactly do you want to know?" She didn't want to be interrogated yet again, but if it got him off her back, she would talk to him.

He looked remarkably calm in the light of the danger that faced them all. For a few seconds he looked at her with an enquiring expression. Then he said, "Tell me about your relationship with Captain MacNabb."

She frowned. Why was he asking about that? He probably knew most of it anyway. But if it kept him happy, she'd tell him. "I know him quite well socially. He's a great guy in his own way."

"You sleep with him?"

"Boy, you don't beat about the bush do you? Okay, so I've slept with him in the past. And I still sleep with him now and then. There's no law against it, is there?"

"What do you get out of it?"

"A good shag."

"Don't play games with me, Miss Loughlin. What do you get

out of the relationship?"

Maggie stared into his eyes. A direct gaze that stabbed right back at her. It frightened her, but she fought to control her reactions. She chose her words carefully. "What exactly are you insinuating?"

"I'm not insinuating anything, Miss Loughlin. I'm asking. Did he give you anything—" He paused to emphasise the word 'anything'. "Did he ever give you anything at all in return for sleeping with him?"

A surge of anger rose inside her, bringing the taste of bile to her gullet. "He didn't pay me, if that's what you're suggesting. I'm not a prostitute. So just you watch what you say."

"He needn't have paid you in cash. What about drugs? Did he ever supply you with drugs?"

She leaned back and clenched her teeth, her mind whirling with disparate thoughts. Unable to keep her voice steady, she turned away from him. "No."

"Now look me in the face and say that."

"Who do you think you are?" She was still unable to face him. "This aircraft is in imminent danger of crashing into the sea and you're wasting my time making stupid suggestions about my private life."

"Nice act, Miss Loughlin. But it doesn't cut any ice with me. We know about your drug habit. We've known for some time. So how about you cut out the little girl innocence with me, eh?"

She suddenly swung her head back to look him in the eye. "Just what the hell are you after?"

"Narcotics, Miss Loughlin. We want to know who organises the transatlantic cocaine run on Sinclair International flights, who carries the stuff and who supplies it. And the answers to those questions are tied up with one more question. Who killed Sally Scrimgeour?"

Maggie shook her head and tried to marshal her thoughts into some cogent response.

When she failed to reply, the DEA agent continued, "You might as well tell me, I'll find out sooner or later."

"Or die with the rest of us when the aircraft crashes."

"In which case it won't harm you to tell me the truth."

She thought fast, her face warm with annoyance and indecision. If there was any chance that she would come out of this alive, she had to make sure that she wouldn't be promptly arrested for involvement in Fergus MacNabb's drug operation. She had to offload the blame while the opportunity existed. She thought fast. Could she offload the blame and leave her own slate squeaky clean? Probably not that clean, but clean enough. Besides, she didn't have any other option in her mind.

"Okay, I'll talk," she said.

"Good." The agent smiled easily. "Tell me all about it in your own words."

"Captain—" She had hardly begun before the words dried in her throat.

"Take your time. We ain't gonna crash in the next few seconds."

"Fergus MacNabb is involved in an operation to smuggle cocaine across the Atlantic. Is that what you wanted to know?"

"We know that already. Tell me the rest."

"Okay. He has contacts among the ground staff at Kennedy: cleaners, engineers, those sorts of people. And they get the stuff through security checks. There are others who collect it when it's been through security. They take it on board the aircraft, carry it across the ocean and pass it on to contacts at the other end. Fergus usually goes for a lot of small consignments rather than one big one."

"You know a lot about it?"

"Fergus talked."

"And you said nothing to the cops?"

"He threatened me."

"Really?" The DEA man looked sceptical. "Who supplies the stuff?"

"I don't know his name. Fergus simply calls him 'the big man'. You'll have to ask Fergus."

"All right. Now tell me, how did Mrs Scrimgeour get involved?"

"She was having an affair with Fergus. Somehow — I don't know how — she and Fergus got themselves into a real bust-up. I guess Fergus must have been pretty mad at her because he planted some cocaine in her handbag. His plan was to use her as a dupe. But she found the coke by accident and she got really rattled about it. First she was going to tell her husband and then she threatened to tell the cops."

"MacNabb killed her?"

"I don't know. He didn't tell me." Maggie countered the contraction in her throat with a hoarse cough.

"I bet he did."

"All right, I'll tell you. It was some guy Fergus knows." She wondered if he would notice how much her hands were shaking or whether he would be clued up enough to interpret the telltale body-language signs that indicated she was lying. "The first I heard of Sally's death was when I got to Kennedy just before the flight."

"I'm not sure I believe you, Miss Loughlin. You had some cosy arrangement going with MacNabb. You know who did the knifing, don't you?" It was a direct accusation.

She flinched. "No." Once again she had to look away as she replied.

"Okay. Let's go back to your own involvement. When did you last get a fix from Captain MacNabb?"

"Yesterday."

"And what did he tell you about his plans for Scrimgeour?"

"Nothing more than I've already I told you. I don't know the guy he got to do it. Or maybe he did it himself. That's enough. Now, leave me alone!" Before she realised what she was doing, she was on her feet, running back into the economy-class cabin, her whole body shaking with fear.

Chapter 14

The dark grey shape of the Nimrod sat in precarious formation about one hundred metres ahead and slightly to the right of the 747. Dougie tried to hold his aircraft steady, keeping the Nimrod fuselage visible in the right-hand side of his windscreen. It was an impossible task. The buffeting air caused the two aeroplanes to gently see-saw up and down in relation to each other. His father had once said that when he was flying that close to another aircraft, he wanted to shoot it down.

It had been a day out for Eric and his two schoolboy sons. They hired a flying club Cessna 172 and flew across the Solent to the Isle of Wight. It was a gin-clear day, and Eric Nyle was enjoying the experience of showing off his flying skills. Dougie and his brother listened intently as their father related, yet again, the excitement of his combat experience in Korea. They saw another club aircraft flying at the same altitude just five hundred yards off on their starboard side.

Instantly, Eric jerked the column and turned the Cessna on a sixpence, positioning it behind the other craft, a perfect position from which to loose off a single deadly burst of canon fire.

"Now I have him!" he shouted with exhilaration. "Now I can shoot him down and he'll never know what hit him."

Dougie had been horrified. They were close enough to the other aircraft to see the passengers, maybe a family out for a fun ride, and his father was talking of killing them. He was thinking only of other people's deaths. It suddenly hit young Dougie that fighter aircraft were instruments of slaughter. They were designed purely for killing. In the space of a few seconds he knew with total certainty that he did not have the stomach to kill people.

All he wanted to do now was to save four hundred lives.

The chances of getting the 747 safely down rapidly receded as the minutes ticked away and the big Boeing's fuel tanks grew steadily drier. Would he ever see Jenny again? The odds were getting longer and longer. His only genuine glimmer of hope lay some miles away to the left where he could see a darker shade of grey, a hazy line drawn along the boundary where the water met the cloud. That line was a comforting reassurance that they were flying close to the Ayrshire coast.

Dougie shot another quick glance at his panel. The VOR beam bar was nicely lined up with the direction of the radio beacon at Turnberry, confirming that he was on the correct course. Even if the Nimrod were to suddenly disappear from the scene, he would be able to follow the bearing of the signals and arrive over the top of the radio beacon.

A sudden thought jarred him. They were approaching Prestwick from the north-west and the VOR radio beacon at Turnberry was some miles south of Prestwick. If they continued heading directly towards the beacon, they would bypass the airport.

They couldn't afford to fly on past their only hope of getting down alive. They should have made a left turn by now. They should be heading towards a point north of the beacon to make an approach into Prestwick.

He jabbed his transmit switch. "Watchdog from Sinclair 984. We're still heading directly towards the Turnberry VOR."

"Affirmative, Sinclair 984." Just the one short reply. Nothing else. No sign of realisation in the Englishman's voice, no change of course, not even an explanation.

Dougie stabbed at the button again. "When can we peel off towards the airport?"

"Not yet, Sinclair 984. Prestwick ATC is still refusing landing permission. They want you to hold over the VOR at Turnberry until they decide what to do about you."

"Hold? Christ, man. We're—"

"They know."

Dougie allowed his unbridled anger to erupt over the airwaves. "What's the matter with those guys? Don't they know we just can't hang on up here much longer? We're getting short of fuel."

"I've told them all the details, Sinclair 984. But they have some major problems at the moment."

"So have we! Look, maybe I should call them direct."

"If you wish. They're dealing with another emergency on the radar frequency, but you could give them a call on the tower frequency. However, I should warn you they are being a tad stubborn."

"I can be stubborn, too, Watchdog."

"Fair enough, old chap. But I honestly don't think you'll get much change out of them at the moment."

"We'll see about that!"

*

Mission Commander Sharpe gritted his teeth and glanced across at the *Washington* shuttle pilot. Guthrie looked calm, but what was going through his mind right then? Regrets for getting involved in this mission? Well, there was no turning back now; they had long since passed the point of no return.

"Propellants are gone." Guthrie acknowledged the instruments indicating their main engine fuel was now fully discharged. They would not need it from here on.

Sharpe drew a long breath. "Time for a bit of central heating."

The *Washington* was just hitting the upper reaches of the atmosphere five thousand miles from its landing point, flying at an altitude of four hundred thousand feet. From here on things would get more than a touch dangerous. As it fell, belly first, through the upper levels of the atmosphere, friction would heat the craft's lower surface. Parts of the craft would reach 2750 degrees Fahrenheit and the air surrounding the shuttle would form a plasma wave, causing a radio blackout.

Sharpe fisted his hands. He was an experienced military pilot but he'd never felt fear like this before. He forced himself to concentrate — keep a clear picture of what was about to happen.

From twenty-five minutes before landing until approximately

thirteen minutes before landing, they would have no radio contact with the ground while the shuttle gradually changed from a spacecraft into a very large and heavy glider.

They had only one chance to get this right.

*

The Prestwick visual control room was crowded. Trisha wasn't sure who most of them were, or where they had come from, so she quietly ignored them and stared out of the window at the murky approach to the main runway.

Behind her, Colonel Lawrence muttered, "Ten minutes to touchdown." His comment was followed by a short buzz of excitement from the other military personnel.

The shuttle pilot kept his radio tuned to the airport radar control frequency throughout his final approach manoeuvres and Trisha monitored the frequency from her aerodrome control console. She had a number of other radio frequencies set up on her selector box.

A new voice suddenly broke into her headset, using the aerodrome control frequency.

"Prestwick Tower, this is Sinclair 984, do you read me? Over." The voice was sharp, but tinged with fatigue.

Trisha hastily leaned forward to reply. "Sinclair 984, this is Prestwick Tower. I read you strength four. Pass your message."

"Tower from Sinclair 984, we are a badly damaged 747 flying low level about five miles due west of you. I request immediate diversion into Prestwick and immediate landing clearance. Over."

"Roger, Sinclair 984. Standby." Forgetting her tower discipline, Trisha craned her neck towards the dark mass of faces behind her. "It's Sinclair 984, the 747. They're with me on the tower frequency and they want immediate clearance to divert in here."

Lawrence folded his arms across his chest and shook his head. He pointed towards the runway. "It's far too late for that. Less than ten minutes before *Washington's* touchdown."

Trisha turned her attention to Keating, the ATC Business

Manager. His white face betrayed the fact that he was in a state of shock, unable to comprehend the enormity of the situation. Trisha knew she would get no help there.

Beside and behind him, other tower occupants remained silent, as if they too were reluctant to get involved in a problem outside their immediate scope or influence. All that mattered to them was the safe recovery of the *Washington*.

"Well? What should I tell him?" Trisha set her mouth firmly as she turned again and stared in turn at each of the men behind her.

Only Lawrence made a determined reply. "I told you. You must refuse landing permission." He glanced down at the digital clock on the aerodrome control console. "*Washington* is going to block that runway for some time even after it lands, you know that."

"Can't you push it out of the way or something?"

"Not immediately. It's going to take time. Besides, you know now why it must have priority." He lowered his voice. "Damn it all, Trisha, it has a nuclear bomb on board. An armed nuclear bomb. Remember? Tell the 747 crew we can't allow them to land here."

Trisha swung back to her console as the 747 pilot called again.

"Prestwick Tower, this is Sinclair 984. I've turned towards you and I have the airfield in sight. What is your wind and your pressure? Over."

"Sinclair 984, the wind is three four zero degrees at two five knots, gusting to three five knots. Pressure is nine nine six millibars. The runway is three-one."

"Roger. I am joining right-hand downwind for runway three-one." The pilot spoke decisively with a hint of annoyance.

Trisha sympathised. In his shoes, she'd be livid. She pressed the transmit switch firmly. "Standby, Sinclair 984. We may not be able to accept you here."

Again she hesitated, unable to bring herself to refuse the pilot of an aircraft in dire straits. It went against all her training and all her natural inclinations. At the back of her mind was a vague hope that it might be possible to get both craft down safely. But it was only a remote hope.

"Tell him to leave the area, Trisha." Lawrence's voice was sharp and decisive, as if he had taken charge of air traffic control at Prestwick airport.

"And all the people on board?"

"Tell him to leave the area!"

Silence settled over the visual control room. Trisha seethed.

"But where should I instruct him to go? There's no other airport open."

"He'll have to ditch in the sea." Lawrence looked across the runway to where two Royal Navy Sea King helicopters sat on a snow covered landing pad. Their rotors were already winding up.

"But they won't last more than a few minutes."

Lawrence shrugged. "Your Royal Navy's 819 squadron has been alerted. Tell the 747 pilot that rescue services are at hand. Tell him anything, but get that goddamn plane away from here."

Trisha's hand hovered over the transmit switch.

In the background Keating murmured, "Oh, my God!"

Trisha slowly lowered her finger onto the switch.

*

The *Washington* had emerged from the radio blackout. It was now one big unpowered glider with only one place to go. The aerodynamic speedbrake on the fin deployed to continue the process of slowing down.

The radio crackled in Sharpe's ears. "*Washington*, this is Highball, do you read me?"

"Read you loud and clear, Highball."

"Roger. We have you on radar. You're still looking good."

"Looking good?" Sharpe silently cursed. Looking good when they could be fried to a frazzle if they hit the ground the wrong way? Looking good when they could be on course to kill tens of thousands of people down there?

The whole damned show was so offbeat no one could possibly know what might yet go wrong. Their radar guidance came from a variety of improvised sources including an E3A Sentry aircraft positioned over the ocean, US Navy warships sited at various strategic locations and the radar systems at Atlantic House and Prestwick Airport.

Sharpe took a calming breath. He gestured across the flight deck to Guthrie. "It's all yours now, Pete. Just get us down in one piece."

"Had that in mind, George."

*

Dougie listened in disbelief. How could the woman refuse landing permission to a damaged aircraft?

"Prestwick, what is your reason for refusal of landing permission?"

Ten seconds elapsed before the controller replied. "I'm sorry, Sinclair 984. We are dealing with another emergency. Please leave the area at once. Over."

"Negative! Negative!" Dougie blasted the words into his microphone and glanced across the flight deck at Kovak. He kept his thumb firmly on the transmit switch as he added, "To hell with you, Prestwick!" The words were hardly out of his mouth before he regretted them. They showed everyone on the ground he was fast losing his cool.

The flight engineer stared back open-mouthed. "That's telling 'em. All of 'em."

Dougie gritted his teeth. "We're going to put this ship down on that runway, whether they like it or not."

*

Colonel Dan Lawrence moved in closer to the control desk and picked up a spare headset at the standby control desk. He checked the bank of radio selectors and picked out a military UHF frequency.

His finger hovered over the transmit switch. He could not allow that 747 to land, but did he have the guts to take the last-ditch decision to stop it? Could he order one of the fighter chase planes to shoot down an unarmed civilian airliner with four hundred or more people on board? Could he do it?

He glanced sideways at the controller, taking in her ashen face and wide-eyed anxiety. She didn't understand, hadn't a clue what was at stake here. That sort of decision had to be taken by a military mind.

Could he do it? Yes. He could do it.

*

Dougie firmed up his grip on the control yoke. They were close in now, flying low downwind and parallel to the main runway. Dougie peered out of his right-hand screen and studied the snowbound airport. An armada of military aircraft was parked on the short, snow-covered subsidiary runway. RAF trucks were gathered close by the main runway. A mishmash of slushy trails followed the vehicles.

"There's something hellishly odd going on here." Kovak's voice cut across the flight deck, echoing Dougie's own thoughts. "What do you think it is?"

"Another emergency, so they say." A moment of doubt entered Dougie's brain, a sudden thought that there might possibly be a good, justifiable reason for the controller's refusal of landing permission.

"Too bad," Kovak retorted. "We've got four hundred lives up here, and they're all depending on us getting this crate down there on the ground."

"You're right." Dougie cast the doubts from his mind. He had no choice but to land. His priority was the safety of the passengers and crew aboard Sinclair 984. "Gear down please, Sammy."

Kovak leaned forward and selected the undercarriage lever down. He tapped the indicator lights. "The lights are all green, but don't count on it being a correct indication. I doubt if you can rely on the port main undercarriage being fully secure."

"I'll keep the weight off the port side as long as I can. The port wing undercarriage may hold us if we set it down gently at low speed."

"Unless it's also damaged. Why don't you try a tight turn to throw the gear into place? Just in case it's not fully down."

"We're flying too low for that sort of thing."

"Are you afraid the poor cow might fall apart?"

Dougie pressed his transmit switch again. "Tower from Sinclair 984. I am about to turn final for runway three-one. Over."

The response was sudden and immediate. "Negative, Sinclair 984. Negative! Overshoot. I say again, overshoot. We cannot allow you to land off this approach. Over."

"For God's sake, Prestwick! We have to land. We're badly damaged and almost out of fuel!" Even as he spoke he was easing the big Boeing round in a gentle right-hand turn which would take it towards the runway approach path.

"Negative." This time the controller's reply held a clearly perceptible tremble. "You must not land. I say again, you must not land. Overshoot and climb straight ahead. There is a priority flight on approach behind you."

Dougie gripped the control column tighter as the 747 turned onto the final approach path. The runway was sliding into view in what remained of the shattered front windscreen, the edge lights easing into line to create a welcome sight to a pilot who was nursing a sick aircraft.

Who had more priority than a 747 with over four hundred people on board, only two engines running and a severely damaged fuselage? And almost out of fuel, to boot. At any moment from here on the remaining engine power might be cut off as the big RB211s became starved of fuel, and then the 747 would become a giant glider. When such a machine hit the ground, hundreds of lives would be wiped out in a moment.

"Prestwick, this is Sinclair 984. I am continuing my approach."

"Negative, Sinclair 984. You are instructed to abandon your approach. I repeat, you are instructed to abandon your approach. There is a priority flight behind you, closing fast. Overshoot

217

immediately!"

Priority flight? What flight could hold so much priority that they could condemn the passengers and crew of a damaged 747? Whatever it was, it had the controller in one hell of a state. What was going on down there? If Eric Nyle were flying this aeroplane, he would land despite the controller's instructions. He would do whatever was needed to get the 747 down safely. But Eric Nyle was *not* flying the aircraft.

Dougie pressed the transmit switch, fully prepared to refuse to obey the order. Then his sense of discipline pulled him up sharp. If they ordered him to overshoot, there had to be a reason. There had to be.

"Tower, what is that priority flight?"

"The flight behind you is a space shuttle. It is closing with you fast. Abort your approach now!"

It's a what?

Dougie hesitated for little more than a second. In that brief instant of time, something deep inside his brain took a firm hold of his decision-making process. Something instinctive and powerful. His actions had been at fault. He must now believe the aerodrome controller. He *had* to believe her. It was not blind obedience, but rather a matter of trust in what he was hearing over his radio telephone.

He jerked his body forward, grabbed the throttle levers and pushed them into the full thrust position.

"Gear up, Sammy!" he shouted. "Quickly!"

*

Lawrence put down the headset as the 747 began its overshoot. He had psyched himself up to making that decision to shoot it down and he had failed. He had hesitated and he had failed. So, the bastards inside the 747 had done the right thing and abandoned their approach? So what? That didn't alter the fact that he had not been able to order them to be shot down.

He just damned well couldn't do it. And he was ashamed.

He glanced again at the controller. Was she aware of his failing? Damn her! Damn them all!

*

The cloud base at Prestwick was down to seven hundred feet, far below what was considered safe for a shuttle landing. Too late to worry about that now.

Sharpe risked a quick glance across the flight deck at Guthrie. The *Washington* pilot's face was tight with tension. Either they would walk away from this or the world was about to enter a new Dark Age.

The airfield radar controller's voice broke through the excitement. "Surface wind three five zero at twenty knots."

"Roger," Sharpe responded.

At 1750 feet he saw only cloud, but the pilot initiated the first flare to reduce his descent angle from twenty degrees to one and a half degrees. Seconds later, the cloud broke in front of them, giving way to a view of the Ayrshire coast. The long concrete and tarmac runway at Prestwick stretched into the distance.

"Gear down and locked." Sharpe tried to keep the tension from his voice. Snow pounded the windscreen, but not enough to obscure the view for landing.

Guthrie grinned. "We're in with a chance, George. In with a chance."

"Jesus! What's that?" Sharpe suddenly started in his seat and stared ahead. Beyond the upwind end of the runway he caught a short glimpse of a 747 climbing away. A 747 taking off? What were those guys on the ground playing at?

*

As the shuttle descended out of the cloud, a hush fell over the visual control room. Sensing history in the making, Trisha leaned forward and selected the desk loudspeaker so that everyone present would hear the voice of the *Washington's* transmissions. Emerging from the cloud, the shuttle burst into view. Someone at the back of the room made a short incoherent cry of astonishment, but most of the tower occupants remained silent.

The spectacle of the shuttle breaking through the cloud base sent a highly charged shiver through Trisha. She held her breath as the craft crossed the aerodrome boundary fence. Behind her she sensed Dan Lawrence moving closer and grasping the back of her seat.

"Easy, baby. Easy," the big American's voice whispered close to her ear.

Over the threshold, the shuttle's nose came up into landing attitude. The army of military vehicles raced onto the runway behind it.

"Now," Lawrence breathed as the *Washington's* main wheels glided over the touchdown zone markers.

Trisha felt the back of her seat move as the Colonel's grip tightened while they waited for the main landing gear to kiss the ground.

Lawrence's voice grew louder. "Put it down now, for chrissake."

Trisha tapped her pen firmly but anxiously against the desk top. The shuttle touched down less than a third of the way along the runway. A burst of smoke enveloped the wheels and then the craft began to slow down.

"He's going to make it!" Lawrence's excitement got the better of him. "What a pilot! He's going to make it!"

Another swarm of vehicles darkened the runway behind the shuttle; fire appliances and trucks carrying huge tarpaulins that would be draped over the craft as soon as it came to a halt. Hiding the shuttle from public view was now a priority. Suddenly, another puff of white smoke burst around the port main undercarriage wheel.

Trisha jabbed at her transmit switch. "Fire one, Tower. Is that a brake fire on the port wheel?"

"Affirmative, Tower."

The shuttle pilot was using his brakes heavily to pull up before the end of the runway, but the heat of the brake pressure was igniting the wheels.

Trisha quickly selected the approach radar control frequency and called to the shuttle pilot, "*Washington* from Tower. Your port wheel is burning."

Even as she spoke, she saw that the port tyre was disintegrating and the shuttle was swerving across the runway. The pilot tried to correct the drift, but his correction was too sharp and the port tyre burst away from the wheels.

Whatever happened now, the runway would be blocked for some time to come.

There was no longer any remote possibility of allowing the damaged 747 to land.

Chapter 15

Dougie eased forward the thrust levers for the two working engines and prayed that the remaining fuel would last just a little longer. If it didn't, they had little hope of getting out of this mess alive.

At least, he reasoned, their overshoot path took them out over the sea so the 747 would not kill anyone on the ground in the event of it falling out of the sky.

The strain of the two engines working at full power added to the noise on the flight deck. Below, the airport perimeter road disappeared beneath the 747's nose. The aircraft climbed agonisingly slowly as the Prestwick golf course quickly followed the road, vanishing beneath the wing. A narrow strand of beach slipped by, and then they were over the sea.

"God help us now," Dougie breathed.

Kovak leaned forward to peer out of the front windscreen, screwing up his eyes as the force of the air drew tears. "Did you hear what I heard, Dougie?"

"Course I heard it."

"A space shuttle! Goddammit, what was a space shuttle doing back there?" His voice came out as a whisper against the roar of the wind.

"Who knows? Ask NASA, or the controllers at Prestwick." Dougie cut short his response as he levelled off the aircraft at five hundred feet and pulled back the thrust levers a touch. Any higher and they would be swallowed in the cloud. He had yet to decide on where to fly the aircraft.

Kovak continued to stare ahead. "They must reckon one space shuttle is worth more than four hundred people on board a 747."

The aircraft bucked as it hit a patch of turbulence. Dougie clenched the control column. "That seems to be the case, Sammy."

"God forgive them." Kovak sank back into his seat. "But what happens to us now?"

"We could ditch in the sea. But I don't fancy our chances if we do that."

"So we're up shit creek?"

"Well and truly." Dougie gritted his teeth. What other options did he have? Watchdog had mentioned that Tiree had a marginal weather clearance. It was only a small island airfield — and none of the Hebridean Islands airfields were built to cope with a 747 — but it was dry land. That had to be better than putting *Tartan Arrow* down in the cold waters of the Atlantic. Would they be able to divert there before the fuel ran out? It was doubtful.

Tiree had another major problem. To get to the island would mean flying back over the Mull of Kintyre and climbing up into cloud.

But the alternatives didn't bear thinking about.

"Get back to your own seat, Sammy. We're going to see if we can restart the port outer engine."

Kovak unbuckled his seatbelt. "You've a plan?"

"Nothing you can rely on," Dougie said, "but we have to be ready to try everything else before we give up and put the aircraft down in the sea. I figure we may be able to divert to one of the islands." He scanned across his limited panel of instruments. They would need some form of navigation assistance.

He adjusted his radio microphone boom in front of his face, changed his radio frequency back to 121.5 megahertz, and called, "Watchdog, this is Sinclair 984, do you read me?"

"Sinclair 984, this is Watchdog. I read you. Sorry about the fracas at Prestwick, chaps. Nothing I could do to persuade them to let you land. The shuttle's tyres have burst. They can't move it off the runway."

"Roger. We're running out of time, Watchdog. I don't want to ditch in the sea, so I'm going to try to put us down on one of the islands. You said the weather was marginally better over Tiree. Have you any other ideas?"

"None at all, I'm afraid. All the mainland airports are now closed by the weather. Glasgow has fifty metres visibility in snow and Edinburgh has a cloud base of less than one hundred feet. Tiree is the only airfield now available for a visual landing. It had a five hundred foot cloud base when we last checked."

"It has a tarmac runway, doesn't it?"

"Affirmative, but not very strong and not very long. In fact, it has three hard runways and there's a lot of flat empty land all round them. That flat land could be a lifesaver for you.

"Okay, Watchdog. Let's give it a try."

"I'm coming up on your starboard side, Sinclair 984. Let me tuck in close and I'll try to lead you there."

Dougie leaned back in his seat and shouted at Kovak. "We're going to try to put this heap of metal down on Tiree."

"God help us all."

"You'd better pray that he does." Dougie shook his head. He drew a mental picture of the Hebridean Islands. Tiree lay among the inner group, small and remote. Too small and too remote. But he had to try it; there was no other option. Apart from ditching.

"Let's get started, Watchdog. I'm almost out of fuel."

"Follow me, old boy. It's about half an hour's flying at this speed. Can you continue for another thirty minutes?"

"I don't know, Watchdog. I just don't know." Dougie turned to Kovak who now sat at the flight engineer position. "How do our chances look for getting that third engine spooled up, Sammy?"

"That depends. If it stopped because we ran out of fuel in the port tanks, we have a chance."

"I thought you were cross feeding?"

"I was, but the fuel system out in that wing is shot to hell. Look, I'm going to try something different to get fuel across to the port outer. Give me a minute and then get ready to wind it up again."

"Very well. But, don't waste any fuel. We need at least thirty minutes' flying time."

"Thirty minutes?" Kovak snorted. "Now you're asking too much."

"Sammy — I *need* that thirty minutes."

The Watchdog pilot's voice cut in. "Sinclair 984, we'll have to climb back into cloud. There's still no clear route along the Crinan canal."

"Standby, Watchdog. We still only have two engines running, but we're trying to get the port outer relit."

"Roger, Sinclair 984. I suggest the sooner you start your climb the better. Make your heading 340 degrees and, once you have the engine running, climb straight ahead. We'll be watching you on our radar."

"I've heard that before, Watchdog."

"We've just got a weather update. There's a temporary clearance presently sitting around the island of Tiree, but a bank of low cloud is creeping in very fast. We haven't much time so we'll take a direct route if we can. Tune in to the Tiree VOR and let me know once you pick up a signal."

"Roger." Dougie leaned across to his navigation console and retuned the VOR receiver to the Tiree beacon. The aircraft was flying too low to pick up the signals, but he expected the instrument to come on line once he started to climb.

Gripping the column with both hands, he turned again to the flight engineer. "Okay, Sammy. Can we have a go at winding up that engine now?"

*

Jock waited ten minutes before he walked back into the operations room. He pulled up a seat near the Hebrides Sector controller and put a hand to his head. His thoughts swirled frantically. Sally was dead and MacNabb was somehow responsible.

His head was host to a deep penetrating ache, an ache so full of torment that he could not even picture her face. Without any conscious effort, that outrage gradually became a desire for revenge.

The activity about him in the operations room grew to fever pitch, but his own private thoughts narrowed down to just one objective. To hit back at MacNabb.

The direct telephone line from Prestwick Airport buzzed at the Hebrides Sector. The controller stabbed a finger at the lighted button on his panel and listened to the message.

"Thank heavens for that," he responded and deselected the line.

"Well?" The watch manager edged closer to him.

"The shuttle is down more or less in one piece," the controller announced. "They had a brake fire on one wheel, but managed to pull up at the end of the runway. And the Americans got their covers over the whole ship within two minutes. Looks like they've got away with it, and they've hidden the evidence."

"Can they tow the shuttle clear of the runway?"

"No." The controller shook his head. "The undercarriage is damaged so the runway will be blocked for some time."

Jock stood on the sidelines, hearing the message only as a peripheral to his inner thoughts.

"That puts an end to any hope of the 747 landing here." The watch manager folded his arms. About him, chatter broke out as some of the tension began to slowly subside. But it was only a marginal lessening of the stress. The immediate problem of the space shuttle was ended, but they still had a major emergency on their hands.

"Hang on a minute. It's Watchdog calling again." The Hebrides controller listened to a message in his headphones and then responded, "Roger, Watchdog. Keep me informed." He turned to the people about him and announced blandly, "The 747 is diverting to Tiree."

"Tiree? You're joking," the manager gasped. "They think they can land a 747 there? They haven't a cat's chance in hell. For a start, how will they get there?"

The radar controller pulled aside his microphone boom. "According to Watchdog, the 747's VOR receiver is working."

Jock closed in behind the Hebrides Sector suite and watched the radar echo of Sinclair 984 as it headed off towards the Western Islands. From the still empty depths at the back of his mind, a new pinpoint of intent suddenly shone through the murk, the first narrow shaft of light to illuminate his despondency. Like the click of a switch creating light, what he had to do sprang into focus.

He pictured the flight deck of the 747, conjuring up an image of MacNabb struggling to fly his crippled aircraft towards the Tiree VOR beacon, towards some hope of safety. It was no foregone conclusion that he would be able to land the aircraft without massive loss of life, but it was a chance. And that chance would have to be eliminated if MacNabb was to die.

Jock felt no overpowering emotion in the knowledge of what he was about to do. It was just a simple job that would lead to a just and proper conclusion. More people than MacNabb would die, but they were as good as dead anyway. Every last one of them. Not a hope in hell of survival.

He felt strangely lightheaded as he stood up, confident that he was about to do the right thing. Confident in a way he had never felt before, as if some other brain was guiding him. He stopped abruptly as his vision seemed to tunnel in, then open out again. His head swam. Then it cleared and the same positive aim came back into view. I'm doing this for you, Sally. Just for you.

He sidled away to the standby control suite at the end of the room. It was designed for use when any of the main control suites went out of service and was fitted with all the radio frequencies. He selected the emergency frequency, 121.5 megahertz, the frequency the 747 pilot was using to communicate with the Nimrod. He placed a thick operations manual across the transmit switch to hold it down. As long as it was jammed in the 'transmit' position, no one else could use that frequency. Sinclair 984 would have no guidance from Watchdog.

Now for the next step. His head swam again and he paused until it cleared and his eyes refocused. The systems control room — that was where he had to go. It was immediately adjacent to the operations room. This was where the duty engineer had overall control of all radio navigation equipment throughout Scotland. The control equipment was called NARIC — Navigation Aid

Remote Indication and Control — and was operated through two IBM PCs on the system control desk.

Jock was not surprised when he edged into the partitioned area to find the desk unmanned. The duty engineer's tasks often took him away from the system control desk to other parts of the building.

Seating himself in front of one of the PCs, he called up the control link to the Tiree VOR. It was all too easy to access into the radio site on the island and instruct the beacon to close down. It was just too easy by far. That one desk was used to control all the beacon transmitter sites remotely, saving the cost of extra staff on the islands. He pressed the sequence of keys that brought up onto the screen the commands for the Tiree link. *I'm doing this for you, Sally. Just for you.*

Then his head was swimming yet again.

*

The port outer engine was back on line.

Kovak heaved a sigh of relief and tried to make some sense of the instrument readings. He had a thick Boeing 747 Operations Manual open on the ledge at the bottom of the instrument panel. It wasn't much help in finding an answer to his cross-feed problems, but better than nothing.

He studied the fuel flow meters. Three of them showed sensible readings of fuel to the three working engines. He might be able to get a rough idea of the amount of fuel left if he could calculate the amount lost by leakage.

At the bottom right of the panel were four vertical indicators showing the level of engine vibration. The two starboard engines looked healthy, but the port outer was beyond the limit.

"We've got excessive engine vibration on the port side," he called to the first officer.

"Let it ride. Tell me if it gets worse."

The first officer was right. What was the point of worrying about a bit of vibration in one engine when they might fall out of the sky at any moment? Kovak's confidence in Nyle was growing again. He was coping well with the emergency. If anyone could get them safely on the ground, it was this guy.

*

The KC135 tanker was flying close to the Mull of Kintyre and the crew's options were running out. Judson had to do something, and soon.

He reached out a hand to the radio panel and selected the VHF frequency he had used to talk to Highball, the airborne command post. Then he gingerly increased the volume. Youngman looked across at him quizzically, but Judson returned the look with a dark frown. As the volume came up, they heard a general patter of radio-telephone communication, much of it of little value to Judson and his heavily damaged KC135.

"Looking for some clues," he called across to Youngman. His attention picked up when he heard another KC135 check in on the frequency.

"Highball, this is Gasser 61, do you read me?"

"Gasser 61, this is Highball, I read you strength five." It was the same voice Judson had spoken to earlier. It did not sound any more accommodating now.

"Highball, Gasser 61 is a KC135. We've given away all our gas and we need to land and refuel, over."

"Roger, Gasser 61. Have you sufficient fuel for a diversion to Keflavik, Iceland?"

"Affirmative, sir. But we'd prefer to land somewhere nearer if we can."

"That's understood, Gasser 61. The British have positioned a standby fuel supply at Machrihanish aerodrome. That's the closest place to you. Are you game to try landing there?"

"Highball, what sort of place is this Machrihanish?"

"It's a NATO base with ten thousand feet of runway. The British have a radar there to cover the emergency. You can call them on 125.9 VHF. The callsign is Coastwatch Radar."

"Roger. What's their weather like, Highball?"

"It's not too hot, Gasser 61. Our last report was... ah... it was eight eighths cloud at two hundred feet and snow showers. Visibility two hundred metres."

"Roger, Highball. That's well below limits. Guess we'll divert into Keflavik. Can you give us a steer—?"

Judson leaned across and deselected the VHF frequency. He gave Youngman a fierce look. "That's it, buddy. Machrihanish. That's where we're going. Get out the book and tell me what sort of facilities they've got there."

"If you say so, Paul." Youngman pulled a heavy document from behind his seat and studied it for several minutes. "Here we are. Like the man said, it's got a good long runway. If they've got some sort of radar, we could maybe give it a try. You reckon we should call Highball again?"

"No way. The bastards want us to ditch in the sea. They won't want us to block that Machrihanish runway when we put this heap of junk down on it."

"Reckon the Limeys at Machrihanish radar know that?"

"Only one way to find out, Lou." Judson clicked his VHF receiver to 125.9, turned up the volume and licked his lips. "Coastwatch Radar, this is Gasser 29. Do you read me, over?"

"Gasser 29, this is Coastwatch Radar on 125.9. I read you strength five. Pass your message."

"Coastwatch Radar, Gasser 29 is a KC135 tanker about fifteen miles from you on your three one zero VOR radial. We are flying at three hundred feet. We request directions for an immediate landing. Over."

"We have no information on you, Gasser 29."

"Roger, that's understood. We're short of fuel and we have to land quickly. Can you treat this as an emergency?" Judson mentally crossed his fingers. He hadn't let on that they were the collision flight in case Machrihanish had heard about it. But he had given them a reason to get their fingers out.

"Roger Gasser 29. What is your heading?" Contrary to Judson's expectations, the controller's voice remained calm.

"We're heading one three zero degrees. Straight towards you, sir."

"Gasser 29, I have no radar contact, you are below my cover. Continue heading towards the field and I will advise when I see you."

"Okay, Coastwatch. What's your weather?"

This was the important bit.

"Gasser 29, the weather is deteriorating. We now have a cloud base right down on the ground and the visibility is one hundred metres in thick snow. I can give you an emergency radar approach straight in to runway one-one."

Shit! Cloud on the ground. They had little hope of landing in that.

"Okay, Coastwatch. It doesn't sound too good," he said.

"Affirmative. I can give you a talkdown radar approach, but the visibility is against you."

"Let's give it a go, anyway, Coastwatch."

"Roger. I'm now picking up a faint echo on a bearing three one zero degrees from the field at a range of ten miles. Can you take a turn for identification?"

A turn? With the crate in the state it was? No way. They were in too much trouble already to be bothered with bending about the sky, just to confirm identification.

Judson responded, "Negative. Take that radar echo as us and bring us straight in."

"Roger. Check your wheels are down and locked. The approach would normally terminate at half a mile from touchdown, but I will continue to give instructions as long as I am able."

"Understood." As Judson spoke, Youngman leaned forward and selected the landing gear. He pulled down the lever and a triangle of three green lights flashed.

"Gasser 29, you are now nine miles from touchdown. There is no need to acknowledge further instructions." The controller's voice droned on, giving heading directions and distances-to-run.

Judson noted that the cloud was now closing in on them and he transferred his vision onto the aircraft instruments. "You watch for the field, Lou," he called across to Youngman. "And tell me the instant you see anything. And I mean anything!"

Youngman nodded. They had to see the runway to land. With no sight of the tarmac they would have to overshoot and then — he didn't know what then.

"Five miles from touchdown," the controller called. "You are now coming onto final approach track, well below the glide path. Your heading is good."

Too right they were below the glide path; they were still flying at only three hundred feet.

Still the voice crooned on. "Four miles from touchdown. You are well below the glide path. Continue heading one zero five degrees. You are clear to land from this approach."

"Anything out there?" Judson shouted.

"Nothin'," Youngman replied.

"Three miles from touchdown. Well below the glide path."

Judson felt his hands gripping the column with an intensity he had never before felt. It was like the column was welded to his hands.

"Two miles from touchdown. Your heading is good."

Keep your darned eyes peeled, Youngman!

"One mile from touchdown. You should begin your descent now. You are just coming onto the glide path."

This is it. Not much power left for a go-round.

"Half a mile from touchdown. You are on the centreline. Advise me if you get the field in sight."

"Anything?" Judson shouted.

"Nothin'."

*

Archie Curry drove slowly out of Westport in his new Ford Sierra. It was a company-owned car, but Curry loved it as if it were his own. He also loved the young woman sitting beside him although she was not — and could never be — his own.

He headed along the A83 road towards the south end of the Mull of Kintyre. Because of high ground running like a spine down the centre of the long peninsula, the road stuck close to the western coast until it reached the village of Westport. From there Curry cut off across Aros Moss, an area of flat peaty ground, hoping to reach Campbeltown on the east side within the hour.

Curry was a short, deep-chested man in his mid-thirties. He had been unhappily married for five years before he found comfort in the arms of the woman. As a sales rep for the Campbeltown Clansman Wool and Weaving Company, he travelled the country. It was a thriving business that paid him handsomely, even more handsomely since the old, tight-fisted managing director died and the company came into the hands of his generous son, Sandy Kilfedden. Curry's only worry was that the young woman with him was Kirsty Kilfedden, Sandy's wife.

"Ye'll drive carefully in this snow, Archie." The woman chided him as the car plodded across the Aros Moss. They were enveloped in thick cloud and heavy snow beat against the windscreen.

"And do I not always drive carefully?" Curry patted the wheel with a feeling of affection. "Mind you, 'tis a braw excuse tae be a wee bit late arrivin'."

"We'll no be that late."

"We will if we stop a wee while."

The look in Kirsty's eyes told him that he would not need to plead. She wanted him as much as he wanted her. Radio One was suggesting 'Let's Get Physical'. Olivia Newton John was hot as hell and her sexy new hit turned them both on.

"It's very cold out here," she said.

"Ah've a blanket on the back seat and ah'll soon warm ye up a bit."

"Aye. Ah'm sure ye will, at that."

His ardour rising rapidly, Curry drove the car off the road and stopped on the white carpet that bordered it. There was no sign of life about them, just the ghostly swirling cloud and the driving snow.

"Let's go in the back," he said with no preliminaries. None were needed. Kirsty Kilfedden grinned mischievously as he clambered over the front seat and pulled off his trousers. Her eagerness was evident in the way she followed him and pulled up the lower part of her dress.

"It's too cold by far tae strip off," she said flatly as she slipped her panties and tights to the floor. "Ah'd catch a chill fer sure."

Curry was too intent on unbuttoning the front of her dress. His face broke into a grin as he unfastened her bra. This was what he had been waiting for ever since they left Westport. This was why he had asked her to accompany him. His excitement grew as he bent his head to kiss her neck, then her breasts. She had the firmest and finest breasts he had ever felt, far too good to be wasted on just a husband.

She suddenly stiffened, her attention distracted.

"Archie, listen!"

"What is it?" His head came up from her cleavage.

"That noise." She stared ahead, her eyes straining to see something out there in the snow. "It's getting louder. Do you no hear it?"

Curry sat up and looked out of the windscreen into the white blankness ahead of the car.

"What is it, Archie?"

"I dinna ken—" he said.

Kirsty jerked her back upright and clasped a hand across her front. "It sounds awfy like an aeroplane. And it's gettin' louder."

"Aye." Curry untangled his arms from the woman. "And it's awfy low, tae."

He stared ahead into the swirling cloud. A darker patch grew quickly, directly in front of the vehicle. It fast became more solid as the noise rose to a scream. Then, in an instant, he realised what it was.

He pushed her aside with one hand and cried, "Christ! Get oot! Get oot o' the car! It's goin' tae hit us!"

Not waiting for her to follow, he jerked open the rear door and threw himself onto the snow. In that same moment, the huge metallic shape of an aircraft fuselage thundered out of the snow cloud, flying only a few feet above the ground. Its engines were screaming.

As it roared over the car, the noise of the jet engines pounded the ground and made the vehicle shudder violently. Curry held his hands over his head as he lay in the snow, terrified, shouting against the blast. His trousers flew out from the open door and were carried away on the wind. The hysterical screams of Kirsty Kilfedden burst out from inside the car.

The aircraft was flying so low that Curry could see the face of a pilot at the flight-deck windscreen, white and staring. For a moment he thought that one of the engines would hit the Sierra, but it slipped by with what seemed like inches to spare.

Then the blast of the engines hit him and he felt himself being rolled across the snow, bowled over like a ball. He shouted out, but his voice was carried away like a feather in a gale.

When he came to rest, he was dazed and confused. His head buzzed with the reverberation from the jet engines. Vaguely he became aware of the noise receding as the aircraft shot back into the swirling cloud. He levered himself up and looked back at the car. His lovely new Sierra was a mess. The windows were blown in and globules of dirty snow were plastered all over the bodywork.

"Kirsty!" He tried to stand. "Are you all right, Kirsty?"

The young woman staggered out of the rear seat, her dress still open at the front, her panties and tights around her ankles. Her eyes were staring up into the clouds.

"Oh, Archie."

Her staring eyes showed no awareness of the coldness as she stood there, only half-dressed. He felt a twinge of guilt when he realised that she had remained inside the back of the car throughout the ordeal.

"Are ye hurt?" he asked.

She shook her head and looked about. "The car. The poor wee

car. What will Sandy say aboot the car?"

Curry fixed his eyes on the girl's naked breasts. Sod the car, he thought. What will Sandy say if it comes out that they were both in the back seat?

*

"Gasser 29, this is Coastwatch Radar. Do you read me? Over." Tension dripped from the controller's voice.

"Coastwatch, we read you."

"Roger, 29." This time the tone was one of intense relief. "I have lost radar contact with you. What is your present position?"

"Ah, Coastwatch... we, ah... we had to overshoot there. We couldn't see your runway at all. We've made a left turn out and we're now flying back out over the sea, to the west of you." Judson tried to put a calm inflection into his voice, but it was a losing battle. "We, ah... we're at two hundred feet, just in the cloud base over the sea."

"Roger, Gasser 29. What is your intention now?"

"Standby."

Judson wiped away sweat with the back of his hand. What could they do now? There was no point in having a second go at landing here. They had come too darned close to killing themselves already. At least they hadn't hit that car.

"What do you think?" he asked Youngman.

The other pilot raised his eyebrows. "Darned if I know, Paul. Darned if I know. Reckon we're in the shits good and proper this time."

"We gotta do somethin'. And quick."

"Reckon we better do as Ocean Command said. We better ditch the old cow in the sea."

Judson shook his head savagely. "Not yet, buddy. Not yet."

"You got a better idea, Paul?"

"Might have. I guess I just might have. You remember that other airfield we passed a while back? The one on the island"

"Jeez, Paul, that place was too small for us."

"I know, I know. But the weather was better there. Besides, have you got another suggestion? The island is called Tiree, according to the charts. You search through the manual and dig out the VOR beacon frequency."

*

Dougie breathed deeply. Maybe he should have listened to Jenny when she talked about having another baby. If he got out of this alive, he would listen to her. He would make things better.

Meanwhile, the cloud that surrounded them was like a living, breathing animal. It held the 747 and played with it as a naughty child might play with a dying fly. It shook the aircraft fiercely until loose panels vibrated and fell to the floor. The wings flapped alarmingly.

He watched the flickering engine instruments and found himself silently praying. The port outer engine was running reasonably efficiently and Kovak was monitoring its fuel flow. If it would just continue running a little longer — at least until they were clear of the mainland — they were in with a chance.

Then the VOR beam bar came on line. It was reassurance that they were headed directly towards the island airfield.

"We've got past the north end of the Mull of Kintyre, Sammy," he called back to the flight engineer. "I'll need you in the captain's seat again." He studied the chart spread out on his lap. Part of the Isle of Mull now lay in their path, but only the low lying part of it. The high ground was off to their right and mostly the route would be over open sea.

Kovak lowered himself into the captain's seat just as Dougie leaned forward to tap the VOR receiver dial. "I hope it takes us straight there, Dougie. We're down to the dregs in the fuel tanks."

"You're reasonably confident about the fuel flow to the port engine?"

"As sure as I can be with those sick fuel flow dials." Kovak strapped himself into the seat. "At a rough guess, I reckon we now have about twenty minutes left. Give or take some."

Tiree aerodrome was now about twenty minutes' flying time away. This was the moment to confirm their plan with the Nimrod pilot.

"Watchdog, this is Sinclair 984. Over."

There was no reply. The roar of cloud billowing in through the cracked windscreen obliterated the usual background hiss in the headphones.

"Watchdog, this is Sinclair 984, do you read me? Over."

Again, no reply. Dougie cursed out loud. This was one hell of a time to lose radio-telephone contact with the shepherding Nimrod. They needed Watchdog's help to get them to the island.

Kovak's voice suddenly brought him back to the aircraft's instrument panel. "Dougie, look! Your beam bar has gone. The fail flag is out."

Dougie stared at his VOR receiver. A striped red and white flag appeared, indicating that he had lost all his guidance information from the Tiree beacon. That was it, the last straw. They were now flying blind in thick, clogging cloud with no radio and no guidance signals.

He bit his lip, blinked and stared at the instrument again. No mistake. He now had no means of determining where he was.

"What do we do now?" Kovak's voice cut across the flight deck.

Dougie's blood curdled. For some moments, he was at a loss.

*

Thick snow beat against the KC135's front screen. The plane was rounding the south end of the isle of Islay, skirting the cloud mass which sat over the island. The VOR picked up a signal from the Tiree beacon and the beam bar came on line.

"There she blows." Judson announced. "We just home in on that and find us a quiet little ol' Scottish island to put down on."

"*Crash* down on," Youngman corrected.

Youngman was right, Judson reflected. Even if they could see the airfield, they would be committed to a crash landing if only because the runways would be too short.

"Let's hope it — damn!" The VOR radio signal suddenly disappeared and the fail flag slid out. Judson leaned forward and tapped the dial but the flag remained obstinately at fail. "The goddamn thing's gone and screwed up on us, Lou."

Youngman grunted. "You just can't trust electronics when you need them." He leaned forward and tapped the instrument. Still, it remained at fail.

Judson looked out at the low cloud skimming above the aircraft. There were precious few visual contacts to help them navigate, just the mass of cloud around the southern islands. And the wild sea below.

"You reckon we can find Tiree without the VOR, Paul?"

"Guess — ah, I guess we have to, buddy. We just have to. We just stay on this heading and hope we see that friggin' island."

Chapter 16

Pamela MacReady glared at the two RAF security guards. Earlier in the morning the same two men had prevented her from entering the operations room. This time they were not going to stop her. One way or another, she was determined to get in.

"I work here," she insisted, staring down at the sergeant at his small desk, fixing him with a dark look of vexation. "I don't think you have the right to stop me from going inside."

The sergeant turned to his colleague with a grin and a shake of the head. Neither man appeared to remember the previous encounter.

The younger of the two men sighed. The older one adopted a pseudo-severe tone, as if he was addressing a child. "Young lady, if we choose to stop you coming into this building, we will."

"I want to get in there to do my job," she insisted, wondering if other staff had been treated the same way.

Suddenly the sergeant's manner changed and he leaned back in his seat, smiling. "Show me your ID card, honey."

Pamela fished in her handbag. When she presented her plastic security card to the sergeant, he waved her past with an almost casual air.

"That's it?" She was surprised at the abrupt change in atmosphere. "You mean I can go inside?"

"That's what you want, isn't it? There's no longer any reason to stop you."

"Why did you stop me last time?"

"If you want to go to work, just get on in there and don't ask questions."

She walked away from the desk with a purposeful gait, still determined to assert her right to be in the building.

She had barely left the foyer area before she came face-to-face with a group of air traffic assistants heading away from the operations room. "Will someone tell me what's going on here?" she demanded.

*

Maggie Loughlin leaned across Fergus MacNabb's prostrate body and felt the heat from his burning brow. The air turbulence outside was getting worse and the fuselage shuddered violently, forcing her to throw out a hand to steady herself.

She glanced towards the windows. Driving snow was brushing frantically across each glazed hole. The nightmare was becoming worse with each passing minute. She needed something to calm her nerves, but the only effective measure she knew was out of the question now. The DEA man was watching her every move too closely for her to reach her single remaining fix without being seen.

She started when Devereaux came up behind her. Silently cursing him, she pushed herself back into an upright stance, grasping a seat to hold herself steady. There was only one way she knew to handle such a man. Confrontation, not submission.

When he spoke, she was surprised by the icy coldness in his tone.

"How is he now?" The American nodded towards MacNabb.

"Feverish. You know anything about first aid?"

"A little." His voice was still sharp, but she now detected an underlying calm.

"Hmm. Pity you weren't down on the main deck when I needed someone. Like, when the collision occurred."

"Is Captain MacNabb able to talk?"

"He's not conscious."

"I'll wait until he is."

"Forget it, Yank. You've no right here, and you know it." She felt her muscles tighten, wondering if she could force the issue without getting herself deeper in the mire.

He responded calmly. "I'm briefed to watch and listen. And

pass on information for other people to follow up. People who do have jurisdiction."

"Why don't you piss off?" She looked down at MacNabb's face for some indication that the captain might be able to hear what was being said. His eyes remained closed. "He'll not talk to you."

"He doesn't have to. But he's gonna have to talk to someone when we land."

"*If* we land."

"Let's look on the bright side, eh? Let's work on the idea that we all get down on the ground safely and I give the British police enough information to get them looking in the right places." He suddenly sharpened his voice. "How d'you feel about that, Miss Loughlin? How d'you feel about the British customs guys doing a strip search on you? And a urine test? And a forensic examination on all your clothes? Eh?"

"You bastard!" The words came out as a venomous hiss, uttered before she found the effort to control her composure. He knew. He was stringing her along because he knew what she had done.

MacNabb groaned and moved in the seat. He opened his eyes and looked up at the narcotics investigator and groaned again, as if clawing his way out of a deep dream, pulling his thoughts slowly into the dawn of reality. His face was ashen and creased with pain.

"What's going on here?" MacNabb tried to rise but Maggie held him down with a hand on his shoulder.

She said, "Don't let this bastard worry you, Fergus. He's out to trick you."

MacNabb shook his head and put a hand to his face. He looked slowly around the cabin until his attention came to rest on the DEA agent and then his eyes flared. He said thickly, "For chrissake, what are you after?"

"He wants to pin Sally Scrimgeour's death on you." Maggie kept her gaze on Devereaux, wondering how he would react. Apart from a brief raising of his eyebrows, he remained calm. He could afford to, the bastard had tricked her and now he was about to pull the noose round her neck.

"Want to tell me how she died, Captain?" he asked.

"Leave him alone, won't you." She knew it was a vain hope. Would the agent reveal to MacNabb that she had shopped him?

He addressed MacNabb again. "There are people back home in New York who want to know who killed the stewardess. And why."

Maggie bit her lip. If Fergus MacNabb was cornered he would do everything to save his own skin. "Don't say anything, Fergus."

Devereaux stared coolly at her from his seated position. "Would you mind leaving us alone for a few minutes, Miss Loughlin?"

When she remained rooted to the spot, he nodded towards the rear of the cabin. He had no need to speak, his body language said it all. Then his eyes erupted into fiery torches, remaining alight for just a second before extinguishing themselves as quickly as they had lit up.

Apparently satisfied that he had subdued her, he waved her away. "Just give us a few minutes together. If you please."

Angrily, she swung round and stormed off. Almost instinctively, her hand went to the hem of her uniform jacket. Her fingers wrapped round the slight bulge in the lining, the comforting feel of her emergency fix.

She needed it now, needed it badly.

Devereaux had no official jurisdiction on this aircraft, but that was no obstacle. All he had to do was talk. Any customs search would find traces of the stuff on her clothes. As for a urine test... that would spell the end of her life with Sinclair International. But it wouldn't stop there. The police would piece together a story of what happened in the States and that would spell the end of everything for her.

Face up to it, Maggie. You've lost this game.

*

Pamela was subdued as she left the staff canteen. Two emergencies had fallen to the staff of Atlantic House: the space shuttle and the oceanic collision. In a sense they were the same emergency because without the American military presence over the Atlantic — those aircraft involved in the *Washington* rescue operation — there would have been no collision between the 747 and the KC135.

The Air Traffic Control Centre had been exceptionally busy when she first arrived in the building, but it was fast emptying now. The military was pulling out. The corridor leading toward the domestic operations room was almost deserted.

She caught sight of Jock as she approached the air lock doors. He stood alone beside a coffee machine. His eyes were glazed and unfocussed. He turned slowly towards her as she came closer and his face suddenly lit up with recognition.

"Pamela. What are you doing here?" His voice was thick.

"I came looking for you, Jock. I had to talk to you."

"This is not the time, Pamela. Too many things going on."

"I know. I've been talking to other people. They filled me in on the business of the space shuttle and the collision over the ocean. Is that why they wouldn't let me in earlier?"

"I suppose so." He lapsed into silence.

"What else is going on, Jock? What else has happened?"

"The Sinclair 747? Did they tell you what happened to it?"

"Only that there was a collision." She saw tears in his eyes. "You look absolutely washed out. What happened, Jock?" She suddenly felt a very deep need to be close to him.

"Sally should have been on that flight." He looked down at his hands, studying them as if they were objects of morbid fascination.

"You mean she's on board—"

"No." His voice cut across hers with a shrill edge. "She's not on board. She was murdered in New York."

"Murdered? Oh, God! No!" She threw a hand to her mouth.

"The police were here."

"Oh no, Jock. When? How?" Pamela took an involuntary step backwards and she felt her jaw drop.

244

"In New York," he whispered. "Someone knifed her in a subway station."

She stepped back another pace and pressed both hands against her face. For a few seconds she stood silent, shocked. "I don't know what to say, Jock. It's just too terrible to think about. I've read about people being mugged on the—"

"It wasn't a mugging." He looked up and his expression was insistent, demanding even though he was still unable to look her fully in the face. "It was premeditated, cold-blooded murder."

"But why?"

"Drugs. The police found cocaine in her bag."

"Oh, Jock! She wasn't a user, was she?"

"A user?" He drifted off into thought for a couple of seconds. "No. Not to my knowledge. The way I figure it out, she was being duped into carrying the stuff. Someone must have planted the drugs in her bag without her knowing. It has to be that way. Sally would never knowingly—"

"I'm sure you're right, Jock."

He wasn't listening to her now. His voice droned on. "Of course, I can't be certain what happened. But I know who's behind it. I know who was responsible."

"How? How can you know? You just said you can't be sure what happened."

He looked at her with a strange, faraway expression in his eyes. As if he had only just noticed her presence. He put out a steadying hand to the coffee machine. "What? What was that?"

"You can't be sure, Jock."

"Of course I'm sure! I know who's responsible. Two policemen came here to speak to me. They knew. I could see it from the questions they were asking me. They wanted to know if I had heard of a guy called Fergus MacNabb."

"And had you?"

"Sally's talked about him more than once. He's a senior captain with Sinclair International."

"And you think he—?"

"Yes. He's behind it, I'm sure of that. For all I know, he may actually have been the one who knifed her. If he didn't, he certainly had a hand in it."

Pamela shivered. "But you can't be certain, Jock. It's only guesswork."

"I'm certain." His voice became distant once again. He was drifting like a lost boat afloat in his own mind. "The handbag... the one the cocaine was in... he gave it to her as a present."

"But that's not conclusive evidence, Jock. The police didn't actually tell you who did it, did they?"

He suddenly snapped into complete awareness. His eyes flashed with intense anger. "I'm sure. As bloody sure as I can be. MacNabb was her lover and he gave her the drugs."

"But that doesn't make him a killer."

"The bastard was using her!"

"It could have been a straightforward mugging."

"It could have been—" His eyes seemed to go out of focus for a few seconds, as if he was suddenly drained of all emotion. When the moment passed, he spoke hesitantly. "You think—"

Pamela put a reassuring hand round his shoulders and came closer to him, softly whispering. "Oh, Jock. Even if it was true that he killed her, and I very much doubt it, you can't actually do anything about it."

"Can't I? Don't count on it." He swung round, so quickly that she was momentarily caught off balance. "MacNabb is flying the 747, the one that's in trouble. It can't land here at Prestwick so it's diverting to Tiree."

"What are you going to do, Jock?"

"Do?" He looked away and his voice fell to a faint inquisitive murmur. "You mean, what have I done?" He staggered backwards. His mouth gaped open for a couple of seconds. "Oh God. What have I done?"

*

Lightning backlit the opaque front screen. For a moment Dougie was blinded and he shook his head to clear his vision. The driving snow continued to splatter against the fractured glass and roar through the hole on the left side. His hands held the control column so tightly he could feel them going numb. Even when a deep pain set into his wrist muscles, he was unable to ease his grip. He blinked and focussed again on the compass because it was the only means of navigation left to him.

God, get us out of this and I will be a better husband. In a flash of understanding he could see where he had gone wrong. He and Jenny. They had allowed their grief to chill their lives. After Edward's death they had turned their home into something cold and unfeeling. He could see that now. The spotless lounge with every item of decoration in its place and every piece of furniture polished and dusted day after day. The mealtimes when he sat opposite his wife and read the newspaper with barely a word exchanged. The times when they sat in silence because neither wanted to give vent to their true feelings. They had been living in a tomb.

If he got out of this alive, Jenny would have the baby she craved. Their house would, once again, become a family home.

If he got out of this alive.

Outside the aircraft, the thick cloud continued to clasp the 747 in its choking blanket. The grey-whiteness swirled past the screen and through the gaping hole, blocking off all means of establishing the aircraft's position visually. Unsure of where they were, Dougie's mind worked feverishly. He had continued holding the 747 in level flight for some minutes after losing the VOR signal and the radio. In the back of his mind he had a continuing hope that one or other would come back on line.

Then the snow storm had hit them. Without warning they were thrown about by fierce cumulus cloud and the screen turned black as blown snow hit them head on. Should they descend? He was fairly certain they had still not passed the southern end of the Isle of Mull. Just a minor error in navigation could send them crashing into the island's high ground. Besides, he had no accurate means of determining the altitude they were flying at.

They had to descend before they ran out of fuel, but he had to be sure of the aircraft's position before starting a descent. And the only accurate means of navigation, the VOR indicator, was now dead.

Maybe there was a chance that the beacon would come back on line soon. They had no certain way of knowing whether it was a ground fault that was even now being repaired or an aircraft fault that would never be fixed. But blind hope was not a realistic option. He had to act, quickly and decisively.

"We have to do something, Dougie." Kovak's voice across the flight deck brought him to a sudden decision.

He looked over at the flight engineer and saw that his uniform was soaked by the snow driven in through the broken screen like arrows. Kovak held one arm across his eyes to protect them.

"We'll start a slow descent on this heading," Dougie said evenly. "If we're lucky, the cloud will break before we hit anything."

"We don't have much choice. There can't be much fuel left now."

"Know how much longer the engines will keep running?"

"Not with any certainty. It's probably around ten or maybe fifteen minutes if we're really lucky, but those instruments are just haywire."

"Okay. Keep your eyes peeled, Sammy, we're going down now. I want you to shout out as soon as you spot anything solid."

"You bet."

Dougie pulled back on the thrust levers and eased the column forward. And he prayed.

*

Jock sidled into the operations room in Pamela's wake. He felt like death. He also felt sheepish and ashamed.

He would rather not have been in the operations room and he hoped that no one would notice him. Confessing to Pamela that he had sabotaged the emergency radio frequency and the Tiree VOR had not been easy, but it had crystallised in his own mind the enormity of what he had done. Then he had felt numbed.

Why had he done it? He wasn't sure, and that was almost as worrying as the deed itself. Was he losing control of his sanity? The reasons and the rightness of his actions had been so clear at the time. But now—

"Where's the R/T switch?" Pamela asked quietly, searching for the correct radio-telephone transmit button.

Jock pointed towards the standby suite. The heavy operations manual was still lying on the radio-telephone selector panel. Clearly, no one else in the room had noticed it. Untidiness was taken for granted in the ops room.

Jock scanned anxiously around. Tension was still evident among the control room staff. Voices were raised and people moved about with a sense of urgency. But no one seemed to notice either him or Pamela.

"You must do it now, Jock." Pamela spoke quietly, but firmly. "You have to put things right yourself. While you still have the chance."

Jock edged towards the standby suite, his eyes darting about the room in case anyone saw him. When he slipped the manual away from the switch, he felt a weight fall from his mind. Only partially, because the VOR was still switched out. He had to do something to bring the beacon back on line.

*

"Sinclair 984, this is Watchdog. Do you read me?" The voice burst into Dougie's headphones like a welcome guest. Just when he had given up hope of hearing any further transmissions over his radio telephone, there was that quintessentially English voice again. Worried and slightly edgy, but solidly there. He had no idea how the radio-telephone fault had been repaired, but the effect was music to his ears.

"I read you, Watchdog. I read you." In his relief, his voice rose an octave.

"Well, thank the Lord for that."

"What happened, Watchdog?"

"We don't know. Just be thankful the frequency is back on line. What is your aircraft's condition now?"

"No change, Watchdog. But we're very short of fuel. We haven't much time left. Ten or eleven minutes at the very most."

"Roger. We have you on our aircraft radar. Your heading is good and you're just coming up on twenty miles from Tiree. Any idea what altitude you are flying at?"

"Negative. I'm in a slow descent. I have to get down below this cloud."

"Roger, in that case continue slow descent on your present heading. But go easy, will you? Things don't look too good on the ground. Cloud base is now five hundred feet over the airfield but there's a heavy cloud bank right down to ground level over the western half of the island. And it's creeping towards the aerodrome. There are also heavy snow storms in your present area."

"We know that, Watchdog. We're in snow at the moment."

"Roger, 984. That doesn't look so good. We may already be too late to attempt to get in visually."

"It's got to be a visual approach, Watchdog. We've lost all our VOR indications."

"So have we, old chap. It's the ground station that's cut out. We hope they can get it back on line. In the meantime you must try to get down below this cloud. You can't see me, but I'm about five miles off on your starboard beam at two thousand feet. Hold your present altitude for a minute or two while we drop down to low level and assess the cloud base."

"Thanks, Watchdog."

Dougie eased back on the column and watched the artificial horizon. He was flying as much by instinct as by technology. He turned to Kovak. "You okay, Sammy?"

"Bloody soaked. And cold. Ask me again in half an hour."

"I'll buy you a beer in half an hour. Meantime, I'll drive the ship while you watch the front screen and keep a sharp look out."

"A sharp look out? You're joking! What front screen? And how can I see through this snow?" Kovak screwed up his eyes as he peered into the howling cold precipitation that knifed through the shattered front windscreen.

"With luck we'll be able to drop down out of it. I hope that Nimrod pilot can find us a clear patch."

"He'd better be quick. We can't fly on empty tanks."

"We might have to." Dougie lapsed into silence. According to Watchdog, they were twenty miles from Tiree. The 747 airspeed was now reduced to 120 knots — two miles per minute. That put them ten minutes flying time from the airfield. At a guess they had only ten minutes' worth of fuel left. It was going to be a close run thing.

*

Ros Dyson staggered down the cabin aisle towards the senior stewardess. The aircraft was heaving about and a violent downdraught caused her to fall against the passenger seats. At that same moment, a jagged flash of lightning lit up the starboard row of windows. Frightened voices cried out among the passengers. Rows of oxygen masks dangled loose in front of them, shaking like crazy marionettes.

"Maggie!" Ros recovered her balance and pushed herself on down the aisle.

Maggie Loughlin was slumped, half-standing and half-kneeling, against a wrecked seat. Just a few feet away, another lightning flash illuminated the ugly hole in the fuselage. Ros threw a hand in front of her face as the brilliant whiteness stung her eyes. She blinked and then saw that Maggie Loughlin had fallen to the floor. Another sharp lurch told her the aircraft had hit yet another air pocket.

"Are you all right, Maggie?" Ros put out a hand to the senior stewardess. Nearby a passenger was vomiting, another was weeping bitterly.

"Maggie! What's the matter with you?"

The senior stewardess turned her head slowly and straightaway Ros understood. The dull, drugged expression in Loughlin's eyes turned to one of bemusement, then pain.

"You bastard, Maggie!" Ros knelt down and grabbed the other woman's arm. What could she do to get Loughlin out of sight of the passengers?

Another violent judder shook the aircraft and a rush of cold, wet air ran down the aisle. Ros held on to the damaged seat frame, but it shifted under the motion of the fuselage.

When the movement stopped, she grabbed Maggie by her arms and tried to pull her upright. "Get up, damn you!" she shouted, oblivious now of the passengers nearby. They were all as good as dead anyway. Why bother with niceties?

An angry expression flickered across Loughlin's face.

"Walk. Come on, walk!" Ros helped the senior stewardess down the aisle, shuffling feet scuffing against seats and wreckage. "We'll need you if we get down."

They stopped suddenly and Ros allowed the senior stewardess to fall heavily into an empty aisle seat. Blood was spattered across the seat cushion where an injured passenger had once sat. She looked round at the white-faced passengers and drew a deep breath. The nightmare had to end soon, one way or another.

She gulped, turned and hurried down the aisle towards the front of the aircraft, anxious to find someone who could take charge. Someone she could trust. She stopped at the front of the cabin and looked back.

Maggie Loughlin was rising awkwardly to her feet, reaching out for non-existent support. A shudder down the cabin floor made her loose her balance and she fell into the aisle.

*

Jock sat at the systems control desk and studied the VDU in front of him. Pamela stood nearby, half-watching him and half-keeping an eye open for the duty engineer.

"Shout if anyone comes." Jock's voice trembled, fearful of more than an approaching engineer. This was his chance to put things right before anyone else was killed. His whole body shook as he reached out to the keyboard.

"Go on, Jock. Put it back on line again." Still using her quiet, insistent voice, Pamela moved in close beside him.

Jock, rubbed his hands together to stop the shaking, leaned further forward and tapped the keyboard. Then he breathed deeply, waiting for the response to appear on the screen.

He sat back for a long moment and then leaned again towards the VDU.

"What's wrong, Jock?"

"The lines to Tiree are down. I can't get through to the transmitter site."

"Try again. You've got to get through."

"I can't. It's the British Telecom lines. They must be down because of the storms."

"What else can you do?"

"Nothing. We've lost the only way to switch the transmitter back on."

"There must be some other way."

"Not from here. The only people who can switch it on now are the local engineers at Tiree aerodrome."

"Well—"

"Pamela." Jack stood up slowly. "The only way to get that beacon working again is to contact the engineers at Tiree."

"Can you do that?"

"I don't know. It might be possible to get a message down the radio-transmitter lines. But you know what that means?"

"No."

Jock walked slowly away from the desk, his hand clamped tightly to his forehead. When he turned back to Pamela, his face was frozen a deathly white. "It means getting other people involved. The only thing I can do now is to tell the watch manager what I've done."

*

"Sinclair 984, this is Watchdog."

"Go ahead, Watchdog."

253

"We've broken through the cloud base at three hundred feet. It's a very uneven base. I can see the island, and the cloud base now looks to be even lower over there."

"Can we get in visually?"

"I don't know. We're picking up heavy cumulonimbus on our weather radar. It looks like a band of frontal cloud spread out in a line north-south right across the island. And it's moving directly towards the airfield."

"What do you suggest, Watchdog?"

"No point in pretending it's going to be easy. We really need that VOR back on line. But we don't have the bloody thing to help us. We'll have to try to make a quick dash in before the front reaches the airfield. I suggest you continue your descent and keep your eyes open."

Dougie pushed the column forward to take the aeroplane on down through the cloud. He glanced across at Kovak. The other man was shivering, taking the full force of the driving snow as it poured in through the holed screen. His headphones hung loose around his ears.

"You heard that?" Dougie asked.

The flight engineer nodded. "You still buying the beer?"

*

They were skimming beneath the cloud when a sudden explosion shook the airframe of the KC135. The control column jerked violently and Judson found himself struggling to keep the airplane level. He had so little height to spare, so little margin for error.

"For chrissake, help me hold the wheel steady," he bellowed.

"I'm doin' my best, Paul." Youngman fought with his column. The pressure slowly eased and Judson let out a long sigh.

He jerked in his seat as a loud blast from the intercom assaulted his ears. "It's the starboard wing again, Major!" The voice was Bryzjinsky's. High-pitched, almost screaming.

Judson wondered how the starboard wing stayed glued on. It sure couldn't keep them airborne much longer. "What happened?"

"The starboard outer engine," Bryzjinsky replied. "It just broke away. It fell clean into the sea."

"Shit!"

"I can see flames out there again, Major. Coming from around the inner engine. It sure looks bad from here."

"Okay, Bryzjinsky. Get all the crew prepared in case we have to ditch."

Youngman looked across at him. "You figure we ought to give Ocean Command a call?"

Judson was tempted. There was no doubt that Ocean Command would order them to put down in the sea immediately, but they would also bring up extra help. The catch was the state of the sea. He had no confidence in being able to survive ditching in that. If he could only reach dry land. Any dry land.

He snapped his mind into top gear. "And have them order us to ditch? No way. We'll only call them if we have to. Last resort. If we can make it to that goddamn island, we'll have a better chance of survival."

"You reckon we can make it, Paul? What with a fire out there in the wing."

"I dunno if we can make it. But we sure are gonna give it a try." He swung his head round towards Hewson. "You got an ETA for that island?"

"About ten minutes, Major. I reckon we'll be over it in about ten minutes."

"You sure of that?"

"Sort of."

*

Jock felt physically sick as he hurried up to the watch manager's desk. After the news of Sally's death, he had been treated well by the staff at the centre. Now he had let them down. Let everyone down. He had only one way out, only one painful answer to the problems he had created.

Angus Cameron had been telephoning the General Manager when Jock came to a halt in front of him. He slammed his telephone down on its cradle and looked up with a sharp eye.

"What is it, Jock?"

"The Tiree VOR. It—"

"I know, it's out of service. What about it?"

"I switched it off." Jock felt the sense of deflation drain through him like water through a pipe. He would rather have crept away from the operations room without a word to anyone, but he must see this through.

"Why the hell did you do that?"

"Never mind why, Angus. The fact is I switched it off from the systems control desk. But I can't switch it back on again because the lines to Tiree are down. You'll have to get the Tiree station engineer to reset the transmitter locally."

"Tell me why you did it."

"There's no time now!" Exasperation was fast taking the place of contrition. "Can you get the Tiree people to switch it back on?"

"No. All the telecom lines are down. There's no way to contact anyone out there."

"You could try the intercom lines through the radio transmitter site."

Cameron studied Jock's face as he considered the option. There was a chance they might get a message through to the island that way, but it was dependant on the Tiree engineers being out at the transmitter site. Most of the time the site was unmanned.

"Okay, we'll give it a try." He rose hurriedly and gave Jock a withering look. "But, why, Jock? Why did you do it?"

Jock choked. "The pilot... Captain MacNabb... he and Sally..."

"For God's sake! Captain MacNabb was seriously injured when the collision occurred. We don't even know if the poor devil is still alive. Last report we had, he was in a pretty bad way and they didn't know if he would survive."

"You mean, maybe he's not flying the aeroplane?"

"Almost certainly he isn't."

Jock gulped. It felt like someone had just punched him hard in the stomach.

Chapter 17

"If you want to fly, there is only one way to do it," Eric Nyle had told his son. "You must join the Air Force. They'll teach you to be a good pilot and they'll give you the chance to fly to your heart's content."

Dougie had listened to his father's words and tried to come to terms with them. It wasn't easy. He had left high school with the chance to go to Edinburgh University, but he wanted to fly. Not to kill people, just to fly.

Eric had put a lot of pressure on both his sons to follow in his footsteps. "You don't need to worry about who'll pay for your flying instruction. You don't need to worry about keeping up your flying hours. It will all be given to you, for free."

Overwhelmed by their father's words, both boys had joined the RAF. That was when Dougie discovered that the military saw little distinction between flying and killing. When he announced his move to Transport Command, his father had been incredulous. "Transports? You can't fly transports! I'll get that stopped. I'll speak to someone about it."

But Dougie had been happy with the posting. Against his father's wishes, he flew military transports until he left the air force to get his commercial pilot's licence. Then he joined Sinclair International.

Maybe it had been a mistake.

"I can see the water." Kovak gestured ahead through the broken screen. His voice was pinched with excitement.

Dougie looked up. The cloud was parting to reveal the dark, heaving waves below them, waves that would, in an instant, swallow them and consign the broken remains of the 747 to the bottom. He pulled back on the control column. At a guess they were now flying at no more than two hundred feet above sea level.

"There's the island. Dead ahead!" Kovak's voice rang out again.

"I see it." Dougie made out a smudge of land at the point where cloud met sea. His first reaction was one of relief. He would be able to get the aircraft down in some sort of semi-controlled fashion. But his quick burst of hope was short-lived. Much of the island was already obscured by thick, low cloud, and it was steadily eating up what remained in sight. He eased forward the thrust levers to buy himself an extra minute.

"Watchdog from Sinclair 984," he said as calmly as his tense body would allow. "We are below cloud and have the island in sight."

"Roger. I have you in sight also, old chap. I'll pull ahead and lead you in."

"Roger, Watchdog. Are they ready for us at the aerodrome?"

"You could say that. Frankly, they sound as though they're scared fartless at the prospect of a 747 touching down on their little patch."

Dougie flexed his fingers to ease the tension. "I know how they feel, Watchdog."

"Perhaps you do, old chap."

Dougie wondered what the rest of the crew aboard the Nimrod was like. There might be a whole team of Englishmen aboard the aircraft: navigators, radar operators, communications operators, people trained to operate the sophisticated submarine detection gear. But the only interface they had with the 747 was through that single pilot and his cut-glass accent.

Dougie mentally ran through an outline of how he intended to get the damaged aircraft onto the ground. He blinked and realised that his eyes had, for some time, been screwed up in an attempt to shield them from the blast of cold air that still pounded in through the broken front screen. They felt sore and tired. This landing would be far from a controlled experience and there was precious little on the ground to help them. He would have to call upon every ounce of experience to prevent further loss of life.

He stabbed suddenly at the transmit button. "Watchdog, are

you in contact with ATC at the airfield?"

The response was not immediate. "Ah, negative. They don't have any ATC at Tiree. But I'm in contact with the fire crew."

"Well, that's better than nothing. At least they have a fire crew."

"Affirmative." A short pause. "But they're not geared up to your sort of aircraft, old chap. They have only minimal equipment."

"Roger." What else could he say?

He turned his attention to his next main problem, getting the undercarriage down with a loss of hydraulic pressure to the main body oleo. He had already decided that, with so many other factors against them landing safely at Tiree, he had to make an attempt to get the gear fully down. One way or another. At Prestwick he would have had a long, strong runway and full emergency services. Here he had a weak runway which was far too short, minimal fire cover and not even an ATC service.

Getting the oleo down was not an impossible task. He had switches on the flight deck that would operate electric motors to unlock the uplatches and wheel bay doors. Getting the wheels down without hydraulics was primarily a matter of using gravity and a short prayer to help them lock into position. He leaned forward, selected the undercarriage down and watched the lights turn green. Then he jabbed his transmit switch.

"Watchdog from Sinclair 984. How does my main body undercarriage look?"

"No joy. The port side leg is only partly extended. You won't get any support from it."

"Roger. In that case, I'm going to try throwing the leg down with a bit of G."

"Good luck."

Dougie paused to compose himself before he put the airframe under stress. This was not a good idea but he had little option. "I'm going to use a spot of G, Sammy. Brace yourself."

"What about the passengers? Shouldn't we warn them?"

"What with, Sammy? We've no working PA system, and the phone to the cabin crew isn't working. If they're not strapped in, they'll have to take their chances."

"Okay." Kovak gritted his teeth. "You want to know what my Uncle Lemmy used to say about flying?"

"No."

"He said the guy at the front always gets to the accident first. If aircraft were unsafe, the pilot would sit at the back."

"That's not funny." Dougie ran his hands round the control column, feeling for a state of equilibrium. This would be a big gamble. Throwing a fully functional 747 about the sky was no great problem, but this was no fully functional ship. This was a damaged relic that could fall apart at any moment. He eased the nose down again to build up speed and then pulled back sharply on the control column in an attempt to throw the undercarriage down.

The fuselage groaned under the additional strain. Suddenly the rudder pedals exploded against his feet with a loud bang, throwing his legs back against his seat. His headset flew off, stinging his ears.

"Christ! What was that?" Kovak shouted across the flight deck.

Dougie ignored him and rubbed one hand over his ears. Whatever had caused the bang, it had happened at a bad time. One hell of a bad time.

He reached to recover his headset and shouted across the flight deck, "You okay, Sammy?"

"Guess so." Kovak's face looked noticeably whiter. "What about the ship? Is she hurt bad?"

"Let's find out." Dougie gingerly felt the column. It responded normally in the lateral, aileron, direction, but felt stiff when he tried to move the elevators on the tailplane. When he released the pressure on the column, the 747 was flying slightly nose down.

"What is it?" Kovak asked.

"The elevator controls. I think we've just lost our elevator controls."

"Oh shite! Not now!"

*

Ros Dyson felt herself being lifted into the air as the floor heaved upwards like an erupting mountain. Moments later she was sinking down again, sinking too far down as the floor buckled and dropped towards the depth of the rear hold. As she fell, she heard a wild scream. It was only when the downward motion began to even out that she realised it was the airframe screaming. Death throes, she thought, the death throes of the 747 and every person on board. And she screamed along with the terrible noise.

When both the unreal movement and the noise had stopped, she found herself splayed across the floor which was angled awkwardly towards the port side. All about her she could hear the cries of alarm and the frantic noise of confusion that told her the passengers were in trouble.

Her mind was a blaze of confused thoughts and feelings, emotions she fought hard to keep under control. She had been at the rear of the aircraft, desperately searching for someone who could take charge. In the front cabin she had found only younger girls, juniors who looked to her for support. Angrily, she had rushed back to the rear cabin, hoping to find someone onto whom she could offload responsibility.

She brushed off her blue uniform and tried to stand, but her legs felt numb. They crumpled beneath her and she fell suddenly and heavily into a sitting position. In the same instant, the cabin went quiet as if the noise of the passengers had been suddenly switched off. Shock, she guessed, just pure undiluted shock. Give it another moment or two and they would recover.

As the seconds passed and feeling slowly returned to her limbs, she wondered how the other cabin crew would have taken this latest setback. She knew the answer well enough. Most would be pissing in their pants. Never mind all that crap about keeping cool and setting a good example to the passengers. Never mind the company image of calmness under duress. When the chips were down, you were as scared as the next person and you showed it. How would Maggie Loughlin have taken it?

On the way back down through the cabin she had seen Maggie wandering about in a daze. The reason had been pretty obvious. She was doped up to the eyeballs.

Sound suddenly burst back into Ros's head, the bedlam of people in torment.

"Keep calm!" she shouted as she pulled herself into a half-standing position. The shout was a useless gesture, but it was all she could think of.

She scanned around, desperate for help, desperate for someone she could rely upon. Someone who could help control this dreadful mess. But there was no one. No one except a young stewardess called Sue who staggered awkwardly towards her, eyes wide with horror.

"What shall we do?" the other girl called out.

"Help me get upright."

"The whole floor is gone!" Sue's voice quavered as she grabbed Ros's hand and helped her to her feet. Almost immediately she staggered back against a set of crumpled seats.

Ros rubbed her arm as she stood upright again, feeling the last of the numbness fall away. "Is anyone hurt?"

"Anyone hurt? Are you kidding?"

"You know what I mean, Sue. Anyone hurt by that last bit of excitement?"

"I don't know. I just don't know."

"Well, go and find out."

Ros looked about as the other girl staggered away. The floor was now angled sharply downwards towards the port side and sharp, jagged edges of the support beams stood out starkly against the inside fuselage wall. Many passengers had released themselves from their seats and were making their way forward towards the centre of the aeroplane. Others were crying out or frozen in their seats, too horrified to move.

"This is too much," Ros muttered. She was certain that the end was near for all of them. Maybe it was just as well. Maybe they would all be better off dead.

Especially Maggie Loughlin.

*

Dougie gripped the control column tightly. With no one at the engineer's panel, he had little idea how much fuel remained. Maybe none at all. Maybe they were running on fumes.

"The tanks must be almost dry," Kovak echoed his thoughts.

"Nothing we can do but hope. Keep your eyes straight ahead, Sammy."

The snow had eased off since they had broken through the cloud, the view less of a strain. But Kovak was still shuddering violently in the cold blast of air that pummelled his face and chest. Dougie felt the muscles in his stomach tighten.

"We'll make a straight in approach," he called out. "We can't afford to hang about any longer."

"Can you control the descent?"

"The elevators seem to be partly jammed in a nose down attitude. There is some movement left but all we want to do is go down."

"You know what you've gotta do, Dougie. You've got to make a greaser of a landing first time."

"I don't intend to overshoot, if that's what you're thinking." He had no option. With the elevators jammed he would be unable to climb away.

The Nimrod had fallen into position just ahead of the 747. It was a welcome sight, but of little help if the Sinclair aircraft fell apart at this final moment. Dougie allowed the nose to ease down again and he watched the sea come up to meet them. The question of whether the main body undercarriage would hold was now immaterial. There was nothing they could do about it.

Directly ahead, the island loomed large in the remains of the front windscreen. The shore stood out clearly where white breakers rolled up onto a long line of sand. Just beyond the shore was the airfield. Beyond that was a black bank of cloud creeping towards the airfield like a huge rolling carpet, drowning everything in its path as it moved closer to the runways.

Dougie stabbed his transmit button and a sharp pain ran up his arm from his thumb. "Watchdog from Sinclair 984. I now have damage to my elevator controls. I can't do any more out here so I'm going straight in for a landing."

"Roger, 984. Do you have the field in sight?"

"Affirmative."

"In that case I'll peel away and give you a clear run in."

"Roger, Watchdog. What runway should I use?"

"Runway two-four has been opened up for you. Come in on a left base and touch down as early as you can and ignore any obstructions. They're all frangible and they'll break as soon you hit them."

"Don't count on it. This old lady's acting a bit frangible herself at the moment and I don't think we're strong enough to take too much obstruction on the ground. Follow me round while I join on a left base for runway two-four and tell me if I look like I'm headed for more trouble."

"Roger, we'll do that. The runway load bearing strength is nowhere near enough for a 747, but I guess you can't be too choosy at the moment."

"Not really. Can you still see my undercarriage? I'd appreciate a last visual check on what we've got left down there."

"Standby. I'll drop down to look." A few moments later the Nimrod pilot said, "I see it now, Sinclair 984. Your port main undercarriage leg isn't fully extended but you know that. The rest looks pretty good."

"Okay, Watchdog. Thanks for your help."

"Good luck, old chap."

*

Maggie Loughlin stared at the open hatch and felt her blood run cold. It was a brief moment of full consciousness, a short return to reality which, she knew, would be quickly swallowed up by a return to her dazed dream. She hated that short period of truth.

From where she stood, gazing down into the hole in the floor, the port main wheel assembly appeared to be extended. She had no experience of assessing undercarriage damage, but she guessed there was a fair chance that it might give way just as the aircraft touched down. Kovak should have clamped down the open hatch once he had finished investigating the wheel assembly. He must have forgotten. Unlucky for Trudy.

The logical thoughts, which had so troubled her, were now beginning to roll aside, replaced by the glazed effect of the drug. Her fear was slowly subsiding. She looked down once more. The cloud below had given way to a cold, uninviting scene, dancing spume on a dark grey sea. From above, the water looked icily solid, deadly. She suddenly realised that her fingernails had cut so sharply into her hands that blood was trickling down to the floor. She stepped closer to the open hatch. It wasn't necessary to end things like this, there was more than a chance they would all be killed when Nyle tried to land the aircraft. But this was more certain, less painful. Then the effect of the drug began to take a deeper hold once more and the prospect of death became suddenly inviting.

But for chance and bad luck, it needn't have ended like this. She could have gone on for much longer if only Sally Scrimgeour had kept her nose out of things. If only Fergus MacNabb had been more careful in his dealings. If only she had not been so eager to help him out of a hole by murdering the girl. She took another step closer to the edge and noticed that the sea was now a bright blue. She blinked and then saw that it was pink, warm beautiful pink, like a soft bed.

She smiled and raised her hands. One more step. Her foot met the draught coming up from below. She followed Trudy Bodenstadt into the chilly North Atlantic.

*

Jock wiped a sweaty hand across his eyes and followed the watch manager across to the Hebrides Sector suite.

"No luck on that score. We can't get through on the radiotelephone links." Angus Cameron stood behind the Hebrides Sector radar controller and faced Jock with his arms folded across his chest.

"That's it then? You can't alert the local engineers?" Jock asked.

"Maybe, maybe not. But we're not giving up, if that's what you mean. Those people out there need that beacon and we'll do everything we can to get it switched on. We've passed a message to the Nimrod pilot and he's trying to pass it on through the Tiree fire crew."

The visual memory of Sally flittered across Jock's mind like a moth. He would never see her again. She was now a cold, lifeless body in a mortuary. Never again. He jerked himself back to life.

"The fire crew should be able to contact the engineers."

"Maybe — probably." Cameron sounded doubtful. "But there's no guarantee they'll be in time."

"I don't know what to say."

Pamela stepped closer to him and he felt her take his hand.

*

"Hold her steady." Dougie pulled back on the column. The pressure needed to hold the aircraft in the sky was getting greater. The chances of landing safely were running away from him. Running away from them all.

"Dougie, she doesn't want to fly anymore."

"She'll fly as long as we stop her from killing herself."

"You better use a bit more persuasion. She's giving up."

"Shut up and heave on that column!"

"Sure. Say, you still buying that beer?"

Before Dougie could answer, the radio telephone crackled in his ears. "Sinclair 984, this is Watchdog."

"Go ahead, Watchdog."

"The Tiree VOR will be coming back on line very shortly."

"Big deal, Watchdog. Where was it when we needed it?"

"Problems on the ground. They seem to have fixed things now."

"Too bloody late, Watchdog. Too bloody late!"

*

MacNabb had been dreaming. His mind drifted around that other world where he was in total control of his own life. And other people's lives.

Devereaux knew too much about him, that much was certain. MacNabb had tried to counter all the DEA agent's questions with convincing responses, but he hadn't been clever enough. His mind was still too groggy with the effects of loss of blood. After Devereaux had left him, he had experienced a few lucid thoughts which put into perspective his own stupid answers to the cop's questions, and in those moments it all became clear to him. He had played the game once too often and he had lost.

Earlier, soon after the collision, they had tried to make him sleep. He hadn't wanted to sleep, but they had given him some sort of sedative and that had dulled his senses even more than the blood loss. After his talk with the DEA agent, he felt himself becoming drowsy again for a short time. Then sharper consciousness came back to him, slowly but surely, as if he was emerging from a restless sleep.

Now it was all over, he was certain of that. His career, his narcotics arrangements, his life. All over now. If Nyle landed the aircraft safely, there was no hope for Fergus MacNabb. And his downfall would seep into the lives of his father and mother, bringing disgrace to the family name. His only hope was that they would not land safely.

He had no fear of death. He was too strong-minded to be worried by the prospect of an unknown that awaited him in an afterlife. His only concern was that Devereaux and Loughlin must pass into that afterlife with him. He was certain that, right now, they held the only concrete evidence against him. If the DEA or the FBI had any other hard evidence, they wouldn't have let him make the flight. So they had nothing positive, nothing except what Loughlin and Devereaux could tell them. It all had to end here, for all three of them. But where was here? He had no idea where Nyle was aiming to take the aircraft or what stage the flight had reached. He had to find out. He had no clear-cut idea of how he would ensure they never landed safely, just a vague notion that he had to do something now.

One of the stewardesses was sitting beside him, calmly watching him return to reality. A coloured woman with black, frizzled hair. He didn't recognise her, couldn't pin a name on her, probably because she was not the sort of woman who took his eye.

"Are you all right, Captain?" she asked.

"Help me up," he replied thickly.

"You'd better just lie still. You're not too well, Captain."

"I said help me up! I should be in charge up there on the flight deck." He groaned and roughly pushed her aside. She gave only token resistance as he struggled to his feet. She probably feared him, as did many others in Sinclair International.

"You're in no fit condition, Captain." She put both hands to his chest in an effort to restrain him. "Mr Nyle knows what he's doing."

"It's my ship." MacNabb staggered forward, his good arm holding the seat backs as he moved towards the flight deck.

"But, Captain—"

He pushed open the flight-deck door with his good shoulder and immediately felt the force of the howling wind smash into him. Two heads turned towards him.

*

"Captain!" Dougie gaped. The last person he expected to see on the flight deck was MacNabb.

"Can I give you a hand, Captain?" Kovak rose up from the left-hand seat, reaching out towards him.

"For chrissake, Sammy! Help me hold the aircraft level!" Dougie roared. He waved his hand to order the flight engineer back into the seat. At that moment he desperately needed the eyes of a fully conscious person to help him land the aircraft. He also needed the other man's strength to help him hold the aircraft in a stable attitude. The dazed look on MacNabb's face told him that he could not rely on the captain's assistance.

Kovak returned his attention to the controls. But, before he could fully slide back into the seat, MacNabb waved him aside with a loose brush of his good arm. "Let me get into that seat. It's mine!"

Kovak looked enquiringly at Dougie who shook his head emphatically. "No, Captain. You must get back into the cabin. You can't do anything to help us here."

"It's my ship." MacNabb jolted as the floor swayed beneath his feet. He reached out a hand and grabbed the back of Dougie's seat.

"Oh, dear God!" Dougie found his voice choked. They were so close to landing the 747, so close to a chance of survival.

His arms ached, searing pain tore through his muscles. "Get back in that seat, Sammy!"

He looked again at the pilot and registered that MacNabb was on the verge of collapse. The man had to be ushered off the flight deck before he passed out.

He shouted at Kovak. "On second thoughts, get him out of here, quick as you can."

"Can you hold the column?"

"Do as I damned well say!"

The pain in his arms was turning to numbness. A bad sign. Not waiting to see how Kovak tackled the captain, he peered ahead to where the island aerodrome was coming into clearer focus. They were making a good approach and the runway was directly ahead of them. But the grey cloud bank was now just beyond the upwind end, crawling doggedly closer to the runway. There was little time left to get the 747 down before the ground became obliterated by the cloud.

His muscles screamed with pain.

He made out the remains of the fences across the tarmac and two small red fire appliances stopped on an old taxiway to either side of the touchdown area. Just a little more time, just a few minutes. A little extra strength.

He was still studying the scene on the airfield when MacNabb launched himself at the first officer's back. As the captain's body fell across his shoulders, Dougie released his hold on the control column and the 747's nose dipped suddenly and sharply towards the ground.

*

The steady march of flames had consumed much of the wing and they were now flying on the two port engines only. Thank God for the man who decided to fit four engines to the KC135, Judson reflected. A pity he didn't think of adding another engine for luck. As the thoughts went through his head, he felt his teeth grind together with a rasping sensation that ran like electricity through his jaw.

"Think that might be the island, Paul?" Youngman broke suddenly into his thoughts. "You can see a land mass dead ahead, just where the sea meets the cloud. Do you see it?"

"Yeah. Could be it," Judson responded with something less than full conviction. He glanced out at the glowing red reflections in the cloud. Reflections of the flames that were burning the airplane apart. How much longer would that starboard wing hold? It was a miracle they were still in the air.

He turned towards Hewson. "Is that it? The island straight ahead, is that it?"

The navigator was poring over a chart of the Western Islands. He raised a pale, tired face and then stood up to look over Judson's shoulder. "That could be it. I can't be quite certain. But it could be—"

"You just don't know, do you?" Judson was more than pissed off. He was on his last legs. "You just don't know!"

"For chrissake, sir!" Hewson suddenly exploded. "We're flying low level in a place I ain't never seen before. The VOR is off line. The weather is crap. And you want me to pinpoint exactly where we are?" He suddenly turned and threw himself back into his seat.

"Take it easy, Paul," Youngman said calmly.

"We gotta know where we are," Judson replied. "They got one helluva lot of islands round here. How can we be sure it's the right one?"

"Reckon it's gotta be it, Paul. I don't see any others."

"Yeah, reckon you're right. Reckon we're in with half a chance." Judson put the navigator's outburst from his mind and allowed himself a momentary period of optimism. Hope was, after all, pretty much all they had going for them right now.

"Gimme the chart, willya," he shouted back at Hewson. "The local chart."

The navigator sniffed loudly and pushed the chart into Judson's open right hand. The pilot took it and studied it briefly. As near as he could judge, they had passed the island of Islay, where there was no chance of making an emergency landing, and were now headed north by north-east towards Tiree. At least they hoped they were headed towards Tiree and its marginal weather clearance. There was so much empty sea and so many small islands dotted through it, most with bad weather and no airfield.

He had expected his first view of Tiree to be around thirty degrees off the port side so that they could turn and approach the island airfield from due south, but it was coming at them from straight ahead. If this was the wrong island, they were in big trouble.

"You sure that's the island with the airfield?" Youngman asked.

Judson glanced up and stared out through the front screen. "It's gotta be. If we attack the island from this direction, the airfield's on the coast nearest us, about halfway along."

"You wouldn't like to be more precise — there's the VOR! It's back on line."

Youngman jerked a finger at the instrument. The fail flags had gone and the beam bar was settling into place. "And here comes the DME." He swung his finger towards the Distance Measuring Equipment. "We got it, Paul. We got it. Hallelujah, boy. We got it!"

"Shit!" Judson shot a dampening cry into the face of Youngman's shout of elation. "It's showing the Tiree beacon off to our left. Are we tuned to the right frequency?"

Youngman leaned towards the frequency switches on the console. "Yep. That's it all right."

"In which case that ain't the right island in front of us. We're not where we think we are. What the hell is that island dead ahead?"

"Dunno, Paul. What's on the chart to the east of Tiree?"

Judson stared at the chart for a full thirty seconds. "Shit! It's Mull. And they've got some petty high ground on Mull. Highest land mass hereabouts."

"Higher than we're flying?"

"One helluva lot higher than we're flying." Judson reached out to grab at the control column. "Let's get us into a left turn before we get any closer. Don't fancy hitting them hills in this old crate."

"At least we got some guidance now." Youngman sounded far happier than Judson felt. "Follow that beam bar, Paul. The DME reading says we got twenty miles to run to the island. We're bound to see it soon."

"Don't get so pleased about it," Judson said. "It ain't all over yet. We've gotta make some sort of emergency letdown on some darned small island and we ain't even found it yet."

"We will, Paul. We will."

The nose of the KC135 swung round, away from the brown graze on the horizon that was Mull. Almost instantly Judson saw a smaller, lighter smudge in line where the VOR indicator was directing them.

"What's that?" Youngman jerked forward in his seat and pointed slightly off to their left. "Over there, Paul. It's another aircraft. You see it?"

"Sure, I see it. It's a 747." Judson's voice came over dull and emotionless. "What d'you think a 747 is doing that low down out here?"

"Whaddya mean, Paul?"

"Think about it! Why would a 747 be flying that low down over the sea, flying around a tiny little island? That's gotta be the ship we hit!"

"If you're right, they're sure in trouble, Paul. Look at the way they're diving towards the sea. They're going down. They're still over the sea and they're going down. God help the people inside that crate!"

Chapter 18

Trisha Ruskin felt the tension oozing out of her, like the sweat seeping from her body. And, like the sweat, the more tension she shed, the more there was left behind. She could be dead now. If that damned bomb had detonated, thousands of people would be dead. Tens of thousands. Hundreds of thousands.

Her vision drifted about the control room, looking for something tangible to latch onto. Anything to grab her mind and take it away from those thoughts. The only object which came into sharp focus was the frame of the big American, bent over the supervisor's desk.

"Do you feel frightened now it's over?" she asked.

Lawrence looked up from the form he was completing. His face was placid, his composure totally unaffected by the emergency he had witnessed. "More to the point, do *you*?"

"A bit." A bit? That was a lie. She was downright scared, and then some. She was shaking, her whole body trembling like a low-frequency tuning fork. "What will they do with the *Washington* now?"

"Who knows? There's talk of breaking it up and shipping the parts back to the States in secret. It's unlikely that it will ever fly again."

"And the public will never know what happened?"

"That's the nature of state security." He eyed her thoughtfully for a moment. "What time do you finish duty?" He straightened his body and casually clipped his pen into his pocket.

"One o'clock."

He glanced at his watch. "I'll take you out to lunch. That might help."

She smiled awkwardly. "It might." Whatever her opinions about his morals, he was one big hunk of male and she wanted to be with him now. She sensed that he wanted her, and that was more than she had a right to expect. Okay, so he was party to a political deal that had put the lives of thousands of innocent people at risk. It was over now. She preferred not to think any more about that.

A driver called on her ground movement control frequency and requested permission to enter the runway. She replied with a sharp affirmative, her voice back on top line. Around the huge camouflaged mound that now covered the space shuttle, vehicles and distant figures mingled and merged into a general melee. But they were no longer important.

Her hands now trembled for quite a different reason.

*

Life was a pig, Judson thought. If the Air Force didn't get you, some woman would. He did everything the base commanders wanted from him and what thanks did he get? None. He married Ruby so that she could have respectability. And what did she do? She trashed him.

"You know what she done to me, Buddy. You know what Ruby did?" Judson glanced across the flight deck. He felt the blood drain from his face as he recalled the moment he learned how Ruby had humiliated him in front of the whole base camp. "She trashed me good. As good as finished me."

"Sure, Paul. I know." Youngman had his eyes fixed straight ahead. "But you can rise above it. You gotta. Otherwise she's won."

"Yeah. Reckon so." Judson turned his attention back to the flying controls. In a few more minutes his flying skills would be tested to the limits. "God knows how I'll do it, but I reckon you're right. In any case, what she did is gonna seem like nothin' compared to what the US Air Force is gonna do to me. Eh?"

Youngman said nothing.

The KC135 was an old airplane with too many miles on the clock, fit for little more than routine training missions. There were one or two B52s older than the tanker and still flying, but not many. Judson fully understood why Ocean Command had no reservations about burying the old crate at sea. He had less understanding about the reasons for putting the crew at risk.

"Don't see the 747, Paul." Youngman interrupted Judson's thoughts as they came closer to the island. "You reckon they were trying to put down on Tiree?"

"Ain't no other place with a weather clearance," Judson replied. "Don't suppose they were allowed to land at Prestwick so they probably had the same idea as us. There's the airfield." He pointed to a flat area near the centre of the long, narrow island where the ground was scarred by a triangle of black runways. They looked dangerously short.

On one side, the airfield was bounded by a white sandy beach. The other boundaries looked like wet and desolate grassland. And yet, in a sense, it was a relief to see that inhospitable landscape because it represented their only opportunity to land on the ground.

"What's the longest runway?" Judson called.

Youngman studied the thick book of landing charts in front of him. "According to this, they're all shortened anyway. Reckon we just point ourselves into wind and take it as it comes. It's a southwesterly so try for runway two-four."

Judson took a moment to adjust himself to the runway configuration. The length of tarmac Youngman had selected was aligned north-east or south-west, depending upon the landing direction. By pointing the aircraft onto a south-westerly heading as they prepared to land, Judson would be committed to runway two-four.

"Seems a long way from home for the old cow to end her days," he said. "They'll never fly her out of this place whatever sort of landing we make."

"As long as we get down alive, that won't worry me none, Paul."

"Suppose you're right. We gonna call ATC now?"

"They don't have none. According to this chart, they got airfield information. That's all. You give 'em a call and see what they say about that cloud bank coming in from the north."

Judson selected the frequency on the console panel and turned up the radio volume control. "Let's hope Highball isn't listening into this. We don't want no more orders to put down in the sea. Not now."

*

The Section Leader of the Tiree fire crew stood in the doorway of a small hut adjacent to the hangar where the emergency appliances were warming up their engines. He was a short, dour man with a thin spill of grey hair peeping out from beneath his cap. His eyes were on the airfield, but his ears were tightly tuned to the radio loudspeaker inside the hut.

In his long career, he had never experienced anything like this. No one on that tiny island had ever come up against an emergency like this.

One of his crew was at a radio desk, talking to the 747 that was about to make an approach to the airfield. Several minutes had passed since the last call from the pilot and both men were on tenterhooks as they waited for an indication that the flight was about to land.

Suddenly the loudspeaker cackled with another transmission. "Tiree, this is Gasser 29. Do you read me? Over." The accent was distinctly American.

The seated fireman glanced up at his superior and then put a hand microphone to his mouth. "Gasser 29, this is Tiree. I read you strength five. Pass your message."

"Tiree, from Gasser 29. We're a KC135 in an emergency. We've lost two engines and we aim to put down on your runway two-four. We're presently about five or six miles from the airfield. How long is that weather clearance gonna last with you? Over."

The fireman was lost for a reply. While his mind worked around the problem, his section leader reached out and grabbed the microphone. "Gasser 29, you cannot land here. There is a 747 also in emergency about to land." He lowered the microphone and stared at the other fireman, waiting for a reply. Neither of them spoke.

A full minute passed before the pilot responded. The voice held a dull, resigned edge to it. "We hear you, Tiree. But we ain't got much option at this moment. Either we land at your airfield or we're all dead."

The section leader opened his mouth but no words came out. At the desk, the fireman looked stunned. After a lifetime of watching small aircraft take off and land from Tiree's short runways, this was beyond both of them. Two big aircraft, both damaged, and both intent on landing.

The section leader's mind could not cope with the enormity of it. "Tell them to keep away." He handed the microphone back to the fireman. Already he was halfway to the door when he called back, "I'm going out onto the airfield. We'll need every man out there."

*

Ros Dyson had just buckled her seatbelt when she felt the aircraft begin its descent towards the aerodrome. What aerodrome? She hadn't a clue, just knew they were going down. There had been no warning from the crew, but she had seen the outline of a low-lying island from one of the windows.

Maggie Loughlin had disappeared. Ros had no idea where or when, so she had reluctantly assumed responsibility and briefed the crew. They had gone among the passengers, calming and reassuring them as well as telling them how to prepare for the possibility of a crash.

Now it all depended upon the flight deck men up front. God help them both.

*

"For chrissake, get him off!" Dougie made a one-handed grab at the control column. He tried to push MacNabb away with his other, but the burly pilot's weight was too much for him.

"I can't!" Kovak yelled back. Both his hands were reaching out for the left-hand column.

Dougie felt a lightning jag of pure animal fear. Through the cracked windscreen he saw the ground rushing up towards them. Not the runway this time, but flat, snow-covered heathland speckled with pools of lying water. The 747 was veering off course and diving towards the ground away from the runway. He reached out with his free hand, grabbed the yoke, and heaved back on the control column. Once again, his muscles were straining against the snagged control lines. His whole body ached agonisingly.

"Pull, damn you! Pull!" he shouted across to the flight engineer. "Pull with me!"

The sweat on his palms caused his one hand to lose its hold. Then MacNabb's grip on him relaxed and he shifted both hands back to the column. A quick glance showed that Kovak was also exerting his strength against the effect of the damaged elevator controls.

"Turn to port," Dougie called. "Turn back towards the runway and pull with me."

The ground rushed closer. Variegated white. Blurred.

"I am pulling!" Kovak yelled back.

Dougie's muscles tightened into knots. Still he heaved on the column. It was the only hope left.

He sensed a shuffling movement behind the seat. As the 747 turned back towards the runway, MacNabb was taken off guard by the movement and he fell backwards, bouncing against the rear wall of the flight deck.

Slowly the Boeing's nose began to assume a shallower dive, hurtling suicidally towards the ground. As the two men eased the 747 back onto its intended course, the airframe groaned under the strain.

Don't let us fall apart now, Dougie prayed. Not now. Not when we're almost on the ground.

The runway was now no more than one hundred feet below, off-centre and speeding closer as each second ticked away. Either side of it was a cold, alien landscape none of them wanted to see.

Dougie felt his arm muscles stinging now, stinging with the intense pain as he made the last turn back onto the approach path. He watched the runway come slowly back into line.

Then MacNabb grabbed Dougie roughly by the shoulders. His voice was thick and slurred. "Give me control. Give me my ship!"

The goddamn madman! Dougie pushed at him and shouted, "Get off of me, you maniac! Get off!"

But MacNabb fell on him again.

Dougie called across the flight deck, "Sammy! Take the column. For God's sake, take control!"

As the flight engineer took the strain on the column, Dougie turned in his seat and reached out his hands to force MacNabb away. The pilot's eyes were dull. Dougie released his seatbelt, rose to his feet. He drew back his fist and slammed in into MacNabb's jaw. The man fell back and collapsed across the flight engineer's seat.

"We're losing power again!" Kovak shouted.

Dougie scrambled back into his seat at the front of the flight deck, thrusting his legs into the well. It was too late now. They were too close to the ground. He gasped as he saw the runway coming up fast.

"It's the port outer again," Kovak yelled. "It's winding down."

"I see it." Dougie sized up the situation in an instant. The port outer engine had failed again and the speed was dropping off. Kovak had lowered the nose to compensate and was increasing the power on the remaining engines.

"Keep the ship steady," Dougie yelled.

They were at fifty feet and coming over the airfield boundary fence.

Fence? It was just a bloody ramshackle wire grill.

Kovak had the aircraft stabilised under lateral control but the speed was rapidly falling off. Dougie took in the wrecked fence across the tarmac, and the small, insignificant fire appliances waiting on the disused taxiways either side of the runway ends. He quickly weighed up the options of allowing Kovak to land the aircraft or taking back the column to land it himself.

He hesitated. It was too late.

Like hell it was! He reached out and grabbed the column decisively.

"I have control!"

Even as he made the call, he saw the power bleed away from the starboard outer engine. Empty tanks.

They were undershooting, aiming at a point short of the runway. Dougie pulled back on the yoke, easing up the nose to drag out every last inch of flight from the dying aircraft. The stall warning indicator suddenly erupted into a deafening screech. Dougie ignored it.

The runway looked much too short, even with the two disused extensions opened up.

He began easing back for the round-out, his left hand reaching towards the thrust levers.

"Cover me on throttle and stick!" he called to Kovak. The words were hardly out of his mouth before the weight of a heavy body fell across his shoulders.

MacNabb's sluggish voice rasped, "It's my ship!"

*

"There they are, Paul." Youngman tipped his head in the direction of the airfield. The 747 was on very short final, the last leg before they hit the runway. His voice dropped to display his disappointment. "Reckon they got there before us. No way we'll be able to use that runway now."

"It had to be their chance anyway," Judson replied soberly. "They must've got over four hundred people on that ship. We've got the fuel, but they've got the people."

"Reckon so. But where does that leave us? The sea?"

"Nope." Judson compressed his lips. That would be to give in to Ocean Command. He would be damned before he gave in to what Ocean Command wanted him to do.

"We got just one more chance. The beach. You see that beach

alongside the airfield? Reckon it must be long enough to get this old girl down in one piece."

Both men stared out at the stretch of sand that ran along the shore on the seaward side of the airfield. It looked uniformly white even in the dull light. A glint of reflection from the grey sky showed where dampness had been left behind by the receding tide.

Youngman sniffed. "Looks like the tide is out. Hope no one is sunbathing down there. It's gonna spoil their day if we kick sand in their eyes."

"You got any other suggestion?"

"None at all, Paul. None at all."

"Okay. Let's get the gear and flaps down." He reached out a hand to the flap switch. "We'll get just one chance at this so let's get it right."

"What's right in a situation like this, buddy?"

"Darned if I know." Judson selected the crew intercom. "Bryzjinsky, get the men bedded down back there. We're about to make a landing. Evacuate the ship as soon as we stop moving."

*

The Tiree section leader sat in the left-hand seat of a Range Rover fire appliance. It was the smaller of the two appliances, but the more manoeuvrable, and he wanted to be first at the 747 when it hit the ground. The vehicle was parked, engine running, on an overgrown disused taxiway where the old paving was uneven and pockmarked with untended holes.

As the damaged aircraft came over the boundary fence, he held his breath. It looked even bigger than he expected, far too big for them to cope with. They had only two appliances and a crew of five men. How on earth could they tackle a blaze in a 747? They were trained to deal with emergencies on little Islanders and Twin Otters, with the occasional Trislander when passenger numbers demanded. But a 747!

"Get ready."

The driver, a young and inexperienced fireman, slipped the clutch and the vehicle began to inch towards the runway.

*

Devereaux loosened his seatbelt and rose to his feet. He had played it cautiously when he saw MacNabb stagger up towards the flight deck. Technically, MacNabb was still the captain of the airplane and if he chose to go up front, he had the right.

Even so—

Devereaux's mind began to dig up unpalatable possibilities. A stewardess at the front of the cabin called to him to return to his seat but he brushed her aside and made his way forward.

The first thing he felt when he burst onto the flight deck was the blast of cold air rushing in through the cracked screen. There was worse damage back in the passenger cabins, but the broken screen unnerved him. At the same time he saw the aerodrome runway racing forward to meet them. A bleak wintery scene and a ridiculously short runway.

A split second later he focussed his eyes on the sight of MacNabb struggling to grab control of the aeroplane from the first officer. The guy flying the airplane was doing his best to hold MacNabb at bay. But he wasn't succeeding.

Devereaux leapt across the flight deck and grabbed the captain's body, heaving it back from the first officer's shoulders. The DEA agent fell backwards, his arms wrapped round the struggling pilot. In that same moment, the 747's undercarriage bounced onto the tarmac.

"Cut the throttles!" someone shouted. The cry was followed by a wild cacophony of ear-splitting noises.

"Shite! It's a tyre burst!" the man in the left seat screamed.

"Straighten her up!" the other pilot shouted. Then the fuselage slewed round, jolted and swerved so that Devereaux found himself trapped under MacNabb's weight. He felt the deck beneath him rise and fall. A loud bang echoed through the skeleton of the plane.

The man in the left screamed, "I can't hold her!"

"Hold tight!" pilot in the right seat called back. "We've lost the main undercarriage!"

*

As the 747 swept past them, the two firemen in the Range Rover scanned the fuselage of the big Boeing. Their disbelieving eyes took in the tangled remains of the port inner engine and the damaged body. The older man's sharp eye also caught the awkward angle of the port main undercarriage oleo. This was going to be a day they would remember for the rest of their lives.

"Now!" he shouted.

The Range Rover leapt forward as the driver suddenly let out the clutch. At the moment the aeroplane hit the runway, both appliances were already racing in close pursuit.

*

Dougie felt the reverberation burst through the fuselage as the port undercarriage collapsed. The port side of the aeroplane was now supported by only the wing undercarriage assembly and, with the likelihood of structural damage around the port side, it might not hold the aircraft weight by itself.

As he struggled to hold the nose straight, he felt Kovak's right hand following his own left hand, pulling back on the thrust levers. But the speed was far too high. The sound of tearing, scraping metal invaded the flight deck, but he had no time to wonder where it came from. They were past the first broken fence in a flash and the second was rapidly approaching.

Dougie pumped the rudder pedals in a desperate attempt to keep the nose pointed down the line of the runway. And all the time his mind was working at lightning speed. Any second now the port wing assembly could collapse and they would slew round off the runway. There was just the possibility of a saving grace in the fact that the fuel tanks were virtually dry and were unlikely to burn. It was only a possibility of salvation because the fumes left in the tanks might explode on impact with the ground.

Explosion or fire. What a choice!

"Hold tight!" It had to be the decision of an instant, a command decision that weighed up all the possibilities of saving lives and losing lives. And if he was wrong, he would never be able to go back and put things right.

In one swift move he leaned forward and selected the undercarriage up.

*

The fireman section leader saw the undercarriage begin to collapse, almost as if he was watching a slow-motion replay. The body of the big Boeing slumped down on the runway like a dying beast.

"Pull in towards the dead engine. But stay well back until she comes to a halt." The section leader pointed towards the port side and the Range Rover driver headed in that direction. But the agony of screeching metal drowned out his leader's voice.

*

Jock Scrimgeour felt physically sick. He sat in an easy chair in the General Manager's office, his head hung loosely on his heaving chest. The only other person in the room was Pamela MacReady.

"It's over, Jock. Whatever happens to the 747 when it lands, there's nothing more anyone here can do."

"I've killed people."

"You were under stress, Jock." She crouched down beside him and took his hands in hers. "You need help."

"Help? Who'll help someone like me?" His voice and body were wracked with dejection. Utter despair was only moments away.

"I will." She squeezed his hand gently.

*

Judson knew instinctively that he had lined up the crippled aircraft with the most promising part of beach and it was as perfect an approach as any man could reasonably accomplish in the circumstances. The approach angle looked right and the speed was right. He had only two working engines and the yaw was awkward, but the aircraft was making a reasonably controlled approach to the ground. His main concern now was the fuel in the tanks behind him. When they hit the beach, would the tanks stay intact, or would they burst and blow them all to kingdom come?

He could have elected to land wheels up, but the risk of rupturing the hull and sparks igniting the fuel was too great. It was a calculated risk to land with the gear down and he fervently hoped they would not dig into soft sand and rip the oleos from the wings. That would spell disaster for sure.

"Major." The voice in Judson's earphones cut into his concentration. "We got more problems."

"What is it Bryzjinsky?"

"You seen that fire on the port-side wing, Major?"

Judson briefly looked across the flight deck at Youngman. From where he sat, he was unable to look back towards the wings without losing his concentration on the approach to the beach. "No. What the—"

"Look, Paul." Youngman pointed to the instrument panel.

Judson felt his tension rise several-fold when he saw the power winding down from the port outer engine. Only one engine was now left delivering power and they had another fire to contend with.

Chapter 19

The 747 had come to a standstill. There was a split second of appalling silence in which Dougie felt detached from reality, a moment when his mind was detached from his body and the horror of the incident was something he could view from afar. But the moment was too short to be taken objectively and he rapidly returned to reality with the noises of the dying airplane once again erupting into his consciousness.

Then the evacuation of the aircraft began. He heard Devereaux and MacNabb struggle to their feet behind him, extricating their bodies from the heap into which they had crumpled. At the same time Kovak began to lever himself out of the left-hand seat.

Despite all the noise about him, the flight deck was oddly calm and, at first, Dougie couldn't puzzle out why. Then his eyes caught the smashed windscreen. There was no blast of cold, howling air rushing in through the gaping hole. Just an unreal calm.

"You'd better get out, all of you. Quickly." He released himself from his harness and gestured to the others.

Devereaux was already pulling at the door with one hand while the other grasped MacNabb's arm. "This one comes with me," he said. He heaved the captain to his feet and roughly pushed him at the door.

"You?" Dougie queried.

"Sure." Devereaux grimaced. "Drugs Enforcement. But don't worry. I'll hand him over to your British police. I know my place."

"Because of what he did here?"

"No. Because he's into narcotics smuggling."

Dougie raised his eyebrows and said nothing more. He had more important things on his mind.

As soon as the DEA agent and MacNabb were clear of the flight deck, Dougie pushed Kovak ahead of him and made his way out into the upper-deck cabin where the evacuation was in full swing. The passengers were leaving the aircraft without panic. Their panic had been used up.

He stopped at the head of the spiral stair to allow a group to descend. A matronly lady in a fur coat put out a hand to him. "How is the captain? I was with him, you know."

"He's alive, madam."

*

From farther out it had looked like a huge beach but it grew smaller the closer they came to it. Smaller and shrinking still. Maybe he had misjudged it, Judson thought. Maybe he would not be able to get the airplane down in one piece on that small piece of Hebridean real estate. But it was too late to think about that. There was no power left for a go-around. He was committed to putting down on the sand.

"Shit! That's the end of another engine." He fought with the control column as the thrust finally died in the port outer engine and he was left with minimal power. One hundred and forty knots on the airspeed indicator and one mile from touchdown. Three hundred feet on the altimeter. He could do it, he told himself, he could do this. He reached out his right hand to cover the one remaining useful thrust lever.

"Follow me through," he hollered across to Youngman. "You know what to do if we get down on the ground in one piece. If anything happens to me—"

"We'll make it, Paul."

"Give me the speed." Judson fixed his eyes on the ground ahead. He put both hands back on the column and added, "You cover the thrust lever."

"One twenty knots." Youngman sounded calm but Judson knew it was only an act. "And I have the thrust lever."

They passed over a rocky outcrop at the start of the bay alongside the airfield and the sand flew in beneath the airplane. Fifty feet above the ground and sinking towards the sandy runway.

White, even sand that had been ground down by years of Atlantic waves. Judson kicked off the drift and felt Youngman's helping boot bring the KC135's nose round to line up with the landing run.

"Power off," Judson said and pulled back on the column. The stall warning alarm blared. Moments later the whole fuselage shook violently as the undercarriage hit the sand.

*

Dougie stepped out of the fire crew's Range Rover, slowly setting his feet onto the ground as if he was afraid it might not be safe. It was.

"Thanks, my friend." He gave the driver a nod and walked towards the radio hut at the end of the small terminal building. The emergency was almost ended, the remaining passengers were safely down on dry land and the aircraft was just an inert mass of aluminium on the runway. It was down to others to mop up. He felt strangely deflated now that the adrenaline had ceased to race through his body.

He had faced a situation his father had never met and he had brought all these people safely back to earth. His father would have approved. Of course, he would not have been proud of his son. Such sentiment would never have entered the head of Eric Nyle. But he would have shown his approval. And that would be enough for Dougie.

He had one more duty before the emergency was finally over and it was, to him, an important duty.

"Can I come in?" he asked. But he was inside the hut before the fireman who was seated at the radio desk noticed him.

"You're—?" The fireman stood up deferentially, as if he was in the presence of someone important.

"I'm the pilot of the 747."

"Aye. Of course." The soft, lilting voice sounded surprised.

"I want to ask a favour," Dougie said.

"Aye?"

"Can I use your radio? Just for a few moments."

"Of course." The man slipped away from the set, indicating the vacated seat as if it were an honour to have Dougie sit there.

When he sat down, Dougie knew what he had to say and he needed no rehearsal. He picked up the hand microphone and pressed the transmit switch.

"Watchdog, this is... this is Tiree."

"Go ahead, Tiree."

Dougie drew a deep breath. "Watchdog, my name is Douglas Nyle. First officer on Sinclair 984."

"Nice landing."

Dougie grinned. "It was a damned terrible landing. But most of us are alive. And I want to thank you for helping us."

"Only doing my job, sir."

"Even so... you ever get to land at Prestwick?"

"Affirmative. Sometimes."

"Good. My wife and I would like to welcome you into our home when you next get the chance."

"It will be a pleasure, sir. A real pleasure."

"Can I ask your name?"

"Hannam. Flight Lieutenant Tony Hannam."

"I'm glad to know you, old chap." Dougie nodded to the fireman and set the microphone back in its harness.

His whole body ached with weariness as he went back to the door of the hut. It was an aching sort of exhaustion he had never before encountered in his flying career. He needed to sleep for twelve hours, and then some. His footsteps were faltering noticeably as he made to leave the hut. In the periphery of his vision, he noticed two Americans in USAF uniform approaching the door from outside, blocking his way.

One of them spoke. "Captain Nyle?"

"First officer Nyle," Dougie responded, struggling hard to focus his tired eyes on the American. "The captain was injured in the collision. He's... somewhere else."

"We're from the aircraft you hit. We put down on a beach over there." The American pointed with a vague wave of his hand. He looked so young to be a pilot, and as tired as Dougie felt.

"Glad you got down safely," Dougie said.

"Sure." The American wiped his eyes and then reached out his hand. "The name's Paul Judson. Major, US Air Force. This here's Lieutenant Youngman, my first officer."

Dougie took the hand and shook it warmly. "Thank God you're not down in the ocean."

"My decision," Judson replied enigmatically. "That was *my* choice."

Author's Note

My own experiences were in my mind when I came to write *Prestwick*. I worked in civil air traffic control for forty years. This story is based in the 1980s when I was an Area Controller at the Scottish Air Traffic Control Centre. I was off duty when a friend and colleague called by to tell me about an incident over the North Atlantic, an area entirely devoid of radar cover. Two aircraft had come uncomfortably close because one of the pilots input the wrong waypoint coordinates into his flight management system.

At the time I had developed an interest in writing and it occurred to me that this could form the basis for a good adventure yarn. Several years passed before I had a crack at actually writing it.

The result bore little resemblance to the real incident — quite rightly, as I did not want to end up in court. However, I detected that there was something missing from the plot. I needed another element to bind it all together. Reluctantly, I put away the manuscript and all but forgot about it until the day I happened to read a report on Ronald Reagan's Star Wars programme. And there it was: the missing element I was looking for. It was the X-ray laser, an awesome device designed to kill itself in the very act of killing an enemy missile. Now I could complete my novel to my own satisfaction.

One reader described how he felt when he was reading *Prestwick*, "As the story unfolded I found myself immersed in both aircraft and rooting for safe outcomes. I was flying by the seat of my pants." I hope you felt the same.

David Hough
January 2016

Heathrow by David Hough

Danger in the Sky (Book 2)

Thousands of passengers
Hundreds of aircraft
One plan to end it all

When a fire disrupts the London Air Traffic Control Centre, the controllers move to an emergency control room at Heathrow — which is exactly where a group of terrorists want them.

The crisis deepens and the whole of London's Air Traffic Control system comes under attack. Despite facing personal danger, the controllers struggle to keep the airspace safe.

Desperate measures are needed to discover who is behind the attack, and what they want. Measures that put innocent lives at risk. As the answers begin to emerge, it becomes clear that far more is at stake than the safety of aircraft and passengers.

By then, there seems no way to stop a terrorist attack far more shocking than anyone had imagined.

David Hough takes his reader on a nail-biting journey:
the clock is ticking, the stakes are getting higher and higher —
and the disaster is getting close and closer.
A rip-roaring, page-turner of a novel.

Printed in Great Britain
by Amazon